Louise Candlish studied English at University College London and worked as an editor and copywriter before writing her debut novel *Prickly Heat*. She is the author of three further novels, the bestsellers *The Double Life of Anna Day*, *Since I Don't Have You* and *The Second Husband*, also published by Sphere. She lives in London with her partner and daughter.

Visit her website at www.louisecandlish.co.uk.

Also by Louise Candlish

The Double Life of Anna Day
Since I Don't Have You
The Second Husband

I'll Be There For You

Louise Candlish

sphere

SPHERE

First published in Great Britain as *Sisters Avenue* in 2005 by Arrow Books
This paperback edition published in 2009 by Sphere
Reprinted 2009

Copyright © Louise Candlish 2005

The moral right of the author has been asserted.

*All characters and events in this publication, other than those
clearly in the public domain, are fictitious and any resemblance
to real persons, living or dead, is purely coincidental.*

All rights reserved.
No part of this publication may be reproduced, stored in a
retrieval system, or transmitted, in any form or by any means, without
the prior permission in writing of the publisher, nor be otherwise circulated
in any form of binding or cover other than that in which it is published
and without a similar condition including this condition being
imposed on the subsequent purchaser.

A CIP catalogue record for this book
is available from the British Library.

ISBN 978-0-7515-4123-6

Typeset in Sabon by M Rules
Printed and bound in Great Britain by
Clays Ltd, St Ives plc

Papers used by Little, Brown are natural, renewable and
recyclable products sourced from well-managed forests and certified
in accordance with the rules of the Forest Stewardship Council.

Sphere
An imprint of
Little, Brown Book Group
100 Victoria Embankment
London EC4Y 0DY

An Hachette UK Company
www.hachette.co.uk

www.littlebrown.co.uk

For Jane

Acknowledgements

Thank you to Claire Paterson and all at Janklow & Nesbit who've supported me so invaluably. Also to Caroline Hogg, Helen Gibbs, Emma Stonex, Nathalie Morse, Hannah Torjussen and the rest of the fantastic Sphere team to whom this book owes its second life – and above all my wonderful editor Jo Dickinson.

Thanks to Steve Freeman, Seb Halse, Neil, Duncan and others from the agency life who might have inspired a memory or two; also Heather, Dawn, Mats 'n' Jo, Jake, Mikey B, Chuck and Ian for saying funny things.

Thank you to Tracey, Tara and Roni at i-Village, and to 'the mothers', especially Mandy and Sharon.

To the sisters I've come across who've fascinated me with their friendships. And, of course, thanks to Nips and Greta.

I'll Be There
For You

Chapter 1

Leaving the restaurant at just after three thirty, Juliet watched her client grin tipsily at her from the back of a cab before crossing Piccadilly to Albermarle Street for the office. She was hot, a little drunk, and very relieved. Mark obviously hadn't noticed anything odd about her at lunch; she'd been right not to take the day off work, not to treat it differently from any other.

'Watch out, mate!' Another cab was accelerating towards her and she skipped out of its way onto the kerb. Since when had cabbies stopped calling her 'love' and started calling her 'mate'? Did she look more comradely these days, less female, somehow? She looked down at her bare arms and legs: it would be hard to wear fewer clothes and still get seated in the kind of restaurant she'd just eaten in.

She wondered if Larry and Kate had come up with any ideas about where the three of them should have drinks that evening. Anywhere would do, just so long as she didn't have to spend the evening alone. Perhaps they could get a table outside somewhere; it was the third sultry July day in a row, already christened a heatwave by the papers but novel enough for her to look forward to passing through each slant of sunlight on the shaded path ahead. The French café near the office had set up a couple of tables on the pavement outside and the sight of coffees being

1

stirred and cigarettes lit in the open air caused a shot of pure, searing abandon to hit her bloodstream. It was a shock, today of all days, to feel real joy. At best she'd expected a kind of suffocated despair.

Her mood changed the second she reached the Imagineer reception.

'Juliet!' Jo cried. 'Where've you been? Dominic's been looking for you!' Although hers was a relatively relaxed reception job, Jo was wearing that silly headset thing that made her look like an air-traffic controller. For once she was actually smiling, looking at Juliet with naked glee, like the Vegas tourist who'd stumbled on a VIP ticket to the big fight and suddenly found herself within flirting distance of Jack Nicholson. 'They're all in the boardroom,' she added happily.

'What d'you mean, "all"?' Juliet asked her. In the cool, lily-scented space she was suddenly conscious of the sweat on her skin. She knew her clothes and hair must reek of cigarettes; Mark was one of the few people left in the developed world who smoked more than she did.

'I mean the *whole company*. For Dominic's presentation!'

'Fine, right, OK.' She remembered Dominic's email now, flagged 'urgent' and followed up with two reminders. God, how could she have forgotten? For Jo's instinct was right: this was bad. Dominic would be far too vain not to take her oversight personally. Rushing down the corridor to the boardroom, she saw her colleagues crammed against the sliding doors. It was not going to be possible to slink in unseen. Damn.

She peered at her face in the glass: nothing like the Oliver Reed glaze she'd seen Larry get away with in the past, but flushed from drinking nonetheless. Nor was it ideal that she looked as though she'd been sleeping rough: her eyes, a pale apple-green, had gone sludgy, her short highlighted hair resembled tinsel, and her make-up had either smudged or melted. It was nine months since she'd returned to London office life, but the air of the traveller still lingered about her appearance. Her body had that particular kind of missed-meals leanness, that stain of a tan that never quite washed off the skin of someone who'd once spent half a year on a Mexican beach. She'd never got back into working-girl grooming to the same degree. It seemed to suit her better this way.

Flattening her hair behind her ears, she waited for the next round of laughs before easing the door across, head dipped. Unfortunately it clattered shut behind her and seventy-five heads turned her way, a many-headed monster hearing the rustle of prey. She caught Dominic's eye straight away, hoping to transmit her contrition in a single end-of-the-matter glance, but saw at once that there was no hope. His face was alight with egomania and the insult of her lateness was plain to see.

'Ah, Juliet, good of you to join us.'

Dominic loved public speaking, standing at the front, commanding his troops. And he looked the part, too, with his six-foot-plus authority, the deft way his body moved in the dark, well-cut suit, the faux mussed-up hair – 'bed head' you could imagine the stylist telling him as they shared a saucy frisson in front of the salon mirror. Every day he presented himself to his staff as though for a magazine shoot celebrating media millionaires under thirty. She'd never met anyone so intoxicated with his own success. He'd once told her, straight up, that he saw himself as the baron of brand builders. Actually, he'd used capitals: The Baron of Brand Builders.

But he had something, she had to admit, and seeing him now at his most magnetic it seemed less extraordinary that they'd once slept together. Twice slept together, she corrected herself.

'I'm so sorry, Dominic,' she said, meaning it. 'I took Mark Kendall to lunch to talk about the new Smithfield's brief and I couldn't get away. He sends his best.'

Dominic just clicked the mouse in his hand and said, 'So, moving on . . .' The image on the far wall changed and the seventy-five heads turned back again. 'Any thoughts on this one, Juliet?'

Apology not accepted, then. She squinted at the image: the room wasn't quite dark enough to make it out. It seemed to resemble a child's join-the-dots drawing, until she saw that there were annotations, too small for her to read from her position by the door. Perhaps it was some sort of engineering diagram: Dominic had just bagged business with a French car manufacturer.

'Come on, Juliet, we're all agog.'

Maybe it was the effort she'd expended on all that false beaming across the table at Mark K, and maybe it was the wine, but she sensed herself weakening now, *allowing* herself to lose control. She was going to say the wrong thing. 'Er, is this your take on the British land-speed record?' There was just one clear shout of laughter amid the titters and she didn't need to look around to know it was Larry.

'You *do* split my sides,' Dominic said, voice dangerously pleasant. 'Actually, this is my projection of revenue streams for the last quarter of the year. Stick around and you might learn something. If you're not too busy with your briefs, of course.'

There were a few uncertain sniggers at that. This was deadly. They'd never bickered publicly before, though she'd been aware for a while that her star had slipped. She tried to remember how much she'd had to drink. Mark had ordered the third bottle of wine when she was in the loo; it would have been rude not to share it and a waste of Imagineer funds to leave it. A bottle and a half each: was that so wayward for the end of the week? Not if she'd made it back in time for Dominic's presentation it wasn't. She looked across to Larry for support. He had his hand over his mouth, rubbing at the tip of his nose with his knuckles in that way he did, hardly bothering to disguise his enjoyment.

Dominic was still glaring at her. 'Cuff him, somebody,' he said finally, with that slow-motion blink of disdain he did so well. *Cuff him*: this was his customary expression of dismissal, as though some trusty sergeant stood by to escort the object of his displeasure to a holding cell below. Like everyone else, Juliet usually communicated silent sympathy to the victim. She supposed others would be doing that to her now, didn't dare look. She didn't think she could deal with sympathy today.

Mercifully, the land-speed slide was one of the last and Dominic was soon taking questions from the floor. 'Dominic, it's fantastic to see this sort of growth ahead of us,' said a disembodied voice at the front that Juliet recognised as belonging to Emma from HR. 'Does that mean there'll be organic expansion in terms of staff?' She was speaking in that bright, rehearsed sort of way that meant Dominic had planted the question.

'Yes,' Dominic said. 'We'll be actively recruiting across the board. But I'll also be thinking about a radical restructure in the New Year, so it will vary from team to team.'

A current of paranoia now buzzed around the room. Radical Restructure: the dreaded double 'R'. There'd been one last year when Juliet had first joined and she'd never experienced such wholesale backstabbing and credit snatching. It had been like working in a bad Eighties movie. In the end, no one had been laid off anyway, which was just as well for her as she'd lacked any instinct for self-preservation at that time. It had been all she could do to lift her head off the pillow and go through the motions of each day.

'Any more questions?'

'Dominic?' It was Juliet's friend Kate. She stood silhouetted against the window with a fleecy outline of orange around her red-blonde ponytail. 'I was just wondering,' she said, 'if there was any news on the leak in the ladies? I mean, it's really grim, especially when you're getting ready to go out.'

'Yes, Kate,' Dominic said. 'That could put you right off your stride, couldn't it? Do you want to catch up with Jo about that afterwards? She's organising plumbing repairs, I believe. Anything sensible, anyone?' He wasn't looking at Kate, but

5

making clear eye-contact with Juliet, daring her to come up with something intelligent, confident she would not. All at once she felt close to tears, kept her eyelids closed for a second or two, willing someone, *anyone*, to ask another question.

'Dominic,' she heard Larry say. 'Since we're all here, this is probably a good time for me to tell you I've got a few ideas for the Christmas party. There's a great restaurant on Brewer Street, where they do . . .'

'Are you aware we're in the month of *July*?' Dominic interrupted with a nasty little chuckle.

'. . . Elvis karaoke . . .' Larry tailed off.

'*Five* months away. How do you know you'll still *have* your job then?'

Juliet watched. Larry had rescued her; she *had* to return the favour. 'It's just that this place is so popular,' she said carefully. 'They're already taking bookings. After all, who wants their Christmas do on a Monday in November?'

Most people shuffled to life at that. A restructure was one thing, a duff Christmas party quite another.

'Who indeed?' Dominic snapped. 'Well, I've got something special in mind this year, Larry and Juliet, so you needn't worry, delighted though I am by your continuing work as unofficial Imagineer social secretaries. Perhaps we can all enjoy your rendition of "Love Me Tender" on another occasion?'

That Dominic blink again. But he was pleased with the round of laughter raised by that last remark, she could tell. He pulled at his bed head and said, 'OK, well if that's all guys, let's get back to business. I'll see account directors at five and don't forget Amir's "Yolk of the Brand" show 'n' tell tomorrow lunchtime. Sign up if you can. Branding begins at home, don't forget.'

Juliet waited in the corridor for Larry, who came out grumbling. 'What does he mean "branding begins at home"?'

'He made it sound like the sort of branding they do to sheep and cattle,' Kate said, a step behind.

'Well, we're treated like livestock, so I suppose it makes perfect sense.' Dominic's little rally had obviously done little for Larry's motivation.

'Well, I for one can certainly do without any disfigurements before the weekend,' Juliet grinned. 'I'm going to a thirtieth birthday party on Saturday. God, doesn't it make you feel old?'

'Not when you're already thirty-four,' Larry said. 'Then it makes you feel irrelevant. Thanks very much, Juliet, I can see you're on a roll today.'

They'd reached reception, pausing for a moment under the gleaming metallic lettering of the company name, along with the slogan: '*everybody think*'. This never failed to annoy Larry, the team copywriter: he wanted to see an exclamation mark after 'think' to show the phrase was declamatory. Every so often he would dash off an email to Dominic about it: '*Otherwise it just looks like the "s" has dropped off the end and is lying on the floor somewhere.*' 'Does anyone really care?' Juliet would appease him. 'Nobody here thinks anyway.'

'Let's take the stairs,' she said to him as they shuffled along again. 'I'm coming with you to the pit. Thanks for rescuing me in there, by the way.'

'What *have* you done to Dominic?' Larry asked. 'He looked like he was ready to burn you at the stake. How come you missed the presentation? That's not like you.'

'I was at Smithfield's all morning and we went straight to lunch. You know, I bet he wouldn't have even noticed if I hadn't turned up at all.'

'Better never than late,' Larry agreed.

'He has been very rude to you recently,' Kate said. 'Maybe he's overcompensating, still pissed off you didn't want to extend your . . .' she broke into a whisper, '*relationship*.'

'Oh, is that what it was?' Larry laughed. He was still amused by the idea of Juliet and Dominic together. She thanked God for the twentieth time that he hadn't been in the bar that night in

April when they'd first got together and was therefore unable to torture her with details of the grisly seduction. Then again, if he had been there, maybe she *wouldn't* have taken Dominic back to her flat. Just how *had* that happened anyway?

Her memory of the morning after was clear enough: she'd woken up to find that the purring shape under the duvet next to her was the Baron of Brand Builders himself. The bed was surrounded by taped-up boxes and half-packed bags – she was moving out that weekend – and Dominic just looked around the room and said, 'If you were planning a quick getaway, Jules, I'd remind you that you're the one who lives here!' Even now it made her cringe: all those years of fidelity at home and professionalism at work and within six months of her first job back she'd slept with her boss. How predictable. And now she seemed to have progressed to cheeking him in company meetings, too.

They had emerged into the half-light of the pit, as it was known, the low-ceilinged space where Larry, Kate and the rest of the creative team worked. It was distinctive for its animal smell, the smell of too many men in their twenties walking around with their shoes off; too many flat-sharers who'd missed their slot for the shower; too many McNuggets with curry sauce. Clients were never brought to the pit.

'So what are we doing tonight . . . ?' Juliet started, but was interrupted by the approach of Emma. As usual, she couldn't help staring at her colleague's layered blonde hair, which was so perfectly blow-dried it looked like she had a wig sitting on top of her normal hair. Emma was one of those people who dressed for the job she wanted (HR director) rather than the one she had (HR executive). She was just like Jo: buttoned up, self-promoting, a pain.

'Just who I wanted to see!' Emma exclaimed, though it could hardly have been a surprise to find Larry and Kate at their designated workstations. 'Have you guys got your job descriptions for me? The deadline is tomorrow morning. Dominic wants to read them over the weekend.'

'Why do we have to do these again?' Kate asked. 'I hate writing.'

'You could always draw yours,' Larry suggested. 'I've got some nice jumbo crayons somewhere.'

Juliet and Kate giggled but Emma didn't. 'It's a highly constructive exercise whereby Dominic can assess your own perception of your contribution to Imagineer and update his personal templates. It's enormously helpful for recruiting.'

'Right. We'll get straight on to it,' Larry said, flicking through the *Standard*. 'I see David Beckham's been at it again . . .' Juliet looked affectionately at him. Even though his dark hair was cropped and he dressed in the same skater-boy clothes all the creatives wore, she could still recognise the Larry she'd seen in those old photos he'd shown her one night at his place: the Larry of the late Eighties, with long metal-head locks and battered leathers. His face was not good-looking, exactly, but it had a sort of friendly sneer you couldn't help wanting to share. He looked smart, like a cleverer-than-average busker.

'What is this?' Larry said as Emma swished off. 'Job descriptions? When the weekend's almost upon us!' It was another of Larry's pet theories that since Thursday was widely accepted as the new Friday, no one need worry about doing any *real* work on either day. Juliet, whose job it was to coax Larry to meet his deadlines and to manage the client if he didn't, usually protested this. But today was different, today she knew exactly what he meant. 'Yeah, what if the world ends tonight and the last thing we used our brains for was a *job description*. What's Emma on?'

'Perhaps, like me, she simply views Thursday as a normal working day, an opportunity for revenue generation . . . and *not* the day before the apocalypse. Extraordinary, eh?' It was Dominic, of course, having popped up like Mr Benn about an inch from where Juliet leaned over Larry's desk. Just what she needed.

She thought quickly and picked up a pen. 'So, Larry, how long did you spend on that Smithfield's aisle-end copy last week? I'm just catching up on billing.'

'Two, maybe three,' Larry said, not bothering to look up from the paper.

'OK, three days, I'll put you down for a week, once you've done corrections and checks.' That should please Dominic at least; he was always reminding the planners to round creative hours up not down.

'No, three minutes, not three days,' Larry said, bored.

'Three *minutes*?'

'It was only about fifty words.'

'He does write very fast,' Kate confirmed. 'But you can make it up on my design time if you like, Juliet. I haven't even started it yet, I'm way behind.'

This was going from bad to worse, but when Juliet looked up she saw that Dominic had grown bored and was already eavesdropping on a conversation at the neighbouring team desks. Thank God, she couldn't face another cuffing.

'Hey, listen,' Kate said when he'd moved away. 'I thought maybe we could go to that Canadian sportsbar place after work.'

'I'd rather eat my own arm than hang out with all those jocks,' Larry scoffed.

'But there are *men* there,' Kate protested.

'Yeah, men watching sport,' Larry said. 'I mean, is that the sort of man you want? Someone who drinks in a *Canadian* bar? Someone who wears one of those stupid elk baseball caps?'

Kate sighed and Juliet smiled sympathetically at her. She was the youngest of their three, only twenty-five, and for all their teasing Juliet liked it that Kate hadn't let the world jade her, not yet.

'How about a margarita?' she said. 'That's if Mexican sympathisers are more acceptable to Larry than Canadians.'

'How about we just go straight to Guy's bar?' Larry said. 'You know we'll end up there eventually.'

'Not necessarily,' Juliet smiled, 'Guy and I are not joined at the hip.'

'I thought that was precisely where you *were* joined,' Larry said, grinning. Why else do we have to spend the only decent summer evenings this year in a *basement*?'

'You suggested it,' Juliet pointed out.

'Guy's, then?' Kate said.

'OK.' But Juliet wasn't sure if seeing Guy was such a good idea. Would she be able to get through the night without comparing him with Luke? Seven years versus two and a half months. The man she had known as well as herself versus the one she'd known so briefly he had yet to appear in her dreams. *Then* versus *now*. Everything versus . . . what, exactly?

'See you by the lifts at six,' she said to Larry and Kate.

Back upstairs in the account suite, an altogether more civilised space than the pit with its glass desks and leather chairs, she spent the next half-hour moving her eyes restlessly between the computer clock and the empty seat opposite. Until recently it had been occupied by Michelle, the Smithfield's team's account director, not yet three months pregnant but already with some unpronounceable complication that kept her bed-rested for most of the time. Michelle's work was now being shared between Juliet and another account planner at no additional reward – monetary or verbal. Instead, Dominic had hinted that he would make an internal promotion during Michelle's official maternity leave, which started in the New Year. Juliet was the natural choice – though relatively new to Imagineer she had more experience than the others overall – but a leapfrog was never out of the question with Dominic. He prided himself on spotting talent in the lower ranks and shaking everyone up with a sudden reshuffle of seniority. Dominic the starmaker.

She checked her email for new tasks. A reminder from Mark

Kendall to send the proposal they'd discussed at lunch. That took forty-five seconds. A meeting request from the head of production. Clicking 'Accept' took less than five. Then she noticed the job description template attached to Emma's message.

There were three parts.

1. *Encapsulate your role at Imagineer in a single sentence.*

She thought for a moment and then typed, '*I push paper.*' That would make Larry and Kate laugh.

2. *What key strengths are required for the role?*

   '*Paper-pushing.*'

3. *Suggest any Talent Evolution that could enrich your role and add value to brand-building within Imagineer?*

Talent Evolution: that was what HR called staff training. It was a wonder they still called themselves HR, though Larry had a few ideas for an alternative. She thought again, was tempted to write '*Sex with Dominic*', but decided against it and typed: '*Wrist-strengthening exercises for longer, faster paper-pushing.*' Then she attached the file to an email and selected Larry's name.

Perhaps it was the lunchtime drinking, perhaps it was the run-in with Dominic, or perhaps it was the fact that it was 16th July and she was struggling to care if the world was still turning by the end of it, but she suddenly wanted to hit the self-destruct button good and hard. So she replaced Larry's name with Emma's and pressed 'Send'.

Chapter 2

Thanks to a jug of margaritas at the touristy Mexican place where they were forced by staff into sombreros, by the time they reached Guy's bar on Kingly Street a smattering of Imagineer staff had beaten them to it. Jo was there, sipping wine and talking to a couple of juniors at the bar with the same expression of self-importance she wore on reception. She was like an electoral candidate securing her votes. Juliet had no doubt that one day they'd all be working for Jo.

'Since when has Guy's become the staff bar?' Larry grumbled, filling their wine glasses to the brim. 'There are loads of pubs between here and the office. Must they choose *our* smoky underworld?'

'They're probably just out roaming randomly, on the hunt for males,' Juliet said. 'It's mating season according to the *Sun*. This is when spring babies are conceived, you know.' It was so hot in the bar she was already down to a tiny strapless top.

Kate pulled a face. 'It's all right for you, Juliet, with men coming out of your ears.'

'Do you want to rephrase that?' Larry said, lighting up. 'Anyway, you know what they say about men, Kate?'

'What?'

'They're like buses . . .'

'Yes,' Juliet said. 'You're never quite sure you're on the right one.'

Larry groaned with laughter, but Kate just sighed. 'I'm *serious*, you two. I know it's supposed to be feast or famine when you're single, but I'm going to waste away here.'

The other two looked at her radiant plump cheeks and laughed.

'Well, you know my view,' Larry said.

'Yes, dearest, I hear it every day.'

'He's right,' Juliet said. 'You've got to move out of your parents' place. You must be giving off that "still living at home" vibe. You want people to think you've got a sex den set-up a quick taxi ride away. Do we need another bottle yet? How about a vodka shot as well?'

'That's another thing,' Kate said. 'I've decided I'm not going to drink anything but wine from now on. Spirits cloud my judgement when it comes to men.'

'What, can't tell your elbow from an arsehole?' Larry grinned.

'Well, *I* can't do that when I'm stone-cold sober,' Juliet said. 'No point blaming the booze.'

'Oh, Guy's all right,' said Larry.

'Guy's *gorgeous*,' Kate added. 'Especially the Kiwi accent.'

'He's certainly ideal for Juliet,' Larry said. 'Who better than the owner of a bar? Hang on, the chief exec of Jacob's Creek could be in with a shot.'

'Ha, ha,' said Juliet.

'There's more to their relationship than drinking,' Kate said loyally. 'Isn't there, Juliet?'

But suddenly Juliet wasn't listening. Her heart had gone into near arrest and it felt like she was being held underwater. Over Larry's shoulder the figure of a middle-aged woman blurred in front of her: Jan Newell. She fought for breath, trying to work out if this were real. She'd known that it would happen at some point, that she'd see one or other of them, but today? And here?

14

In her new sanctuary, where she was supposed to be protected from her old life? Surely Jan wasn't looking for *her*?

'What's up?' Larry asked, following her gaze.

'Nothing, just don't move, I don't want that woman to see me.'

'Who?' He looked at her curiously. She felt inert, colourless under her make-up.

'It doesn't matter, it's nothing important. Just keep me covered.'

'This is like *Cagney and Lacey*,' Kate giggled.

'You're far too young to remember that,' Larry told her.

'Cable,' Kate said.

But Jan wasn't looking for anyone, she was simply making her way through the clusters of drinkers from the loos to the stairs. She must be eating in the restaurant upstairs, Juliet thought. How surreal to see her brush past Jo, apparently with no clue that the girl who'd almost been her daughter-in-law, almost shared her name, was less than ten feet away. She was smartly dressed, freshly lipsticked, and – what was the word they always used for older women who'd kept their figure? – *trim*, that was it. She looked cheerful and trim. Perhaps Tony was waiting for her upstairs, the two of them in London for the theatre or opera. They'd probably been advised to do something civilised today, something life affirming. Look forward, not back, that's the phrase the bereavement counsellor kept using before Juliet had been able to bear it no longer and stopped attending the sessions.

She watched Jan's sandalled feet disappearing up the spiral staircase and took a big gulp of wine. Finally, she remembered to breathe.

Larry was still watching. 'Are you with a witness protection programme or something, Jules? Who *was* that?'

'No one, just a friend of my mum's.' She couldn't bring herself to explain and, with it, risk breaking down in tears. It was only then that she saw that today had been, above all, about avoiding crying.

Luckily Larry changed the subject. 'So who's coming to your birthday bash on the seventh?'

She tried to think. 'Oh, the usual suspects, a few friends, Hannah and Michael, and I suppose I'd better invite work people as well.'

'I'm looking forward to meeting your sister,' Kate said. 'I love it that you're so unlike each other. I mean, the idea of her hunting down a wealthy husband – it's so *ruthless*.'

'It wasn't quite like that,' Juliet said, feeling guilty for drunken exaggerations of the past. Hannah didn't deserve that. It was unfortunate that her friendship with Larry and Kate had developed just as her closeness with Hannah seemed to have slipped. It struck her that she'd never really shared with them how great her sister could be. Hannah was back from her honeymoon now, had called that morning and left a message. She'd remembered the day, of course. 'It's not that she doesn't love Michael,' Juliet went on. 'Because I think she does. It's just so hard to see why when he's such an arrogant pig. Other than the money, of course. Larry's met him, haven't you?'

'He's just a PSS,' Larry said.

'What?' Kate asked.

'Public School Stereotype.'

'I need to make a list of all your three-letter acronyms,' Kate said.

'TLAs, please,' Larry said. 'Though some are four and some . . .' He had to raise his voice slightly over the buzz that had just started up. The air seemed to get even sultrier, a little more charged, as though the studio audience had spotted the star waiting side stage: Guy had arrived. Out of the corner of her eye Juliet watched him check in with his bar staff and immediately start chatting with some lonester at the bar. Jo and co had gone, thank God, but had they stayed Guy would have been equally as

16

attentive to them. That was the thing about Guy, he treated everyone, *everyone*, the same. That was how it had begun with her, a chat at the bar when she'd gone straight from a presentation at Smithfield's to meet Kate for a drink. Kate had been late and Guy had kept her company. There'd been an attraction, they'd both sensed it at once.

She watched him through the smoke. He must have come straight out of the shower, she thought, his hair was in those loose dark curls, his face damp. For a man who had spent the last five years of his life in this cave he was ridiculously *glossy*. She'd seen no evidence of laundry facilities in his rooms upstairs but he was always in a fresh shirt. She looked forward to smelling his smell, pressing her skin against his, feeling that sudden lurch of lust.

'Hi guys!' Finally, he came over to their table, nicked a cigarette from the nearest pack and kissed her. There was a new casualness in the weight of his hand on her shoulder, it was more proprietorial pat than lustful pawing. This was puzzling; they'd only been seeing each other for a few months, it was far too early for proprietorial pats.

She tried to catch his eye and communicate some of her need: the look that came back was admiring, respectful. There was something so courtly about Guy. Or was it that she didn't know him well enough to judge? Maybe he was just another charmer in the mould of Hannah's new husband – maybe Hannah laughed with *her* friends about *Juliet's* taste. As Guy moved away she was suddenly submerged by the underwater feeling again, but this time she was close to drowning. It was all too much: she'd been wrong to think she could treat today like any other.

'If you were a type of song, what would you be?' Larry was badgering Kate.

'Oh, not the Kipling game again,' Kate protested. 'He makes me do this twenty times a day, Juliet, and I can never think of anything.'

17

'I'd be a stadium rock anthem,' Larry said. 'No, correction: a *power ballad.*'

'I can see that,' Kate laughed. 'I suppose if I had to be something I'd be a love song. Preferably a duet.'

'Juliet?'

'God, I have no idea.'

Larry began ordering drinks with an urgency she recognised from every other night they'd been out together. Martinis, double vodkas, a round of tequila shots. They all kept pace, Kate's pledge of exclusivity to the vine forgotten already, Juliet hardly distinguishing one drink from the next as she hurled the liquid down her throat and felt the sting behind her nose and eyes. Finally she got what she was waiting for, that wash of reassurance that life wasn't always going to be such a tragedy after all. What a relief to just *surrender.* She smiled at Larry and Kate, her best friends these days, though she'd known neither as long as a year. Now what were those silly little niggles again?

She drained her glass of wine and Larry swiftly refilled it. Peering through the smoke she watched Guy again, leaning against the packed bar, being fluttered at by one of his waitresses. They all engaged flirt gear with him as a matter of course: shoulders back, breasts to attention, fingers twirling hair; except for the head waitress Martine, who had short hair and twiddled her earlobes instead.

Juliet got to her feet and eased through the humid forest of bodies to reach him. She pressed her body against his while her hand searched his pocket for the keys. 'Babe, there's a queue for the ladies. Can I use upstairs?' Then she was backstage, wading through the sweat and steam of the galley kitchen, down the cramped corridor and up the back stairs, windowless, pictureless, and into the main studio room where Guy lived. He followed her, as she knew he would, had intended him to.

'Sorry, am I being a pest?' She pronounced it 'pissed', the way he did, her favourite word of his. She agreed with Kate, the accent was great, and he loved that she loved it.

18

'Oh, a *terrible* pest . . .'

When he pulled her skirt up and put his fingers inside her she felt a resurgence of spirit as well as desire. So it was still the same, after all. He was on his knees, even better, not just interested but *enslaved*. Her top was off, the roller blind on the window still up, taxi lights blinking outside.

Afterwards, Guy's face was unusually intense. 'Take the day off tomorrow. I want you in bed all day.' A command, not a request.

'Sorry,' she said. 'Today's been weird at work. I have to go in tomorrow.'

'Saturday, then,' he said, more than once. 'Come back on Saturday.' He'd never done this before, and nor had she, pressed the other to know when they'd next be meeting. It pleased and scared her at the same time.

'I have to go,' she said, kissing him.

'Where've you been?' Larry asked, close to slurring, when she returned. The bar was emptier, but the hard core that remained was making twice as much noise as the after-work crowd had. How long had she been? Larry and Kate had stacked up the drinks she'd missed: something murky, something clear, something layered.

'Just catching up with Guy,' she said.

'We're doing, If you were a Hollywood star . . .'

'Must be living,' Kate chipped in.

'Oh,' Juliet smiled. 'I'm not sure.'

'You're hopeless today!' Kate protested. 'I'm Nicole Kidman.' She got up to go to the loo and Larry steadied her as she wobbled off. Then he turned back to Juliet. 'Are you all right? I mean, really?'

'Yes. No. *No*. It's exactly a year since Luke died.'

'Ah,' Larry said, eyes sad. 'I had a feeling it might be something like that.'

'Do you mind if I don't talk about it?'

'Course not.'

They lit cigarettes and Larry said, 'Have you noticed that the best part of smoking is lighting the thing?'

'Yes, it is,' Juliet agreed. 'Maybe if we just light them and watch them burn we'll live longer?'

They sat in easy silence waiting for Kate.

'By the way, I think I know what I'd be if I were type of song,' Juliet said.

'What?' Larry asked.

'I'd be a cover version.'

He raised an eyebrow. 'A cover version of what?'

'Oh, I don't know. Just of the better original.'

Chapter 3

Hannah had been back from her honeymoon less than a week when she discovered she was pregnant. Looking up from the blue line on the test kit she faced herself in the pristine oval mirror, fingers still clutching the funny little stick thing. Was this really happening or was that actually an electric toothbrush in her hand, the big cartoon grin she presented to the glass just a routine check for particles between her teeth?

It didn't take long to decide to tuck the news away in some secret corner. It would be just for her for now. After all, pleasing herself was the easy bit; whether or not Michael would share her delight was a thornier issue. He was one of those people who liked to take one life-changing event at a time and, to be fair, they hadn't even finished unwrapping their wedding gifts yet. But she was confident it would just be a matter of timing with Michael. After all, everyone agreed that she was the only woman who'd ever been able to *manage* him. He'd been the last in his circle to get married and it was common knowledge that she hadn't been the first girlfriend to entertain hopes of tying the knot. His legal expertise in Joint Ventures had never quite extended to his private life, or so his friends joked. Until Hannah.

She wrapped the tester in several layers of loo roll and buried it under the phials and packets and bits of soggy tissue in the bin.

Pregnant. Already? It must have been a honeymoon conception, or perhaps just before. There wasn't time to work out dates, pull together her diary or even her thoughts: she was meeting Lottie in Northcote Road for lunch in twenty minutes and needed to leave now. She couldn't resist another look in the mirror on her way out – this time without the Cheshire Cat grin – to see if she looked any different. She was glowing, certainly, but that was probably just the benefits of three weeks in Italy, which had left her skin glossy and ripe with good living and her dark hair highlighted a little from the sun. But the pink across the cheekbones and tip of her nose was new – she wasn't usually a flusher. Shock, perhaps.

She took a new route down to Northcote Road, crossing Clapham Common by the children's playground and slicing right through the heart of Nappy Valley towards Wandsworth Common. She'd laughed when Michael had told her of the neighbourhood's nickname. 'Nappy Valley. It's where people go to *breed*.' He'd said it in the same foreboding way he might say '*die*'.

Nappy Valley. There was no denying its aptness. From houses left and right came mothers and their babies: it was like watching the opening sequence of a soap set in Fertilityville. There wasn't a woman in sight without a sling, pram or pushchair, mostly the expensive all-terrain type, about as necessary in this clean, villagey neighbourhood as the SUVs that lined the kerbs.

Skipping down Bennerley Road, she smiled with new eagerness at the sight of a mother adjusting a parasol over her buggy. That will be me, she thought, protecting my baby's skin from the sun, making sure the hat doesn't slip down over his eyes and stop him from admiring his brand-new world. Perhaps he'd be wearing one of those sweet little animal hats with the ears, or a mini sheepskin deerstalker – they could make even the scrunchiest baby face look cute.

How eagerly her mind leaped forward; it was a well-known susceptibility of hers. 'Don't be so *previous*,' her father had once

22

warned her when she was small, 'you'll only be disappointed.' Juliet, who was four years younger and listening as usual, had argued that 'previous' couldn't possibly be the right word because it was on her spelling list and meant the one before. But it was. Hannah *was* previous. She just couldn't help herself. She'd known Michael about ten minutes before allowing the wedding fantasies to take grip. She'd lived in his flat less than a fortnight before dreaming about double-fronted family houses overlooking the common. And now she was at it again. Weren't you supposed to wait until the fourth month before you even admitted to having thoughts about baby clothes?

She realised she'd come to a halt behind a car and the woman she was watching had straightened up, seen her staring and begun to zap back a great beam of suspicion. Hannah hurried on, hurt. Clearly, admittance into Nappy Valley was not automatic, whether one was in possession of an embryo or not. Now she came to think of it, they were odd, these women. They lived in immaculate houses in idyllic tree-lined streets, they gathered together in cafés to coo over perfect babies whose ages always seemed to match, but catch them *alone* and they were unsmiling, totally preoccupied with themselves. She hoped she'd be friendlier when she became one of them.

She reached the pushchair traffic of Northcote Road and, driven by the adrenaline that now seemed to control her body, pushed open the door of the first estate agent's she came to. Michael's bachelor loft with its spiral staircases and tiny, vertiginous roof terrace would be no good now.

'Hello?'

The man on the phone mouthed a 'Hold on' and she hung back by the door. The agents were on their feet at their desks, talking into phones like City traders, fences of polished teeth on display. They all wore dark business suits, incongruous against the country-cottage décor with its stained-glass windows and fresh flowers. She shivered beneath the icy breath of the air con.

23

'Right, is anyone helping you?'

'No, not yet,' Hannah beamed. 'I've just started thinking about buying a house in this area.'

She spied the beginnings of a gleam. 'Take a seat.'

Hannah sat. 'I'm just looking,' she added.

'What's your budget?'

She realised her daydreams had never involved such practicalities as cost. Her only reference point was her flat in Tufnell Park, sold in haste earlier in the year. But Tufnell Park was not like Nappy Valley; as far as she knew, people didn't go there to breed.

'About five hundred thousand?' The terminal riser was a mistake, she saw at once, she should have been flatter, more commanding. 'I mean seven,' she added firmly. The agent looked as though he might actually laugh out loud. 'You won't get a tit on a bird table for that around here.' This was met with snorts from a colleague at the back of the room, who was watching the exchange over the top of his computer monitor.

Hannah waited. She didn't blame them for their disrespect. Having never been wealthy before, she recognised that she must lack the natural authority that went with it. She should have checked some of the details in the window before going in and come up with a more realistic sum.

'I take it you're looking for Edwardian or Victorian?' the man went on. 'Not a Tezza?'

'Tezza?'

'Terry and June-style, you know, Thirties terraces, *storm* porches.'

'Oh, no.'

'Well, I haven't got much in your price range, then. We've got a nice conversion loft, two bedrooms, not actually Between the Commons, though, closer to Balham.'

'Oh, we've already got a loft,' Hannah said. They could have been talking about kettles or coffee makers. 'We're looking for a house, a family house. With a garden.' The sense that she was the spokesperson for a whole family unit renewed her confidence.

But the guy was practically shrugging his shoulders in front of her. 'OK,' he said, as though he'd heard quite enough of this nonsense. 'Well, if you can up your budget a bit, come back and register with us and I'll dig out some details.' He passed her a card – she almost expected him to let it fall to the ground as her own hand reached forward – and began stabbing at his phone. Her conversation with Mitch Evans, Senior Property Negotiator, was evidently over.

But nothing was going to quell her spirits today. Only yesterday she'd been reading an article about post-nuptial depression and had marvelled at how anyone could feel despondent at the start of a marriage. Her own situation felt like a fantasy: she was married to Michael, the man she loved, and now she was going to be the mother of his child. The house would come in time.

Lottie was already sitting in the café when she arrived. 'Welcome back, lovebird! How was the honeymoon? All sweet and gooey, I hope?' She immediately turned away from Hannah to dab at her baby daughter, who lay wrapped like a crispy duck pancake in some sort of complicated pushchair system parked by the table.

'Hi, Ophelia,' Hannah said to the tiny exposure of cross pink face. 'Her nose is all runny. Is she not well?'

'We think she's got her first cold, she's so grizzly today, in a right state.' No one could accuse Lottie of the same: her hair looked freshly highlighted and blow-dried, the sand-coloured suede jacket unblemished by snot or sick or other infant matter. Clothes always looked fantastic on Lottie, who had long limbs and small breasts; she was the only woman Hannah had met who had managed to look elegant in her pregnancy.

'Poor Ophelia,' she said, blowing her a kiss.

'Hilary's gone off to take some presents back,' Lottie said. 'Newborn stuff is just too small for Ophelia – I told you she's in the ninety-fifth centile for length, didn't I? But she shouldn't wake-up, anyway.' The implication was that Lottie wouldn't have a clue what to do with the baby if she did wake before schedule, not without trusty Hilary. Hilary, the nanny from Virginia or somewhere equally homely, was a distant relative of Lottie's husband Rob and Lottie's dealings with her were imbued with that brand of affable equality that only someone experienced with staff could carry off, an equality that only *seemed* like equality. Which wasn't far off how Hannah had once felt about her own place in Lottie's world. But ever since she'd moved in with Michael, Lottie had become her closest friend, coming to her rescue when the increasingly elaborate wedding arrangements had threatened to implode, keeping her sane with her good-heartedness. It helped that she lived within walking distance, on the edge of Wandsworth Common. Just the sloping streets of Nappy Valley separated their homes.

The waitress approached and Hannah scanned the specials board. 'Goats cheese bake and some olive ciabatta, please.'

'Just the soup for me,' Lottie said. 'No bread. God, I'm desperate to shift this weight. Much as I love the little creature, I want my body back!'

'You look really slim,' Hannah said truthfully. 'I'm much bigger and I'm not even . . . haven't even had a baby.'

'Oh, but you've got that sexy, voluptuous build. What are you again, an *endomorph*? You've got boobs. Anyway, how was Italy? I want to hear *all*.'

'Oh, it was fantastic,' Hannah said, feeling contentment swaddle her body as she rewound her mind: ten days ago they were in Capri, two weeks ago Ravello; a month ago they were just a day away from the wedding itself. 'I loved everywhere, Amalfi, Positano . . .'

'Even that rat-hole Naples?'

'*Everywhere* was perfect.'

Lottie nodded in that expectant way that sometimes made

26

Hannah feel she'd better serve up something rather tastier if she was going to keep her place at the queen's table.

She rushed on: 'But I couldn't help thinking, I don't know, it's just that towards the end I felt like Michael was, not bored, but just sort of itching to get back to work. He even phoned the office a few times, whereas I could have stayed out there forever and never made contact with home again!' Her outburst struck a hysterical note in the cool, reasonable space of the café.

Lottie smiled indulgently. 'Oh, you know what these law bores are like. I'm surprised he managed three weeks at all, especially having just been made partner.'

'But it was our *honeymoon*.'

'Well, you know my opinion,' Lottie said, motioning to the waitress for more mineral water. 'Oh, could I have a fresh lemon wedge as well, please? You should never have married a lawyer, you should have gone for a banker boy like me – they're far more naturally predisposed to timewasting. It's all I can do to stop Rob booking holidays. He's already on about skiing and it's hardly August. I had to remind him that children need to be able to stand before they can ski, so I suppose that means shelling out for Hilary to come along too . . .'

Still struggling to regain her cool, Hannah interrupted: 'Lottie, I didn't choose to marry Michael *because* he's a successful lawyer. I just fell in love with someone who happened to be one.'

'Yes, a partner at one of the highest-paying firms in the City and wealthy enough not to have to work in the first place, what a stroke of luck!' Lottie was leaning into the table, winking at her. 'Come on, babe, I'm only kidding. Anyway, there's nothing wrong with opting for a decent lifestyle. Otherwise, where would you be? Somewhere like *her*?'

Hannah followed her friend's critical squint to a woman sitting a couple of tables away. She looked conspicuously unkempt among this well-heeled crowd. As she struggled to strap her baby to her chest in an outdated-looking side-sling, her shirt flopped off her shoulder to reveal a stained collar and chunky grey bra strap.

'Now *that's* why there's nothing wrong with marrying a lawyer,' Lottie continued. 'You don't need to see her naked ring finger to know she's, how can I put it, of *limited means*.'

'Lottie!' Hannah giggled. 'You sound like Queen Victoria – she might hear you! Besides, she might be the au pair or something.'

'Too old.'

'She looks younger than us.'

'Yeah, but too old,' Lottie shrugged. 'Take my word for it, I've interviewed dozens of the creatures and they're barely out of nappies themselves. Anyway, she could do with a recommendation for a decent hairdresser, you have to agree? Those roots must be at least a year old.'

As the woman lifted her head from kissing her baby's face to glance up at them, Hannah saw how radiant she looked, how entirely unflustered by Lottie's inspection. There was something childlike about her face, with its pale skin and neat little nose, like the face of an actress who could go on playing ingénue roles well into her thirties.

'Have you seen the baby?' Hannah asked quietly. 'That thick hair! It's absolutely gorgeous.' She was horrified to find her eyes filling up. Could it be the hormones kicking in already? That would explain her overreaction to those remarks about Michael that would normally have made her laugh.

'The ones with hair always look cuter,' Lottie agreed. 'Poor Ophelia's still totally bald.' As the waitress returned with their food she caught the other woman's eye and called out, 'Hi there, how old's yours?'

'Seven weeks. You?'

'Twelve. Chelsea and Westminster?'

'No,' the woman looked back to her child and Hannah saw how their eyes were now locked together. To avoid fresh water-

28

falls, she tucked into one of the melted cheese croutons on her plate.

'St Tommy's?' Lottie pursued. Totally unprompted, she then treated the stranger to an account of her own delivery-room experience, episiotomy and all. 'They tried to claim they had no private rooms and had to put me on a *ward*, it was a nightmare. I mean, with an *infected wound*?'

Hannah put down her fork.

'Have you got a little one?' the woman asked her. Her accent was blunter than theirs; something else to mark her out in this enclave. There was little evidence of a regional mix in Nappy Valley, the odd New World nanny notwithstanding.

'Oh no, I'm only just married.' Hannah flushed, remembering the woman's ringless status. 'I mean, not that you have to be married, of course . . .'

'Well no,' the woman giggled. 'You just need to have sex. Once.'

'Tell that to the IVF brigade,' Lottie said.

Now it was the other woman's turn to look awkward. 'I mean, if everything's in working order, of course.'

Hannah tried to rescue the situation with some introductions. 'I'm Hannah and this is Lottie.'

'Don't forget Ophelia,' Lottie said.

'I'm Siobhan, and this little one is Nora.'

'Nora?' Again Lottie dripped contempt. 'That's an *unusual* name.'

'Yes, after her great-grandmother.'

'Oh, what a nice thing to do,' Hannah said.

'So long as you don't offend the other side,' Lottie said with a smile. 'God, you won't believe the politics involved, Han. Names are the least of it!'

'OK, well, good to meet you,' Siobhan said, with a finality Hannah couldn't help admiring. She'd obviously had enough of Lottie's nitpicking.' 'Scuse me, can I have the bill please.'

As the waitress fussed around Nora, Lottie ate a couple of mouthfuls of soup before pushing it away, swirl of crème fraîche still intact. 'When are you back at work?' she asked Hannah. 'You are still going back, aren't you?'

Hannah hadn't given her part-time job at a local art school a second thought since being waved off before the wedding with low-fat cupcakes and white wine. 'Tuesday,' she said. 'I'm still just doing three days a week, not sure for how long . . .' She wondered why she didn't tell Lottie about the pregnancy test. It was wonderful news, after all, and who more likely to be delighted than a new mother? Then, once she'd confided in Lottie, she'd have no choice but to tell Michael, too, straight away, before he found out from Rob, before she could become obsessed with finding the perfect moment. *Tell her.* 'How about your work?' she asked instead. 'Have you had much time for it?'

Lottie's business as a personal property shopper was highly lucrative, Michael reported, especially considering it involved little more than eavesdropping in estate agents and cafés and having access to every private phone number in the area. It occurred to Hannah that perhaps she hadn't shown due interest in Lottie's business in the past, that there was much to be learned from her friend before she resumed dealings with the local estate agents.

Lottie sighed. 'Well, I've had to make time, really, the market's been going crazy this summer. And there's no excuse not to since I'm based at home and have Hilary and Kasia to help . . .'

'Kasia?'

'Our new au pair. She must have arrived while you were away. She's from Poland, gorgeous-looking girl, but her English is hopeless.'

'Oh dear.'

'Anyway, I've just taken on a couple of new clients this week, actually,' Lottie said, flicking invisible dust from her shoulder.

'What are they looking for?'

30

'Oh, same old, same old. Everyone wants a four- or five-bed-roomed Victorian Between the Commons, preferably double-fronted or with a basement kitchen – *they'll* be lucky. Mostly got a baby on the way, first or second. Where's their sense of adventure, for God's sake? I mean, when will someone surprise me?'

Just then, Ophelia began hiccupping and Hannah decided not to share her news today after all.

Chapter 4

Michael and Hannah's loft was in a converted Victorian school on the corner of Clapham Common Northside and Sisters Avenue. Sisters Avenue was one of Hannah's favourite streets in the area, except of course for the short stretch of dank little boxes put up to replace the terraces lost to bomb damage (they made her think of neglected front teeth in an otherwise well-flossed mouth). She particularly liked the large houses at the Lavender Hill end, with their curved facades and pretty patio gardens. And she loved the name. For her it evoked the Bennets and the Marches and all those other clever sets of siblings who bantered and squabbled and shared their dreams under the same roof.

By the time she got home the sun was lost in a clotted sky and it had turned into the sort of sticky, lightless afternoon that showed their own flat to its least advantage. It looked dusty, though it had just been cleaned; drab, though it was freshly decorated in the chalky greys Michael liked; and cold, though the air was humid. She still remembered the first time Michael had brought her here, soon after they met, on a Sunday afternoon last spring. He had proudly pointed out the brickwork over the door, 'Boys' spelled out in black, which had been the side entrance of the original infants' school. It was hard to imagine lines of living, breathing children pouring through the corridors now that the developers had picked through the buildings and turned all that infants needed into all that adults could ask for – which from what she could work out amounted to lots of walnut and granite. For Hannah, the 'Boys' sign merely reinforced the flat's bachelor interior. From the slate and stainless-steel kitchen to the tile and sandblasted-glass bathrooms, it was pure masculinity. Even the taps were like joysticks for some state-of-the-art game console.

She'd moved in with Michael back in March, by then a whole year since they'd met and just three months before the wedding. It was later than planned because she hadn't wanted to uproot Juliet from the Tufnell Park flat until it was absolutely necessary.

'What the hell is all this,' Michael had laughed as she unloaded her soft furnishings from the car, the sari cushions and framed textile fragments, the striped runner that looked small enough for a doll's house in Michael's grand hallway. But he'd welcomed them all, right down to the last scented candle, installing his wife-to-be in a spirit of fond resignation. His expression had put her in mind of a parent clearing space for the cage of a child's new guinea pig. Try not to scratch the woodwork, he might have said. She'd found it sweet; he'd never lived with a girlfriend before, it was a historic offering for him.

But somehow it had never come to feel like home. The cold surfaces she'd got used to easily enough (at least once a day she would silently thank Lottie for her insistence that Michael install under-floor heating everywhere there was tiled flooring). What still made her uneasy, however, was the internal structure, the spiral staircase that rocked underfoot, the dividing walls that felt so fragile, as though she could bring one down with a single stumble. It seemed temporary. It made her *feel* temporary.

Only the windows pleased her, the double-height originals of the school's assembly hall. She sat under one now in their living room as she flicked through Michael's phone book for a doctor's number. She'd need to talk to a GP about the pregnancy, but was still registered with her old doctor in North London.

'Welcome to The Northside Surgery. Our lines are open between ten a.m. and twelve noon and from three p.m. to four thirty p.m.'

It was two fifty-eight. She couldn't wait two minutes, but wanted to speak to someone immediately. After a moment's indecision she rang Juliet's work number.

'Hi, this is Juliet Goodwin, senior account handler at Imagineer Brand Builders. I'm not available to take your call . . .'

She hung up. She'd left a message for Juliet last week but hadn't heard back from her. She supposed her sister must still be feeling low about Luke; they'd talked often about how difficult it would be on the first anniversary of his death. She could just imagine what was going through Juliet's head: 'This time last year we were walking to the restaurant . . .'; 'This time last year he suggested another drink, but I wanted to leave; if only I'd said yes . . .' – that sort of thing, and worse, no doubt.

Of course, those conversations were months old now, from back in the days when Hannah would have been the first port of call for Juliet *while* she was feeling low, not after. Equally, she'd have had no thoughts of her own then about telling Lottie important news before her sister. But not now. She wasn't sure quite why this distance had opened up between them. Wedding madness, presumably. She'd need to devote some time to Juliet again, she decided, now all that was over.

The dialling tone signalled a new message and she entered the code. 'Hey, Tappy mate, it's Blakey. Are you back yet? We're having a party down here next Saturday, put it in the diary.'

She couldn't help smiling. Tappy: that silly, cryptic nickname of Michael's, though many of his friends just went with Fawcett, his actual surname at least ('Faucet, tap, geddit?' they'd told her in the beginning, as though sharing some ancient code). Their collective use of surnames and juvenile corruptions still amused her. These men were in their thirties, some getting close to forty, but spoke to each other as though still in prep school. It was like *Goodbye, Mr Chips*. It had only been when addressing the wedding invitations that she'd even discovered some of their Christian names, that 'Blakey' was Marcus Blake and 'Scummings' was Adam Cummings; she'd wondered if they'd even be able to recognise their own place names at the table.

Yes, 'Tappy' was going to need delicate handling with her explosive news. The Juliet situation would have to wait a little longer. First stop, the kitchen.

'What is this, my very own domestic goddess?' Michael asked, cuddling Hannah from behind as she began ladling the lamb onto plates.

She laughed. 'I just wanted to cook, especially as I'm not working this week. But don't worry, we can go back to eating out next week.'

'I'm not complaining, this is great. What can I do?'

'Just take the potatoes. Oh, and open the wine.'

He did as he was told, making that satisfied tutting sound in the roof of his mouth. She no longer wished he were five inches taller when she watched him walk away, just registered the blank where the thought used to be. The two of them were exactly the same height; it was a shame she had to limit her outings in high heels, but it had never been in danger of being a deal-breaker. At least he's got a good head of hair, her mother had said, ever the optimist. Indeed, there was no sign of thinning, and, besides, he was arrestingly handsome: high cheekbones, thick-lashed dark eyes, aquiline nose – that patrician sort of face that cried out to be painted, in her opinion, though that was never going to happen as Michael couldn't sit still for more than two minutes.

The air was thick with a variety of expensive smells: her own perfume, the rich food, scent from the candles she was burning, ginger and something, a wedding gift from Michael's assistant Charlotte – it was from a shop on Sloane Street where a box of four cost the price of a meal for two in a decent restaurant. Hannah had deliberated before lighting them, wondered if she shouldn't save or ration these precious wedding trinkets, observe some sort of togetherly ritual in their usage, like the cutting of the cake. But Michael wouldn't mind, she was sure; he'd scarcely looked up from his paper when she'd opened the first round of gifts, seemed more delighted by her excitement than by the generous gestures his friends had made.

'God, it's hell being back,' he said, scoffing down the food as though a rival hound waited to push its head into the bowl. 'Max is such a pain in the arse. He's just not going to forgive me for making partner. Fuck knows what sort of skulduggery's been going on while I was away"

Skulduggery. The word made her think of the baby and for the first time she recognised a sense of guilt alongside the exhilaration. Ridiculous, she told herself, she'd done nothing wrong, the whole run-up to the wedding was a complete blur and as that girl in the café had pointed out, all it took was the simple act of sex – once. As Michael complained on about the obstructive Max, all she could think was that she should tell him now. Married couples – especially newlyweds – were bursting to share their news, weren't they? It was precisely that togetherness, that finishing each other's sentences togetherness, that irritated everyone else on the planet. What was it the best man had said in his speech, something about the unique joy of finding someone who shares your spirit?

'It's quite fun being at home during the day,' she began. 'I'm not sure I want to go back to work at all.'

He chuckled at this, not taking her seriously.

'I was thinking, since my job's so casual, maybe we shouldn't wait at all, you know . . .'

'What?'

'Well, start thinking about having a baby sooner rather than later.'

'A baby?' Michael looked up agape. 'God, we've only been married a month, not even that! Didn't we have this conversation in Italy?'

She raised her eyebrows in amused reproach, as one might at an outspoken child who'd overstepped the mark. This, she'd found, was the way to deal with Michael when he was troublesome. 'Well then,' she said. 'We'd better start using contraception again, hadn't we?'

'Again? Aren't you on the pill?' He was stupefied, knife and fork suspended in midair.

'Michael, you know I came off it to lose weight for the wedding.'

Michael lowered his cutlery again. 'God, yeah, you did mention it, I suppose. Well, we've obviously been lucky. Better sort ourselves out again sharpish. Have you registered with my doctor yet?'

'Not yet.' She was right not to have made a sudden, bald announcement; far better to let the idea trickle down through the terraces of his consciousness until it collected at ground level and appealed to him afresh. She turned to her plate. The lamb was delicious, the sundried tomatoes plump from all the wine. It struck her as ridiculous that she should have taken expensively dehydrated food and pumped it full of liquid again.

'It's bloody Lottie isn't it,' Michael said, with the bright-eyed satisfaction of a sleuth finally arriving at his solution. 'Putting ideas in your head, dragging around that slug. You know she doesn't do a thing with it herself, she's got a nanny *and* an au pair, whatever the difference is.'

'*It's* got a name, Michael. *She* is called Ophelia. And don't call her a slug. Anyway, this is nothing to do with Lottie. I mean, it's hardly a novel idea, is it? Most of the married population get

37

around to reproducing at some point. Eighty per cent, or something like that.'

Michael, who usually responded well to statistics, just snapped at a forkful of potato.

'And Rob adores Ophelia,' Hannah added.

'Maccas would have been just as happy to have waited five years. He's still a young man.'

'Since when do you have to be an *old* man to have a baby?' Hannah asked, reasonably, subconsciously leaning back in her chair, arms hooked behind her so her full breasts would get his attention. 'The younger the better, surely? What about that guy from your work at our wedding, you know, the one with the pictures of his baby? Damon, was it? He's not even thirty and he said it was the best day of his life when his son was born.'

'Only because it was St Patrick's Day!' Michael chortled away to himself but something had flared in him and watching his face more closely she saw that it was fear. She felt sympathy for him. The prospect of parenthood *was* scary; that was why you were given nine months to get used to it.

'Think about it,' she said to him. 'You're thirty-five already, almost thirty-six. Leave it another ten years and you'll be in your sixties when our children are teenagers!'

'*Children*? They're multiplying! Let's just calm down for a bit.'

'I'm quite calm,' Hannah said, smiling.

He sat observing her for a minute. 'Come here.'

'I'm still eating.'

'It'll wait.'

He positioned her straddling him at the table, unbuttoned her top, slid his nose in her cleavage, tongue at her left nipple. 'I don't mean to argue,' he said, resurfacing. 'I love the idea of kids, of course I do. I just want you to myself for a bit.'

'I know, darling.'

38

'Besides, I don't think the world's ready for a mini-Mikey quite yet.'

'Hmm.' It was hard to argue with that.

'I'd better get a condom,' Michael grinned.

'OK, fine.'

Chapter 5

Was it Dominic who said that Camden Town was the wrong place at the wrong time *all* the time? You could see his point when you came out of the tube and faced the assembled crazed and dazed – this was surely where lepers would collect if the disease ever took North London. Juliet had moved to the area in March and was still no less wary than on that first Monday when she'd come back from work and been followed up Camden Road by a man with one leg shorter than the other who seemed to think she wanted to listen to his unintelligible diatribe. Only in Camden was it hard to shake off a man with a *limp*.

Today she hurried straight into Sainsbury's and made short work of emptying her bank account on a haul of cheap wine and cigarettes, plus an economy stack of candles. Someone else would have to bring the champagne. She wondered if it were sad or just inevitable that by her twenty-ninth birthday she still couldn't afford to fill her trolley without checking the prices. A taxi was essential, though, she couldn't possibly get all this home without the clinking of bottles attracting a train of winos behind her.

There was a note on the coffee table from her flatmate Sasha: '*Happy birthday, J! We're just grabbing some food. Back later, S & C x*'.

So it was official: Sasha was no longer a single initial. Well, that hadn't taken long; the air in the bathroom was barely clear of the last one's winter pine lotions and potions. Matthew, he'd been called. Now she came to think of it, hadn't there been a bit of an overlap between M and C? God forbid that Sasha might have had to revert to the first-person singular for a day or two. *We'll* be in the bar, that should be fine with *us*, let me just check what *we're* doing this weekend. Had Juliet been as slavish to the plural all those years with Luke? She supposed she must have been. 'Juke', close friends had called them, other couples from college who'd never known them apart. She saw very little of those couples now.

'We'll be single girls together!' Sasha had said, soon after Juliet and she had been introduced and the fit between one's impending homelessness and the other's newly spare room had been established. 'It'll be such fun!' She was a friend of a friend of Hannah's and had shared Juliet's bemusement with the wedding mania that had engulfed their circle. Yes, while everyone else was wetting their knickers over cabbage roses and four-poster beds in Capri, they'd get busy being single girls together.

But Juliet had been installed less than two weeks before discovering that Sasha was neither single nor fun. She was also permanently in residence, leaving for work in the morning after Juliet and routinely arriving home before her. The first time Juliet found the bathroom occupied by Matthew and his alpine aura she'd had to wonder where Sasha had ever managed to meet him. Work, was the short answer, though Sasha, who enjoyed talking about herself, could also supply a long one.

But all of this was fair enough. Matthew was a nice enough guy, fun in a family entertainer sort of way, and if he was around a lot during the week then at least he tended to return to his own place at weekends. Besides, it was hardly a case for the trade descriptions act; by May Juliet had met Guy and acquired a man herself.

No, the let-down was everything else. For starters, Sasha

41

turned out to be very mean with money, the sort of person who was incapable of splitting a phone bill fifty-fifty. She was also a non-drinker and rabid anti-smoker who had blackout blinds on her bedroom windows and whose eight hours a night could be achieved only in absolute silence.

But it was when Matthew was dismissed and Callum presented that things really took a plunge beyond the pale. Now there were no weekends, or even occasional nights, spent away by either of them. 'He's only got a single bed at his place,' was Sasha's explanation when Juliet pointed out that Callum had stayed over eleven nights in a row. 'It's easier here.' Which came back to one thing: it was Sasha's flat, Sasha's run of play. Juliet couldn't finish a roll of toilet paper without having an invoice thrust in her face, but Sasha had the right to set up a halfway house of Callum's in the hallway if she so chose and there would be nothing Juliet could do about it. You could *never* have equality when your flatmate was also the flat owner.

Putting the note in the bin, she unpacked the booze. A sharpener, that was what she needed, hadn't drunk a drop all day thanks to a meeting that had overrun into her lunch hour. She poured herself a glass of red wine and tried to remember how many people she'd invited that evening. Too few to move furniture, but enough to make it worth mixing up a couple of large jugs of punch – she'd use some of those expired liqueurs Sasha kept on top of the fridge and brought out for hot toddies when someone was ill.

Once that was done and the candles were haphazardly alight on every surface, she carried the wine bottle into her bedroom and started getting ready. Now she was feeling excited. She hadn't hosted a party for years, the last had been a Christmas do she and Luke had thrown after he'd come back with a caseload of vodka from a trip to Poland. This was the first party she'd ever held on her own. It had seemed essential somehow, worth the hours spent coaxing Sasha to allow it.

What a shame, then, that everyone turned out to be coming later rather than sooner: Guy not until at least eleven, and only if he could get away from the bar early; Larry after he'd detoured to his place in Holloway to pick up music; Fulton, another new drinking friend, was held up at work; and Kate had gone all the way home to Palmers Green to get changed – she'd forgotten to bring her gear into the office and was determined to wear a particular dress, which made Juliet wonder which particular Imagineer male it was in aid of. She'd been hinting at a new interest lately and Larry and Juliet were desperate to find out who he was. No doubt he was currently with the rest of the work mob in the pub, paying for their own drinks for an hour or two in preference to being the first to turn up. By Juliet's reckoning Hannah and Michael should be the first to arrive.

Hannah. She hadn't quite decided if she'd forgiven her sister for leaving her in the lurch before the wedding, turning her out of the flat they'd shared with only a hair's breadth of notice. How could Hannah possibly have needed the money from the flat once she'd ensnared the fabulous Mr Fawcett, a sure cash cow if that amazing loft near Clapham Common was anything to go by? She'd tried not to be churlish about it, the property was Hannah's to do with as she pleased, but it would take a while to forget that morning in February when she'd come home early from work to find the estate agent taking photos – he already had keys and Hannah *still* hadn't told her. But there hadn't been time to make a fuss. Hannah had got it into her head that she should pay for the wedding and with just four months to go she needed a quick sale. Juliet's future accommodation had probably been the last thing on her mind. Certainly, she hadn't noticed the irony of her upping sticks to a street called *Sisters* Avenue while sacrificing her own to this, this S & C purgatory.

She was still feeling hurt, she knew that. But, as she glugged down the wine, Juliet felt her natural generosity resurface. No, she wouldn't make a scene with Hannah today: it was her birthday, her hair was perfect after a three-hour cut and colour, both sleek and floppy, exactly the way she liked it, and the dress – a vintage sleeveless shift in blood-red – was stunning *and* a bargain.

The intercom was buzzing. 'Happy birthday,' Hannah said, handing her a black box tied with silver ribbon. 'Something from Florence. You look lovely, what a wonderful dress.'

'Thank you. Red wine OK? Where's Michael?'

'Coming later, he's caught up at work.' Hannah took a doubtful sip of the enormous balloon of wine handed to her. She seemed different, Juliet thought, looking. Her sister's beauty had an expensive sheen to it these days, but she was used to that by now. No, there was something else as well, something more intrinsic than the surface benefits of a real tan and regular facials.

'So how's married life?' she asked. 'How was Italy?'

'Fantastic, thanks. It seems like ages since the wedding, doesn't it? It's weird to get back to real life.'

'You'll have to show me the photos, Mum's been raving about them. Oh, what a pretty scarf, thank you.' It was silk and obviously costly, but not really Juliet's style. The old Hannah wouldn't have picked this out for her.

'The photos *have* come out well, I must admit,' Hannah said. 'There're some really good ones of you, Juliet. How's everything going with Sasha? She's so nice, isn't she?'

'Oh, OK,' Juliet said brightly. 'It's a bit crowded, though, you know, when the boys are around.'

'Are you still going out with Guy?'

'It's only been a month since I saw you, Han!'

'Sorry, I just thought . . .'

'Anyway, we're not "going out". It's far too soon for anything big.' Juliet was instantly sorry for snapping, all too aware that observers of her relationship with Guy couldn't win either way: she liked suggestions that she wasn't serious about him as little as those that she was.

'I liked him very much,' Hannah said carefully. 'I'm glad you decided to bring him to the wedding in the end. How's his bar doing? Where is it again?' She was obviously making a big effort to show interest, but the fact that she needed to make an effort at all irritated Juliet and then made her feel guilty for her own irritation.

They both turned at the sound of a key in the door. It was Sasha. She wasn't dressed for a party, just jeans and a vest top, and Juliet couldn't decide whether to take her casualness as a compliment or an insult. Her flatmate had that rosy pony-club wholesomeness that could easily be transformed into beauty with some basic updating, but at twenty-eight showed no signs of letting go of the reins. GND, Larry called her – Girl Next Door – and there had been times recently when Juliet would have been glad to relocate her there.

'Happy birthday!' Sasha said, eyes scanning the living room for early signs of disturbance. 'I *will* get you a pressie, I just haven't had a chance to go shopping today.' There would be no gift, Juliet knew. 'I hope this isn't going to be an all-nighter, mind you, Juliet, I've got a *terrible* migraine.'

They'd discussed this, or 'negotiated' it to be more accurate. Sasha *knew* it might be a late night, even though it was a Thursday; it was a 'for one night only' licence for Juliet to play music and dance and smoke. 'Well, it won't be Horlicks at ten, I can tell you that,' she grinned. 'I intend to get my last year of youth off to a decent start.'

'Don't say that, I'm only a year behind you! D'you think I look thirty already? People at work always think I'm more senior than I am. I'm sure it's because my forehead is more wrinkled, or maybe it's just the headache.' As usual, Sasha could think only of herself. It was all she could do to acknowledge Hannah. 'Hello,

Hannah, how's married life? Oh, I don't think you've met *my* new chap. This is Callum . . .'

Callum trotted forward. Long of face and with fur for hair, he was either canine or lupine, Juliet could never decide which, but the point was he was more that than he was human. In her more honest moments, she might admit that what really annoyed her about him was not so much the impurity of his looks – who was perfect, after all? – but the fact that for him she functioned merely as an unfavourable contrast with The Goddess Sasha. 'That's an *interesting* skirt. Sasha only wears black on the bottom.' ('Yes, Callum, that's because Sasha's got a big arse.') 'Don't you need a shower? Sasha washes *her* hair every day.' ('Yes, Callum, that's because hers is the texture of hundred-year-old rope.') It was only a matter of time before she really lost it and said something out loud. It would be worth it to see the look on his canine/lupine face.

Hannah offered him her hand and he shook it dispassionately, giving an imitation of a smile. Just like a pet that had been trained in human behaviours, Juliet thought, wanting to giggle.

'Sasha's got a bag like that,' he said to Hannah. 'Only hers is smaller, more discreet.'

Juliet hoped Hannah might club him around the head with it, but she just smiled at him in that cool, tolerant way of hers and said, 'Lovely, isn't it? A honeymoon present to myself. Callum's a nice name. Is it Scottish? How do you spell it?'

'Otherwise known as Caliban,' Juliet muttered, as Sasha swept him out of sight into the kitchen. 'They won't be long, she's just got to feed him his Chum.'

'Juliet!' Hannah said. 'I know what you mean, though, he's not quite in the same league as her, is he?'

'It's what they call dating down,' Juliet said, and Hannah laughed. This was nice, this felt more like their old companiable banter.

'What does he do?' Hannah asked.

'Works with her – that's how they met. What would we all do without the hunting ground of the office?'

But this time Hannah looked puzzled and the camaraderie seemed to vanish as quickly as it had arrived. She didn't know about her sister's shenanigans with Dominic, for Juliet had stopped telling her everything by then. There'd seemed little point unless she could somehow relate the tale to beaded bodices or the prevailing wisdom on the correct ratio of ushers to guests. Nor could Hannah now remember what Sasha did, Juliet saw, and suddenly she didn't feel like helping her out. It bothered her that Hannah never seemed to remember any of the details about her life any more.

'At the British Museum,' she said finally. 'He's not in the press office with Sasha, though. Does something underground with tools, I think. Best place for him. No windows.'

'Oh, the museum, OK, that's right.'

The buzzer went again and suddenly everyone arrived at once. First in were the Imagineer lot, dozens of them, shiftless, heads down, like buffalo seeking shade from the heat; then Larry, who'd obviously had something stronger than Fanta to keep his energies up as he lugged cases of vinyl and CDs into the living room; and Kate, wearing black denim and lots of dark eye make-up. She looked gorgeous and smudgy against the white walls, like a charcoal drawing.

'Is that the sister?' Juliet heard her ask Larry as she began distributing drinks to the new arrivals.

'Yep, by the window. Pretty drop dead, isn't she?'

'She's *beautiful*.'

'You can say that again, mate. Where's the liquor?' The vowels were pure East Coast, the ennui straight out of West London: it had to be Fulton. Fulton was the only American Juliet had ever met who didn't consider Brits to be especially big drinkers. He'd taken to London life like a fish to water, or, as Larry put it, like a fish, period.

'Hi Fulton!' Kate said, enthusiastically enough for Juliet to suspect he might be the target of her friend's attentions that evening. And who could blame her? Fulton, who looked like a youngish Kevin Costner but behaved like an oldish Hugh Hefner, was *very* sexy. She'd considered him for herself when they'd first met, at a party last Christmas, but it had been too soon for her, and by the time she *was* ready she'd got to know him well enough to see that his approach to relationships was too dismissive even for her. Fulton was fun: no more, no less.

'How're you doing?' Larry asked, offering him a cigarette.

'Cool,' Fulton said. 'Just don't tell me if you hear my mobile. I've had enough for one day.' Fulton worked for an online financial news service, but claimed that he would give up work as soon as his father died or he married for money, whichever came first. Juliet took him at his word: like most of the other men she met these days, Fulton had no appetite for an office-based career. 'Might pull a sickie tomorrow,' he said. 'Depending how shit-faced I get tonight.' It was always funny hearing him roll out those British colloquialisms, though she and Larry had agreed he might have to be ostracised if he ever discovered cockney rhyming slang.

'So what have you lot been up to today?' Fulton asked them.

'Oh, you know,' said Larry. 'Leveraging the brand. Developing strategic wisdom. Advising Kate on breaking her, er, dry spell.'

'Larry!' Kate protested.

'Didn't know London women ever had dry spells,' Fulton said, and launched into an account of a female colleague who'd now notched up a football team's worth of 'covers' in his office. 'And I'm talking an *American* football team . . .'

'No "cover" yourself tonight?' Larry asked.

'No, but there may be one coming through soon.'

'Ooh! A new squeeze?' Juliet passed him a glass of her punch, which looked like turps drained from a jar of old paintbrushes. She watched him wince slightly at the first mouthful.

'Jesus, Juliet! Yeah, we just met last weekend.'

'What does this one do?' Larry asked.

'Sports sponsorship, maybe. Something that involves a lot of smiling. She's cute,' Fulton grinned. 'You'll like her. She's from Swansea.'

'*Swansea?*'

'Where is that, anyway?' She said it was near Bristol. Like that's gonna help me out!'

Juliet laughed and started to explain, while Larry drifted off to take over the music. Then Sasha came to announce her intent to 'mingle' and Juliet slipped off to continue her rounds with the punch, making sure to keep her own glass filled, topping up her good mood like a spinal anaesthetic. After a while she stopped to look at the dying light outside, lovely even through the smog of cigarette smoke. The flat overlooked the southern end of Camden Square where some strange lopsided construction served as the neighbourhood's playground. She thought of summer birthdays, remembering with a flood of warmth, a feeling close to desire, how she'd loved having the family's only summer celebration.

Suddenly this felt like the perfect party. Larry was playing the most perfect mellow music, everyone was perfectly drunk, gushing out compliments, loving her dress, loving *her*. It seemed impossible to think that a year ago she'd been a basket case. Then, her losses had seemed too huge to overcome: not only Luke himself, but also the security their shared life had guaranteed. And by the time she'd got used, with Hannah's help, to losing all of that, she'd lost Hannah, too – at least that's how it had felt. But now the wedding was over perhaps Hannah would be back down to earth and back in Juliet's life, too. The two of them needed to have a proper talk, that much was clear, but not here, not tonight.

'Juliet, Guy's here!'

He was early – more perfection! He'd brought flowers and a case of wine, sorted them out before coming to join her. He always took care of the practical stuff before getting around to the greetings, an occupational hazard, she supposed, but it gave her the opportunity to watch him out of context, away from the bar. According to Larry, she sometimes treated him like an alternative to the cigarette machine, and in a way it was true. That night last month, the weird anniversary night, had somehow confirmed for her a new fear of being in a couple again. However powerful her natural liking – and physical attraction – for Guy, she lacked the stamina for anything that might involve relationship maintenance. It was as though Luke had left her with the heart but not the stomach. But it was impossible to explain to anyone else something she didn't even understand herself, which was why she struggled to answer when Kate kept asking, 'Don't you ever want to see Guy *away* from the bar?'

Yes. Tonight, the answer was yes. She liked seeing him here, she liked how he fell into easy conversation with Michael, who had been stuck with Callum since his arrival an hour ago, liked how he was the only one who seemed like a proper, uncomplicated grown-up man.

'I'm so glad you came.' She clung to him for a long time.

'Are you OK?' Guy asked, seeming to sense that this clutch was more than alcoholic affection.

'Yes, fine, a bit drunk. I was just thinking about when I was younger. My birthday parties were always held in the garden, because it was summer. I was trying to remember the first one, when I'd started school and had real friends.'

'What did you do? What games?'

'There were dolls in the wigwam, they were hosting a tea party. You had to know the password to get in. I remember Hannah didn't know it. We said she was too big to come in, she would take up too much room.'

'That's not very nice,' Guy grinned. 'Was this before Laura was born?'

'Yes, quite a bit before.' They didn't talk about their past lives much and she knew it was she who had forced them into this peculiar state of blankness. She just couldn't do it, had even briefed her family not to talk to him about Luke at Hannah's wedding. And whenever he introduced references to his own history, she tried not to listen, anxious to keep herself as unencumbered by his past as he was by hers. She'd never asked about previous jobs or old girlfriends, would be hard pushed to remember his brother's name or which part of New Zealand he was from. It was as though they'd met as amnesiacs and could relate purely in the present.

'Guy! Been back to South Africa recently?' Michael asked. 'I've just been doing a bit of business with some Cape Town companies . . .'

Juliet couldn't help turning a critical eye on her new brother-in-law. She supposed he really was a permanent fixture now, legally joined to the Goodwins. She'd distrusted him from the start, as had Luke, who'd met him several times in the early days. They'd agreed he was insincere and, for his age, unnaturally attached to his posse of male friends. Of course, part of the problem was this womanising past of his; everyone talked about it, even Hannah. And it hadn't helped that Sasha had added a few tales, too. Michael had once come on to her at a Sunday lunch party, she said, and then again a month or two later and she could have sworn he didn't even remember her from the first time. She'd been vague about the dates and Juliet hadn't pressed it. At least he'd never approached *her*, though when they were first introduced he did wink at her. For some reason she'd never been able to forget that image. Fulton had made her laugh the other day when he'd said, 'Come on, Juliet, I think you need to get over the fact that your sister has married a winker.'

He was right, of course. She knew she had to learn to like

Michael. Michael made Hannah happy, and she should have no argument with that. But, still, it was going to take more than private money and a City career to gain *her* respect. Been back to South Africa! For all his expensive education he was still the sort of crass Brit who had trouble differentiating between Antipodeans and South Africans.

She tuned out and noticed Hannah talking to Larry in the corner. The candlelight reflected in those wide, dark eyes made her look like the heroine of a costume drama, enigmatic, untouchable. It occurred to Juliet that Hannah and Larry had had their heads together for quite a while. The two of them were getting on, *really* getting on. That hadn't happened before, Larry was always by *her* side. She edged towards them, pulling Guy and Michael with her. Did she detect the tiniest reluctance on Hannah's part to step back and welcome them before repositioning herself, glowing-eyed, between Larry and her husband?

'Congratulations,' Larry said to Michael, with an exaggerated heartiness that signalled he was far drunker than anyone else. 'Tell us, then, what's it like to be *joined*?'

'Joined?'

'Y'know, man and wife.'

'Oh,' Michael said. 'Well, what can I say? It passes the time.' His hand appeared on the other side of Hannah's waist and from where Juliet stood it looked as though he'd plunged his arm right through her body.

'Well, I have to say I'm surprised,' Larry said, and they all turned to him to see what he meant.

'You know, death by matrimony and all that,' Larry said, stumbling slightly to the side. 'Nobody said it better than Wham,' he added. Juliet giggled.

'*Wham*? Isn't it time you moved on, mate?' Michael said, rattled.

'Good idea,' Larry cried. 'Care to dance?' He lunged towards the stereo, racked up the volume and set about the kind of comedy pogoing that Juliet usually left parties to avoid. The room was ridiculously small and he stumbled against the sofa before being absorbed into the crowd. Suddenly it seemed like there were hundreds of people in the room, not tens, as though the floor were going to give way beneath their feet.

'Who *is* that bloke?' Michael asked Hannah.

'Juliet's friend Larry. He's very nice. Incredibly clever.'

'He wrote a novel when he was twelve,' Juliet told them. 'He's totally wasted at Imagineer. He does his work in a tenth of the time of anyone else.'

'Bit of a muppet, if you ask me,' Michael said.

Juliet danced, careful to keep out of Larry's range, though others were less fortunate and there were already a couple of spilled drinks and an ashtray on the floor. Lucky the professional carpet cleaners were already booked for Saturday – one of Sasha's conditions. Where *was* Sasha anyway? She hadn't seen her for hours. Scanning the room, she was aware of an insistent buzzing noise in her head.

'We're making a move now, Juliet,' Hannah said, hugging her. She was surprised to feel herself resist a little. Maybe she wasn't quite ready for that heart-to-heart after all. 'I'll give you a call tomorrow.'

'Bye, sis,' Michael said, still draining his glass as he was guided to the door. 'Let's hope my car hasn't been looted.'

'It's not that bad around here!' Hannah protested. 'This isn't far from where I used to live, you know.'

'Thank God I took you away from all that . . .' Michael laughed.

Kate joined Juliet at the door and watched them leave. 'You know, sometimes I think I'd quite like that,' she said.

Juliet examined her friend's downcast face. Had the chosen one failed to turn up or was it the suggestion of a new flame for Fulton that had brought this on? 'What?' she said, slipping her arm through Kate's. 'You want an arrogant bastard? Well, I'm sure we could arrange that. London's full of them. *Imagineer's* full of them . . .'

'No, you know what I mean, just *marriage* and all that. Knowing there's always going to be someone else, I suppose. Bloody hell, what's that noise?'

Sasha's voice was screaming out from her bedroom: 'Juliet! Juliet! The *door*!'

Two bored-looking blokes stood outside, one leaning against the hallway wall. 'We're from Camden Council Noise Pollution Service. We've had several phone calls about the music . . .'

'Tell them to supply their own if they don't like my taste,' Larry said camply, appearing at Juliet's side. 'I've tried to cater for a variety of genre lovers, but I'm *never* going to be able to please all of my listeners all of the time.'

It wasn't funny but he was so indignant Juliet doubled over with laughter, sloshing her drink down her bare leg and onto the carpet. 'Bugger.'

'What's happening?' Fulton asked, coming out of the bathroom and flicking cigarette ash into the hallway at the men's feet.

'The *volume* of the music is what's disturbing them,' the Camden man said, addressing Juliet. 'Now, are you the occupant, Miss . . . ? Can I take your name, please?'

'Juliet, what's going on?' Sasha now emerged from her bedroom in a towelling robe.

'Oh, is it bedtime?' Larry asked, pulling at the sash. She backed away from him, glowering.

'Don't let the bed bugs bite,' Fulton said, throwing his cigarette end over the banister.

'*Juliet!*'

'All under control,' Juliet said weakly. 'All under control.' When she finally turned back into the living room, music subdued and orders to wind down the party understood, the place was still heaving. Someone had transferred Baileys into Sasha's prized glass flowers from Prague and was tipping them towards a line of waiting open mouths. Bits and pieces of clothing had been discarded and there was an awful lot of bare flesh crammed into a very small space. Bring back the days of wigwams and tea parties, she thought, I could just about handle that.

Chapter 6

Luckily, two client teams were out on Talent Evolution training so the office was half-empty when Juliet turned up at ten the next morning.

'Just so you know, I can't do a thing today,' she announced to the Smithfield's corner. 'My head just does not compute.' She wrapped her cardigan over the back of her chair and watched it slide straight to the floor. The energy to pick it up eluded her for the moment: the double espresso and brownie consumed in the lift didn't seem to be having any effect. 'Oh,' she said, looking up. 'Are *you* sitting there now?'

A small man with a moon face and a suit slightly too roomy for him was in Michelle's seat and judging by the coffee, mobile and pair of ailing succulents arranged in front of him he was there to stay. 'Not gunna let a window seat go to waste,' he said. 'Dom OKed it.'

This was all she needed, the Swine within spitting distance. It was just too tempting for the saliva glands. Ever since Phil 'The Swine' Swain had joined their team three months ago that face had come to represent for Juliet Imagineer itself: pleased with itself, avid for success, contemptuous of competition. He was the most experienced planner in the team after Michelle and her; in title she and Phil were separated only by one word, the 'senior' that prefixed hers, but in truth they might have been working for rival firms. God, she would rather look across at *Callum* than Phil Swain.

'Heavy night?' he asked pleasantly. She knew he knew she'd had a party, that she'd sent out individual emails to invite her colleagues rather than using the team alias that would have included him automatically.

'Not really,' she said, 'just a few birthday drinks.'

'Oh, that's right, the big three-oh.'

'No,' Juliet said testily, 'the big two-nine.'

'Right, if you say so.'

'I do say so.' She wanted to lasso him with her cardigan and watch his lungs empty in front of her, but she still didn't have the strength to pick it up.

'Juliet, just the girl I want.' Dominic was standing over them, so immaculate she could almost smell the hot iron on pure cotton. She felt grubby, despite her own snatched shower. 'I see you've discovered your new neighbour?'

'I have. But I thought window spots were for account directors and senior planners only?'

Phil's eyes narrowed with yakuza viciousness. She kept her own wide and blithe, waiting for him to look away first.

'There's no hard and fast rule,' Dominic shrugged. 'I thought Phil deserved a pew with a view and now you two can share knowledge while Michelle's away. Why's your hair wet, anyway?' he asked her. 'Is it raining?' As they were not only standing by but also *discussing* the window that framed another blue-skied day his question was preposterous.

'Just been to the gym,' she lied, ignoring Phil's growl of disbelief.

'Listen,' Dominic said. 'I need you to join me for an induction session.'

'Induction? Is someone giving birth?'

Dominic sniggered. 'No flies on you today, eh, Jules? Look,

Emma's booked in a couple of new junior planners for a chat before they start next week. It's the usual spiel: I'll stir them up a bit with the company philosophy stuff, then you talk them through an average day, show them what they'll be aspiring to.'

If he was being sarcastic it was with more subtlety than they were used to. Phil even looked slightly sulky at being overlooked for this good cop, bad cop assignment.

'I thought we were about to lose staff, not take on new people?' Juliet said.

'We're about to *restructure*,' Dominic said. 'I've always got places for talented new faces.'

Please let the rhyming be accidental, Juliet thought. 'Of course,' she said. 'I'd love to meet them. What time?'

'Now,' Dominic said. 'We're in meeting room two, and don't shilly-shally on the way. Oh, your computer seems to have crashed, Jules. Better get Support to have a look.'

There was no disguising the sarcasm now as she'd yet to turn on the monitor and her bag was sitting on the keyboard, Travelcard visible. It was so typical. She could count on one hand the number of times she'd been late in the last ten months, but Dominic seemed to have had a front row seat for each. She wouldn't put it past Phil to be tipping him off by email. '*Hi Dominic, is Juliet with you? No one's seen her today and I've got the client on the phone . . .*'

'Are you still on for our status meeting later?' Phil asked her, half an eye on Dominic as he hovered to check texts on his phone. 'I've booked the boardroom and emailed everyone for contributions to the agenda.'

'Sure, great.'

'I can chair it if you're not feeling up to it?' Phil really was a master, Juliet thought. He managed to inject genuine compassion into his voice, even though he'd be the first to celebrate if she announced she had a week to live. Clearly Michelle's seat was not the only thing he planned to hijack around here.

'No, I'm fine,' she said brightly. 'We do need to catch up; though I guess there's not much to report. It's been quite a slow summer.'

'Has it now?' Dominic was interested again. 'Well, do something about it, guys, that's your job, isn't it?'

'Yes, in fact, I've just sent out . . .'

'New phone, Dom?' Phil interrupted. 'It's really cool.'

'. . . two new proposals . . .' Juliet tailed off, giving up.

'Yeah,' Dominic grinned at Phil. 'Have a look at this picture, Swainy, I think it must be someone's arse. What d'you think?'

The two rookies were alarmingly bright of eye and Juliet found herself regarding them as she might a pair of seal pups at the zoo, barely registering their features, even their gender. They had the kind of early twenties faces Dominic liked to see around the place, with that shiny new skin even three years of college substance abuse couldn't blemish. But there was something else: unlike the majority of Imagineer's staff, they didn't appear to be hungover, they were healthy, they were *alert*. Had she too been like this once? The high of last night was long gone; she felt jaded beyond levels she'd ever thought possible.

Dominic pushed his glasses up onto his head, leaned back in his chair and began rotating a silver pen like a cheerleader's baton. 'So if you get used to thinking of the client company as the earth, it's easier. It has an inner core, outer core, mantle and crust. Now, tell me, which of those layers is the *brand*?'

The pups glanced at each other and then one spoke. 'The outer bit, because it's the bit we see.'

Wrong, Juliet cringed.

'Cuff him, Juliet!' cried Dominic.

Juliet turned, half-apologetically, to Pup A. 'We believe that the inner core is the brand.'

'The inner core is the brand,' he repeated.

59

'So, if the inner core is the brand, what's the crust?' Pup B asked suddenly.

'Juliet?' Dominic said.

She took a deep breath and began to recite. 'The crust would be the media we use to express the brand and basically any outer expression of the brand, for example, the logo, the corporate colours, the tone of voice. But you need to understand the qualities of the inner core before you can start to think about the mantle or the crust.'

'Or if you prefer, imagine a scotch egg,' Dominic said. This was the bit where they were supposed to laugh, but the faces looked unsure.

'What's the sausage meat, then?' Pup A asked.

'I'm vegetarian,' Pup B added.

This is a farce, Juliet thought. My head is the bloody scotch egg. Performing her piece about account planning felt like being pushed to the very brink of human endurance, but she was pleased to see Dominic's nod of approval as she wound up. 'And, of course, we take our key contacts out to lunch regularly, keep in close touch even if there's not a project active. We're always looking for mindshare, we want Imagineer to be Smithfield's' first port of call.'

'Yes, we're very close to our clients,' Dominic said. 'We like to think of our staff as interchangeable with theirs in many ways. In fact, Juliet will be the first to take part in our new job-swap scheme.'

This was news to Juliet, but she knew she couldn't show it.

'Excellent,' said Pup A gamely, and the other one nodded energetically, suddenly aware, apparently, that he was being overshadowed by his keener litter-mate.

'Yes, I'm very excited about it,' she said. 'I'm sure it will be very, er, *illuminating*. Anyway,' she laughed, 'how bad can it be, it's only for a week . . .'

'A month,' Dominic corrected, getting jollier by the moment.

'At the client's HQ. Where are Smithfield's based again, Jules?'

'Vauxhall,' she smiled. 'Not the most glamorous of offices, I'm afraid.' In fact, they were in a building earmarked for demolition by the council, where the smell in the lifts was just a shade away from a public lavatory and where the staff had stopped believing that their new glass tower near Tower Bridge would ever be finished.

'Well, good luck,' Pup A said, and she smiled weakly back at him.

'Oh, Juliet knows never to rely on luck,' Dominic cut in, rising from his seat. 'So we'll see you a week on Monday, shall we? Nine a.m. sharp. We'll walk you to the lifts.'

As the lift doors closed, Juliet turned to Dominic. 'What's this about a job swap? Were you serious?'

'Of course. Don't look so put out. I don't see this happening for a month or so. October, I thought. We're just trying to decide who you'll swap with. Probably Lucy or Jessica.'

Both juniors in the marketing team at Smithfield's. This would mean that in her dealings with the team at Imagineer she'd barely be on an equal footing with the Swine.

'Who will cover my work while I'm there?'

'Your job swapper, of course. Get with the programme, Juliet, it's not that difficult a concept, surely? Of course, Phil will handle anything confidential.'

Great, now all she needed was to have her salary adjusted to the supermarket's slave pay structure and her degradation would be complete.

'You'll be on your normal Imagineer salary, of course,' Dominic said, with his infuriatingly acute antennae for other people's anxieties. 'But you won't be eligible for any team bonus that month.'

And the next bonus just happened to be paid in October. It wasn't worth arguing that it covered the July to September quarter, which would be spent grafting in the Imagineer office as usual. Dominic already knew that, of course, having devised the bonus structure himself.

'Fine.'

'There's a meeting with the client about it on Monday morning,' he said. 'Eight a.m. Not a problem, I hope?'

'Of course not, I'll put it straight in the diary.'

'Don't forget. Oh, BTW . . .'

Juliet hated the way he spelled out acronyms when it was fewer syllables to say the phrase in full. Larry did it as well, it was obviously a male thing.

'Yes?'

'Your job description, I enjoyed reading it. Very droll.'

'Oh. Thank you.'

So that was what this was all about, she thought, the pushing-paper rubbish.

'See you later alligator,' he said.

I'd like to see an alligator swallow him live, she thought, smiling her goodbyes – feet first, so he'd be forced to watch his own agonising, bone-crunching death. She pressed the lift button. A cigarette break was in order.

Kate and Larry were already standing in the street, Larry's head bowed over cupped hands. Juliet told them about the job swap. 'And if that's not bad enough, Phil Swain is now sitting opposite me in Michelle's old seat!'

'Not the Swine?' Larry said. 'You poor sod.'

'I think you're both very mean to call him that,' Kate said. 'He's OK, you know.'

'She actually thinks he's sexy,' Larry said to Juliet, grimacing.

'And so he is,' Juliet said. 'Compared to a *goblin*.' She lit a cigarette. So *that* was who Kate was hoping to see last night. Not Fulton, but Phil. But she was less amused when she saw the dismay on Kate's face. 'Sorry, darling, I'm sure he can be a perfectly decent person. It's just a shame we seem to be rivals for Michelle's job. Makes it difficult, y'know?'

'I understand,' Kate said.

She was so sweet, Juliet thought, so willing to see the best in people. Starting from Monday she was going to try to be more like Kate.

Chapter 7

'You'll have to see our locum,' the receptionist said to Hannah, her voice as frazzled as the thicket of brown hair fast defeating the restraints of its band. 'It's all a bit chaotic this morning, we've got a baby clinic on.'

The last piece of information was only too obvious, as Hannah had stumbled twice on her way from door to reception desk in the gridlock of rubber wheels and dripping rain covers. All around lay fleecy bundles of sneezing, hiccupping, runny-eyed new flesh. It was an overwhelming sight. In her pregnancy book, the babies were all curled up in their amniotic sacs, innocent little kittens breaking their sleep only to indulge in the occasional recreational somersault. How different they looked once hatched, how *frightening*. 'All babies look like Winston Churchill,' that was what Rob had said at Ophelia's christening. 'Everyone knows that.' But there was nothing Churchillian about this bunch, they were more like alien life-forms. Was there really one of these increasing its cell count inside her?

'Hannah Fawcett, please! Hannah Fawcett?' She still took a second to respond to her new name, instinctively thinking of herself as a Goodwin. Her heart sank slightly when she saw that the doctor was male and much younger than she was. He reminded her of one of the estate agents on Northcote Road.

'Mrs Fawcett. You're new with us, I see. Is your husband registered here?' Michael didn't do the NHS, was registered privately at a practice near their flat, but after some thought Hannah had sought independent ground. 'Well, you'll need to book in to see the nurse another time so she can take all your details.'

'OK.' There was something about his delivery that gave her the impression he was improvising. Perhaps it was his first session as a GP; after all, someone had to be the one to submit to the freshman's manhandling. Hopefully no internal examination would be necessary. She noticed the scales on the floor next to her and wondered if she'd put on any weight yet. She'd always feared she had the sort of build that would double in size during pregnancy. Michael might not like that; more than once he'd praised Lottie for keeping her shape when pregnant.

'So what can I do to help you today, Mrs Fawcett?'

'Er, I've just discovered I'm pregnant.'

'And how do you feel about this?'

'Oh, very happy.'

'Excellent, well you're in good company. Clapham has the highest birth-rate in Europe, you know.'

'Does that mean I won't get a place at the hospital, you know, on the night?' She'd already been playing out the worst-case scenarios in her head.

The doctor laughed. 'Let's not worry about that quite yet, eh? There's a long way to go. Now, let me get my wheel.'

She had visions of him leaping up to perform for her on a unicycle, couldn't shake the thought that he was some sort of imposter. But instead he pulled out a grubby plastic disc that looked like a protractor and placed it on the notepad in front of him.

'So when was the first day of your last period?'

Hannah wasn't sure and spent a moment grappling with images of the wedding, the hair and make-up dry runs, the dress fittings. Was all that excitement really so recent?

65

'So, the twenty-third of March is your EDD. Estimated date of delivery, that is. You're exactly eight weeks pregnant. Now, how have you been feeling?'

'Fine, a bit sick.'

'Poor you. Sick as a parrot, I bet, that's quite common, as I'm sure you know. Get your husband to bring you a dry biscuit to nibble on before you get out of bed in the morning.'

The idea that he took her for an uncomplicated married woman with devoted father-to-be delivering snacks to her bed-side caused Hannah a twinge of misgiving. She considered asking his advice about breaking the news to Michael – he probably came across women like her all the time, women who took their time over big announcements, whose husbands worked week-ends and who, before they knew it, had let eight weeks of pregnancy slip away. Eight weeks! That was almost a quarter of the whole thing.

'Even though I feel sick,' she said, 'at the same time, I feel hungry, all the time, *really* hungry, like . . .' She felt suddenly inarticulate.

He cocked his head to join her search for the perfect simile. 'Hungry like a wolf?'

'Yes, I suppose so.' Parrots, wolves, she was starting to wonder if this conversation were taking place inside her head. She looked at the door, all that separated her from the squealing mini aliens on the other side. She felt no safer inside than out.

'Also quite typical,' the doctor said. 'OK, while we're at it, why don't we run through the foods you should be trying to avoid.'

Again, the information he gave sounded as though he was making it up on the spot and Hannah found she wanted to laugh. She couldn't rid her head of the image of this drama-student figure in the delivery room, waving his protractor between her legs, talking about blue-veined cheeses. Eventually, when the giggles neared eruption point, she sensed that he was winding down and decided to experiment with eye contact again. His face was kind and weary; he couldn't possibly be newly qualified. '. . . So, we'll write to them and they'll send you a date for your twelve-week scan. If you haven't heard by eleven weeks you should call them. OK?'

Outside, the chaos had subsided and immediately her sense of surreality disappeared. She wondered what had come over her during the consultation; not only had she not listened but she'd also wasted her first opportunity to ask questions. She supposed it didn't matter much; as soon as Michael knew she'd be signed up for a private antenatal package and she'd never see this doctor again.

'Hi there! Hannah, isn't it?' Hannah turned to a nearby mother and pushchair. 'I'm Siobhan, I don't know if you remember, we met a few weeks ago in that organic place on Northcote Road?' It was the girl from the café and the pretty baby with the storm of dark hair. The girl's own hair was shorter, the blonde ends chopped off, which made her navy blue eyes very large in her face. There was a gap between her front teeth and her skin was pale and petal soft. She looked totally natural. Hannah felt suddenly overtanned, over-groomed, old.

'Siobhan, yes, of course, how are you?'

'Fine, just here for Nora's jabs. We had to wait forever, but luckily she was good as gold.' Siobhan looked with interest at Hannah, who saw that she was waiting for her to reciprocate with an update of her own ailment, as people so readily did in doctors' surgeries. Uncomfortable with the scrutiny, she turned to look at Nora, who was sleeping in her pushchair, arms up in surrender above her head. 'What a sweetie,' she said. 'Whatever they've done to her it's obviously done the trick!'

'I know, I wouldn't mind a shot of something myself. I think I got exactly three hours' sleep last night, and not all in one go. Hey, if you're not doing anything, why don't we get a coffee?'

'That would be lovely.' Hannah felt instantly thirsty, as

though she was choking on hot sand. She looked around for a water dispenser, but the assault course of buggies put her off.

'Come on, Nora,' said Siobhan. 'Time to go, no more nasty needles for a while!' They all did this, the mothers, supplied a running commentary to life's daily doings, even if the baby was fast asleep. Instinct, Hannah supposed, or sleep-deprived derangement, perhaps. They didn't even seem to notice they were doing it. But three hours' sleep! That wasn't enough. She would never be able to survive on that. Would Michael be persuaded to help in the night? She couldn't be sure.

Siobhan expertly manoeuvred Nora's pushchair around waiting patients like a mother hoovering around teenage legs and Hannah rushed to get the door. But the change in air seemed to jolt the baby awake and she'd soon begun crying.

'What's wrong?' Hannah asked, squatting by the buggy. 'It's OK, sweet pea . . .'

'She's fine,' Siobhan said. 'She probably needs a nappy change. I really ought to get her home, actually. But you're welcome to come and have a cuppa at mine, if you haven't got to rush off?'

'Sure, I have no plans.'

'The bus stop's just across the road, if that's OK?' Siobhan said.

'Bus stop?'

'I don't live in Clapham any more. I registered at this surgery years ago when I was staying with a friend and I've never bothered moving. Should, really, now Nora's jabs are up-to-date. I live in Herne Hill, near Brixton.'

'Brixton?' It seemed Hannah couldn't come up with anything but an echo. Siobhan just chuckled. 'It's only a few stops on the thirty-seven . . . look, here's the bus already.'

On the lower deck there was some grumbling as Siobhan uprooted two old men to access the pushchair bay. 'Just had a bleedin' hip replacement,' one muttered at her and a couple of nearby passengers tutted their allegiance. Hannah was surprised by their hostility, but Siobhan just smiled at the man and said, 'Thank you,' in the politest of tones. Then she turned back to Hannah and whispered, 'Well, if the hip was bleeding, it's just as well it was replaced. Sorry, that was very poor. But these old codgers really seem to hate babies, don't they.'

Hannah didn't know what to say. She'd never seen anyone over forty-five in Nappy Valley.

'So that can't be *your* nearest GP either,' Siobhan said, 'if you live over near Northcote Road?'

'We live on Clapham Common Northside actually. No, I needed to register quickly and none of the local places were taking new patients.'

'Nothing wrong, I hope?' Siobhan asked, concerned. Hannah saw that she was one of those people whose every emotion streaked across her face before she could catch it. So different from Lottie's composed mask, so different from her own.

'Actually, I've just found out I'm pregnant,' she said, astonished by her own announcement. Now that she'd told the doctor and Siobhan – not to mention a bus full of baby-haters – it was starting to sound more real.

'How wonderful!' Siobhan exclaimed. Her face was pink with pleasure. 'I'm so pleased for you. You must both be so chuffed?'

'Yes.'

'How many weeks?'

'Eight, apparently.'

'It's funny at first how they do it all in weeks,' Siobhan said. 'But you soon get used to it.'

Now Hannah felt overwhelmed, bewildered to find her body swinging from side to side on a packed, stinking bus. It had been raining that morning and the smell of damp trainers mingled with last week's fried chicken was overpowering. She was desperate to change the subject. 'Where are we?' she asked, looking out the window at the crowds.

'Brixton. That's the town hall, there's the cinema. They do a

69

baby club there, by the way. Might be useful to know this time next year!'

'I don't think I've been here before.' Ridiculously, she was nervous. Outside the comfort zone of her own postcode she felt like she was leaving London altogether, as though she'd been snatched by a stranger. She wanted to prise open the doors and dash all the way home. 'I mean, I lived in North London until recently.'

'Don't worry, it's perfectly civilised!' Siobhan smiled at her confusion. 'I'm on the Dulwich Road. Do you know it?'

'Dulwich Road, no, I don't think so.'

'We're almost there.'

Once they arrived at Siobhan's flat Hannah relaxed again. It was on the basement floor of a large redbrick house, with its own entrance and a little front patio crowded with potted flowers. Most were close to extinction. 'I got very green fingered when I was pregnant,' Siobhan said. 'Now I don't have time to water myself.'

Inside, the ceilings were surprisingly high, the rooms large and square. The flat smelled of baby smells: warm milk, washing powder, tumble-dried laundry. Siobhan showed Hannah the little patio garden at the back, which led steeply up to a lawn and the park beyond. There were more steps, rather grander wrought-iron ones, running down to the lawn from a balcony on the raised ground floor.

'We all share,' Siobhan explained. 'The upstairs flats have a key to the side gate.'

'What's all that screaming?' Hannah asked.

'The lido in the park. You wouldn't believe how many people don't seem to work at this time of year!'

'There's a lido?' She was still doing the silly echo.

'Yes, it's a huge one. Bit too manic for Nora, she's still getting used to her baby bath, but next summer she'll love it.'

Back inside, Siobhan whisked Nora off to change her nappy

and Hannah looked around the kitchen. It was comforting somehow to see the piles of baby clothes and scrubbed woodwork; a
far cry from the gleaming laboratory of their kitchen at home.
Try as she might she simply couldn't imagine BabyGros sitting
next to the stainless-steel espresso machine.

'Right, coffee!' Siobhan was back. 'Let me just put Nora in
her chair. I've only got Nescafé and I'm afraid it's not decaf. Is
that OK?'

'Yes, of course.'

There was something about watching hot water being poured
into mugs and biscuits arranged on a big white plate that opened
the floodgates for Hannah. 'You know I said we were both
pleased? About the baby, I mean. Actually, I haven't told
Michael – my husband – not yet, anyway.'

'Oh? Why not?' Siobhan had a calm way about her, lulling,
almost. Hannah couldn't imagine her raising her voice.

'I've been waiting for the right moment, but we haven't had
much time to ourselves,' she said. 'He's been working a lot. So I
thought maybe I should get it confirmed at the doctor's and then
tell him. But they didn't do a blood test or anything.'

'They just take your word for it,' Siobhan laughed. 'Those
pregnancy tests are practically a hundred per cent accurate. You
should tell him soon, though, because you really need support
during this time. It's all very confusing.'

'I know. I just didn't want to tell him when he was halfway
out the door . . .'

'It's OK, I know how you feel,' Siobhan said. 'Just because the
pregnancy test is positive doesn't necessarily mean the family
reaction will be!'

'Oh, no,' Hannah protested. Siobhan obviously thought she
was too *scared* to tell Michael. Somehow she'd cast him in a
role – a not very heroic one at that – of which he was neither
aware nor deserving. OK, so he'd been less than enthusiastic that
evening when she'd dropped a few hints, but that had been an

71

abstract discussion. Once he realised the baby was a reality, he'd be delighted, wouldn't he? She felt guilty. Poor Michael, it wasn't right that virtual strangers knew his affairs better than he did. 'I'm sure he'll be really happy,' she told Siobhan firmly. 'I'm going to tell him tonight.'

'Good,' Siobhan said. 'Let's go and sit on the sofa, Nora needs a stretch.'

'Are you with anyone?' Hannah asked. The flat showed no signs or smells of maleness.

'No, I'm on my own. *We're* on our own, I should say.'

'Where's Nora's father?' Her directness was met with a defensive flicker, though Siobhan still smiled. 'Sorry,' Hannah added, 'it's none of my business.'

'No, don't worry, it's fine. Suffice to say he's no longer in the picture. It was just a one-night thing, I haven't seen him since.'

'So he doesn't know about the baby?'

'No.' Siobhan's face remained cheerful.

'I suppose it's a long story?' Hannah asked.

'Actually, no, quite a short story, and not very interesting. To be honest I don't give it any thought from one day to the next.'

Hannah bit into a Jaffa Cake. This was weird, sitting here perfectly companionably, dismissing life-altering dilemmas in a few words. It felt as though Siobhan was an old schoolfriend she'd bumped into, as though they'd had such a close friendship in the past that they were able to pick it up again with only the most basic updating.

'Who was that other woman in the café that day?' Siobhan asked, settling on the sofa. 'The sharp one who didn't eat anything.'

Her bluntness reminded Hannah of Juliet. 'Oh, you mean Lottie?' she laughed. 'She's actually a lovely person. Maybe seems a bit arrogant if you don't know her.'

'A bit?' Siobhan laughed. 'Sorry, I shouldn't be rude. She reminded me of that actress my mum likes, y'know, from *The Good Life*?'

'Penelope Keith? She'd be *horrified* to hear that.'

'Who, Penelope?'

Hannah couldn't help laughing at this.

'Are you and Lottie really good mates, then?' Siobhan asked.

'Yes, we've become very close. She's also Michael's best friend's wife,' Hannah said. 'That's how I know her. They've got this very close-knit circle, all been friends since university, and it was nice to have a friendly face around when I first started going out with him. She helped me with the wedding a lot – we just got married in June. She's one of those people who seems to know everyone. Even when she was heavily pregnant she was running around sorting stuff out for me.'

'Really? Well, it's always good to have people around to help. Are your family not in London?'

'My sister Juliet is, but my parents are in Norfolk now. We grew up in Berkshire, but they had a bit of a financial disaster earlier in the year when Dad's pension was lost. His old company folded, it was all a bit of a shock. Anyway, they had to sell the old house.'

'How awful.' Siobhan was sipping her tea, waiting for Hannah to go on; she looked as though she'd be happy to wait just as long as Hannah needed. It was nice that she was so comfortable with silence. Most people couldn't wait to fill a pause with their own voice.

'So have you got lots of family and friends around you?' Hannah asked. 'It must be hard work looking after Nora on your own.'

'Not family, they're all in Cheshire, except my brother who works in the Middle East. It didn't go down too well, the whole no-father thing. That's what I meant about the positive reaction. But they'll come around, I expect. They were exactly the same when I dropped out of college after the first year. They waited until I had a regular job and had bought this place before admitting it might have been an acceptable move. But sometimes I wonder if they wouldn't prefer it if I *had* made a mistake and lived to regret it for the rest of my life.'

'Really?' Hannah said. She hoped she didn't look too appalled. 'Surely not?'

'You wouldn't put up with that from friends, would you?' Siobhan sighed. 'I suppose it's because families know you'll always be connected that they can indulge in such strong disapproval. Friends just wouldn't take the risk.'

Again Hannah thought of Juliet. No friend had been so lukewarm about Michael, about the wedding. If it hadn't been for Lottie bullying her into it, Juliet probably wouldn't have participated at all.

'But anyway,' Siobhan said, 'things could be much harder. I mean, imagine twins!'

Immediately Hannah began fretting again. Did multiple births run in Michael's family? She couldn't remember seeing any identical faces at the wedding.

'So how did you meet your man?' Siobhan asked.

'I was working as a conference organiser. It was hell, all City and foreign clients. Far too pressurised for me. He was speaking at one of the telecom events. We sort of hit it off. I'd been seeing this other guy, but he kind of stole me away.' Though she chuckled, she still felt that lurch of panic when she thought about life before Michael. It hadn't been unpleasant by any means, but it had felt like it was starting to dribble off in the wrong direction. She'd never quite thrown off the thought that Michael had rescued her, saved her from taking that B road through her thirties where everything she wanted remained out of reach.

'How romantic,' Siobhan said. 'Are you working now?'

'I help out three days a week at an adult education art school, just admin, but the business seems to be winding down. The courses are barely half-full next term.'

'Good timing, then,' Siobhan said. 'I worked right until the ninth month, I was shattered by the end, but I needed to save cash so I could spend as much time as possible with Nora once she arrived.'

'What d'you do?'

'Secretarial, and a bit of project management. My last job was temping for an American bank. Good money, but . . . well, you know if you've worked in the City. It wasn't really my kind of thing.'

'Will you go back?'

'I'm not sure. I mean, what's the point of having a child if you never see it?'

What's the point of having a career if you're just going to give it up at the first whiff of a nappy, that was Lottie's view, but Hannah thought better than to repeat it here. Siobhan's lifestyle was obviously rather different from Lottie's – and her own. As Siobhan cuddled Nora into position for feeding, she didn't ask about Hannah's plans for future work, no doubt assuming that Hannah wouldn't be needing to work after her baby was born. 'Helping out', that was how Hannah had described her job; it was true that she even thought of the word job in inverted commas. She felt pathetic. What kind of example would that be to a daughter?

She wanted to try to explain, as much to herself as to Siobhan. 'I do want to find something I'm good at, but I'm not cut out for that corporate environment. I'm not really sure how I even started in conferences. I'd done a bit of PR before, but never really specialised. I suppose I never felt I had the natural talent for that. I can't see myself going back to either of those careers.'

Siobhan nodded.

'Besides,' Hannah finished, 'I'm sure raising a child is harder than any office job.'

'I don't like to be the one to disillusion you,' Siobhan said, raising an eyebrow, 'but yes. Except when they're sleeping, of course – then it all seems manageable again.'

All at once Hannah longed for a pillow against her own

cheek. She was so tired these days; thank God her non-job was within walking distance of home. She wondered if she'd be able to get a cab anywhere nearby.

'This has been lovely,' she said as she was leaving. 'Let's do it again.' She was glad she meant it, wasn't just being polite.

'We'd like that,' Siobhan beamed. 'Let me put your number in my phone. Come and lie on your ladybird for a second, Nora.'

'I'll hold her if you like,' Hannah offered. She couldn't resist kissing Nora's forehead and touching the little eyebrows, palely sketched above fascinated dark eyes.

'Do you know how to get home?' Siobhan asked. 'It's the thirty-seven bus going towards Putney. This side of the road.'

'Thanks, yes, I'll be fine.' And at the feel of the baby in her arms, both soft and solid at the same time, Hannah had a powerful instinct that everything was going to be all right.

Chapter 8

'*The embryo is 10–14 mm in size*,' Hannah read, covering most of the browser with a Word document and using the arrow keys to read the text line by line. '*The fingers and toes are well defined. The eyelids are developed, although they will stay closed for several months. The construction of the heart is complete.*'

The father is still in the dark. She *had* to tell Michael, it was getting crazy. Not only had she now been sent her appointment details for the scan, but if, as she hoped, they were going to sell the loft for something more practical they'd need to get a move on – according to Lottie, the market had started to slow down a bit recently.

After that conversation with Siobhan she'd been determined to tell him the same night and had booked a table at their favourite restaurant on Lavender Hill. But he'd called to say he'd be working late and she shouldn't wait up for him. By ten o'clock she'd been in a deep sleep. '*I'll tell him if you like*,' Siobhan had joked when they'd met up again a few days later. Hannah had laughed, but she knew it must look peculiar. It *felt* peculiar.

The worst thing was that with each new day of silence came the growing suspicion that the introverted girl she'd once been was worming her way back in again. As a child she'd been secretive and dreamy, while Juliet, though younger, had been the loud one who blurted out her every opinion. Hannah remembered feeling very proud when her mother had once admonished Juliet for asking a shop assistant why she had so many spots: 'You should learn to keep your own counsel, young lady, like your sister.' But later, at university, Hannah saw that keeping your counsel was far less popular than spilling every last bean, and if you didn't have enough beans to spill you needed to grow some more pretty damn quickly. She'd worked hard at opening up, joining in the girls' talk, and by the time Michael had entered her life she'd become really quite confident at confidences.

Tonight, she'd do it tonight, definitely, straight after Juliet had left. She hoped Juliet would bring Guy to dinner, he was so easy and relaxed; Juliet was less testy around him. But his job meant he didn't have many nights free; he probably wouldn't want to waste one schlepping down to South London for an evening with the married dullards. And now she came to think of it, hadn't Michael offended him at Juliet's party by taking him for an South African? Even Juliet had been reluctant to come tonight, refusing Hannah's offer to stay overnight as though she feared her visa would be withdrawn and she'd never get back across the river again.

'Hannah, shall we break the back of these September registrations?' The voice of her colleague Rani broke her reverie.

'Yes, of course, just give me a second.'

'Maybe I'll make some tea first,' Rani said. 'Cuppa for you?'

'Yes please, decaf.'

'You still doing this detoxing thingy?'

'Yes, it's going really well.'

Hannah closed the web page and stretched her arms above her head. Sitting at the computer was already getting more uncomfortable. How on earth could Michael not have noticed the difference in her, whether she'd actually told him or not? She was clumsy, self-absorbed, eating non-stop. Surely these were all behavioural changes a newlywed would notice of his mate?

78

There was no bump yet, but her breasts were a cup-size bigger already and bullet firm. Rani set down the mug with a little slop and the sight of it made Hannah sigh inwardly with the pleasure of the familiar. That was another thing pregnancy had brought, this heightened sense of the preciousness of normality; the sight of people queuing at the post office or a dog being walked on the common, snuffling away at the bushes and tree trunks. They wouldn't have caught her eye in the past; now they engulfed her with security.

'Doughnut?' Rani offered, holding out the box.

'Ooh, thank you.' For the hundredth time Hannah wondered how old Rani was. Her skin was unlined, apparently ageless, but the teeth were yellowing, gums receding; it wasn't a young person's mouth. She should have just asked her straight away, or found out through skilful contextual questioning, along with the other personal details colleagues usually exchanged. Instead, week after week, the two of them had sat side by side in an atmosphere of amiable detachment. There'd been none of the intimacy she'd shared within minutes with Siobhan. What on earth must Rani think of her? She'd probably dismissed her as another spoiled Nappy Valley wife with artistic pretensions, too snooty to bother getting to know an outsider.

And in a way it was true. When Hannah had seen the ad in the local magazine she'd told herself it might open up new career paths for her, she might learn how to run her own art school or retrain as a teacher. She'd fantasised about owning her own gallery on Northcote Road and beating more experienced rivals to the fresh new talent up for grabs at local degree shows. But if she was honest, this had never been more than something to do during the run-up to the wedding – something to stop her becoming one of those obsessed brides-to-be you saw on TV who didn't seem to care who it was they were actually marrying so long as they'd been granted their Big Day.

Sessions at work were dull. Together, she and Rani handled all

79

the paperwork: logging the student registrations, printing off contracts for teachers, chasing up tuition fees, booking models. But all real decisions were made by the absent owner, Grace, a moderately successful painter in her day, but now losing her marbles, according to Rani. 'Though she's still got her own two eyes,' she said. 'They are the crucial marbles in this playing field.'

The occasional phone call from Grace's son Christian kept things ticking over for now: Grace had an idea for a guest teacher, he'd changed accountants, they'd decided to sell one of the portraits that hung in the entrance hall. All of this Rani reported; Hannah had never even met Grace herself, Christian just twice. In the end, her days had turned out to be about marking time, just like any other desk job. A job injecting jam into the doughnuts she and Rani now shared would be more artistic. Yes, she would have to leave. She already thought of it in retrospect.

'Looking forward to your holiday?' she asked Rani, eager to show willing, even though Rani had pushed her to the brink of a coma lately with her itineraries for Crete and Santorini.

'Very much so, I spoke to my sister-in-law and the tickets have now arrived.'

'How lovely, some nice September sun.'

'Still eighty-five degrees,' said Rani proudly.

'I'm jealous!'

'Oh, did I tell you,' Rani said through sugared lips, 'Christian has asked to see us next week. Can you pop in on Monday?'

'Sure.'

'I think they really are closing this place down. I heard he's getting the building valued.' Grace owned outright the crumbling building on Clapham Common Southside where the school was housed, a substantial asset by anyone's standards. Lottie would know its value, Hannah thought.

'Really?'

'It's craziness not to,' Rani said. 'The school makes only

peanuts and they could get millions if they sold this place. Make it into flats for lawyers, you know?'

'How soon d'you think it will happen?' Hannah asked.

'I don't know. End of the term? Maybe before then. We'll have to sort out refunds, I suppose. But this is no skin off my bones.'

'Oh?'

'I paid for my holiday already. Lucky, eh?' She sighed and turned to look at the whitewashed island on her screensaver. It was as though life after her holiday would never come around. That was the way to do it, Hannah thought, cursing herself for her habit of long-term worry. In fact, hadn't that been one of her New Year's resolutions this year, to never look beyond a fortnight ahead? ('Take off the "fort" and you're getting closer,' Juliet had said.)

'Yes,' she said to Rani. 'Lucky.'

That evening Hannah watched Juliet's face on the video intercom as it peered at the buttons for the right flat number. She was definitely alone, her face would look different if Guy were down there with her, less closed. Hannah wondered if her own expression changed when her husband was nearby. She'd seen her face in repose a couple of days ago, when she caught sight of herself in a shop mirror for a split second before recognising who it was. It was vague, vacant even. It was the face of the echo girl.

'Hannah, it's me.'

'Come on up.'

She felt a surge of longing for how it was when they were younger, how it was until a year or two ago, in fact, before Michael, before Juliet's last trip with Luke. When Juliet had come back from Mexico and had been living with her in Tufnell Park to save for the next leg of her travels, she'd still been the real Juliet then, the Juliet whose kindness underpinned all of those outrageous opinions, the Juliet who saw the best in everyone. But ever since Luke's death she'd seemed determined to hunt

81

out the worst. Hannah had bought a book about bereavement and had dutifully followed her sister's every move up the ladder of grief. It was her suspicion that Juliet had got stuck on the 'Anger' rung and had forgotten that 'Acceptance' was well within sight.

Juliet was brittle from the moment she stepped through the door, offering Hannah just a cursory hug before casting around the living room, systematically poking at things and making remarks about all the new items on display.

'Wedding list,' Hannah said, handing her a vodka and tonic in a brand-new tumbler – Chrysler Highball, the shop had called it.

'God, what a haul,' Juliet said. 'Remind me to get married sometime.'

'Oh, I'm sure you will,' Hannah said. Two minutes in and she already felt uneasy. Juliet settled in the corner of the L-shaped leather sofa and looked at her as though awaiting the first question in a job interview, an interview that someone had persuaded her to turn up to for practice purposes only. She wasn't being impolite exactly, just unengaged. As usual, she looked fantastic, in some sort of shimmering pink top and denim skirt with funny woven pockets. She had that ability everyone seemed to want of making high-street tat look like vintage designer, and since she complained ceaselessly about having no money this was quite a blessing.

'So how's work going?'

'Oh, grim, you know.' So that was it. Juliet took work very seriously and became unsettled if she felt it was going badly.

'Why?'

'Dominic's on my case big-time at the moment.'

'I thought he was your biggest fan?'

'*Was*, yes. Now he hates me. But I'm sick of Imagineer, anyway. Sick of working my arse off to finance his holidays sailing to Zanzibar or boarding down the Matterhorn or whatever it is he's into this season. And I'm definitely paid less than the other senior handlers. I saw Phil Swain's payslip and even *he*'s paid more than me and he's not even a senior!'

'Men always get more,' Hannah tutted, not sure if she knew who Phil Swain was.

'You know Dominic's less than a *year* older than me and he's worth fifty million?'

'He's obviously some sort of genius, though, isn't he?' Hannah said.

'He's obviously some sort of knob,' Juliet grumbled.

Hannah was determined to stay positive. 'What about the account director job?'

'Oh, I've got a cat's chance in hell of getting that. It's only maternity cover anyway. Michelle'll be back as soon as she's popped the kid out.'

Hannah felt herself touch her lower abdomen. 'So d'you think you might move on then?'

Juliet shrugged. 'No point, I just can't deal with interviews and all that at the moment. And there are projects I'm working on that I need to see through to the end myself. December's always fun, though. I don't think I paid for a single drink last Christmas.' She sighed and crossed her long legs; they were deeply tanned and very slender. Too skinny, Hannah thought; her ankles looked too delicate to support her body weight.

'I'm just going to the loo,' she said. 'Help yourself to whatever you need . . .'

She was a while upstairs, squeezing away at her empty bladder (Siobhan had warned her about that particular symptom) and checking her profile in the full-length mirror. When she came back Juliet was in the kitchen topping up her vodka.

'I just *love* Michael's ice dispenser,' she said. 'I've *always* wanted one of these big American fridges. They're so *Knots Landing*, aren't they? Does it do crushed ice as well?' She'd done that the last time she was here, referred to things in the flat as Michael's rather than as jointly owned. Technically, that had been correct in the past, Hannah supposed, but not now. Obviously Juliet was not just in a mood about work, she was also annoyed with *her* about something. Perhaps it was the conspicuous display of Fawcett wealth that was the problem tonight, the spectacular flat with its expensive furniture and paintings, the countless wedding gifts on every surface, not a mass-market trinket among them. But Juliet would have her eyelashes pulled out with rusty tweezers before admitting to envy, Hannah knew. She *had* to get this straightened out, or the two of them would be strangers by the time the baby was born.

'Juliet, I've got so much to tell you.' The wide waif eyes looked up at her and Hannah got a glimpse of the dutiful younger sister, the big-eyed nine-year-old ready to take her assigned role in the next game, willing to sing Cindi Lauper to Hannah's Madonna.

'Yes? Sorry, I've been going on about work again. Just tell me to shut up.'

'I've got some news . . .' Hannah blurted, but stopped at the sound of the key in the door. Michael was home, before eight thirty for the first time in weeks.

'Hey, Juliet! How's my second favourite Goodwin? You look brown. Been away for the weekend?'

Juliet turned to him with that same interview posture of polite attention. 'God, no,' she said, 'I'm far too broke for a holiday. The arms and legs are fake.'

'Well, what wonders they work with prosthetics these days,' Michael laughed. 'I could've sworn they were the real McCoy. Can we go straight out, girls? I'm starving, haven't eaten all day.'

'Sure,' Juliet said, glugging back her drink and making for the door.

Hannah hadn't touched her own drink. Wearily, she rinsed out their glasses before following.

'All right babe?' Michael asked Hannah, nuzzling her neck,

when Juliet went to find the cigarette machine. His hand was under her skirt, between her thighs, deft as a tailor. 'You look very sexy at the moment.'

She didn't feel sexy and the prospect of a curry didn't help, but the other two had insisted.

'The food here is the best in South London,' Michael said to Juliet when she settled back into the booth, cigarettes and mobile phone in front of her as though she couldn't breathe with them out of her sight. 'The menu makes me laugh, though. You know, their big thing is that all the food is "colour-free".'

'What, it's all transparent blobs? Yuk!'

'They mean they don't use any artificial colourings,' Hannah said.

'Hey, you think?' Juliet snorted and Michael joined in the laughter, increasing the pressure on her thigh. Hannah tried very hard not to feel that the two of them were ganging up on her. Their matching expressions of horror when she ordered a soft drink rather than the oversized Cobras they'd chosen hadn't been the greatest of starts. And Juliet's rhythmic sucking and stubbing of cigarettes was making her nauseous.

'So, Juliet, what happened that night at your place?' Michael asked once they'd ordered. 'Last we saw of you, you were about to be removed by the boys in blue.'

'Oh, that was nothing,' Juliet said. 'Just a complaint about the music. Sasha threw a bit of a strop about it, actually. Can't blame her, I suppose. But these things happen at parties, don't they? You know she made me get the carpet professionally cleaned as well, *and* the windows.'

'Jesus, what a neat freak,' Michael said, crunching a poppadum.

'I don't know how you can still share,' Hannah said without thinking. 'Waiting for your turn for the shower and all that . . .'

'Some of us have no choice,' Juliet interrupted. 'It's called rent, real life, you must remember it, sis? Anyway, just as soon as my overdraft is cleared I'll look for something else. Maybe Kate will want to share.'

'Well, you're welcome to stay with us for a while,' Michael said generously. Juliet always had brought out the best in him, Hannah thought, despite – or perhaps because of – her clear lack of admiration for him. 'We've got an extra room. It'd keep the parents from coming up too often, for one thing. Fortunately, my father's done his back in so they don't like staying with us at the moment – too many steep stairs. Funny how spiral steps seem to fox the over-sixties.'

Juliet giggled.

'Seriously, come and stay whenever you like. It is *Sisters* Avenue, after all. Perfect for the Goodwin girls.'

Now Hannah felt she needed to explain why *she'd* not yet offered to have Juliet stay with them, or *live* with them – was that not what Michael was suggesting? After all, he had no idea the second bedroom would be needed for a nursery, unless they moved, in which case there'd be room for the whole family. She felt a shiver of anxiety as she thought about the pile of house details she'd now amassed, most stuffed away in a box of wedding swatches. *Another* secret.

'Technically, we're on Clapham Common Northside,' she pointed out to Michael, trying to sound light-hearted.

Michael just shrugged. 'I mean, that Camden place is like something out of Legoland, isn't it? The bathroom is so small, I practically had to reverse out after I took a leak.'

'Thanks for the offer, Michael,' Juliet said, 'that's very kind. But living with loved-up newlyweds might be the only thing worse than putting up with Sasha and her one-man admiration society.'

'*That* hairy little runt,' Michael agreed and Juliet beamed. Michael really was very good at judging what it took to win someone over, Hannah thought. She was pleased he was making such an effort with her sister. 'Great party,' he added.

'Shame you guys had to leave so early,' Juliet said.

'That was my fault,' Hannah said, 'I wasn't feeling well. It was quite late, anyway, almost midnight.' Well, midnight on a Thursday was late for her, she thought, and Friday was one of the days she worked.

Juliet looked at her with an expression of quizzical indulgence, as though faced with an ancient relative who was never going to grasp the fact that the young were no longer subject to strict night curfews. 'So what were you going to tell me?' she asked Hannah suddenly. 'Back in the flat?'

'Oh,' Hannah struggled to cover up her alarm. 'Just that I'm thinking of giving up work, or cutting down my hours at least. Looks like the school's in trouble.'

'I've never been able to see how it makes any money,' Michael said.

'You should do something different,' said Juliet, 'a proper job again. I mean, do you ever come into the West End any more? That art school must be about as fun as an old people's home. All those wee-soaked old biddies drawing bits of bark. I can just imagine a life class. Urgh!'

Michael snorted. 'It's the models who're naked, not the old biddies painting them. At least I hope so.' He signalled to the waiter for more drinks.

'Just because it's an art class it doesn't mean everyone's a hundred years old,' Hannah laughed. 'People of all ages want to learn how to paint.'

'Do they?' Juliet asked. 'I don't know anyone who's got the time.'

'Anyway, that's the least of it,' Michael said. 'Has she told you her latest scheme? She's wanting a kid!'

'Michael!' Hannah said. 'Children are not a *scheme*.' So he'd remembered that conversation, then. Good, that meant he'd been giving the subject some thought and it wouldn't be such a shock when she broke the news.

'Oh yeah?' Juliet looked as though nothing could surprise her less. 'You must be nuts,' she added. 'We had Sasha's nieces over the other day and it was a nightmare. One of them burned her finger playing with my lighter and Sasha's sister-in-law spoke to me like I was Myra Hindley. The wailing went on for hours.'

'Oh, you shouldn't let the little buggers make you cry,' Michael said.

'Ha, ha.' Juliet rolled her eyes. 'Anyway, Larry came over and saved the day. He made up a great story about a rhinoceros who'd lost his horn and some kids came along and knitted it a new one. They loved it.'

'I can't imagine Larry with small children,' said Hannah, eyes softening.

'He's very good, actually. Men often are, aren't they? So much closer to the state of infancy than we are.'

'Well, infantile is exactly how I'd describe him, anyway,' Michael said with a sneer.

'I think you got the wrong impression that night,' Hannah said. 'He's such a gentle person, isn't he, Juliet? And I suppose he would be good with stories, being a word person.'

'Yeah, a regular Hans Christian Andersen,' Michael said.

Juliet was watching them with amusement. 'Well, you'll be interested to know he's thinking about moving down here. He's finally buying a place of his own.'

'Is he?' Hannah said. 'How exciting!'

But Michael had clearly had enough of the Larry talk. 'And how's the littlest Miss Goodwin getting on?' he asked Juliet.

'Laura? She's still on holiday at the moment,' Juliet said.

'She must be back at college soon?' Hannah hadn't spoken to their younger sister since the wedding, and recent phone conversations with her mother had been entirely taken up with the wedding debrief and stories of the honeymoon. She heaped chopped onion onto her poppadum and tried to stop her mood sliding.

'End of September,' Juliet said. 'Oh, did you hear the latest? It's hilarious!'

'The latest?' Hannah asked.

'Laura's signed up for an Arctic trek!'

'An Arctic trek?' She *had* to stop this ridiculous new echoing habit.

'Yeah, apparently you can only take one pair of knickers or something, for three weeks.'

'Who's financing this expedition?' asked Michael.

'She's raising the money herself. I'm surprised she hasn't squeezed you two for a few quid.'

'Well I think subsisting on one pair of knickers for three weeks is a cause well worth sponsoring,' Michael said, his hand now much higher under Hannah's skirt.

'Food, fantastic!' Hannah squirmed from his touch as trays of curries were unloaded in front of them. Now there seemed like no other food in the world she wanted more.

'I'm not hungry any more,' Juliet announced, reluctantly grinding out the cigarette she'd just lit.

'Come on, eat,' Michael said. 'Think of all those starving polar bear cubs.'

'Hey, it's not me who's planning to freeze my arse off in an igloo,' Juliet said, 'I don't need a coat of blubber, thank you very much.'

She and Michael watched Hannah slop huge spoonfuls onto her plate and tear off a palm-sized hunk of naan bread.

'You might not get the chance,' Michael said to Juliet with a guffaw. 'Looks like the pre-wedding diet's well and truly off. Only joking, babe . . .'

But Hannah had switched off. She'd already decided to tell Michael the news tomorrow instead.

Chapter 9

A message from Kate popped up onscreen. '*I'm sooo jealous you sit opposite him. He's gorgeous!*'

Juliet smiled and typed back: '*You don't still fancy the Swine?*'

'*You promised you wouldn't call him that!*'

Juliet squinted across at Phil, who was talking on the phone – to someone at Smithfield's judging by the steady beat of keen-to-please nods. 'Leave it with me, I'm sure I can find the resource to handle it.' As he grinned into the phone, she tried to imagine how he would appear to a complete stranger and not a bitter rival with the world's worst hangover. Mild-mannered, solicitous, the consummate team player. But *gorgeous?*

She typed: '*I suppose he has good teeth.*'

'*He's not a horse! Try harder! P.S. Get him to come out for a drink sometime . . .*'

That reminded Juliet she'd been going to check her drawer for a Nurofen. She hadn't slept very well last night, thanks to the puffing and hissing that passed for strife between Sasha and Callum, and the inevitable hangover didn't help. She'd fallen into quite a pattern with the weekday drinking: Monday nights were spent with Larry and Kate, taking advantage of the many happy hours available on the traditionally quietest of week nights; they took a break most Tuesdays and Wednesdays, but if Juliet was seeing anyone else she'd slot them in on those nights, invariably meeting up in some drinking hole or other; Fulton usually joined them on a Thursday for their regular night at Guy's bar; then on Fridays they would follow the path of least resistance to whichever bar the latest Imagineer leaving/birthday/promotion drinks were taking place. Juliet saw Guy on Saturdays, meeting him at the bar around closing time and spending most of Sunday with him in the flat upstairs. By Monday, she was ready for a session with Larry and Kate again.

Putting it in timetable form like that, she supposed it did sound like a lot of drinking. It *was* a lot of drinking, certainly more than she'd knocked back a year, two years, *any* number of years ago. With Luke she'd just carried on the traditions of college life without once needing to wonder whether they drank too much or too little; with Hannah, she'd shared a bottle of Pinot Grigio most nights, but food had been equally as important, if not more so. But these days, with Larry and Kate and Fulton, well, their collective tolerance was just so *epic*. What worried her more, though, was the fact that she was starting to hate it when other people *didn't* drink. Sasha and Callum with their one bottle of wine between two lasting several nights, that made her unhappy. And what about Hannah refusing a beer the last time they went out? For a drink made from yoghurt! She felt like her sister had been making a point: *I can do without a drink, Juliet, can you?*

Phil was off the phone, looking very pleased with himself. 'Result! I think they might ask me to speak at this year's marketing village.'

Kate's message was still in the box on her screen: *'Try harder!'*

'Great,' Juliet said. 'That will be fantastic exposure. Listen, I'm just popping out for a coffee, can I get you one?'

Phil looked so astounded she felt genuinely taken aback. 'Where're you going?' he asked, as though suspecting it might be the Dr Crippen Centre for Poisoned Cappuccinos.

'Starbucks. Or maybe the Italian place by Boots.'

He fished in his trouser pockets for change.

'It's all right, it's on me,' Juliet said.

Now Phil actually gasped.

It was so nice to get some air that she decided to walk past the local Starbucks and head for the one near Berkeley Square. She would use the time to prepare for her meeting with Dominic that afternoon in which she hoped to discuss her salary. She'd gone in early that morning to look up some websites, concentrating mainly on one called 'How to Lose that Sinking Feeling: A Salary Negotiation Strategy for Nice Girls'. Apparently, the mere act of asking would be an improvement on most women's strategy.

It was outside Fenwick's that she spotted a face she recognised. Lottie, that was who it was, the very bossy friend of Hannah's who'd practically organised Hannah's wedding as some kind of minor sideline while she waited to deliver a baby. Now *there* was someone who'd know how to squeeze every last penny out of Dominic's coffers. She'd probably never had a sinking feeling in her life. She looked effortlessly smart today, wearing a white trouser suit with fabulous 1940s trousers – obviously hadn't travelled in on the tube, then – and spiky high heels with beaded straps. Juliet, not meeting the client today so in trainers and combats, felt like a down-and-out.

'Juliet!' Lottie exclaimed. 'How *are* you? How's the world of brand consultancy? Are you still on that supermarket account?' She remembered everything, Juliet marvelled.

'No baby?' she asked in return, straining to remember Lottie's daughter's name.

'No, Ophelia's at home with her nanny. I'm treating myself to an Elemis Spa day and a few bits and pieces in the sales.' She held up bags from shops Juliet had visited only in lottery-win fantasies and let the rope handles swing back and forth on her wrists. 'I'm a great believer in self-gifting, aren't you?'

92

Juliet smiled, thinking this was better preparation for her meeting than any website, but Lottie didn't wait for an answer. 'Well, if you're anything like Hannah, you are!' She laughed. 'She's been going *beserk*, lately. I wish I had shares in that new maternity shop on Northcote Road, I can tell you.'

'Maternity shop?' Juliet frowned.

Lottie's eyes went very narrow and then very wide. 'God, I'm so sorry. She hasn't told you, has she?'

'She's *pregnant*?'

'I'm sure she'll tell you herself very soon. Give her a call.'

'Hmm.'

'She was probably waiting for the safe period,' Lottie said smoothly. 'I've only known for a few days myself.'

'She did leave a message for me the other day,' Juliet said, trying to remember when that was.

'There you go, then. They're so excited, as you can imagine. Michael won't shut up about it.'

'Really.'

'I'm due for a treatment,' Lottie said, looking at her watch. 'Which way are you walking?'

'Oh, down Brook Street.'

'OK, I'm this way. Well, see you soon, Juliet.'

She swept off, leaving Juliet immobilised in the middle of the pavement like someone who'd just had her bag snatched. She had no idea how she felt about this news. She was delighted, hurt, lifted up, shot down. One moment it seemed that everything had changed for the better, the next that it had merely confirmed the worst.

She wandered back to the office. 'No coffee?' Phil asked, as though she'd satisfied all his expectations of a wind-up of some sort.

'God, I forgot! I'm so sorry, I'll make us one in the kitchen.'

'Don't worry,' he said. 'I've got a meeting in five, so I'll brave Jo's brew.'

'Sorry,' Juliet said again, absently. He just gave her an odd look and turned back to his monitor.

Larry and Kate were out of the office on a creative away-day so she couldn't tell them the news. It was strange, she felt that until someone else helped her shape her response she couldn't risk calling Hannah. She checked her work voicemail and then her mobile. Nothing.

Then, soon after two, the internal line rang. 'Juliet, I have your sister in reception.'

'Which one?' Two guesses.

'Hannah.'

'I wonder what she's doing here.' Three guesses.

'I don't know,' Jo sighed.

'OK, I'll come straight down.'

Even if she hadn't already been told she would have known as soon as she saw her sister. Hannah was a great one for showcasing her curves in snug, tailored clothes and almost always chose a skirt over trousers, but today she was wearing black flares with some kind of Moroccan floaty thing on top.

'Juliet! Sorry to just turn up like this. I couldn't get hold of you.'

'That's OK.' Juliet found she was having trouble meeting Hannah's eye, as though she were the one with the secret. Eye contact was point number three on the 'Lose that Sinking Feeling' website. 'My mobile's been playing up.'

'Can you pop out for a coffee?' Hannah asked.

'If we're quick. I've got a meeting with Dominic at two thirty.'

'OK. We could just grab a drink at the French place downstairs?'

In the lift she could sense Hannah's nervous excitement. 'Spoken to Mum this week?' her sister asked casually.

She wants to know if I know, Juliet thought. 'No,' she said. 'Not for ages. She's never in when I try. Is she well?'

'Yes, fine, missing Laura, I think. They got used to having her

94

around again over the summer. Weird to think of them as empty nesters, isn't it?'

On the subject of nests . . . , Juliet thought. What a pair we are. My not telling her I already know is almost as silly as her not telling me in the first place.

In the café they ordered drinks and Hannah studied the snack menu. Now they were face to face and stationary, Juliet could inspect her sister more closely. Even in the maternity tunic she was exquisitely turned out, not an eyelash out of place. She wore lipstick that wouldn't, like Juliet's, be transferred to her cup like a block print after one sip, and the symmetrical winged lines of her eyebrows had to be the work of a professional. But, unlike her friend Lottie, Hannah had the kind of face that would be beautiful without the grooming. She'd always been the classic beauty of their family, with her pale skin and dark hair. Juliet remembered an essay she'd written in English class that began: 'My sister has coal-black eyes and tumbling raven hair.' She'd never thought to be jealous, not about that. It was just part of who Hannah was.

The café was busy. It took the waitress ages to come with the drinks and take Hannah's sandwich order. She was glad the venue had been Hannah's suggestion because it was very smoky. Hannah must have noticed, too, because she suddenly asked, 'You're not smoking. Have you given up?'

'No, I just didn't want to in front of you,' Juliet said simply. 'I know about the baby, Hannah.'

Hannah stared, startled. 'Do you? How?'

'I bumped into Lottie.'

'When?'

'This morning. On Bond Street.'

'Oh! I didn't know she was in town, we could have driven up together!' That was a South London thing, referring to central London as 'town', as though they lived in the country rather than within walking distance of the Thames. When they'd been in Tufnell Park, no more urban than Battersea, Hannah had never referred to the West End as 'town'. Juliet didn't know why this should irritate her so much.

'What a shame,' Hannah went on. 'I wanted to tell you myself. But never mind.'

'So how many months?' Juliet asked.

'Just over three. They do it in weeks, so it's fourteen.'

'Fourteen weeks!' Juliet was shocked. 'Why didn't you tell me earlier? How long has Mum known?'

'Er, I can't remember. Not long. Does it matter?'

'Yes! You *always* do this, Hannah.'

'What d'you mean?' She looked so crestfallen that Juliet felt guilty for her own heartlessness, but that soon gave way to exasperation.

'I mean always, whenever there's anything important. You just, I don't know, *retreat*.'

'No I don't!'

'You *do*.'

'Like when?'

Juliet remembered the first time she'd noticed it. Hannah had promised her her cherry lipgloss, still over half-full, just as soon as their mother gave way on its bubblegum-flavoured successor. But suddenly Hannah's friend Kerry was brandishing it, said Hannah had given it to her days ago, and Hannah was avoiding Juliet like the plague. When Juliet was finally able to confront her, Hannah denied ever promising it, but Juliet knew she was fully aware of her treachery. Otherwise why make herself scarce like that?

This didn't seem like a very useful example now, but Hannah was clearly still waiting for one. 'Even when we were younger,' Juliet said. 'Don't you remember you didn't tell Mum you'd started your periods for ages?'

'I told *you*,' Hannah protested. 'Come on, Juliet, I was twelve, I was *embarrassed*.'

Juliet knew she was allowing herself to be riled by other frustrations, like Lottie's shopping budget and Phil's marketing village, not to mention the thousands of tiny, vicious drill bits boring away at her head, but she found she couldn't let Hannah off the hook. 'And like when you got engaged to Michael. I had to find that out from Dad!'

Hannah's eyes filled first with protest and then tears. 'Juliet, you were already in Peru when he asked me to marry him. And the first time I spoke to you after that . . . Well, it was hardly appropriate, was it?'

Hannah's baguette arrived and she eyed it as though it were out of bounds until Juliet gave the nod. Juliet felt terrible. It was time for a concession. 'Anyway, forget that, it doesn't matter. I know now. Congratulations, by the way!'

'Thank you.'

'So what did Michael say?'

'He's really pleased,' Hannah beamed. 'He hopes it will be a boy.' She took a corner of the sandwich.

'I think a girl would be cute,' Juliet said. 'All those gorgeous gingham dresses and little shoes! They had a whole page of them in *Elle* last month.'

Hannah munched away. 'To be honest, I'd been a bit worried he might think it was too soon. He wasn't as keen as me to start a family.'

'Yeah, I got that impression that night at the curry place,' Juliet said. 'I was surprised, I would have expected him to be much keener to continue the blood line.'

'You make him sound like some vain old duke!' Hannah said. 'He really is just a nice, normal guy, you know.'

Juliet itched for a cigarette. 'I know, sorry. Look, I'm pleased about the baby, really I am. Have you been getting any practice in with Lottie's little girl?'

'Not really. Lottie has a nanny and an au pair and a mother-in-law all quite willing to get to the dirty nappies before me. But

I've been seeing a lot of a new friend, Siobhan, and she's got a baby, too.'

'Oh yeah? Who's Siobhan?'

'We met in a café in Battersea. She's . . .' Hannah searched for the word. 'Well, amazing.'

'In what way?'

'Well, for starters, she's a single mother and doesn't care what anyone thinks.'

'It's hardly a great stigma these days,' Juliet said. 'Judging by the number of celebrities at it it's positively unfashionable to be anything else.'

Hannah laughed. 'That's true. What I mean is she's just so *certain* about everything, very direct. You'd like her. She reminds me of you, actually.'

Juliet raised an eyebrow. 'Well, I'm glad to know someone thinks of me as certain.'

Hannah looked worried that she might have offended her again. Surely she's not *scared* of me, Juliet thought. She smiled as broadly as her lips would allow and tried to think of something more constructive to say. 'So where does this Siobhan live? Near you?'

'Herne Hill, the other side of Brixton.'

'If it's south, I won't know it,' Juliet said, only half-joking. 'I just about know my way from the station to your flat, but that's about it.'

Hannah's eyes glowed. 'Actually, we won't be there much longer, Michael and I have just started house hunting.'

'How did that happen? I thought he'd have to be surgically removed from that bachelor pad?' This was met with another dejected dip of the eyes from Hannah. Juliet felt as though she had no control over her own tongue. 'I mean, I'm sure that's the right decision. Those stairs *are* a bit impractical, aren't they? So are you coming back to North London?'

'No, we're looking Between the Commons,' Hannah said,

rather proudly it seemed to Juliet. 'You know, Nappy Valley, where I took you to that French street market once.'

'Oh yes.' She remembered a market selling overpriced olives and cheeses, where lots of couples called out things like, 'Darling, have we already got a tagine dish? I can't remember.' Preposterous though it was to remember her time of grief in Tufnell Park with any kind of nostalgia, Juliet now thought with fondness of their fruitless hunts for decent nibbles at the off-licence on the corner. There was no contrived villagey atmosphere there. You had to get on a bus to Highgate for the nearest deli.

'I know it probably seems boring,' Hannah said. 'But it's perfect for families. We won't be going out as much, we'll have a completely different lifestyle.'

Was Michael aware of that, Juliet wondered, managing to catch the thought before she could say it out loud, but Hannah had stopped listening anyway, and was smiling over her shoulder.

'Aha! Jo said you might be here!'

Juliet jumped at the weight of a hand on her arm. She gazed up. 'Dominic! I'm so sorry, I had to pop out. But I was just on my way back.' She considered passing Hannah off as a new Smithfield's trainee, but it was implausible: Smithfield's trainees didn't have professional eyebrow jobs and £200 haircuts. 'This is my sister, Hannah. Hannah, this is Dominic.'

'This is totally my fault,' Hannah smiled, half-rising before Dominic motioned for her to sit back down. 'But lovely to meet you, Dominic. I've heard so much about you.'

'God, don't say that, please!' He was suddenly dripping charm. 'Don't you sometimes wish you had one of those devices that you can just zap and erase what the other person knows about you? You know, like in *Men in Black?*'

'I don't think I saw that one,' Hannah said. 'But you needn't worry, they've all been good reports. God, I sound like a headmistress, don't I?'

99

Dominic clearly had no objections to this particular analogy judging by the way he rumpled his hair and chortled away in a most uncharacteristic schoolboyish style.

'You're doing so well,' Hannah went on. 'It's fantastic how quickly the company's grown. And Juliet tells me she's had a great year with her client . . .'

The old PR Hannah had sprung into action. Grateful for the diversion, Juliet sat back and watched for a minute or two. Hannah was doing pretty well considering she obviously couldn't remember any specifics. But it didn't matter, she was like a music video – first time around ninety per cent of her effect was visual. Dominic practically had his tongue hanging out, barely looking up when the waitress came by and thanked him by name for his order. Since he'd started appearing on those newspaper rich lists *everyone* knew his name, Juliet thought. Just like Rupert the Bear. She tried not to giggle.

'Do join us,' Hannah said, adjusting her seat to make room.

'Hannah's got some exciting news,' Juliet told him. 'That's why I got distracted.'

'I'm pregnant,' Hannah said. The beam was broader than ever.

'Congratulations!' Dominic said. 'Of course, I've never met you before so I don't know whether your radiance is a new feature . . .'

Juliet rolled her eyes.

'Girl or boy?'

'We don't know yet,' Hannah said. 'But we should find out at the next scan.'

'I always wonder why people don't want to know,' Dominic said. 'Why would you turn down useful information?'

'I agree!' Hannah exclaimed. 'Actually, my husband would be happy not to know, but I want to make decisions about decorating. I mean, I don't want pink fairies and sequins all over the place only to find it's a boy!'

'Absolutely,' Dominic said. 'You'd only blame yourself if he turned out to bat for the opposition.'

That last remark was pure Michael, thought Juliet, as Hannah chuckled wickedly. Hannah really knew how to handle this type of male; she reinforced all their illusions about themselves while somehow emerging with exactly what *she* wanted. And what about her own type of male, what was that, exactly? The Guy type, perhaps. She couldn't even define what that was. Why was it that she and Larry could come up with categories for people they passed on the street, but not Guy? They were meeting that evening, he'd arranged to take the night off, and she'd been feeling uneasy about it again, as though she feared he might be trying to pin her down to something. It was crazy. Not long ago she'd had it all mapped out for her, she knew the man she was going to marry and the life she was going to lead; back then, *Hannah* had been the unsettled one. But now Hannah was married, pregnant, totally assured of her place in the world (Nappy Valley, evidently), while Juliet sat there getting cold feet about *dinner*.

She tried to re-enter the conversation. 'Wouldn't sequins be a choking hazard anyway?' she asked, but they both ignored her.

'It's amazing, isn't it, how much kit you're supposed to have?' Dominic said to Hannah, as though on the verge of parenthood himself and not the child-unfriendly buffoon who'd once suggested a notorious coke addict as the face of a new range of baby food.

'God, I know,' Hannah agreed. 'And I thought planning a wedding was difficult!'

As they talked on, Juliet tried several times to catch her sister's eye, eventually resorting to prodding her knee under the table. It worked. 'Look, I should leave you two,' Hannah said. 'I feel terrible I made Juliet late for a meeting.'

'No hurry,' Dominic said, just as Juliet replied, 'OK, if you're sure . . .'

Hannah looked at her watch, a soft silvery band on tanned wrist. More self-gifting, Juliet thought. 'No, really, I must go. I've got a massage booked back at home. A friend told me about this antenatal treatment that sounds incredible. It lasts ninety minutes! I hope they don't mind if I fall asleep during it.'

What lives these women had! Ninety-minute massages and Bond Street treats, while the rest of the city sat at its desk with only an M&S chocolate finger to pass for a luxury item. Kate was right. This was enviable stuff. Meanwhile she was going to have to get on her knees to grovel for a few extra hundred a month.

'What a very charming woman,' Dominic said when Hannah had gone. 'I can see who got the looks in the Goodwin family.'

He was joking, but Juliet was irritated anyway.

'Where does she work? Isn't it something to do with conferences?'

She remembered now, she'd talked about Hannah in her interview for the job, told him how close they were and what fun it was to be two office girls sharing a flat, helping each other out. Like Lottie, Dominic had one of those sponge brains that could soak up and squeeze out information as the occasion demanded. Very successful people tended to be sponges. Lately Juliet had been feeling more like a sieve herself.

'Not any more,' she said. 'She works in an art school. She's always been interested in painting.'

'Sounds like the perfect set-up,' Dominic replied.

'Mmm, maybe a bit too perfect.' She added a smile to show she had nothing but delight in her sister's fortune, but Dominic raised an eyebrow and said, 'Jealousy's a sad game, Juliet.'

'I'm not jealous,' she protested. 'I'm pleased for her.'

'Yeah, yeah. Where did it all go wrong for you, eh?' He was so merciless it made her catch her breath. She was glad she'd never told him about Luke, and if he'd heard any of her history on the grapevine and was still saying all this then he was even crueller than she'd thought. Either way, she preferred it to pity.

She decided it was time to get this conversation on track and try her Negotiation Strategy for Nice Girls. 'Sorry again for not getting back for our meeting, Dominic, but if you've still got a minute I want to talk to you about my salary.'

'Can't it wait?' he said. 'Pay reviews are in January.'

'That's four months away!'

Luckily, he'd not yet touched the black coffee sitting steaming in front of him and saw that she'd noticed. 'OK. Shoot.' He leaned back into the shadows. 'I assume you're not going to tell me you're overpaid?'

'No,' she said firmly. 'I'm feeling very strongly that I'm, well, *under*paid.'

'How so?'

She had to tilt her own head out of the sunlight to make eye contact with him. 'Well, for one thing, I've brought in a lot of business this year. The kids' project and the home delivery rebrand. I've also taken on a lot of Michelle's responsibilities while she's been away.'

'Is that a problem?'

'No, I enjoy it. But I feel I'm worth more.'

'What *are* you worth, exactly?'

She tried to think. What did that website say again: *No professional athlete competes without a precise target. Know yours.* 'Well, just more, say five thousand a year more?'

He was looking at her dispassionately as though she'd asked him to advise on the best haircut for her facial type. 'To be honest, Juliet, I've been getting the feeling your heart isn't in it any more.'

'What? I'm doing at least fifty hours a week!' *Always keep in mind that this is a business negotiation. Do not get emotional . . .*

'It's not about the number of hours, you know that. It's about commitment to the brand. I'm not convinced you're as proud of the Imagineer brand as you could be.' As Dominic sat pontificating in the shadows it was starting to feel like an audience with a Bond supervillain. She tried to remember the name of the one he reminded her of. *Stay focused on the negotiation. Do not succumb to distractions . . .*

'How so?' she asked crisply, mimicking his own line.

'Well, people should meet you and know instantly you're with Imagineer. Like someone might be recognised as a McKinsey girl. Do you think they do that, Juliet?'

'Well, McKinsey's a globally recognisable . . . but I suppose if . . .' she tailed off.

He leaned forward. 'Look at someone like Phil Swain. I constantly come across people who say they've met him at a party or a dinner and remember him talking about Imagineer. He and Imagineer are *the same thing*. He's always *thinking*, Phil.'

'Phil's very professional,' Juliet agreed truthfully.

'Whereas you don't really give me the impression that you're committed to this job swap, for instance.'

'Yes I am!' *Negotiation does not mean confrontation.* 'I mean, it's a great opportunity. I get on very well with the Smithfield's team. It's just the logistics, it's so out of the way. There's not even anywhere to buy lunch.' She might as well have said flip-flops for all the sympathy this got her.

'Then take something in.' He was half-scowling now. 'If you're not sitting in cafés with your sister then you can concentrate totally on your work, can't you?'

'Yes.'

'And when you come back, we'll have a rethink about your salary. That's fair, isn't it?'

If you can't seal the deal, state a date . . . 'Yes, OK. So we'll meet as soon as I'm back in the office. What day?'

'Well, I don't have my diary on me, do I?' Nor did he have any change on him and Juliet realised that Hannah had gone in such a hurry she hadn't left any money either. With a sinking feeling, she picked up the bill.

Guy had to cancel dinner because Martine had phoned in sick, so

Juliet left work on time and popped into the pub by Camden tube to have a drink on her own. Next to her at the bar was a typical Camdenite, young, male, weathered skin and dirty fingers, the sort of character who would puncture your throat with a burning roll-up if you happened to misjudge your facial expression by a whisker. She decided to sit at a table instead. The warning on her cigarette pack was, 'Smoking seriously harms your unborn child.'

She was still trying to digest Hannah's news. It had taken her the whole afternoon to come to the conclusion that she was ecstatically pleased that she was going to have her first niece or nephew, but terrified that the new Nappy Valley-based Hannah wouldn't want her to bring her all-smoking, all-drinking ways within ten miles of the infant.

Tufnell Park was well and truly over; Hannah had sold up and left her behind. And the distance between them was not just geographical, it was there in the absence of any apology or explanation, in the denial that any business remained unfinished, it was there in the fourteen weeks it took Hannah to get around to telling her she was having a baby.

Juliet felt reshuffled. A natural feeling, she supposed, when one's closest sibling gets married, but just because it was understandable didn't make it any more pleasant. And now she was being shuffled even deeper into the pack. The new baby, the first of a brood, no doubt, would rightfully take priority, followed by the new friend who, being so like Juliet, had as good as replaced her.

She finished her drink and decided to pick up some shopping and offer to cook for Sasha and Callum that evening. She'd been meaning to do this since last week, when she'd been complaining to Guy about Phil and he'd just turned to her and said, 'More enemies, Juliet?' It had stopped her in her tracks; she couldn't speak. None of this is your fault, Juliet, that was what the bereavement counsellor had said to her, several times, in fact, and she'd used it like an inflatable ring every time she'd thought she was going under. But it was well over a year since Luke's death and weren't things starting to be a little bit her fault by now? When was she supposed to take full responsibility again? Guy was right. *More enemies, Juliet?* All these stand-offs and fall-outs and feuds everywhere she turned: however trying these people were, it was *she* who was the common denominator.

But when she got back to the flat, Sasha and Callum were already sitting at the coffee table, heads bent over twin bowls of pasta. There was enough for a battalion in the big dish set between them but Sasha didn't invite Juliet to join them. Instead she said, 'I thought you were going out tonight?'

'I was, but Guy had to work at the last minute.'

'I'm so glad I don't run my own business,' Sasha said by way of sympathy.

'I bought dinner,' Juliet said, 'but I guess you're already sorted. How about some wine, though?'

Callum didn't even bother to look up, but Sasha got to her feet and followed Juliet into the kitchen. 'I know it sounds a bit bad, but do you mind going back out? It's just that this evening is special for us.'

Juliet tried not to sigh. What did Sasha mean, 'special'? Some minor anniversary, no doubt. She tried to work it out. Five months, maybe? Or perhaps it was a hundred and fifty days. As she knew from the torturous sessions with utilities bills, Sasha worked in very precise small units. 'I could read in my room?' she suggested finally.

Sasha pulled an intense face and began mouthing the words, 'I think he's going to propose!'

'Oh.' Juliet poked her head around the corner. 'I suppose he *is* already on his knees – one benefit of not having a dining table, eh?' Sasha didn't laugh. 'But you've only been together, what, five months?' Juliet whispered. Jesus, that was less time than Guy and her and she'd run a mile if he started talking about marriage.

106

'So what?' Sasha snapped. 'When you know, you just *know*.'

'OK, OK. Let me just put the shopping away and I'll go to the cinema.'

'Thanks,' Sasha said, amiable again. 'Roll on the hen night, eh?'

The Odeon in Camden was quiet. Juliet bought a tub of Häagen-Dazs and watched a movie about pirates, quickly becoming distracted by the assortment of accents and losing track of the plot. When she got back to the flat Sasha was flossing her teeth in the bathroom and she could hear Callum moving about in the main bedroom.

'Well?' She tried her best to summon up some edge-of-the-seat excitement.

'Oh, nothing happened,' Sasha grumbled, mouth sulky.

'What a shame!'

'I think you must have totally broken the mood.'

'I'm sorry. I had no idea.'

'It's all right, you weren't to know,' Sasha said, magnanimously, though it was obviously quite a stretch for her. 'See you in the morning.'

Finally, at just after midnight, Juliet was able to get to her bedroom and close the door.

Chapter 10

'I can't see anything,' said Hannah, peering over her shoulder at the screen where a milky way of grey and white sucked and swirled. Could that remote dappled moon be the baby's head?

'I can, look!' said Michael. 'It's ET sucking his thumb! '

The sonographer laughed. 'There's baby's spine and I'm just going to measure the head.'

The gel on her tummy felt warm and comforting. She still couldn't get over how pregnant she looked. Recently she'd begun to feel in a permanent state of post-prandial discomfort, as though every meal was a six-course Christmas lunch. She felt sure people looked her waistless body over and took her for a compulsive eater.

'Baby's not in a great position for me to check the heart and lungs,' the sonographer said. Hannah felt her stomach being pressed a little more insistently and stole a look at Michael. He looked diminished sitting on that chair in the dark corner, stripped of his authority in this humming oestrogen-rich zone. His eyes were uncharacteristically uncertain and it took her a while to identify the expression she'd seen just once or twice before as vulnerability. The last time had been on their wedding day, when he'd been at the top of the aisle with Rob by his side, shuffling about, smoothing back his hair. In contrast, she'd proceeded solid and calm towards him, like a ship setting sail, faces cast up from the dockside to wish her well.

She squeezed his hand. 'All right, darling?' She knew it shouldn't feel anything other than right and proper that he now sat, the nervous father-to-be, by her side, but the truth was she was still relieved he'd taken the news so well.

She'd told him in bed on the Saturday morning before the first scan, protected, at least, by the half-light.

'Are you serious?' He'd snapped upright, like a child suddenly realising it was Christmas morning, and turned towards her in delight. He'd wanted to know everything, was aghast that she'd waited so long to tell him.

'You haven't been around, all those trips . . .' Already it sounded so flimsy.

'I would have swum home from China for this news.'

'Really?' Hannah was amazed. 'But I thought you weren't that keen?'

Michael frowned. 'If I said that then I was a fool.'

'You said you wanted me to yourself?'

'I'll still have you to myself, won't I? You and our little man.'

Hannah had laughed then. 'Don't be so sure it's a boy.' She'd prepared herself for everything but textbook delight. In a strange way she'd almost felt *cheated*. Now, of course, she just put the whole thing down to the hormones.

'*There* we are,' exclaimed the sonographer. 'There's baby's heart! I'll just check all four chambers are present and correct.' It was beating fast and light as a bird.

'Can you see what sex it is?' Michael asked out of the darkness.

'Do you both want to know?' the girl asked, looking at Hannah.

'Yes,' she breathed.

'OK. Let me just get the right angle and I'll show you.'

A boy. It was a boy. The image of a miniature Michael filled her head and she felt a horrible premonition of her own inadequacy for the task. *Stop it*, she told herself at once. She wasn't going to allow another false crisis to take hostage of her head.

'Result!' Michael exclaimed.

'Lots of people cry,' the girl said, as Hannah, still gazing at the monitor, made no attempt to stop a tear from rolling towards her ear. 'Aww, what a cutie he is.'

'A Fawcett son and heir,' Hannah whispered, remembering what Juliet had said. She wanted to commit to memory the contours of that little face, the deep eye sockets, little nose bud, the jaw that moved like an old lady trying to speak without her teeth. The next time she saw it – him – he would be in the outside world with them, locking his trusting eyes with hers in that precious way Nora did with Siobhan.

'Well done, darling,' Michael said afterwards. 'This is all getting very exciting, isn't it?'

'Yes, I'm so glad he's all healthy. Those little fingers! And quite long legs, too.'

'Yeah, we don't want a shortarse. Already doing tricks as well, did you see him bend his knees and kick into that black hole bit?'

'My uterus, yes.' Hannah laughed and clutched his hand. 'I've got to get some blood taken now. Will you come with me?'

'Sorry, I've got to shoot. Charlotte moved my eleven o'clock but I've got a client lunch in half an hour. I'll only just make it as it is.'

'Oh, fine. It's just I'm a bit weird about blood.'

'Need to get over that, babe,' he laughed. 'It'll be like Vietnam down there in a few months' time. I'm sorry I have to go. I would stay if I could, I promise.'

'It's OK,' Hannah said. 'Don't worry, I'm just being silly.'

He kissed her on the mouth and dashed out, arm raised for a taxi even as he exited the revolving door.

Hannah waited in reception to be called by the blood person whose job title she couldn't pronounce. She felt much more like her real self now. At this moment in time *nothing* stood in her way, *their* way. The news was broken, the baby was healthy, and Michael was on board. He'd even agreed to the move, in fact he'd suggested it himself after looking at one of her baby catalogues and seeing all the safety devices they'd need. Perhaps he'd been a little surprised by the speed with which she'd produced sheaves of property details, but he understood the natural deadline of the situation. And now Lottie thought she'd found them a house – she'd referred to it as The One on the phone last night. Hannah would be viewing it in just a couple of hours; she felt her heart quicken at the thought.

Lottie locked her BMW and turned to kiss Hannah's cheek. 'Don't let me influence you,' she said, 'but I think this is it. I've got that feeling, y'know?'

It was the tenth house Hannah had seen Between the Commons and on one of her target streets, Salcott Road. As Lottie click-clacked up the tiled path to the front door with a jingle of the keys, Hannah felt her own mood lift a notch higher.

'Hang on a bit while I sort out the alarm.' The front door was the milky green of French farmhouse shutters, one of Hannah's favourite colours. The tiles ran the length of the wide hallway, burnt orange, white and chocolate brown, polished like glass. 'Original, of course,' Lottie said. 'Let's look in the sitting room first, then we'll go down to the kitchen – that's the showpiece, you'll love it.'

It was true what they said about knowing as soon as you saw the right house. It came like a bolt, an instant recognition that you'd found somewhere you could be happy. People took longer deciding on a pair of shoes, said Lottie, who likened the house-buying instinct to the way you felt when you met your future husband: he might need a bit of decorative work but you knew at once if you could live with him.

As they walked into the living room, Lottie gave her arm a

little squeeze and Hannah felt instantly infected with a sense of shared entitlement. Lottie's manner was perfect. *Of course* such stylish surrounds were nothing less than the right of her client. She'd brought the two together, after all, and she wouldn't show such a special property to any old punter, would she?

The large windows, full-length shutters, dividing doors and original cornicing were all immaculately delineated against clotted-cream walls. Clearly someone with a fine eye had chosen these paintings, mirrors and rugs. There were two seascapes that she particularly liked by the main window. They must have been recently reframed, Hannah thought. What was that lovely grain, pearwood, perhaps? Looking more closely, she saw with a start that they were signed by her employer, Grace. It was a sign, it *had* to be.

'Helena did the interior design herself,' Lottie said, peeking inside a glass box on the mantelpiece. 'She almost gave it up, can you believe it? Had the kiddies and forgot she had a life of her own for a few years. Now she's incredibly in demand – especially now she's doing a commission in the Dordogne for someone rather famous.'

'Ooh, who?'

'Let's just say he's no stranger to Number Ten at the moment.'

'Right.' Hannah, who couldn't remember the last time she'd followed politics or even read the main section of the Sunday paper, had no idea who Lottie meant.

'Anyway,' Lottie said. 'Helena's *awash* with cash now, let me tell you.'

'*Awash* with cash,' Hannah repeated. 'You're right, Lottie, this really is a lovely house.'

'And not badly priced.'

'Oh, how much?' It felt awkward asking; of course Michael would already be in possession of the facts.

'One point three.'

More than the budget he'd set, then, but Hannah had no doubt Lottie already knew this.

'I've already told Michael I don't think they'll take an offer on that, I'm afraid,' Lottie said, leading the way down glass steps to the basement kitchen. 'They just don't need to. It's the sort of place where people fall in love with the atmosphere. All I can do is give you first refusal, but you'll need to offer straight away if you want it, so they'll agree to stop showing it. Otherwise someone else will come along and get in there before you.' Someone else introduced by Lottie, Hannah presumed. How long did their first-refusal grace period last? Until Monday morning, perhaps? She knew already that she'd feel betrayed if they lost out.

The kitchen, a whole open-plan floor of the house, had more original tiling, more Victorian fireplaces, even some original wood panelling, all set off by a pair of extraordinary green glass chandeliers. Lottie snapped on the light switch with the flourish of a magician's assistant and sent spears of light onto the surfaces below. Hannah imagined herself warning Michael Junior of the perils of spiked glass as the child sat over his breakfast cereal, mesmerised by the coloured light.

'They're taking them with them,' Lottie said preemptively. 'Unless you want to pay cash separately. Those things cost thousands apiece. We were thinking of commissioning one for our master bedroom, but Rob's worried we'll be decapitated in the night!'

'So there's no chance Helena and her husband will change their mind about selling?' Hannah asked, anxiously.

'Oh, no, they're totally committed.'

Michael had told her that Lottie once persuaded a couple to continue with the sale of their house when they'd just lost their only daughter in a car accident.

'That's so terrible,' Hannah had said.

'Why?' Michael said. 'It's just business. The world doesn't stop turning.'

'Yes it does,' she protested, distressed, and he stroked her hair in surprise. She knew he'd feel differently now he was having a child of his own.

It was funny, but in many ways Lottie would make a more natural match for Michael than she did, Hannah thought, watching her friend fiddle with the locks on the French windows. She was surprised this hadn't occurred to her before. All Michael's previous girlfriends had been high-flying types in banking or law. 'The higher the achiever the lower the maintenance,' he'd joked once. 'They don't trust you to do anything yourself so they do it for you. Well, that's fine by me.'

But she'd never been worried by that sort of remark. It was precisely her more absent-minded approach to things that had made Michael love her in the first place. 'Scummings says you're away with the fairies,' he'd happily reported. 'But you don't know how great that is. How *different*.'

'Coming out?' Lottie called from outside.

The walled garden was another delight, the whole place might have been lifted from Hannah's daydreams. She picked her way between the pots, counting oleanders and lemon trees, lavender and rosemary, then followed Lottie's kitten heels back into the house and up the stairs to the bedrooms.

'Little Isobel's room is so cute!' Lottie threw open a door on another vast space. A big curled iron bed dominated the room, strings of fairy lights wound around the headboard. A line of soft toys were tucked into the satin eiderdown, wide-eyed insomniacs all.

'She helped Helena plan it,' said Lottie. 'A princess's grotto. No good for you guys, of course. Junior will probably want Thomas the Tank Engine!'

Hannah thought of Juliet as a child, insisting on the smallest room in the house, a pale pink cell right at the top. At night she would sleep under the sloping roof with enough yellow-haired dolls beside her to staff a league of cheerleaders. Hannah, having moved on to Duran Duran and eyeliner, would still come and mop up the tears when in the morning the dolls were discovered to have fallen out of the bed in the night. When did Juliet stop coming to her to make things better, she wondered? And what on earth would her sister say to this place, where the kitchen alone was bigger than the whole flat they'd shared in Tufnell Park? Well, she wasn't going to feel guilty about it. The house was modest compared to Lottie's place on Bolingbroke Grove and, besides, Juliet would know that she could treat this place as her own.

'So what d'you think?' Lottie asked, retracing her route, alarm reset, heel on polished tile as she click-clicked back to the car.

'I love it,' Hannah said, grabbing her arm. 'Michael should definitely see it before you show anyone else.'

'Oh, I'm showing him tomorrow morning, didn't he tell you?'

'No, but great. I'll come, too.'

'He said you'd probably be resting,' said Lottie. 'We have planned a bit of an early start. Of course you should come back for a second viewing together afterwards, it's your first family home, after all.'

'Yes, maybe the next day, what is that?'

'Sunday,' Lottie said patiently. 'I don't usually schedule Sunday viewings. Besides, Michael's going to the rugby club, isn't he?'

Hannah sometimes wished these things weren't left to Lottie to point out. But who was she to complain? She who'd kept huge life-altering issues from Michael for weeks on end. 'Well, *I* love it, anyway!'

'I knew you would, sweetie. Let's see what he thinks before I talk to Helena. Speak soon, I've got to be in Nightingale Lane in exactly thirty seconds.'

For the second time that day Hannah was left alone to contemplate the exit dash of someone in conspicuously greater demand than she was. That was one of the things about 'just helping out' rather than working all the hours God sent at a real job – life lacked the same dash.

115

Heading for Northcote Road, she kicked her way happily through the leaves, all soggy and clogged together like the remains of someone's breakfast cornflakes. She had nothing planned for the day, thought about calling Siobhan and persuading her to bring Nora out for lunch. And then she bumped into Larry.

'Hello, what are you doing down here?' Like all of Juliet's circle, he lived north of the river.

'Flat hunting,' Larry said, looking slightly sheepish.

Hannah gazed up at his face, eyes behind big seventies-style tinted glasses. 'Oh yes, Juliet said! How exciting! What are you looking for?'

'Just a one-bedder, I've just seen six in a row, not one bigger than a coffin. Looks like I'm moving south to be buried alive!'

She laughed. 'Where do you live at the moment again, is it Kentish Town?'

'Holloway. I have unparalleled views of the prison walls. But now I'm buying I want somewhere a bit greener. My sister used to live around here before she left London, so I know it quite well.'

How could he afford it on his Imagineer salary, Hannah wondered. Juliet could barely scrape together the cash to buy wine glasses (though there always seemed to be funds available for what went in them, Hannah noticed). Of course, she didn't believe for a moment that either of them were quite as poorly paid as Juliet liked to claim, but flats around Northcote Road did start at a quarter of a million and someone buying on his own would need a six-figure salary to get that kind of mortgage. She laughed at her own nosiness; she'd become quite the property expert when you considered that first conversation with the agent, the one who said she couldn't afford a bird table, or whatever it was.

'I was left some money,' Larry said, apparently reading her thoughts. 'My father died last year. The money's finally come through.'

116

'Oh, I'm so sorry, that's awful.'

Larry shrugged. 'We weren't that close to be honest, but I still miss him.'

'Poor you. God, I can't imagine not having Mum or Dad.'

'It is a weird feeling,' Larry said, 'hard to explain, it's sort of inside your *marrow*, if you know what I mean.'

Hannah thought about this. It felt like the most candid thing she'd heard in months. How articulate he was, how open about the way he felt, but in such a modest way. She'd noticed that quality in him at Juliet's party, had been drawn to it. Everyone else was always so quick to shout his or her credentials it made life exhausting. She wanted to throw her arms around his waist and hug him.

'Have you got time for some lunch?' she asked, surprising herself.

'Sure, where?'

'Here?' They were standing outside a packed café, the door to which now opened to unleash a string of infants batting plastic swords at each other, followed by a woman in her thirties who was hissing into a mobile phone: 'I said I'd do it if I've got time. Just give me a break, will you?'

'Er, OK,' Larry said.

They sat with their knees squashed together at a corner table and looked at the sticky menu. Hannah jumped as a pink and brown painted face suddenly appeared an inch from her elbow.

'Archie,' boomed a businesslike female voice. 'I've *asked* you to come and sit down so will you please come and *sit down*.'

This was obviously how one spoke to a small child, she thought, stressing key verbs as though training a pet monkey. The painted face only accentuated the effect.

'Mum, I need to do a wee.'

'I said *do not* blow the whistle until we're outside.'

'*Come on in*, Millie! You're making a draught!'

'You've got all this ahead of you,' Larry smiled, pulling out his

117

cigarettes and then, looking around, stuffing them back in his pocket. His presence was gentle and soothing against the hot, high-pitched background noise; he seemed like a guide murmuring in an aviary of agitated birds.

'Scary, isn't it,' she said, meaning it. 'Right, what are you going to eat?'

'Everything. A fry-up *and* a smoked-salmon bagel. I'm starving.'

'Hangover?'

'I do feel a bit rough,' he said.

She ordered an all-day breakfast, with scrambled eggs, mushrooms, tomatoes, extra toast, and a mug of hot chocolate with whipped cream.

'Are pregnant people allowed eggs?' Larry asked. It struck her that Michael had not paid any attention to her changing diet, other than to comment on its increased volume.

'Oh, I expect not,' she smiled. 'But for God's sake, what harm can it do? It's protein, after all.'

'I suppose not drinking and smoking is enough of a sacrifice for anyone,' Larry said with genuine admiration and she saw his fingers stray towards his cigarettes again.

'I haven't smoked for years,' she said. 'And the not-drinking isn't as hard as I thought. I suppose because it's for a good cause.' She wondered if it was possible for him to imagine her as a normal woman, an attractive, slimmish female carrying nothing but her mobile phone and Marlboro Lights; a Juliet figure. How maternal she must seem, especially now the bump was showing, every pore of her skin advertising her fertility, her state of being possessed by her man.

As their food arrived, a toddler at the next table burst into tears and began thrashing around in his mother's arms. This set off a smaller child and between them they incorporated most of the farmyard sound-effects Hannah could think of. She and Larry ate without speaking for a minute or two, slotted together like a pair of spectators at some avant-garde play, unsure how to react now the actors had started rushing through the stalls.

'So how's Imagineer?' she asked when the noise had died down to a few snotty sobs. 'Juliet seems to hate it these days.'

'Oh it's basically a pile of wa . . . rubbish,' Larry said.

My God, she thought, he's censoring his language around me, he's afraid of offending me, as if I'm the Queen.

'Sounds to me like Dominic's being a bit of an arsehole,' she added. A Michael word, it sounded so shocking from her mouth she might just as well have *been* the Queen. The sharp glance from a nearby mother wasn't lost on her either.

'Oh, he's just playing up to the role,' Larry said, biting at a triangle of toast to leave what looked like the corner piece of a jigsaw. 'I suppose I'd be pretty pleased with myself if I owned a company with a fifteen million a year turnover – before the age of thirty.'

'Is he really that young?' Hannah asked.

'Thirty in December. He's having a big celebration at the same time as the staff Christmas party. Only Dominic could throw a joint birthday party with Jesus Christ.'

They were interrupted again as two women squeezed into the booth next to them and settled another pair of mutinous-looking pre-schoolers. 'Now, Izzy, would you like sausage and beans?'

'Yes.'

'Or toast and egg?'

'Yes!'

'You can only have one, darling, which do you want?'

'Chicken nuggets!'

Outside, a boy beat his fists on the metal tabletop and began howling when adult hands tried to prise him away.

'This is a zoo,' Larry said. 'And someone's opened all the cage doors.'

She laughed. 'You'll have to get used to it if you live around here.' She felt suddenly gloriously detached from Nappy Valley

119

and all its *Chitty Chitty Bang Bang* emphasis on The Child. She had months to go, *years* before she was required to take part in this kind of public animal training. For now, she was on the outside with Larry. 'When's your next appointment?' she asked.

'Half an hour. Bijou garden flat. Ideal pied-à-terre or investment property. That means you wouldn't imagine actually *living* there in your worst nightmares.'

'It might be all right,' Hannah laughed. 'Could I come, too? I know it's a bit nosy but as I've just found my own dream house I might bring a bit of good luck!'

'Sure, that would be great, but you might be shocked after what you're used to.'

There it was again, the assumption that she was visiting from some higher, rarified ground, that she needed special handling. But he was smiling, pleased by her suggestion, she could tell. 'Which street?' she asked. 'I'm a bit of an expert these days.'

'Sisters Avenue, up past the top of Battersea Rise.'

'Sisters? That's where we live! How funny! Which end?'

'No idea.' He fished out the details from a flattened bundle in his pocket. 'Here we go, one hundred and two.'

'That's the other side of the S-bend,' Hannah said, thinking. 'I always think it's so appropriate that a road called Sisters Avenue is all sort of curvy and . . .'

'Round the bend?' Larry interrupted with a snort. 'Well, *Juliet*'s certainly that, though I'm not sure about the curvy bit . . .'

Hannah was at once conscious of her own unfeasibly expanded bust. There was definitely a trend in maternity wear to display swelling rather than hide it, which was fine in theory but in practice made her feel a little exposed. 'Juliet's getting too thin, if anything,' she said. 'But I suppose I would say that in my new elephantine state, wouldn't I?' Why had she said that? It was an open invitation to him to size her up.

'I think you look great,' Larry said simply.

She blushed. She used to be able to take a compliment without embarrassment, but this was happening all the time lately, a pregnancy thing, perhaps, like the tiny burst blood vessels across her face and collarbone. Too much blood. At least that was what she told herself.

'Josh! Do you want to be sick on your new shirt? Your *birthday* shirt?'

'Yes!'

'Just *finish* your mouthful and *breathe*.'

'I think that boy is choking,' Hannah said, glad of the diversion.

Larry pulled out his wallet. 'Come on then. Step away from the table and move slowly towards the door. Do not make eye contact. It could be fatal.'

'Hey, this is quite nice,' said Larry, looking above his head at the high-ceilinged hallway. 'I like these bumpy things . . .'

'Corbels,' Hannah said.

'Very good! We should play Scrabble some time,' Larry replied. 'Now which of these three doors d'you think leads to the "compact open-plan living/kitchen space"?'

They were on their own, the agent had just handed over the keys and left them to find the flat and let themselves in.

'Are they supposed to let us come on our own?' Hannah asked Larry.

'I don't know, but it would be perfect for couples having illicit affairs, wouldn't it? No need to pay for hotel rooms. I bet there are people whose thing is to do exactly that – the thrill is in deceiving the estate agent!'

That remark made her feel all the more self-conscious as they examined the little bedroom, duvet rumpled and slept-in, smelling of Chanel.

'I like the satin cushions,' she said to Larry. 'Oh, and what a lovely lamp! Is that mother-of-pearl?'

'Funny how everyone looks at the personal things rather than the actual space,' Larry said. 'I find myself examining wedding photos like I'm a detective putting together a psychological profile. Then afterwards I can't even remember if the place had a shower or not.'

'It's true. I suppose nosing around someone else's home is one of the few ways you can work out how you're doing yourself.'

'I suspect I'm not doing very well then,' Larry said. 'I own no satin or mother-of-pearl, that's for sure.'

A funny little barn-style door led to a tiny patio, where they sat on garden chairs and Larry lit a cigarette.

'In a strange way I could see myself living here,' he said. 'I know its small, but the ceilings are high. I suppose being tall I notice that more.'

'I guess with your lifestyle you're not in much anyway,' Hannah said.

'You'd be surprised. Sometimes I spend the whole weekend in my flat, catching up on sleep, watching TV.'

'Don't you go out raging on Saturday nights?' *Raging*? Oh dear, she was the Queen again. Down to the Criterion Ballroom, she might have added, with that nice young thing you're courting.

Larry just shrugged. 'Thursday and Friday are the big nights. Especially Thursdays. Of course, Thursday's the new Friday.'

'Juliet used to say that, too. I suppose that makes Friday the new Saturday?' Hannah laughed.

'Oh yes, and Saturday's the new Sunday, hence my TV binge.'

'What's Sunday then?'

'Oh, Sundays are still Sundays,' Larry said. 'Some things have to stay the same. You can't change the fact that you have to go back to work on Monday.'

'I like Sundays,' Hannah said. 'It's the only time Michael isn't working, though he does go to the rugby club some weeks.'

'I'm surprised he leaves you alone so much,' Larry said.

She turned away and pulled at the weeds between the paving stones. 'You and Juliet should get together. You're so similar.' She had no idea what had made her say this, but she couldn't help feeling pleased when she saw how surprised he was.

'Naw,' he said. 'We're just mates. Anyway, she's seeing Guy.'

'Yes, that's true. So you're single?'

'I am. I know you're just married and all that,' Larry said. 'Which I'm sure feels great. But in a way I quite like not knowing.'

'Not knowing? You mean who you'll marry?'

He nodded.

'Statistically you've probably already met her.'

'Maybe. That would be weird.'

She wanted to explain how it felt when you joined your life with someone else, the sheer *peace* of settling the matter. She knew he'd get what she meant straight away, but she stopped herself. It was getting too intimate. The common ground of Juliet rose again.

'I worry about Juliet at the moment,' she said. 'She sort of, well, she doesn't seem to *like* anyone these days.'

'I'm not sure that's fair,' said Larry, tapping ash onto the ground.

'I know she's going out with Guy, so of course she must like *him*. It's just that whenever she talks about people, men especially, she's so *sneering*. What does she call that guy at work, The Hog or something?'

Larry laughed. 'The Swine. Phil "the Swine" Swain. I have to admit responsibility for that one. It is a bit of a rogues' gallery at Imagineer, though. If you spent even an hour there you'd know why she's so negative.'

'And Sasha's boyfriend as well, what about him?'

'Caliban?'

'Yes, that's it. OK, he's not Brad Pitt, but is he such a bad person?'

Larry looked thoughtful. 'I know what you mean, I suppose. But she does have good friends, too, and you can kind of understand that she might have lost her faith a bit after what happened with Luke.'

'You know about that?' Hannah asked.

'Yeah, though she doesn't talk about it much. But she's obviously had a tough time this last year or so.'

'Of course.' It seemed so long ago now, Luke's death, Juliet's return, and, between the two, Michael's marriage proposal. He'd asked her the night before Hannah had got the phone call from their mother. The ring had been on her finger precisely fourteen hours. At first, when she heard the news, all she could feel was shame for having said to Michael at dinner how good it had been to deliver Juliet back to Luke and have her flat to herself again.

'Won't she want to move back in when she's back from South America?' he'd asked.

'Oh no, she and Luke will get a place together again. They would never live apart.'

Instead, Juliet *had* moved back in. She'd been a different person then, a sad, shocked child who was going to have to be Hannah's priority for as long as it took for the horror of her experience to fade. Plans with Michael were suspended until they judged that Juliet was improving.

'How long do you think before she's back in the land of the living?' he asked one weekend when they came across Juliet watching her seventh consecutive hour of television.

'Not long, I hope,' Hannah replied.

Now, looking at Larry's compassionate face, she felt fresh guilt flood her chest. *Not long, I hope.* It seemed so casually cruel, so impatient. How exactly had she gone about judging Juliet's recovery? Hadn't it suited her own plans to believe that her sister no longer needed her as badly? Had she even feared Michael would slip away from her if she neglected him any longer?

124

'We should take the keys back,' Larry said. 'They'll think we're fleecing the place. Or having an illicit affair, of course.' They looked directly at one another for a moment and then he kicked his cigarette butt under a plant pot and stood up.

'At least the owner's not here to care,' Hannah said, following. 'I hate being in when people come for viewings. Traipsing in and out all day long, pawing your toiletries.'

'Pawing your toiletries,' he repeated. 'I like that. Harassing your herbs and spices. Defiling your satin cushions.'

'Don't be mean,' she laughed.

'Have you found a buyer for your place yet?' he asked as they locked up.

'Yes, she's quite frightening, actually, a giantess. I swear she must be six two. Anyway, in this case I get the feeling she'd be more interested in pawing my husband than my toiletries.'

'Oh yeah?'

'I'm only joking,' said Hannah, 'but she is a bit of a flirt.'

'Ah, a common species. I'm sure you can handle it.' Was she flattering herself or was there admiration in that last comment, the implication that she was above the usual petty female politics? She liked that he was so readily on her side.

They reached the corner of Clapham Common Northside and the entrance to her own building. She thought she might ask him to come in but was relieved when she remembered that he needed to return the keys to the estate agent. 'This is me,' she said. 'Give me a shout if you need a viewing companion again. Let me give you my mobile number.'

Why did his keying the digits into his phone seem like something more than the standard process of new friendship? What was going on here? As she watched him lope away, back down towards Battersea Rise, she hugged herself like a teenager who'd just negotiated a rather successful first date.

As chance would have it, the giantess was there again that

evening. Fleur, she was called. She had extraordinarily long legs – no wonder she loved the double-height ceilings so much. Hannah imagined her playing at a full-size grand piano in the middle of the room, those spiky fingers jabbing at the keys.

Fleur had made an offer on the place the first day she viewed it and was proceeding with the purchase with swift efficiency. Her parents were helping her out with a fifty per cent deposit, she was chain-free and because she'd heard about the place from Michael's friend Marcus there wouldn't even be an agent's fee. Michael was delighted with the package and had no objections to her repeated visits. He was even on first-name terms with Fleur's father.

'Time for a quick drink?' he asked her when they'd finished another tour of the loft's five rooms.

'Sure, a quickie, I'm meeting friends in Clapham South.'

'Hannah?' he asked, pouring white wine into the wedding-list crystal.

'No thanks, I'm not supposed to be drinking, remember?' She tried not to sound accusing. Lottie had warned her that men needed to see a real live baby before they could change their social habits. A bump wasn't quite enough of a prompt.

Fleur looked bewildered and turned back to Michael. She must think I'm just fat, Hannah thought.

'We're having a baby,' he said. 'A boy.'

'Oh, how sweet! Congratulations!' In her knee-length boots and fur-trimmed white cardigan she looked like a lofty snow queen about to pat her favourite elf on the head. 'Can I smoke?'

Hannah waited while Michael deliberated. 'Do you mind not,' he said eventually. 'Unless you want to come out onto the terrace? It's stopped raining.'

'Sure, of course,' Fleur said.

'I'll grab you an ashtray.'

'Well, if you've seen everything you need upstairs ... ?' Hannah said to Fleur, aiming for that attitude of polite finality Siobhan did so well, 'I'm going to use the bathroom.'

126

'Yes, thank you.'

Hannah watched from the stairs as Fleur allowed Michael to light her cigarette and then eyed him through the smoke with the air of a young Lauren Bacall. Hadn't Bogart been married when Bacall came along? she thought idly.

By the time she came back down, Fleur had gone and Michael was on the sofa accelerating through the TV channels, settling finally on an old *Star Trek*.

'That's more like it. Seven of Nine, love of my life before you came along, Han. Oh, babes, I meant to say that you're invited on my client trip next month.'

'Client trip? Where to?'

'Cape Town. The Winelands. It's a fantastic hotel.'

'Why do I need to come?'

'It just looks good, sweetie, all the wives will be there.'

'I thought society had moved on from the days of the Stepford Wives?'

'Society, yes. Reed, Warren, McCarry, no.'

'I'm not sure I can fly long-haul,' Hannah said, frowning.

'Why not? You won't be in goat class, don't worry.'

'*Economy*,' she corrected. 'That's not the point, Michael. It might not be safe for the baby.'

'I don't see why,' Michael argued. 'You see bloaters flying all the time.'

'Bloaters! Is that how you describe your pregnant wife?' She knew he was just trying to get a laugh, but this time it felt too harsh, too personal. She couldn't help recalling what Larry had said. 'I think you look great.' That had felt nice. This made her want to cry.

'Oh, come on, I'm joking.' Michael began massaging her fingers. 'I don't want us all to be apart for a whole week. I want you two with me.'

'I'll ask my GP,' Hannah said. 'It might be all right.'

'Good. Now sit down and relax. I'm cooking tonight and then you can tell me all about our new house.'

Chapter 11

Juliet was not at all surprised to see that Fulton's new girlfriend was another Small Town Sex Kitten, a specific female type she and Larry had identified one evening after close observation of the Friday night crowd at Guy's bar. STSKs were blonde, petite, and highly successful in jobs that required good people skills. Fulton tended to go for them, at least had done as long as Juliet had known him, blitzing through six self-contained, monogamous 'relationships' in the last twelve months.

'This is Rachel,' he said, draining the end of a pint of Guinness. A second glass stood empty on the table – not the most promising sign as he was supposed to be driving them through Friday night traffic to Virginia Water that evening.

'Great to meet you, Juliet.'

'I've heard all about you,' she replied. God, it was such a rigmarole, getting to know Fulton's girls. They demanded equal status in the group, but it was hard to care when you knew they wouldn't be around as long as your latest bar tab. But she wanted this weekend away, with its country air and head-clearing walks. They'd been talking about doing something like this for months but had never got around to booking anything. Now Rachel had come along and organised it in a couple of phone calls.

'Can I get you guys another drink?' Juliet asked.

'Yep, same again, cheers,' said Fulton, stretching back in his seat. He was getting a bit of a beer belly, Juliet noticed, his assimilation into British society virtually complete.

Rachel asked for red wine. Probably switched from white when she came to London, Juliet thought, quickly chastising herself for being such a bitch without giving her a chance. *More enemies, Juliet?* Looking more closely she saw that the girl was about twenty-five and strikingly beautiful. Whatever her small town origins, she'd obviously undergone a classic London retouch: regional accent non-existent, long hair expensively honeyed, slim-fitting black clothes from Joseph, finished with a vintage-print scarf, no doubt snuffled out in some corner of Topshop that she was confident no one else in her office had yet reached. Though she was distractingly busty, Juliet didn't suspect a boob job. This girl had natural assets, was so glowingly English in this King's Road bar with its Far Eastern décor that she made the venue seem wrong and not her.

'OK, one Guinness, one red wine. Back in a minute.' She waited at the bar, considered grabbing a shot of vodka while she was there, then remembered it was the first sign of alcoholism to sneak a secret drink at the bar while buying a round. She ordered the shot anyway. What was the last sign of alcoholism? she wondered. Drinking and driving, as Fulton clearly intended to do?

'What time's Larry getting here?' Fulton asked when she got back. 'We should leave pretty sharpish, don't wanna hit a snarl-up.'

Rachel tittered at this, clearly charmed by Fulton's East Coast brand of estuary. 'I'm really looking forward to meeting Larry,' she said.

'Oh, didn't he call you?' Juliet said. 'He's not coming this evening. He got caught up flat hunting and then something went wrong with his car.'

The set of Rachel's jaw told Juliet she was not best pleased with this turn of events.

'He might come down tomorrow, though, in time for lunch.'

Marginal unclenching of the jaw. 'What about your boyfriend, Juliet?' Rachel asked. 'What's he called, is it Guy?'

'Oh, he's definitely not coming, he runs a bar so never has Friday nights off. Sometimes he doesn't get any nights off, except Sunday, and even then he's doing the accounts or whatever.'

'That must be difficult,' Rachel said.

'Not really,' Juliet said, 'it's just a casual thing. Oh, and Kate's doing something with her parents. But between you and me, I think she's got a date with the Swine tomorrow night. Oops, I'm not supposed to call him that any more.'

'Who's the Swine?' Rachel asked.

'Just some perfectly acceptable bloke from her office,' Fulton explained, who Juliet and Larry have decided to victimise. They've made a voodoo doll and stick pins in it.'

'Really? That's horrible.'

'Not literally,' Juliet said. 'We just don't particularly like him. And we don't call him the Swine now that Kate's expressed an interest. But only because it's Kate.'

'Glad to hear Kate's finally getting a bit of satisfaction,' Fulton said, grinning. 'She and Larry seemed to be going for some sort of celibacy record. OK, cool, just my two favourite London girls, then. It'll be great just the three of us. And the house sounds fucking awesome.'

'It's lovely,' Rachel said. 'Right on the Wentworth estate. Andy hardly spends any time there now he's based in Florida. There's an indoor pool, a trampoline, oh, and the garden's just been landscaped.'

That was what she reminded Juliet of: an estate agent. An upmarket agent sitting in her Notting Hill office, working hard at not being impressed by celebrity shoppers. ('They're just like the rest of us, you know, once you get to know them.') Oh dear, she was being bitchy again. It occurred to her that for all her instinctive snobbery towards Rachel she was the one being exposed as the provincial teenager, what with her cruel nick-names, the way she spoke about Guy. *That must be difficult? Not really. It's just a casual thing.* New people didn't understand, she knew that, they thought that she couldn't be a nice person to speak about a relationship so dismissively. It made them feel there was something wrong with them for needing permanence and security from their own partners.

'So how d'you know this Andy?' she asked Rachel, making a new effort.

'Oh, he's a client.'

'A client?'

'I work in sports promotions,' Rachel said. 'He's one of our golfers.'

'That's right, Fulton did tell me,' Juliet said. 'Sounds like a brilliant job. How long have you worked there?'

'A year now.'

'Rach seems to specialise in golfers,' Fulton said. 'God knows what she sees in me.'

'Oh, I'm sure your swing is impressive enough,' Juliet replied, and Rachel giggled.

'Right, one for the road and then we have to go,' Fulton said.

Juliet sat in the back of the car with carrier bags of champagne and vodka, while Rachel alternated between navigating (she held the map upside down, as Juliet herself would have done, to get her bearings as they travelled south) and stroking all available parts of Fulton, who grappled with the gears and grumbled about shift sticks. Juliet hoped she wouldn't die because the driver was getting a hand job. That was no way to go.

It was a dark, wet, unwelcoming evening and by the time they arrived in Virginia Water she'd slipped into a stiff-necked doze and almost forgotten where they were going. She was desperate for another drink. The house was a one-storey ranch affair, with huge

131

rooms in which regular-sized furniture was made dwarfish in acres of carpeted beige. Travel souvenirs, bad hunting oils and garish landscapes decorated the walls; Hannah would gag at such bad taste. The living room opened onto a flashy indoor swimming pool and hot tub, presumably with a view of the fairways. As for the master bathroom, it was about two hundred square feet and featured a free-standing sauna and twin sunken baths with gold taps.

'It's kind of like an over-the-top travel tavern here, isn't it?' Juliet laughed. 'Look, all the bedrooms open onto the patio, with a little table and chairs outside. Is there a carvery as well?'

'Fuck, I knew there was something,' exclaimed Fulton. 'We haven't got any food!'

'Like we sit down every Friday night to a well-balanced meal,' Juliet laughed.

'I've got some Revels,' Rachel said.

'That sounds like a good theme for the weekend,' Fulton said. 'Here's to Rachel's Revels!'

They demolished the champagne while exploring the rooms, then Rachel mixed a jug of something murky-looking at the sitting-room bar. Evidently she knew her way around Andy's home and was comfortable enough to just help herself. Juliet watched as Amaretto, Tia Maria and Cointreau were all sloshed into the brew. Then they all knocked back a succession of shots.

So where is Mr Golfer Man?' Juliet asked, crosslegged on the floor. 'Does he mind us nicking all his booze?'

'He's in the Far East at the moment. He's never here,' Rachel said. 'But his housekeeper'll make sure everything's stocked up for when he's next in the UK.' She spoke with the imperiousness of the maid who'd just married the master, thought Juliet, beginning to warm to her.

'Look at all the male junk,' she said, nodding at the table football and dartboard. 'There's obviously no woman in his life.'

'Puts them off their game,' Fulton said. 'Same for all sportsmen.'

132

'That's not it!' Rachel protested. 'All the golfers I know have wives.'

'There you go,' Fulton said. 'No sex.'

Rachel draped her legs over the side of the sofa and lit a cigarette. 'Andy's just not one to be tied down,' she said.

'Why the iron bedposts, then?' Juliet scoffed.

'I'll show you what they're for later,' Fulton said.

Rachel tinkled with laughter, already very drunk. 'I know, let's go for a swim!'

'Won't we drown in this state?' Juliet asked, struggling to get to her feet.

'Oh, the housekeeper'll move our bodies before Andy gets home,' Fulton laughed. 'Did I tell you to bring your swim gear, Juliet?'

'Yeah, the water looks cold, though.'

'No, it's heated,' Rachel said. 'And the roof's retractable. I don't remember where the switch is, though.'

When Juliet returned from changing in her room she saw Rachel was floating on her back topless, steam rising from her mouth into the sharp black air. They'd got the roof off after all. It was drizzling, felt absurd to be standing freezing in a bikini. But once she got into the water she felt fantastic. It was like a giant outdoor bath, only her face stung with the cold, a nice, tingly sensation.

Fulton sat in the hot tub for a while, ogling them both, then staggered out and shook his whole body like a dog. 'Hey, girls, the rest of the fizz should be cold by now. I'll get it.'

'Good plan.' Juliet tried shaking the drops from her own ears and face, imagined herself as a grinning spaniel. Rachel floated towards her. 'Wow, you do have great boobs,' she laughed.

'Thank you very much,' Rachel said. She was pushing them in Juliet's face, and Juliet couldn't resist seeing how they felt, warm handfuls, the skin hot in the cold water.

'There's something about this house, it's so 1970s . . .'

133

'I know.' Now Rachel was kissing her mouth and tugging at the strap behind her neck.

She must be sleeping with the golfer, Juliet thought, as well as Fulton, who was now pouring wine into their mouths and over their shoulders and breasts. *He* didn't care much about serious relationships, and neither apparently did Rachel, so why was she constantly beating herself up about Guy? It suited him, too, the casualness of the arrangement, when he needed to cancel at short notice and she didn't make a fuss. Didn't it? She pressed her body against Fulton's and he dropped the bottle into the water.

Only in the morning when she woke up in bed with Rachel and saw Fulton naked and snoring in a leather armchair by the window did it occur to her that this might have been a bit of a mistake. Her clearest memory was of trying to light cigarettes, one after another, only to drop them into the pool and spend ages chasing the soggy remains across the surface of the water.

Later, Larry let himself in the unlocked front door and found the three of them seated in separate armchairs in front of the television. 'No way!' he exclaimed with a laugh and Juliet jumped, guiltily. But he was just looking around the room. 'Why's the furniture so out of proportion? This is like the Stonehenge scene in *Spinal Tap*! Hey, is that a *pool*?'

'I'll show you around,' Juliet said, grabbing his arm.

'Hi Larry, I'm Rachel!' Rachel jumped up, all glowing cheeks and bouncing boobs. 'Just take any bedroom you like.'

'What a very friendly way to introduce yourself,' Larry said, grinning at her. 'Is Fulton *asleep*? Lazy bastard.'

'It was a heavy night,' Juliet said, shepherding him out and closing the living room door behind them.

Larry whispered, 'So? Is she an STSK or what?'

'Oh yes,' Juliet said. 'I think we can safely say she is.'

Chapter 12

Three weeks into the job swap at Smithfield's and the atmosphere in the office was stultifying. Imagineer had its irritations, all right, but at the end of the day Juliet enjoyed being good at the job she did there. She loved the planning and briefing, the sessions with the creatives and techies, being part of whatever it was that made someone suddenly come up with an idea that they all knew was exactly right, while all the time keeping the different strands of business neatly embroidered together.

But here there was nothing for her to do and no one for her to not do it with. Mark Kendall, her closest contact, had been on holiday until now and his colleagues made Phil Swain seem like Groucho Marx. No one watched EastEnders or had a hangover, at least not one with origins they were willing to discuss. It felt like she'd been banished to Alcatraz and could only sniff at the air and dream of the action going on in the city across the water. She was counting down the days.

Luckily, she'd been called upon only once to join a Smithfield's social event – a drink in the local pub, when everyone left the building together but lingered one by one as they approached the pub door. Unfamiliar with the trick, Juliet had found herself first at the bar and stumping up for a huge round, only then to be deserted by most of the group – all heading for mainline trains to the suburbs.

The evening had been interesting in a different way, though. After the pub, she'd cabbed to a bar in Clerkenwell with her new smoking buddy Sanjay, a marketing exec of six months' standing who was already scanning the *Guardian* media ads for his next move. There she'd seen Hannah's husband Michael sharing a bottle of wine with a woman she couldn't place. Nothing wrong with that, of course, it was probably only a colleague, but there was something about their faces, an intensity, that stopped her from going over and saying hello. She'd decided to keep an eye on them. Michael did have that history, after all. And a pregnant wife.

At ten, he'd stood up to leave, and as he stooped to kiss the girl, Juliet's view was blocked by a cluster of drinkers breaking apart to make way for someone looking for the loos. But she could have sworn that kiss lasted longer than a pecking moment before he straightened up again. After he'd gone, the girl joined two other men at the bar and Juliet saw that she was very attractive: very tall, with fine, tapered wrists and a slim neck.

'She's fit,' Sanjay said. 'Looks like a swan. Not that I fancy swans, y'know.'

Juliet thought the woman looked a bit freakish but she didn't say so. She feared she might be getting a reputation for being negative. Equally, there was no need to say anything to Hannah, she decided, her sister would only think she was deliberately looking for trouble in paradise because she'd been refused entry herself. She hadn't actually *seen* anything anyway, Michael had probably just been talking into the swan woman's ear as he said goodbye. The bar *was* incredibly noisy.

In any case, all of that was secondary to her concerns about the Guy situation. They'd met up just twice since her transfer to Vauxhall, and, more to the point, since the shenanigans with Fulton and Rachel in Virginia Water. She'd been alarmed by an impulse to confess to him the happenings of that Friday night, not that she could remember enough of it to string together a credible account. How could she explain that her overriding memory of a weekend away with friends was of checking the waste-paper baskets for used condoms? Or that she'd been too embarrassed to ask Fulton if he'd been careful in case there'd been nothing to be careful about. Careful? What a useless euphemism that was.

No, the point was that if she was feeling this guilty then she was getting too close. Surely it was better to end things now and avoid reaching the point when she might hurt Guy, *really* hurt him. She didn't *want* to end things, not exactly, but what were the options? Face up to her waywardness and reinvent herself as a nice girl? That was never going to happen unless she stopped the drinking sessions, and if she did that then where would she be? At home every night with Sasha and Callum, eating separate meals and then retreating to her room because they were having another 'special' moment? The more she thought about it the more complicated the logic became. This was the worst thing about the job swap. Too much time to think.

'Everyone ready for the Acorn Shuttle?' A bright bell of a voice went clanging around her skull, as it did about fifty times a day. Polly, the Smithfield's marketing director, was a large lady with heavy breath and a voice that would surely carry across the river if the windows weren't sealed shut with dirt. 'Come on, Juliet, it's your first time in the Shuttle!' She stood over Juliet's desk, broad, unnavigable, her face lost in its chins as she smiled encouragingly down at her.

'Sure, looking forward to it,' Juliet murmured. She'd been ignoring this entry in her diary; it was apparently a monthly departmental free-for-all in which ideas could be exchanged – 'the blue sky's the limit,' Polly had said when she'd requested details. The official slogan was something like 'No idea is a bad idea', a bad idea in itself, Juliet thought, given that ninety-nine per cent of the concepts bandied about the Imagineer pit were absolute gibberish and they came from some of the best creative minds in the industry. Mark K had told her all about the Acorn Shuttle and how he believed it was so named because ideas would just vanish into the stratosphere never to be heard of again. 'Someone probably suggested mobile phones twenty-five years ago and the little slip of paper is just sitting there on the surface of the moon like a forfeit.' She was glad that Mark was back today. He was the nearest Juliet had to Larry in this place.

They all trooped into the dingy, windowless meeting room and took places on mismatched chairs around the three tables pushed together in the middle of the room. Juliet had a feeling the tables might be disused school desks.

'OK, hit me!' said Polly, flinging back her arms as if to surrender her body to the ecstasy of marketing genius.

Silence. Juliet caught Mark K's eye. He looked tanned and well-fed. She felt pale and hungry.

'Come on, gang! I want something from everyone today!'

Fearful silence.

'I had an idea,' said Becky, who sat at the same bank of desks as Juliet and seemed to spend at least six hours of every day in internal meetings. 'You know how we're all in meetings all the time?'

Everyone groaned their agreement and began plucking at the edges of their plastic coffee beakers.

'Well,' Becky said, smugly, 'instead of spending half our time booking each other for meetings, what about a shared diary, y'know, online or something? Like the Imagineer software Juliet uses?'

'Yep, I hear you,' Polly said, winking for no obvious reason. That made Juliet think of Michael again. Had he winked at the swan that night? She didn't think so. 'You know, Becky, I'd like to focus on really left-field ideas this morning, rather than

138

departmental *gripes* – we've got our marketing forum on Mondays for all those – and Lord knows there are enough of them! No, what I'd like to do is go to Sir Alfie and show him what a fantastically creative team I've got here, a team with a genuine sense of what supermarkets of the future will be like.' She turned to Juliet. 'I meet with Sir Alfie on the first Tuesday of every month, just the two of us, so you can be sure your ideas really will reach the top.'

'Great,' Juliet said. Sir Alfie was Smithfield's chairman and chief executive, who, according to Mark K, Polly was 'banging again'.

'So, supermarkets of the future . . . ?' Polly said.

'What, like astronaut food, you mean?' said Sanjay.

'Well, we'd certainly be able to target much smaller sites, good thinking, Sanjay!' Polly nodded brightly at him, as though offering positive reinforcement to a retard.

'Not necessarily,' put in Mark Bradley, one of the two other Marks in the department besides Kendall. 'I was just thinking the other day how huge newspapers have become. They weigh an absolute ton.'

'Newspapers?' The same humouring smile. 'I don't get you?'

'Well, if papers get any bigger, the supermarket news kiosks will need to expand, won't they? Maybe have a whole aisle to themselves? So it would make sense if food products needed *less* shelf space – hence Sanjay's astronaut food.'

'But in a society of the future where people eat dried pellets, would we still read our news in paper form?' asked Mark K.

'It might not be that far in the future,' said Mark B defensively. 'After all, cats eat pellets already.'

'And fish,' said Sanjay.

'Cats eat fish or fish eat pellets?' Mark K asked Sanjay.

'Both, I suppose,' Sanjay shrugged. Juliet suppressed a snort. This had to be a wind-up. Surely even Polly couldn't imagine this was constructive? She thought about Dominic's sessions, where

139

he pulled five or six people into his corner at random intervals and everyone had to present an idea off the top of their head before rating each other's and awarding the best a prize. The creatives always objected, said there was too much pressure to perform and you didn't come up with good ideas that way. 'I just want you to make sure that *everybody thinks*,' Dominic would say. It really wasn't so dissimilar to this, Juliet thought. Only the furniture was different.

'All valuable observations, but, again, not quite what I had in mind for this brainstorm,' smiled Polly, blinking. 'Let me throw something into the Shuttle: a brand-new food range, say. How about something for the elderly or people with sensitive teeth?'

'We could just repackage our own-brand baby food,' said Becky. 'Organic, maybe?'

'You'd need much bigger jars so they can read the lettering on the label,' Sanjay said. ' 'Cos old people can't see too well.'

'Yes, good,' Polly said. 'Keep it coming.'

'I've got an idea,' said Juliet. 'How about a range of food purely for hangovers? The Morning After range. Gorgeous stuff like bacon sandwiches with avocado mayonnaise, muffins with peanut butter, everything dripping with calories.' Her stomach gurgled at the thought; she hadn't had time for breakfast. Sasha had used the last of the bread for Callum's toast.

'It would need to start cheap for students,' she went on, 'but could have some pricey stuff, too, like great big stuffed smoked-salmon bagels. Our copywriter Larry, for instance, who some of you know, he has to have smoked salmon when he's hungover. Nothing else will do. The range would be all those things you crave when you've really overdone it the night before.'

'You could have something there,' said Mark B. 'Every item could come with a sachet of Resolve.'

'Maybe a morning-after Pill as well,' sniggered Mark K.

Juliet had sensed a stiffening next to her during this exchange and now saw that her neighbour, a tight-lipped woman whose

140

name and job she had forgotten, was waiting to speak. 'The difficulty I have with that, Mark, is market share.'

'Market share?' Juliet asked her, even though the woman was addressing Mark and ignoring her completely. A sudden fizzle of anger took her by surprise.

'We currently claim twenty-five per cent of the market of single women aged twenty-four to thirty-five – that's a phe-*no*-me-nal share – and it's specifically driven by our healthy eating ranges. I just don't see us doing junk food.'

'But you sell loads of junk food,' Juliet laughed. 'What about your new kids' range?'

'We don't use the pronoun "you" at Smithfield's, Juliet,' Polly put in. 'Just "we". We're all a team, even the temporaries and job-swappers.'

'OK, what about *our* new kids' range?' Juliet said. 'It's all burgers and nuggets, isn't it?'

'All portions in our Teeny Tinkers range have been carefully devised to offer the youngsters the balanced nutrition they need,' said the killjoy calmly, still holding her head profile to Juliet.

'What am I, the invisible woman?' Juliet snapped. The table went quiet and she saw the two Marks raise eyebrows at one another.

'Of course not, lovey,' Polly said, clearly relishing a feather-smoothing moment. 'Liz is delighted to hear your contribution. Juliet has joined us from Imagineer, Liz, we're very lucky to have her input.'

Liz finally met Juliet's eye. 'Oh, do you work for Phil Swain?'

'*With* him,' Juliet said flatly.

'Well, Juliet, it may seem like junk to you,' Liz said, 'but it's actually *brain* food. What you're talking about is a completely different emotional bucket.'

'Emotional bucket?' said Juliet. 'What does that mean?' But her energy burst was over now; she checked her watch and started dreaming of a Starbucks hot chocolate with whipped cream, maybe a sprinkle of nutmeg. But there was no Starbucks near the Smithfield's building.

'Anything else?' Polly asked. Her arms were folded across her chest now.

'OK guys, I've got another meeting in five. This has been *very* creative, lots of lovely acorns.'

She gathered up her files, none of which had been opened during the meeting, before rising to her feet. 'Juliet, can I ask you to put a report together by the end of the day and file it on the server under Shuttle?'

'Of course,' Juliet said, shuffling back in her chair. She had nothing else to do that morning, except gnaw at her pen and check her emails from Imagineer.

Her Smithfield's counterpart, Jessica, was now practically indispensable, she learned, though Kate was concerned that she was working a little *too* closely with Phil. She checked her diary. Just eight working days till she was due back at Imagineer. And just eight hours till she was meeting Guy. They were the bright spots on her horizon and yet, if she really thought about it, she wasn't looking forward to either of them.

Finally the stragglers had gone, Martine had buttoned up her coat, the last on the staff rack, and it was just the two of them left in the empty bar. A two-man lock-in. Bars shouldn't be seen empty, Juliet thought, looking around. They were sad little asylums without their inmates.

Guy poured them enormous brandies and kissed her rather determinedly. 'I'm shattered,' he said. 'And it's only just November. This place is a madhouse.'

'Just what I was thinking. But that's why you love it, isn't it?' Juliet said with a yawn. 'You need to stop the bar getting such good reviews.' She admired his dark eyes through her cigarette smoke. He was gorgeous, edibly gorgeous, there was no disputing that.

'I need a break,' Guy said. 'I've been doing this for ten years without any longer than a week off. I'm going to take the whole of February off, hire a relief manager and go and see Craig in France.'

'Cool. Good for you. Where's your brother working again?'

'Morzine.'

'Never been there.'

'Why not come with me for a bit?'

'For a bet or for a bit?' Juliet joked. 'Your accent still confuses me.'

'Well, I don't have any problems understanding yours,' Guy said with an exasperated sigh. 'Have you ever noticed that?'

'All right, keep your hair on,' Juliet said. In a horrible way, a part of her was pleased he seemed tenser, more confrontational than usual. It would make it easier to break things off, perhaps it might even seem the natural result of a disagreement.

'What about coming for a week?' Guy went on. 'Or ten days?'

'I haven't got any money,' Juliet said.

'You don't need money.'

'How can I not need money? Skiing costs a bomb.'

'We'll stay with Craig. His wife works for the ski school, so lift passes will probably be free.'

'Maybe,' Juliet said. 'It does sound like it might be fun. We're out of fags, can I get some change from the till for the cigarette machine?'

'I'll get it,' he said.

The next morning, still in bed, Juliet told Guy she wouldn't be coming to France. 'Holidays just aren't a big priority for me at the moment.'

'Why not? Don't you feel like getting away from here as well? This city is doing my head in at the moment. Come on, Juliet, it would be good to get some proper time together.'

'I'd rather stay in London.' She took a deep breath and was surprised to hear her heartbeat pick up like a drum roll. 'I just don't want to get all serious, Guy. You know, I've been thinking maybe we should forget this whole thing.'

'What whole thing? This isn't serious,' Guy laughed, but with little humour. 'We haven't seen each other for weeks.'

'I know, but I get the feeling you . . . I don't know, I'm just going through a weird time.' She got out of bed and started gathering up her clothes.

He watched her dress. 'You're not making sense,' he said simply.

'Sorry, I just don't know how to explain. It's not you, it's me.' She cringed at her own cliché.

He frowned. 'That's rubbish.'

'Look, I'm going to go,' Juliet said. 'I'm sorry, really.' Sadly, she thought, the cliché was actually quite true in this case. It wasn't him and it *was* her. As she hurried down the stairwell and pulled the door behind her to face the usual rancid Soho morning smell, the dried crusts of last night's vomit, she chilled through. It was only by extinguishing this one flame of tenderness in her life that she saw that that was what it had been.

Chapter 13

'There are plus/minus twenty thousand species of flora in South Africa,' said Derrick, voice raised above the tail end of the coffee-break chatter. He was businesslike again after finally managing to disband the unplanned pit stop. The historic ramble had already lapsed behind schedule because the women had wanted to look in the gallery shop and make more stops for antique shops than he had anticipated. Though he smiled at them with a terrific set of white teeth, Hannah wondered what he really thought of them as they twittered around pots and masks and little bronze cheetahs, asking repeatedly how much one thousand rand 'really' was. They had no intention of prioritising architecture over shopping.

'In Stellenbosch, of course, we are known for our vines, but also our strawberries,' he said, making diligent eye contact with each of the group in turn. Hannah nodded encouragingly.

'Oh, yes, we had some strawberries at breakfast, they were delicious, so incredibly sweet,' said Lucy. Lucy was sweet, too, Hannah thought, a standout among the rest, though all the wives and girlfriends made easy company. Everyone agreed it was such a bonus they'd hit it off, right from the moment they'd arrived in Cape Town two nights ago to beautiful, tart, early summer air and a hotel as luxurious as Michael had promised. Of course, the few female Reed, Warren, McCarry staff in the party had not brought *their* other halves. They, it seemed, had demanding jobs of their own and could not spare the time. No one questioned this.

The group stood clustered around Derrick like dutiful Girl Guides on the corner of a wide street lined with white gabled houses. Dorp, it was called. That was a good word. Actually, Hannah was starting to feel like a bit of a dorp herself: having just reassured everyone she was doing quite well, absolutely blooming, she now realised she felt distinctly unwell. It wasn't just the sensation of having swallowed a turtle whole and being forced to share her body with its frantic flapping, for she was used to that now she was over five months into her pregnancy. What was new was the pressing headache behind her eyes and the little whooshes of dizziness.

Derrick raised his voice a notch, as though they'd been joined by an outer tier of listeners: 'The house in front of you was built in 1789 by the Magistrate H. L. Bletterman. When we go inside, you'll notice the traditional H-shaped layout – a wonderful representation of the eighteenth-century manor house. Now, it may *seem* spacious, but remember families often had between ten and twenty children in those days.'

There was a collective gasp.

'How would you think of enough names for them all?'

'How would you notice if one was missing?'

'Did they not know about the rhythm method?'

There were more than enough bedrooms at Salcott Road for her little family, Hannah thought, picturing its interior as vividly as the last time she'd visited. For most of the trip so far her mind had remained in Battersea. They'd exchanged contracts just days before flying down to Cape Town and would be moving out of Sisters Avenue in mid-December, not long after the art school had closed. She didn't anticipate any sadness at either event. Excitement about the new house overshadowed any fondness

146

she'd managed to summon up for the loft. As for the art school, the hours spent there added up to no more than a couple of months in full-time work. And she'd never even met Grace, who had been one of the reasons she'd wanted to get involved in the first place.

But it would be odd not having a job. January would be the first time since leaving university that she wouldn't have that regular deposit in the 'Paid in' column of her bank statement. Well, she'd just have to make the house her job, she'd devote every spare hour to feathering her new nest, she'd draw up a proper budget and discuss it with Michael as though he were her client – she might even see some bits and pieces while she was here. Michael hadn't said a word about her looking for another job after the baby, and she tried to keep her relief about that to herself. She wouldn't care if she never set foot in an office again, but not all women liked to see such eagerness for a return to traditional arrangements – Lottie and Juliet, for instance.

She staggered back suddenly and supported herself with her hands on her knees. Lucy was at her side at once. 'Are you all right? Hannah?'

'I'm not sure, I feel a bit faint. I think I'd better go back.'

'Derrick! Hannah's unwell, I'll take her back to the hotel.'

'No, don't worry,' Hannah said. 'It's not serious, I can go on my own. Where can I find a taxi?'

Now Derrick was on his cell phone and the group closed in around Hannah.

'I felt like this *all the time* when I was pregnant with Maddy,' said Alice, the wife of Michael's senior partner Simon. 'It's probably the sun – you're not used to the bright light after a London autumn. And that long flight! Go straight to bed when you get back to the hotel, you need a nice long nap and a bath.'

'Take this bottle of water,' Lucy added. 'You might be dehydrated.'

As soon as the taxi turned the corner she felt much better and not a little silly at having caused such a fuss. It was cool and silent in the car as they purred down the suburban streets. The gabled Dutch houses soon gave way to shiny new ranch-style places. Every so often one would pop up with a heavy thatched roof – it looked comical, like someone had put an old person's wig on a young child's head for a joke. There was not a soul in sight, although it was past midday; it felt like a film-set of an American suburb just after the warning had come through that a meteor was about to hit earth. All around, bright signs warned 'Armed Response' and displayed stern silhouettes of biting dogs; a show town for security systems, but no use against the meteor, Hannah thought, smiling to herself.

Deposited at the hotel reception she felt as though she'd been sent home from school early to an empty house she hardly recognised. It was almost half past twelve. Michael and the others would probably be at lunch by now. She picked up the room key and decided to wander the long way back, along the edge of the vineyards, up towards the Chardonnay vines at the back where the grapes were just budding. It was nothing short of idyllic, the hiss of sprinklers a gentle percussion to the birdsong and breeze, the swish of uniforms as staff criss-crossed the lawns with trays of those squat little cans they used here for mixers. Replenishing minibars, she supposed, and remembered the big bar of Dairy Milk she'd seen in theirs. A square or two might be nice in the bath before a sandwich from room service and maybe a plate of dainties. Yes, this was the life, she'd enjoy it while she could – it wouldn't be long before those famous sleepless nights set in.

Passing a shaded plunge pool, she smiled hello to two guests who lay fully clothed on sun loungers, a pile of magazines between them. She felt sorry for Michael and Simon and the others. How could anyone come somewhere so beautiful to *work*?

At that moment the sun was blotted by a rogue string of mucousy cloud and a yelp of laughter made Hannah stop short

148

and turn her head. Nothing. Then it came again: it was Michael's laughter, she was sure. It must be coming from the restaurant terrace; she'd lost track of where the main hotel was in relation to the outbuilding where she stood. Perhaps she should go and join them for lunch; she didn't want to look antisocial. But then she'd have to explain what she was doing back so early and endure the scornful smiles of the female colleagues, all of whom were junior to Michael and not yet married. They had to be nice to her, of course, and at mealtimes they were outnumbered by the wives and girlfriends, but Hannah could just imagine their unspoken response when they found her back at the hotel alone: *we* don't have the luxury of a bit of pregnancy dizziness; we *work* for a living. No, a bath and chocolate were far more tempting.

Now another sound reached her, strained this time. Someone in pain, *Michael* in pain. It was coming from one of the rooms close by. She hurried down the sloping lawn towards a row of neat little bricked patios, each with its own set of wrought-iron furniture and terracotta flowerpots. She listened. Nothing. The French doors with their wooden shutters made her think of something Derrick had told them that morning – all external shutters had been outlawed a few centuries ago after a fire destroyed most of the town.

Then once more she caught Michael's voice. It sounded much closer this time. She paused on one foot on a round paving stone as though caught in the middle of a hopscotch move, aware that the women on the sun loungers were now looking at her over the top of their sunglasses. She stepped onto the nearest patio.

'No, in my face, *that*'s it . . .' said Michael's voice, followed by a groaning sound, a *female* groaning sound. Hannah tiptoed right up to the French doors but all she could hear at first was the whisk of the ceiling fan inside, until the sudden, unmistakable cry of her husband climaxing. This was followed by a long girlish giggle.

'Mmm, that was *very* nice, I must say . . .' Michael again. He sounded so *English*, as though complimenting his hostess on a particularly refreshing G&T. What a thought to pop into her head! Hannah wondered at her own calmness as she strained harder to catch more.

'Can you just move that way a bit, my leg's gone numb.' The voice was female, young, arrogant, clipped. It took just seconds to place the face it matched: Nicola, the trainee Hannah had sat next to at dinner on the first evening. She was petite and dark-haired, full of respectful charm as she asked Hannah about the baby and chatted across the table with Alice and Simon.

'Well, what would your wife say to all this, Mr Fawcett?'

'Don't bring Hannah into this,' Michael said, sounding half-impatient, half-amused. 'I'm sure she's quite happy looking at all that original thatching . . .'

Another giggle. 'She did go on about your perfect new house last night. I thought she was never going to stop! Is there a granny flat for me?'

'No, but there might be a bed you can use . . .'

Still Hannah stood there. Somehow she'd been anaesthetised. It was like listening to a radio play, her brain couldn't make the connection with the reality in front of her.

'What's the time anyway?' Nicola asked.

'Hang on a sec . . . Almost quarter to one,' Michael said. 'We'd better get back to the others. I think our conference call has been a great success, don't you?'

'Oh yes. Except I think there's one more thing on the agenda we haven't addressed . . .'

'Do you now? I must remember to mention your attention to detail when I do your next appraisal . . .'

He was laughing easily now, then doing that Michael snuf-fling-groaning thing, a noise so intimate it hit Hannah's gut with almost physical force and made her draw deeply at the air. At last, her brain buckled. This was her *husband*! This cow he'd just had sex with had been invited to their *wedding*! And this was all far, far too casual to be the first time. She opened her mouth to scream but nothing came out. Her head felt like a bowl of hot blood.

'I'm just going to have a quick fag,' Nicola said.

'Don't smoke in here,' said Michael. 'There are alarms everywhere.'

'God, what is it with this country? You'd think they'd take advantage of the cheap ciggies, they don't know how bloody lucky they are.'

At the sight of slender creamy calves and neat little feet stretching across the tiles, Hannah finally fled. But her brain had forgotten her body's extra weight and she stumbled, heavy and awkward. One of the women on the loungers called out something in German and she turned, held up a hand, could barely bring the woman's face into focus. What was it they said about emergency situations, when a ferry filled with water or a plane split in two, how some people's senses kicked into a kind of supergear and made them capable of feats beyond normal human parameters? But others just could not compute in time the extraordinary information in front of them; they became hopeless jellies unequal to the challenge of survival.

She reached her own room, let herself in and went straight to the dressing room where their suitcases lay open on the floor. She was panting badly. Where were the tickets? She prayed Michael hadn't shut them in the safe; she hadn't listened properly when he'd told her the combination. Then she saw them, folded to make a bookmark in his book: *A History of South Africa*. He'd been reading it on the plane while she devoured *Vanity Fair* and ignored his muttered comments about errors he'd spotted in the text. She'd even felt a bit ashamed because she'd preferred her celebrity profile to his history lecture. What innocent interplay that all seemed now!

She walked over to the bedside table, picked up the phone and dialled '9'.

'Reception?'

'Hi, I need a car to Cape Town Airport as soon as possible, please.'

'You're checking out early, Mrs Fawcett? Is everything fine?' *Is everything fine?* They asked this question fifty times a day, it was like a national catchphrase. *No, everything is not fine, everything* is *fucking awful.* 'Excellent,' they'd say, smiling, regardless of the response. Waitrons, they called them in the restaurants, not waiters.

'Yes, no, I am, but my husband is staying as planned.'

'Of course, I'll call as soon as I've arranged the transfer.'

'Thank you.'

It was agony waiting for the call. Her immediate fear was that Michael would come back to their room before lunch. Might he want a shower, after . . . No, he could get that in Nicola's room and, anyway, wet hair would make it clear to the rest of the group what he'd been up to – no one was swimming today, it was bright but not warm enough to use the hotel's outdoor pool.

She packed what she needed in her carry-on bag and tucked her passport and ticket into her jacket pocket. The blood still crashed around her skull. Still no call, this was interminable. She walked out onto their terrace. It was much larger than the one she'd just been standing on; partners had obviously been allocated more luxurious accommodation than junior staff – Michael's firm was nothing if not hierarchical. No doubt Simon and Alice had the honeymoon suite with the private pool. Beyond the lawn ran the orderly rows of vines, and beyond them a plush band of trees, in the far distance nothing but rock and taut blue sky.

'What a shame it's not just us,' she'd said to Michael, when they'd first seen the view. 'It's so peaceful, isn't it? We could just sit out here all week and read.'

'Yes, well *you* still can, babe,' Michael had said, squeezing her,

152

'but I've got to talk a load of rubbish about South African finance policy.'

For a glorious few seconds she dreamed that life had been rewound, that it was an hour earlier, that she felt exactly as Lucy and Alice and the others imagined, overtired from nurturing new life but perfectly content. All she'd need to worry about was keeping to the shade and swallowing a long cool drink while the bath filled with bubbles. She went back inside and turned on the TV. A black prisoner was bantering with a prison governor, who announced he was going to send his charge back to South Africa. Then the scene froze for the ad break. *There's a Zulu on My Stoep*, the movie was called.

A note, she needed to leave a note, so they wouldn't think she'd been murdered by some unfortunate stray from the townships. She could imagine Michael getting Derrick banged up for suspected abduction. She opened the folder of hotel stationery and took out a sheet of writing paper: '*I've gone. Don't follow me. Enjoy the rest of the trip – I'm sure there are plenty of local attractions to keep you busy . . .*' After reading this through she crumpled it up and threw it in the waste-paper basket, then started again. '*Michael, I've* gone *home early. I'm sure you can* work out why. *Don't bother changing your own plans. Hannah*.' That would do.

The phone rang. 'We have a taxi for you at reception, Mrs Fawcett. I'll send someone for your luggage.'

'I've just got hand luggage, I'll come straight there, thank you.'

She walked, head down, through the main building, through the lounge with its sofa cushions plumped up like soufflés, past reception and into the back of the open taxi, where she shrank low into her seat as the driver pulled out – just as well, for she could see the heads of Simon and the others on the terrace, one or two turned in the direction of the drive to inspect a bottle of wine held out by the waitron. She couldn't see Michael.

It was the same driver who'd brought her back from the town

less than an hour ago. He didn't attempt any small talk, for which Hannah was grateful. The moment felt unreal, cinematic, as though she were watching her twin sister being propelled to disaster by some fit of insanity while she stood by, helpless to intervene. *Helpless to intervene.* That just about summed her up, she thought miserably. Why hadn't she kicked open those doors and confronted them? Pulled their horrible sweaty bodies apart and given them hell? Because she'd been helpless to intervene, that was why. Her instinct was to flee.

'There's Table Mountain ahead,' the driver nodded after a while.

'Yes,' Hannah said, politely looking.

'A climber fell this morning.'

'Oh, how awful.'

There's always someone worse off than you, that's what her mother used to say to them when they'd reported some petty playground injustice. (It was her variation on the mealtime 'Think of the starving Africans' theme when they'd tried to leave their peas.) Hannah, who had accepted the truism with as much humility as she could muster, now remembered Juliet's protest: 'That's their hard luck, Mum, isn't it? But what about me?'

At the airport, changing her flight proved no problem for the British Airways staff, but the next direct service to London didn't leave for four hours. There was the option of flying via Johannesburg but this she dismissed at once as she'd be in the air for an extra three hours and, besides, two takeoffs and two land-ings doubled her chances of crashing and never meeting her son. She'd started to think in this ultra-cautious way recently. She didn't think she'd turn out to be one of the superior beings, but more likely the type to perish trapped in her seat as black smoke filled the cabin and the super-people bounced down the inflatable slide.

She focused all her energy on breathing. If in doubt, breathe out, that's what the midwife had told her when she'd asked how bad the pain would be during labour. It seemed to do the trick for other kinds of pain as well. She couldn't allow herself to break down. Four hours was fine. Michael would have no reason to suspect her escape, but would spend the whole afternoon in the conference wing just as he had the day before. Even if he did pop back to the room he'd have to be near the desk to see her note. And the wives' tour wasn't due back until six o'clock; should Lucy or anyone call to see how she was, she'd surely assume she was napping.

Sitting in the glass cage of the executive lounge she occupied herself with a mental log of each traveller to pass in front of her. First the early arrivals, trickling through to the departure hall, mostly older travellers with slow legs. Cottonheads, that's what Juliet and her friends called elderly people. They always checked in hours earlier than they needed to, clutching bubble-wrapped packages and insisting on far too much hand luggage per person. They'd gather in clusters at inconvenient spots, like the top of a busy escalator or outside the ladies, fussing over minor decisions. Her parents were exactly the same: 'Where did you put the boarding passes, Gayle?' 'I thought *you* had them?' 'Oh God, you don't think I left them on the table in that café, do you? Hang about, no, here they are, in my bag all along. What a relief!'

At last, aloft, she began to whimper, quietly, so as not to bother the man next to her, though he couldn't fail to notice her distress as the seats were the reclining kind that faced each other in pairs. Food arrived and, later, plates were removed. Then the heat was turned up and the lights dimmed. Hannah turned her face away and cried properly.

She woke up thinking of Juliet. They'd been prone to eaves-dropping since very young; one of their favourite games was to hide in cupboards or trees or just around the nearest available corner and listen in to adults' conversations, avid for swearwords or references to sexual acts. She still remembered word for word

155

her parents' conversation in the kitchen that time. They had assumed the girls were upstairs in their rooms but instead the two of them were crouched at the back door by the dustbin.

'They'll be fine,' their father had reassured their mother, voice all serious. 'Kids deal with this all the time.'

'I'm sure Juliet will be OK about it,' their mother had replied, 'but I'm worried about Hannah. She doesn't like things to change, and we've always been so close.'

They'd dashed off when their mother had come out to the bin with a bowl of vegetable peelings, and agreed under the plum tree that their parents must be divorcing. At school, every second child had parents who were divorcing. Juliet, still young enough, had begun weeping.

'Breakfast?'

'Yes, please.' Hannah adjusted her seat and looked forward to the latest business-class offering. No point starving Junior because his father had turned out to be a heartless bastard.

It was Laura. They'd been talking about the arrival of Laura. The family was getting not a divorce but a new baby. 'Eavesdroppers never hear good of themselves,' their mother had said to them when she'd got to the bottom of their moping and clinging. It was the first time Hannah had heard that saying. And so she and Juliet had stopped earwigging, for a while at least.

It was early morning when Hannah arrived at Juliet's. Her sister's had been the address that came out of her mouth when the taxi driver had caught her eye in his mirror to ask her destination. She'd thought about Lottie, Siobhan, of going back to Sisters Avenue to collect her own car before driving up to her parents. But she couldn't bear to go back to the loft. It would feel like facing Michael himself.

Her sister emerged from her bedroom at Sasha's summons, showered and dressed but still looking much the worse for wear. 'Hannah! What's wrong? Is it Mum?'

'No, no. Can I use your loo? I'm desperate!' Hannah asked.

'Caliban's in the bathroom by the sounds,' said Juliet. 'What's up? I take it you're not just here for the facilities?'

Hannah followed her sister into the living room. Someone's sleep-heavy form lay submerged in blankets on the sofa, so she lowered herself onto the floor.

'Sorry, that's Kate. We were at an awards do last night and she stayed over,' Juliet explained. 'What's wrong?'

Hannah hardly knew where to start. 'I've just come from Heathrow, came back from South Africa early.'

'I didn't know you were in South Africa?' Juliet said, frowning. 'Look, sit on the sofa. Kate! Wake up!'

'I found Michael with another woman.'

'Another . . . ? Oh, Hannah, I'm sorry.'

'What's going on?' Sasha was standing at the doorway in her gown, was always standing in doorways in her gown, it seemed to Hannah.

'Sasha, we all need to go to the loo, can you ask Callum when he's going to be finished?' Juliet sounded much sharper than usual. Sasha just scowled and went out again. Relations were clearly deteriorating in NW1.

At that point Kate raised her head. 'Morning. Oh, hi, Hannah! God, I feel *horrendous*. Where are the aspirin, Jules?'

'In the cupboard above the kettle. Turn it on while you're in there, will you? So does he know you've gone?'

'Does who know I've gone where?' Kate said, getting up and pulling her T-shirt down over pale, solid thighs.

'Not you – Hannah!'

'I left him a note,' Hannah said, taking the clump of tissue Juliet passed her. Then Juliet put a hand on her arm, which made her feel a little better.

'What a bastard. What happened, exactly?'

Hannah told her. It still didn't seem real, though Juliet's exclamations of disbelief were authentic enough.

'You poor, poor thing. This is *terrible*.'

'I know. I can't believe it's happening to me. What have I done to deserve something like this?'

'What did she look like?' Juliet asked suddenly.

'Attractive. Very young.' Hannah wanted to open her mouth wide and wail until no more sound came out.

'Is she really tall?'

That was an odd question, Hannah thought, but Juliet was obviously trying to get a full mental picture. 'No, quite short, but thin, sort of feline.'

'Well, she must be sick in the head,' Juliet said. 'How could anyone do that? It's bad enough, but with you in the same hotel! They must have got off on the risk element. Are women getting nastier or what?'

Hannah just sniffed.

'So what are you going to do?' Juliet asked. 'Where will you stay?'

Hannah looked around the flat; it was far smaller than she remembered, the two-seater sofa seemed to take up the whole room.

'I mean, you could stay here,' Juliet said. 'If it was my place there'd be no question, but, well, it's not really my call.'

'That's OK,' Hannah said, starting to recover herself. She didn't want to make Juliet feel guilty that she wasn't in a position to help. 'You're obviously overcrowded as it is, and pregnant women really can't wait for the loo this long every day.' She managed a laugh.

'Nor can *any* woman,' Juliet said. 'The other day I had to pee in a pint glass in my bedroom.'

'Urgh,' Kate giggled, reappearing with three mugs of tea. 'You should get a commode in your room!'

'I would if I could afford it!' Juliet closed her eyes and began massaging the sockets. 'God, that was such a weird night last night, wasn't it? I definitely must have passed out at one point.'

'We thought you'd been abducted by aliens,' Kate said, giggling.

'I barely feel alive,' Juliet groaned.

Me neither, Hannah thought. She sipped her tea.

'You know, you should get the locks changed at the flat and not let the fucker back in,' Juliet said to her.

'Ooh, which fucker is this?' asked Kate.

'Michael. Her husband.'

'What's he done?'

'I can't, really,' Hannah said to Juliet. 'It's his place. It's always felt like his place, even after the wedding. I'd rather be the one to leave.'

'There are other friends, though, where you can stay, aren't there?'

Hannah thought. Who *could* she stay with, who could she trust with this private humiliation so soon after the wedding? Especially as she'd let months go by without returning calls or turning up to drinks when she should have. Who would help her without betraying that glimmer of schadenfreude, that irresistible glee as they bashed out their morning Hotmails. (*'You'll never guess who I've got staying with me? Let's just say the honeymoon is over . . .'*) Lottie was the obvious choice and Lord knew she had the space, but Rob was Michael's best friend. It would be impossible. She wondered for a moment about Rani and realised she didn't even know where her colleague lived.

'I'll try Siobhan,' she said. 'D'you mind if I hang out here for an hour? I don't want to ring this early, she'll be busy with the baby.'

'Sure,' Juliet said. 'There's loads of time. We're allowed to be late after an awards do when we've won something.'

'What did you win?' Hannah asked mechanically. She didn't listen to the answer, tuning back in only when she saw that Kate was trying to get her attention.

'More tea? And does anyone want toast?'

159

'Oh, would you,' Juliet said. 'Thanks, Kate, I'm starving. You should eat something as well, Hannah.'

Hannah unzipped her bag to hunt for a new tissue. 'I ate on the plane. I feel a bit sick now.'

'I'm not surprised after what you've just lived through!'

'Anyway, let's not talk about this any more,' Hannah said. 'I've been thinking about nothing else for a twelve-hour flight. I feel like I'm going insane. How are things with you, Juliet? How's Guy?'

Juliet looked down. 'Oh, that's over as well.'

It was the 'as well' that made Hannah burst into tears.

Chapter 14

Hannah had been at Siobhan's for three weeks and her new friend was displaying all the loyalty and compassion of a very old friend. Six months ago she hadn't known the Dulwich Road even existed, but now that little basement flat by the church was her precious sanctuary. She'd been concerned about crowding Siobhan and Nora, but as it turned out the living room seemed larger once they'd moved the sofa bed into the bay window and reorganised the rest of the furniture. In any case, Hannah had very few possessions with her: a suitcase of clothes collected from the loft while Michael was still in Cape Town; a couple of baby books (the sections on single-parent families newly thumbed); her medical notes. All those pots and vases and wine glasses she'd agonised over when choosing their wedding list and here she was living quite comfortably without a single one of them.

Every day, too early to check the time, she would lie in bed half-listening to the morning routine: first Nora's wail and Siobhan's answering murmurs; then the lullabies from the mobile over Nora's cot and tiptoed steps past Hannah's bed to the kitchen; the opening and closing of the fridge door, followed by the ping of the microwave and whoosh of the milk bottle; finally, Siobhan's footsteps back to Nora's bedroom. One ten-minute cycle, every morning without fail. She couldn't think of a better way to be reminded that day followed night.

'Rather more charming from under a duvet,' Siobhan laughed when Hannah shared her thoughts. 'But, no, don't even think of trying to help in the morning. You do far too much as it is – all this babysitting . . .'

'It's a pleasure, really. It's the least I can do.' Neither wanted to repeat the usual conversation about money, with Hannah offering and Siobhan refusing. By now she'd established other ways of doing her bit: like big Tesco shops with lots of treats and nice wine, evening babysitting and a regular slot during the afternoon for Siobhan to get out on her own or rest in her bedroom. 'House of Naps', Siobhan called the flat, and it was true, there was hardly a moment when one of the three of them wasn't sleeping.

'What did you do before?' Hannah asked her one day. 'Did you just *never* get a break?'

'You have to work with the material in front of you, don't you?' was all Siobhan said.

Hannah thought it was a tragedy that Siobhan was treated so poorly by her family, especially since her own support of others was obviously unconditional. Not once to her knowledge had a relative visited, though friends dropped by every so often, mostly other mothers who Siobhan had met at antenatal groups. She'd lost touch with friends who didn't have children, she said, mainly because they each thought the other had it easy and, all things considered, judged it best to stick with their own. 'I think of it as a temporary separation,' Siobhan said. 'And the same with my parents. Relationships don't die out so easily, not all of them anyway. People come around. Meanwhile, I don't have time to worry.'

'Yes,' Hannah agreed. 'I wish I didn't have quite so much time to worry.'

'Well, you won't for much longer! These next three months will whizz by.'

They'd got into the habit of having a hot lunch together when Nora was down for her nap, and today they'd pulled their kitchen chairs onto the patio to enjoy the freakishly mild December day. It was as warm as September and many of the trees in Brockwell Park still had their leaves. There was even the sound of seagulls over the lido, which in winter had taken on the air of a cool, green square lake, and the only sound of urban life was the faint coughing of the buses on Dulwich Road. It seemed a million miles from Clapham Common and the Fawcett marital home, not the short bus ride that it was.

'So what are you going to do about Michael?' Siobhan asked. 'Made any decisions yet?'

'I don't know,' Hannah said truthfully. 'In some ways I feel exactly the same as I did on the flight home from South Africa. *How could he?* I just don't understand how a man can sleep with someone else under his pregnant wife's nose, so soon after getting married. Since when did the seven-year itch get reduced to five months?'

'I've known people capable of worse,' said Siobhan. 'Men shag bridesmaids at their own weddings! Don't you think this sort of thing probably happens all the time but the other partner just never finds out?'

'That's too depressing,' Hannah said, struck for the hundredth time by the contrast between Siobhan's fresh, wide-eyed appearance and the candid realism of her opinions. And it was all the more striking because she suspected herself of the complete opposite. She *looked* womanly and knowing, everyone said so, and yet she felt as naïve as a fourteen-year-old navigating her first relationship. She frowned at Siobhan. 'I mean, who are these bridesmaids who would *do* that to their friends?'

'People like Nicola, presumably,' Siobhan said. 'The thing is, if you *hadn't* walked by that particular hotel room that day at that moment, you'd still be feeling head over heels, wouldn't you? Especially with the baby and house and everything. You'd still be thinking Michael was the man for you.'

Hannah considered this, just as she had every day since fleeing the Stellenbosch hotel. She didn't always come up with the same answer. 'Well, yes, I suppose so. He does seem, *did* seem, the closest thing to my perfect match.'

'Perfect match?' Siobhan repeated the words slowly, as though savouring a phrase from medieval English. 'Does such a thing exist any more?'

'I don't know. I just thought he was exactly what I wanted in a husband. Clever, exciting, successful, and kind as well. I mean, I knew he'd been a bit of a . . .' She broke off.

'A one?' Siobhan filled in, delicately.

'Yes, exactly. A one. But I still thought he could be *The* One. He seemed proud of having changed.'

'Perhaps he didn't change at all, just wanted to give you that impression?'

'God, I'd like to think that this was a one-off. The first time . . .' She looked pleadingly at Siobhan as though her reassurance was all it would take to make it true. But that instinct she'd had that day, that sense that Michael and Nicola weren't new lovers, she still couldn't shake it. And all those comments in the past from Rob and Marcus and Adam, she'd just dismissed them as so much exaggeration. As far as she'd been concerned, their notion of Michael as the last of London's great ladies' men was more for their own benefit than his, as though he'd become some sort of talisman for their own lost bachelorhood. The wedding had put a stop to the comments, of course, but not, evidently, to Michael. I thought I was so special, she thought to herself now, because I was the one he decided to marry. This must be punishment for my arrogance.

'You know what I think?' Siobhan said. 'I think women are so busy moulding themselves into whatever they think it is that

164

their man expects, they don't notice that *he* hasn't compromised in the slightest.'

'Maybe.' Hannah soon felt adrift in these discussions about men. She had no brothers and had made few male friends over the years, so her experience was of a handful of boyfriends and one husband, a husband with whom she'd separated after five months. She thought about Juliet and her carefully defined categories for each man who crossed her path, and woman, too, for that matter. *Everyone* fits into a category, she insisted. Hannah had never asked which category Michael fell into. There was Public School Stereotype, she supposed that would be it, though by now he'd probably been switched to whichever compartment housed the unfaithful.

'My sister had a perfect match once,' she told Siobhan.

'Oh, the one who was killed?'

'You make it sound as though it was his being dead that made him perfect!'

'You said it,' Siobhan chuckled. 'No, seriously, what was he like, then?'

'He was very attractive, a real adventurer,' Hannah remembered. 'They always seemed totally *together*. They were both very strong characters, but it worked. *Everyone* liked Luke. But I'm not sure she would consider him so wonderful now. He turned out to be, well, not totally what she thought.'

'There you go,' Siobhan said, without relish.

'He seemed perfect, though, for a while.'

'I think "seemed" is the best we can hope for,' Siobhan said.

Yes, Hannah thought, Luke had seemed Juliet's ideal mate, and Michael had seemed hers. Wasn't it just as Siobhan said? If she hadn't felt unwell and gone back to the hotel at that exact time, and if Juliet hadn't joined Luke at that particular point on his travels, then both couples might still be together today. But only because the two women would be none the wiser. 'None the wiser': it was one of those phrases that seemed to have been

165

coined for her, a bit like 'Helpless to intervene'. She pictured the phrase on her gravestone: '*Here lies Hannah Fawcett, née Goodwin. She died none the wiser.*'

She tried to keep her thoughts on track. 'Anyway, Michael's done it now and the first time is the one that matters. I mean, don't they say infidelity just gets easier and easier, a bit like murder?'

'Yes, until you get caught,' Siobhan sighed. 'Then you find you're up for consecutive sentences.'

'What's the sentence? Divorce, I suppose?' Hannah asked. It felt weird saying the 'd' word out loud. It was the first time, but presumably that would get easier, too.

Siobhan cleared away their plates and brought out a bowl of satsumas. 'So what does your sister think about all of this?'

'Oh, Juliet's never liked Michael. She thinks I just married him for his money.'

'That's a bit mean.'

'It's OK, *I* know it's not true. But I can hardly deny he has his faults, can I?' She'd had just one conversation with Juliet since turning up at her flat that awful morning, and she'd asked her outright what she'd do in the same situation.

'Well,' Juliet said. 'I'd start by being honest about whether or not I still loved him.' *Ever* loved him, that's what she really meant, Hannah was sure of it.

'Yes,' she said decisively. 'The answer's yes.'

'Right.' She could tell Juliet was surprised. 'So Michael has been unfaithful within the first six months of marriage, and yet you *still* love him.'

'Yes, I suppose.'

'Well,' Juliet sighed. 'What does that tell you about yourself?'

Hannah had felt insulted by this. 'Well, it tells me that I fell in love with a man who I believed would be faithful to me and I now find it hard to just switch off and pretend I never loved him in the first place.'

Juliet had backtracked a bit then. 'Sorry, I know it's hard. I suppose it's a question of whether you can forgive him or not.'

'Would you?' Hannah asked. She had to know.

'Don't ask me that,' Juliet said.

Now Hannah asked Siobhan the same question and was again denied a straight answer. 'I think I'd give myself a bit more time to think about all this. Anyway,' Siobhan laughed, 'I'm a fine one to advise, aren't I?'

Seeing she'd already peeled four satsumas Hannah shared the segments with Siobhan. 'Have you thought about him lately?' she asked. 'I mean Nora's father?' She'd asked this before and was used to it being dismissed as a 'non-issue', but today Siobhan seemed more willing to talk.

'Not really. I know it's hard for people to understand, but I had no relationship with her father and it's nothing like your situation with Michael. You're married. In my case, the guy's just not a factor.'

'It just seems so weird that she's got grandparents and relatives out there who don't know about her, how gorgeous she is.'

'Her life will be less complicated this way,' Siobhan said. 'I'm not trying to deprive her. It's just the best way after a one-night stand. We don't need some tug-of-love with strangers. And even if I did get it into my head to track down the father, he'd probably just laugh in my face and deny the whole thing.'

'But you'd get the court to order DNA tests and the CSA would force him to make contributions.' Hannah had given the subject deeper thought in recent weeks; what was to say she wouldn't need to follow some of these procedures herself, married or not? 'He wouldn't have to be involved, but at least you'd get some money to help you out. If he still works in the City he can't be that hard to find.'

Siobhan was looking at her in near alarm. 'For God's sake, don't get it into your head to investigate this,' she said. 'I've got enough on my plate without having a Miss Marple on the case.'

167

'But aren't you in touch with anyone from that job?' Hannah persisted. It was a relief, a pleasure almost, to turn her mind to something other than her own dilemma. 'Where were you working again? Morgan Stanley?'

'Proctor Mitchum.'

Hannah's eyes widened. 'That's where Lottie's husband works, I'm sure! What was this guy's name?'

Siobhan looked embarrassed. 'Actually, I don't know.'

'What?' Hannah couldn't help sounding disapproving.

'Well, haven't you ever slept with someone and not known their name?'

'No!'

'Really? I thought everyone had done something like that.' Siobhan's genuine amazement made Hannah feel cross and a little sorry for herself. There seemed to be a lot of comment at the moment from all quarters about the lack of daring in her life choices. Well, Siobhan could keep her one-night stands, because leaving a husband when expecting their child was daring enough for her. But she couldn't help wondering how the other women she knew would answer Siobhan's question. Juliet would be a yes, certainly, as would the chum under the blanket, Kate. And Lottie was probably a yes, too, she was quite proud of her colourful, pre-Rob exploits.

'Do you mean you just can't *remember* his name?' she asked Siobhan, trying to understand.

'No, I mean we just didn't introduce ourselves. It was quite fun in a way,' Siobhan said with an air of surprise that suggested she really hadn't given the episode a moment's thought before now. 'He just came up to me and said something like, "Don't tell me who you are, just tell me who you'd be if you could be anyone else in the world."'

'What did he mean?'

'You know, like a historical figure, a movie star or whatever.'

'Sounds like a game Juliet and her friends used to play,'

Hannah said. 'If you were a Bond girl, who would you be, that sort of thing.'

'Exactly. It seemed sort of sexy at the time.'

'Who did you say?' Hannah asked.

'I said Brigitte Bardot. I'd just been reading a biography of her.'

'I bet he was pleased with that! And who was he?'

'David Niven, if I remember rightly.'

'I could see that working . . .' Hannah was starting to enjoy this. 'I can't believe you haven't told me this before, it's a great story. Did you stay in character all night? Did you talk about Saint-Tropez and animal rights?'

Siobhan giggled. 'No, that's as far as the celebrity role-playing went, sadly. I don't think he knew anything about David Niven, to be honest. But the attraction was amazing, I remember that . . . Maybe there was some kind of primeval urge driving me on – maybe I really wanted a baby and it had to be then and there. Oh, and I was *very* drunk, did I mention that?'

They both laughed.

'Well, personally I think David Niven would want to provide for his child,' Hannah said. 'Why don't I ask Lottie to get Rob to help us track him down?'

Siobhan flushed. 'Hannah, leave it, please! I moved quite soon after the night it happened and it was ages before I realised I was pregnant. Besides, I've got no one to blame but myself for not using anything at the time. The decision to have a baby was mine, not his, so why should he be forced into a situation he had no say in?'

'Well, if you're sure. It's just financially . . .'

'I'm not bothered about money, believe me,' Siobhan said, very firmly now. 'I know it's important to you, but at this moment in time I'd rather have complete freedom.'

Hannah felt slightly offended by this, but couldn't in all honesty deny it. Money *was* important to her, not to the exclusion of all other considerations and certainly not enough to make her return to someone who'd humiliated her, but important just the same. In fact, the contrast between Siobhan's needs and her own was starting to make her panic. Siobhan seemed willing to subsist on so little. What if she and Michael did divorce, would she be able to cope on her own? Would he give her enough money for a nanny? Her mother had moved miles away, Juliet had to have her arm twisted even to cross the river . . . Siobhan might be able to cope with anything, but could she? What about holidays and haircuts and music lessons and school fees . . . ?

'Are you OK?' Siobhan asked. 'Sorry, I didn't mean to be sharp.'

'No, it's not you. I was just thinking, if Michael and I do split up for good, will he want to be involved, you know, with the baby?'

'I'm sure he will,' Siobhan said, leaning towards her, eyes full of sympathy. 'You mustn't feel like we're in the same boat, you know. From what you've said Michael has lots of decent qualities, otherwise you wouldn't have married him, would you?'

'Maybe. Unless I'm a hopeless judge of character.'

'Of course you're not. I bet he'll turn out to be a really good father, even if it's just part-time. You'll be able to make something out of all of this, don't worry.'

'I hope so.'

'I'll have to wake Nora in a minute,' Siobhan said. 'Let's enjoy the peace while we can. Forget about Michael for now, he's not exactly beating down your door, is he?'

Hannah didn't tell Siobhan that she picked up her voicemail religiously every day and there was always a message from Michael. At first he'd pleaded with her, apologised over and over, begged her to get in touch for crisis talks. She never did. He'd never made any attempt to deny his crime, of course. He would have understood her note all right, and a stark account to Lottie, made with no insistence on confidentiality, would probably have relieved him of any remaining hopes for that particular escape route.

After a while his messages had become more matter-of-fact, bulletins of practical information about domestic arrangements that she began to follow with real interest: they were about to complete on the Salcott Road house, just a couple of final queries to clear up; Fleur was ready and waiting, had been around to Sisters Avenue again to measure up for blinds, was thinking about retiling the floor in the kitchen – she had some sort of black-and-white palazzo scheme in mind; he'd got Charlotte to send out Christmas cards from both of them, he hoped that was OK; he'd decided to buy the green chandeliers from the vendors, didn't want to tell her how much he agreed to pay, but daylight and robbery were two words that sprang to mind as it turned out the damn things had been handmade in Venice; they were completing on Friday; they'd completed; he had a set of keys for her to use whenever she wanted, she had only to say the word.

There was something about this final piece of news that Hannah found soothing, the first twinge towards reconciliation. It was as though she'd been expecting the house purchase to fall through as a sign that the marriage was categorically doomed. But it had survived the change in circumstances, and perhaps they could, too, perhaps she would be living in Salcott Road after all. Whenever she pictured the baby it was always in that house, in the child's room with the fairy lights. But one problem remained: she still couldn't bear to see Michael, not *physically*. The thought of his satisfied post-coital voice in that hotel room made her gag.

She jumped at the sound of her phone delivering a text message. It was from Lottie, suggesting afternoon tea the following week. She'd added '*P.S. Please say yes, we miss you!*' Who were 'we', Hannah wondered? Lottie and Ophelia? Lottie and Rob? Lottie and Michael? Before she could respond, the phone rang. It was a number she didn't recognise so she let the voicemail pick it up. 'Hi, Hannah, it's Larry. I'm down in Northcote Road again, wondered if you wanted to meet up?'

She called him straight back. 'Why don't you get on the bus and come down here for lunch? You know I'm in Herne Hill now? You're driving? Even better, just follow the bus route into Brixton and then down onto the Dulwich Road.'

'Was that Larry?' Siobhan asked, appearing with Nora. The baby's eyes were still swollen with sleep, but she was awake enough to start twisting herself out of the snowman fleece her mother was trying to zip her into. 'Not that you'd remembered, of course, but it's my baby massage session now, so I'll have to leave you two alone . . .'

'There's nothing going on,' Hannah protested, though coyly for her. 'He's just being a pal.'

'Of course,' Siobhan twinkled.

Just a pal. Even so, she spent a couple of minutes on her make-up after Siobhan and Nora had left.

She loved seeing his face again, realised it had been in her thoughts regularly since their meeting in Northcote Road three months ago. She had warned herself not to compare him with Michael, not now the context had changed and it would be so easy to make a hero of the next man she spent any time with. It wouldn't be fair on Larry anyway, as he wasn't nearly as good-looking as Michael. Having said that, in her mind's eye Michael's face had now taken on a slyness that wasn't there in reality, probably because the only photo of him in her possession was one from Italy in which the late afternoon shadows had cast a kind of cunning across his features. He'd laughed when she'd shown him the passport-sized version she kept in her purse. 'Why did you choose that one? I look as if I'm plotting to do away with you!'

She smiled over at Larry from the mug tree in the kitchen. No, if she was going to make comparisons, which of course she wasn't, then she would probably say that Larry had less refined features than Michael *physically*, but offered a gentler manner and, perhaps, a more reliable honesty. She caught herself mid-thought: *offered*? Was she taking offers, then? And if she was, was it because she considered that things could never be recovered with Michael and she was now, to all intents and purposes, a free agent? Or was it precisely in order to recover things with Michael that the idea of Larry as anything other than Juliet's friend had even occurred in the first place? What squarer way to reconcile a marriage to a cheat than to notch up a dalliance of one's own? A simple tit for tat. The fact that she was even thinking this way made her sad, but there it was.

'Does Juliet know you're here?' she asked Larry.

'You're very concerned about Juliet, aren't you?' he said, sipping from the scalding coffee she'd presented him with.

'We haven't been so close recently. I feel really out of touch with what's going on with her. But I wouldn't want her to be annoyed about us meeting up. Is she OK?'

'She's doing all right,' Larry said. 'We're all a bit wiped out because of the party season.'

'God, I haven't been to a single Christmas do,' Hannah said. She didn't count the lacklustre drinks she and Rani had shared with Christian on their last day at the school. An agent had been showing the property to developers, stepping around them as they squatted to bubble-wrap paintings from the walls. Even the champagne cork didn't pop properly; Rani had been quite upset. But Hannah had walked down the steps onto the busy pavements of Clapham Common Southside with no sense of significance whatsoever. This had been a working interlude overshadowed by private affairs. She'd probably forget she'd ever done it.

'That's so tragic!' Larry was saying. 'You really haven't been out? I shall have to do something about that. Which night are you free next week?'

It was the word 'night' that made her see that this was the moment, the moment to nip whatever this was going to be in the bud. But instead she heard herself answer, 'Any night. Oh, not Wednesday, Siobhan's going to the cinema and I'm babysitting. But I don't like going to smoky pubs, I hope you don't mind.'

'Of course not. I'll think of something. Tuesday, perhaps?'

'OK, that would be lovely.' So it had begun, whatever it was going to be.

'This flat's all right, isn't it?' Larry said, looking around. 'I always expect basements to be dingy and damp, with students kipping in the hallway. How many bedrooms are there?'

'One and a half – Nora's room is tiny, not big enough for a proper bed, but that's all she needs for her cot. But Siobhan's room is enormous. She could probably split it in two when the time comes.'

'So where do you sleep?'

She felt herself blush and turned her face away to reply, 'On the sofa, right where you're sitting. It pulls out into a bed.' As she watched him give it a prod, it was impossible to dislodge the association with her most private time. It was all so exposed: the special boomerang-shaped cushion for under her hips, the bolster for between her knees, the bottle of Gaviscon on her makeshift bedside table: but of course Larry would have no idea of the complicated sleeping conditions of pregnant women.

'That's very disciplined to fold it back up every day,' he said. 'I'd probably end up doing everything from the bed, you know, eating, watching telly. Like John and Yoko.'

'Well, it is Siobhan's living room,' Hannah said. 'I try not to pull it out until they've gone to bed.' She found she preferred it when he spoke, so she could watch his wide, patient grin. She felt greedy, wanted to lean over and touch his mouth. She took a step back before she could do anything silly. 'Shall I show you the rest of the place?'

'Sure. I find it hard to be in a flat these days without needing to examine the plumbing and electrics.'

She led him through the other rooms: Siobhan's bedroom, now doubling as a laundry room so Hannah didn't have to sleep with sails of underwear flapping overhead; Nora's tiny room, with her cream-painted cot and oversized poster of a tiger. Her collection of soft toys was growing by the day, partly because there was a shop on Half Moon Lane that Hannah was incapable of passing without slipping in and choosing one more little gift. She worried that the lack of known relatives would deprive the baby of toys. Siobhan said Nora would be happy with an empty Fairy Liquid bottle with some beans in it.

'Does she own this place, then?' Larry asked.

'Yes, she bought it for peanuts before the area came up. The mortgage is less than rent would be, so it was a good move.'

'Definitely. God, I wish someone could show me somewhere that hasn't come up in this bloody city. Somewhere nice and impotent.'

'I have no clue,' Hannah said. 'Maybe Holloway?'

Larry laughed. 'Point taken. I wonder what this place is worth? God, it's obsessive, isn't it? I pray my offer will be accepted on the Sisters Avenue flat and I can stop caring about property prices.'

'You'll probably care even more when it is,' Hannah said. 'Are you definitely going for that one? You know it's much cheaper around this area and nicer than Battersea in many ways. The park is beautiful.'

'Don't tell me *you*'re thinking about breaking permanently from the Valley?'

She marvelled at how he picked up on the smallest nuance; their conversation seemed to leapfrog every second sentence, as though they were skipping over whole passages of a longer script. 'A good question,' she said. 'But I haven't actually lived in Nappy Valley yet, you know, not technically.' Insanely, she

175

imagined herself going back to Sisters Avenue, not to Michael's loft but to Larry's one-bedroom flat. The smell of perfume would be gone, as would the shimmering bedside lamps, and Larry's trainers would be stacked by the door because there was no storage for footwear. Every day she'd see those gentle eyes and lap up the humorous, thoughtful words he used to observe the world around him. 'Infantile' Michael had called him after Juliet's party, 'A typical skive-and-survive creative type.' Well, Michael's opinions held no sway now.

He returned to the sofa and this time she joined him. 'So where's all your stuff?' Larry asked, easing back against the cushions.

'Still at Michael's. But I have what I need.' It was then that she seemed to leave her own skin and watch a dark-haired, round-limbed woman lean so closely towards Larry that her hair touched his face. Then they were kissing and he had his fingers in her hair.

'This is a bit of a surprise,' he murmured, after a while.

'A nice one?'

'Yes.' His hands were all over her breasts now, circumnavigating her stomach, down her back and over her bottom. She surrendered for a blissful minute, then unexpectedly thought of Siobhan, chattering with the other mothers as they warmed oil in their hands and tried to steady the bodies of their wriggling babies. Had she any inkling that her lodger, the wronged wife, was rolling about on the sofa with her sister's best friend?

'Why aren't you at work?' she asked suddenly.

'I'm using up leftover holidays,' Larry said, surprised. 'I've got pretty much every Friday off till the end of term.' Their shirts were off, skin pressed warmly together. And then she felt a familiar internal wrestling and whooshing: the baby was joining in, responding to all the rubbing and pressing.

'What was that?' Larry asked, alarmed. 'The baby?'

'This is too weird,' Hannah said. 'Let's put our clothes on.' He

176

followed her and they lay together, snuggled up in front of the blank television screen. 'Sorry,' she said. 'I just don't know what I'm doing at the moment. I'm a bit unstable.'

'That's all right.' He stroked her stomach experimentally and Hannah eased his hand away, worried about hurting his feelings. 'Does it move a lot?'

'Yes, there's just about enough room still for a somersault.'

'A somersault? God, it's the Cirque du Soleil in there.'

'How did this happen?' she asked.

'I'm sure someone once told me it was something to do with a sperm and an egg,' he laughed.

'No, I mean us,' Hannah said, not letting go of his hand.

'I have no idea. But I'm glad it did.'

'I wish I wasn't in such a complicated situation.'

'It's me who wishes you weren't,' Larry said. 'But you shouldn't be wishing anything away.'

'I don't mean the baby,' Hannah said, turning to face him, eyes huge.

'I know exactly who you mean,' Larry said. 'I don't particularly want to hear his name again today.'

'Juliet's told you everything, I suppose?'

'Yes, you're quite a pair, you Goodwin girls.'

'Are we? Actually, there are three of us. There's a little sister, Laura, as well.'

'I'd better not meet her,' Larry smiled. 'I'm not sure my heart could take it.'

Chapter 15

Juliet was not enjoying the party season as much as usual. She felt as though she'd seen and heard it all before a thousand years in a row. Exhaustion, that was what it was. She was bone-weary, washed-out, dog-tired. What was the phrase Fulton used? Something American-sounding, for once. 'Outta gas', that was it. She was totally and utterly outta gas.

It was a few weeks since that peculiar night at the Grosvenor, but she still couldn't get it out of her head. It had been an end-of-year media awards dinner and she'd been at the Imagineer table with the usual suspects: Dominic, Phil, Larry and Kate, as well as some of the Smithfield's contacts Dominic considered it politic to schmooze that month. It was routine stuff: the food was bland, the acoustics horrendous, the MC a TV presenter who did a late-night chart show on Fridays – at least he had done the last time Juliet had watched TV on a Friday night. What was not so routine was that she had no memory whatsoever of a whole segment of the evening. The last thing she recalled before the black hole opened was sneaking into a cloakroom and sitting in the corner, head on her knees, watching fireworks fizz on the underside of her lids. It was only when an attendant found her among the bags and pulled her up that she managed to open her eyes again.

'How long you been here?' the girl asked in broken English.

Juliet just shook her head. She couldn't believe she'd been asleep all that time, but her watch showed a ninety-minute lapse since she'd left the others with their coffees. Luckily Kate had appeared just then to collect her own coat and insisted on taking her back to Camden. She and Dominic had searched all over for her, she said, but they'd assumed she must have gone home early.

She'd still been feeling unsettled the next morning when Hannah had turned up at the flat with her atrocious – though sadly predictable – tale of Michael's misdemeanours in South Africa. Juliet hoped she'd been as kind as she should have been; it hadn't been easy serving up tea and sympathy when it felt like someone was blowing up a balloon inside her skull.

And on top of the exhaustion and memory loss, she'd now developed a strange new hunger confusion. She could never quite decide whether she wanted to eat or not, and if so, what. One Thursday lunchtime, Larry and Kate badgered her to go for sushi – there was nothing like a bit of warm saké to get through a restless pre-Christmas afternoon, Larry said, it moved time along like no other liquor. He'd stepped up his commitment to Thursday lunchtime drinking now he was using up spare holiday and taking Fridays off.

'No thanks,' said Juliet. 'Oh, actually, maybe. I quite fancy some miso soup.'

'Make your mind up,' Larry laughed. 'We're leaving in ten minutes.'

She messaged them to say no, she wasn't hungry after all, couldn't even stomach the saké. But seeing them at the lifts – Kate in her new grey coat and Dr Zhivago fur hat, Larry still in shirtsleeves as though the fact that it was now winter had passed him by – she suddenly imagined the delicious blend of cold salmon and hot ginger and rushed out to join them. In the restaurant she ate nine dishes from the conveyor belt, more even than Larry, who famously ate like a teenager and often ordered enough for two.

'No one ever eats those funny egg ones,' Kate said, watching the pile of plates mount between them.

'Except vegemetarians, of course,' Larry said. Juliet giggled at the Larryism but soon stopped when he added: 'You must be pregnant, Jules.' He sounded casual enough, but she knew he was serious by the way he watched for her reaction.

'You have been a bit weird lately,' Kate said too brightly. She wasn't as good as Larry at acting spontaneous. They'd obviously discussed this in advance.

'Don't think so,' Juliet said, stuffing the last of the ginger slices into her mouth. 'I haven't slept with anyone since that last night with Guy, have I?'

'Don't ask us!' Larry snorted. 'You haven't slept with me, at any rate.'

'Or me,' Kate added, and the two of them exchanged a smirk.

'Ha ha,' Juliet said, rolling her eyes. 'I wish I'd never told you about that Fulton and Rachel thing – like neither of you have ever done something you regretted under the influence! Anyway, I'm sure I've had a period since Guy. When were Jo's promotion drinks?'

'Last Friday in November, the twenty-eighth or something,' Kate said.

'Well, there you go, I changed my Tampax in those grim loos in that pub. I remember it clearly.'

'Delightful,' said Larry, grimacing. 'But point taken, you're obviously not up the spout.'

'Wish I was sometimes,' Juliet grumbled. 'Then I could have a bit of time off like Michelle. It makes you realise how long a pregnancy is when you're doing all of someone else's work while they're away. With Phil's help, of course,' she added for Kate's benefit. 'Well, I guess at least one of us will be celebrating when Dominic finally decides who's taking over from Michelle, so either way you'll be sharing the champagne, Kate.'

'Did Larry not tell you?' said Kate, brow creasing. 'We heard

180

they're bringing in an agency person to cover Michelle's maternity leave.'

'Who told you that?'

'Kev in the tech team. Dominic's been interviewing all week, apparently.'

'Cunt,' said Larry cheerfully.

'Does Phil know?' Juliet asked.

'He's not pleased either,' Kate said. 'He's thinking of looking around.'

Larry sighed. 'For once I agree with him. We all need to get out of this bastard company.'

'I know,' Juliet agreed. She was suddenly too tired to care.

'Let's just walk out, all of us!' Kate suggested, fired up. 'I mean, today, *now*!'

'Yeah!'

The waiter brought them the bill and there was a pause as they sorted out the change, digging around the bottom of bags and pockets for a tip.

'Might as well wait for the Christmas bonus,' Larry said. 'I am about to cripple myself with a mortgage, after all.'

Juliet was glad he'd got there first. She didn't think her bank account could stretch to a revolt. 'Shall we head back? Pass me a few of those sour plum sweets, Kate . . .'

It was two days after the office Christmas party – a double celebration as Dominic had turned thirty that week – and the account suite still smelled of morning-after breath and morning-after bodies. In the pit, where the central heating seemed to blaze several degrees higher than the rest of the building, the key note was warm tuna mayonnaise, worse, somehow, than the human aromas upstairs. All around Juliet and Kate sweaty men were unpacking paper bags and bundling hot food onto their desks, only to demolish the microwaved booty with three snaps of the jaw. Some looked around straight afterwards as if there might be a scrap to spare elsewhere. It made Juliet feel sick. Drinking a can of room-temperature Coke, she seemed to be the only one not feeding up for winter.

'You all set for your presentation?' Kate asked, pressing coleslaw into a shoe-sized jacket potato with the back of a plastic fork. Juliet tried not to look at the yellow pool of butter inside the container.

'Yeah, I think so.'

The job-swap presentation had been put back so many times the swap itself was now a vague memory, but everyone had vowed they would stick to this afternoon's meeting, even though it was just a couple of days before the office closed for Christmas. Juliet couldn't decide if it was a good or bad thing that no one would be paying a blind bit of notice to what she had to say. On the one hand, she had struggled with the document – she knew Dominic would forward a copy to Polly, which severely limited the kind of observations she could include. On the other, if it *was* going to be circulated at director level it was a fantastic opportunity for her to win new fans and get invited to speak at marketing villages or wherever else Phil Swain was making guest appearances these days. Besides, Dominic still hadn't announced who'd be covering Michelle's maternity leave and the latest word was he'd decided not to fork out temporary rates for a senior position after all.

Michelle had been sighted only a handful of days since her pregnancy was made public in the summer, but had returned for one week in order to leave, officially, today. This meant an expensive collection for her team (gifts for mother *and* baby, plus flowers, and everyone knew instantly if you'd skimped and gone to Sainsbury's rather than the floral art 'salon' across the road) and a boozy account-team lunch on the company. Juliet had stayed behind to look at her notes a final time.

'I wish I could just be beamed to a spa in the Caribbean, don't you?' she asked Kate, stretching her aching arms.

Kate nodded, and managed to say, 'Anywhere,' through a steamy mouthful of potato.

'A beach house in Tobago.'

'A beach hut in Brighton!'

'One of those houses on stilts in Koh Samui!'

This was new, this dreaming about travel, new this side of Luke, at any rate.

'I'm glad I'm going skiing in the New Year,' said Kate. 'I know it's only Mum and Dad, but I'm desperate to get away.'

Juliet thought about Guy's offer. Skiing seemed like something you might do in a dream, sliding soundlessly along on a smooth white path through the trees, down and down and down . . .

'D'you think you'll miss Phil when you're away?' she asked.

Kate coloured. 'Nah. It's still early days,' she said warily. 'No big deal.'

'You sound like me!' Juliet cried. It was too awful to think that her cynical ways might be rubbing off on Kate. 'I saw you two last night at the party, you're *really* into each other. It's great. I'm pleased for you.'

Kate avoided further comment by sawing violently at the last of her potato. 'You should call him, you know,' she said.

'Who?' Juliet asked.

Kate pulled a face.

'Guy? No.'

'Why not? I know you still like him.'

Juliet paused. When she tried to think about Guy it felt like English was no longer her first language, she got all twisted and couldn't find the words. 'I'm feeling too weird at the moment. I'd just ruin everything again.'

'You have seemed a bit off-colour recently,' Kate said. 'But you could still talk?'

'I just don't trust myself right now,' Juliet said. 'I don't even *like* myself.'

'Juliet! That's terrible.'

'I wish I could go to sleep and wake up a brand-new person, you know, like having an organ transplant or a complete blood transfusion or something.'

'Everything will be OK,' Kate said simply, but she looked worried.

'You are sweet,' Juliet said. 'I wish you were coming to this presentation. There'll be no one at all from Creative, it's crazy. Why's Larry off again, anyway?'

'He's looking at some more flats in case Sisters Avenue falls through,' Kate said. 'He wants to get it all sorted before Christmas.'

'Can you believe he's going *south of the river*?' Juliet said. 'It's like he's leaving London altogether.'

'Well, he hates Holloway,' Kate said. 'He used to live in Tooting, so it's more his territory if anything.'

'Oh, I didn't know.' Juliet was sometimes reminded of how new her friendship with Larry and Kate was.

'Didn't he run into your sister down in Battersea?' Kate asked.

'Yeah, he said. Bizarre to think of him moving into that Nappy Valley area. Have you ever been there? He's got nothing in common with that crowd.'

'At least he knows your sister.'

'Yes, I suppose so,' Juliet agreed.

'Has she got back with Michael yet?'

'Not that I know of.'

'It must be so awful for her,' Kate said. 'Imagine splitting up with your husband when you're pregnant. With your first child! I don't know what I'd do. I'm sure I'd have a breakdown or something.'

'I know.' Juliet made a mental note to call Hannah again that evening or tomorrow; or soon, anyway. It couldn't possibly be almost Christmas, a month since her sister had left Michael in Cape Town and the last time Juliet had seen her. Now Hannah was holed up with the sassy single mother she didn't ever seem to pick up the phone. Once or twice she'd responded to Juliet's messages, but each time when Juliet had been unable to talk properly herself. Larry was more up to date than she was, it seemed.

'Larry doesn't think much of Michael, does he?' Kate said.

'Who does?' said Juliet. 'He's a class-A shit. It astounds me that she didn't see that before. Look, I'd better go. Wish me luck.'

'Break a leg,' Kate said.

Everyone trickled into the meeting room, opinions lubricated with lunchtime drinking: Dominic, Michelle, Phil, the head of IT – Danny, whose surname Juliet could never remember – and a handful of account directors from other teams.

She drew a long, deep breath. 'Thank you all for coming. As you know, Dominic asked me to take part in a job swap with Smithfield's Supermarkets in October, and this presentation is my report of my time there. I swapped with Jessica Phillips, marketing executive . . .'

'I liked Jessica,' Dominic interrupted.

'She was excellent,' said Phil at once. He was wearing a pair of glittery devil's horns above a noticeably flushed face – it was odd to see him without the waxen lunarscape of his regular face. Juliet stared. Was it really possible that in the last sixteen months this was the only time she'd seen him drunk when she wasn't?

'Don't think I met Jessica,' Danny said, frowning.

'Did I?' Michelle asked.

'Yes, she came over for an induction when she first joined Smithfield's,' Phil said. 'She's the one with the half-and-half body, remember?'

'Half and half? What d'you mean?' Dominic asked. 'Sounds a bit sci-fi.'

'Just that her proportions are a bit odd,' Phil said. 'Her body is as long as her legs. An exact fifty-fifty.'

'What about the head?' Danny asked.

'Not counting the head.'

'What are the proportions supposed to be, then?'

'Well, not fifty-fifty.'

'Doesn't ring a bell,' said Michelle.

'Well, whatever, she fitted in really well, I thought. Maybe we should think about poaching her for good . . .' Dominic crumbled the pastry off a mince pie and regarded Juliet in the challenging new way she'd come to expect whenever she caught his eye. In the middle of the table were boxes of chocolates and cakes, and a pot of coffee that looked like it had been percolating since before they'd been born. One of the side-effects of Jo's promotion to Office Coordinator was the arrival of June, a receptionist even less willing to receive than Jo. Calamity June, they called her. She couldn't work the phone system, couldn't make coffee or order the right sandwiches. Unlike Jo, she had no internal ambitions, but wanted to be in a girl band, kept taking time off for auditions for those pop idol shows.

Juliet waited patiently. 'So, let's begin with a reminder of the team structure over at Smithfield's. They've got a thirty-strong marketing team, with three key contacts for Imagineer staff . . .'

'We know all this, Jules,' Dominic said rudely. 'Anyone want a bit of Chocolate Orange?'

'Ooh, can I have the core?' Michelle asked. 'It's my favourite bit.'

'They should package the cores as a spin-off,' Phil said. 'Like they did with Segsations. Everyone likes the cores best.'

'Only as a contrast to the segments,' Dominic said dismissively. 'You wouldn't want the core if that was all there was to choose from, would you? You wouldn't *know* it was a core. Whereas a segment can be enjoyed independently of the core.'

'Strictly speaking, I'm not sure an orange even has a core,' said Danny. 'I mean, it's not like it's a chocolate *apple*.'

'I'm not fussy, to be honest,' Michelle laughed. 'If it's chocolate, it's mine. We need the iron, don't we, mini-me!' She rubbed her enormous bump.

Juliet felt like throwing her notes down and stuffing a whole chocolate orange into each of their mouths before walking out the door and getting the next bus out of there. Instead, she tried again. 'Mark Kendall is our main client contact; he handles brand development and spends at least half his week on Imagineer projects . . .'

'Yes, we *know*,' Dominic said again. 'What we want you to tell us is how they view us on the *inside*? Do we have a good reputation? Are we inspiring them, giving them great ideas? Who else is pitching for our business? Have they budgeted for us beyond April?'

'I was coming to that. I think . . .' Juliet began.

'I can't believe they'd give that much away, frankly,' said Michelle, talking right over Juliet. 'They'd know there was a certain level of espionage going on. I mean, how much did *you* give away to this half-and-half woman, Phil? And did Juliet have access to the senior management anyway? No offence, Juliet, I'm sure they loved you.'

'I heard they called her the Invisible Woman,' Dominic said slyly. 'At one particular meeting . . .'

'Wouldn't surprise me, they're very suspicious of outsiders,' Michelle said. 'If I hadn't suggested they put together that induction presentation for agencies, no one would know the first thing about their team structure . . .' As Michelle rattled on, Juliet became fixated on the massive baby shape attached to her body. A big stretch of skin was visible above the elasticated waistband: it was disgusting, the texture and colour of a gigantic raw Butterball turkey. Was Hannah going to look like that? Maybe she already did.

She realised she hadn't heard a word Michelle had said and now, of course, they were all silent and looking to her for some sort of answer. She took a punt: 'It's true, the dynamics haven't changed much since you were more, er, active, Michelle . . .'

Phil Swain suddenly let out a splutter of laughter and Juliet looked gratefully across at him.

187

'Phil?' Dominic frowned.

'Sorry, I was just thinking about the Smithfield's Christmas pub quiz and the *dynamics* there.' He must be talking about Dominic's side-stage snog with the client's new graduate trainee, Juliet thought, amused. She was starting to like this new, flushed Phil.

'Pub quiz? Did we let them win again?' Michelle asked.

'Had to,' said Dominic, passing around more chocolate. 'Though obviously we could have whipped the fuckwits' arses if we'd wanted to.'

Juliet watched the line of munching cheeks with growing horror as the skin started to melt onto their shoulders like candle wax.

'Juliet!'

'What happened?'

'Did she hit her head?'

'Open the door, let some air in!'

'Go and get her friend, whatsisface?'

'Larry?'

'No, the girl, you know, the salad dodger in Creative.'

'Kate, d'you mean?'

'Hey, that's very rude. Kate's a lovely feminine size . . .'

'Shut up, Michelle, just go and get her. OK guys, I'll handle this, we'll touch base on the job swap programme in the New Year.'

'OK. Cool.'

'Oh,' said Juliet, finding herself on the floor, propped up against the wall. 'Did I pass out or something?'

'You must have had one too many at lunch,' Dominic said, but not unpleasantly, 'if Michelle and Phil are anything to go by. They're both rat-arsed. I thought pregnant women weren't supposed to drink?'

'No, I worked through lunch, didn't go to Michelle's do.'

She seemed to be on her own with Dominic. He had his arm around her shoulders, was squatted down next to her.

'You really gave us a shock.'

She noticed the smudge of chocolate in the corner of his mouth, could smell the warm orangey sweetness on his breath and focused instead on the arm of his designer glasses: Dolce e Gabbana. Dolce e Gabbana, Dolce e . . .

'Do you want some water?'

Juliet nodded. 'Sorry about the presentation. I'll mail you the PowerPoint file when I get back to my desk.'

'Fuck the presentation.'

'Oh.' He couldn't mean that. She was confused, felt a film of liquid cover her eyes and tried not to blink. Until the tear fell she wasn't technically crying.

Dominic passed her a beaker of water, cocking his head almost sideways in an effort to make eye contact. 'Look, Juliet, about what happened at the Grosvenor that night. I know you've been avoiding me. There's no hard feelings, you know.'

About what happened? What was that, exactly? Did he have something to do with her having passed out in the cloakroom? God, they'd had sex again, hadn't they? Was it possible to have sex and not even remember? Maybe. She was still pretty hazy on the Fulton and Rachel encounter, and she often couldn't remember how she'd got home at night beyond the shadowy slam of a mini-cab door or the changing hands of a ten-pound note.

'You know you can tell me if there's anything wrong,' Dominic was saying. 'We're mates, aren't we?'

She didn't answer.

'You haven't been yourself for a while now. Are you not well?'

'I'm fine, really, just a bit tired and hot.'

'I tried to find you last night at the party,' Dominic persisted. 'I wanted to clear the air before it gets really awkward.'

'Sorry, I left early.' She began to lose the battle against her tears.

'Don't cry,' Dominic said. 'It's OK, really. Look, why don't

189

you get a cab home – charge it to us. And take the last few days off. We'll see you in the New Year. Ah, here's Kate.'

'Juliet, are you all right? What happened?' Kate's eyes were bright with concern but all Juliet noticed was her breath: it smelled of boiled onion. She'd never been so aware of people's breath. 'Come and sit in this chair. Do you want some more water?'

Dominic got June to order a taxi for them and instructed Kate to collect their things and go with her. Then he insisted on helping her into the taxi and hesitated on the kerb for a moment before turning back inside. Juliet stared out of the taxi window at the Christmas shoppers. They were the well-heeled variety in this part of town. There was not a fur collar among them that had taken on, as Juliet's had after months of rainy nights, the look of an old teddy bear. They could have been a swarm of aliens for all she had in common with them. She looked at the sky: white, ominous. It seemed appropriate.

'Here's your Imagineer Christmas card,' Kate said as the taxi pulled off, lurching to a stop almost at once to queue for Regent Street. Now the shoppers were in armies, dashing through the gaps between cars as though someone had just announced it was going to be the last Christmas ever. 'I opened mine in the lift. The December payslip's inside, with our bonuses – an extra month's salary! Much better than last year. Thank God! I'd set myself a twenty-pound-per-person pressie budget, but now I can be a bit more generous.'

Juliet pulled open the envelope, relieved to see the standard slip and not a P45. Perhaps Dominic had been nice to her upstairs because he was, well, a nice guy who really did want to be mates.

'*Imagineer bonus*,' she read, following the line across: '*00.00*'. She imagined him standing at the top-floor window mouthing, 'YP, Juliet.' *Your Problem*, one of his favourites.

'Great, isn't it?' Kate asked, obviously euphoric about the double bonanza of an early finish and refreshed funds.

'Yeah,' Juliet said. 'Fancy a drink when we get to mine? I'm pretty sure there's some red wine somewhere.'

'Sure, are you well enough, though?'

'Oh, I'll survive. I'm not ill, just pregnant.'

Kate's gasp was lost in the sudden shower of hailstones, rapping like a thousand fingernails on the roof of the taxi as it headed north.

Chapter 16

Hannah should have smelled a rat when Lottie proposed for tea not the favoured organic café on Northcote Road but Claridges, a proper grown-up venue that required proper grown-up clothing. It was impossible not to be enchanted by the Christmassy atmosphere in the hotel, the galaxy of decorative silver, the extraordinary central chandelier, the hot festive kisses evaporating in the air. She was glad she'd added a spotted scarlet scarf to her standard extra-large black top and trousers and had bought new shoes on the way. Her trainers – her footwear from that last day in Stellenbosch and since worn almost every day – now sat wrapped in tissue in the bag at her side.

Then, as she was greeted by the maitre'd, she saw at Lottie's table the reason for the venue: the elegant, straight-backed figure of Michael's mother, Marianne. The nearest thing to Michael himself that Lottie would have dared attempt. She felt a thud of fright.

'Hannah, darling,' her mother-in-law cried. 'What a joy to see you and the bump. I'm so excited about the new arrival, and so is Arthur.'

'Lovely to see you too . . .' So this was how it was to be, a straightforward charm offensive. For a moment she'd forgotten that she was the injured party in all of this. And no one did a charm offensive better than Marianne, who was the only person Hannah had ever met who used 'darling' as an adjective. Allowing her coat to be eased off her shoulders she decided she wouldn't pressurise herself into being the initiator here, she would just play along and try to enjoy the tea. It was entirely possible that neither Marianne nor Lottie would even mention the split, if they were indelicate enough to use that term at all. On the phone, Lottie had called it a 'situation'. She supposed Marianne would opt for 'hiccup' or something similarly light and temporary.

'Let's get this coat to the cloakroom,' Lottie said, passing it to a nearby minion and helping Hannah get settled. 'Do you fancy a glass of champagne? We're having one.'

'I won't, thanks. I've been quite good about alcohol so far.' Hannah was genuinely pleased to see Lottie. She deserved better than the one meeting Hannah had conceded since moving in with Siobhan. The problem was she'd found it too hard not to view Lottie as a representative from Michael's camp; at best she could be no more than a mediator. But Hannah didn't think she was ready for mediation yet.

'Full afternoon tea, I think,' Marianne said, twinkling at the waiter. 'We've got an extra mouth to feed. Hannah, the pastries here are absolute nectar.' She waited for the waiter to retreat just out of earshot before adding, 'He's rather edible, too, isn't he?'

Even in such well-heeled surroundings Marianne shone, with her fine-boned face and classic style, the height and bearing of the Fifties deb – she'd told Hannah more than once that she'd yet to find a designer to tempt her from Chanel and would make no apology for her lack of daring until she did. She'd been much admired at the wedding in her bold burnt orange, a colour few half her age could have carried off, yet had never been so ill mannered as to eclipse the bride herself. Hannah had often fantasised about her daughters bypassing her own tendency to fleshiness – 'voluptuous' worked only when maintained at the most precise weight and condition – and inheriting instead Marianne's lovely spare elegance. It seemed to unfurl quite naturally, even in the most mundane acts, like pouring tea and patting cushions.

The others took just one sandwich each so Hannah chomped her way through the rest of the row: her hunger was ignited with a roar, this meeting was going to be worth it just for the food.

'Let's get you some more,' Marianne said. A twitch of one index finger was enough to have the waiter back by her side. 'Maybe more of those chicken ones?' Both she and Lottie were gazing at her as though she was the village runaway who'd been hiding out in the woods for five days.

'I was just saying to Lottie before you arrived, we'd be so happy to see you in Cheltenham at Christmas. And if you don't want to see Michael while he's being such a . . . well, *pickle* . . . then we can always work out a time when he's not around.'

A *pickle*? What was this, an audience with the Mitford sisters? But at least the situation was being acknowledged. Hannah wondered if she'd be accorded quite the same delicacy if she weren't housing that tiny male Fawcett in her body? How valuable he made her by his own preciousness. She might be replaced, but he couldn't be.

'Thank you, but I'm going up to see my parents in Norfolk. Juliet's alone this Christmas and we're going for longer than usual, probably a whole week.'

'How *is* Juliet? Doing well?' There was not a single false note to Marianne's tone, though Hannah had seen her observe Juliet with distaste in the past. She'd never been sure if it was the informal dress-sense or the chain-smoking that was to blame.

'She's fine.'

'Is she still the career girl?'

'Marianne! Everyone's a career girl now,' laughed Lottie. 'We run our own businesses, you know, have our own bank accounts. And did you know we even got the vote not so long ago! A little matter of Mrs Pankhurst and some street railings, or some such nonsense . . .'

Marianne's laughter was as sweet as the tinkle of silver spoon on china as she turned to take delivery of the new sandwiches before reaching across to touch Lottie's arm with her fingertip. She was like a conductor. 'Go ahead, Lottie,' she said. 'I know you love to tease us old girls. But there are still some traditionalists out there, you know, plenty of women only too pleased to prioritise the day-to-day care of a family. Not everyone has your ambition.'

Or her budget for staff, Hannah thought.

'Hannah, *you've* stopped working now, haven't you?'

She couldn't work out if she were being compared favourably or unfavourably with Lottie. In this particular silver-leafed time-warp with this particular mother-in-law, it was more likely to be the former. 'Yes,' she said, 'but only because the art school has closed. I haven't given up on a career altogether.'

They waited for her to go on but she found she had nothing to add, nothing she wanted to share with them, in any case. The truth was that she *had* given up on a career, and with some relish, but was now going to have to rethink. Single mothers, however well provided for, usually did some sort of paid work.

'And what can we buy for the baby?' Marianne asked. 'I don't believe in all this tempting fate business. The biggest things you need right from the off, don't you? Cribs and car seats and so forth.'

'I positively encouraged early gifts,' Lottie agreed. 'We should go and have a look in Daisy and Tom's next week, Hannah. They've got the cutest little ponchos in at the moment. Ophelia looks almost *Peruvian* in hers, even with her fair hair. Oh, I know, a baby shower! I'll throw it for you at my place. They are absolute goldmines! We had the whole nursery kitted out from ours.'

'I still haven't seen Ophelia, you know,' Marianne said. 'Are you and Rob in heaven?'

'Heaven, hell, one of the two . . .' As Lottie and Marianne giggled together Hannah longed to join in, to be back in the group, back among all that privilege and luxury and away from the vexations and frugalities that might lie with single motherhood. Then she thought of Siobhan and felt ashamed of herself.

'You are lucky, though, to have a girl,' Marianne was saying. 'Boys can be really monstrous. I remember we thought Michael was the devil incarnate when he was teething. Of course later we realised that that had been one of his more angelic phases!'

Was this the lead-in to the subject that they were really here to discuss, Hannah wondered, watching as the sandwiches were succeeded by scones and clotted cream and some sort of special jelly. Miniature cakes and fruit mousses were then presented for Marianne's regal inspection. She nibbled a sliver of doll's-size éclair before excusing herself for the ladies.

Lottie gave a conspicuous glance over her shoulder at the older woman's retreating figure, before saying, voice so low Hannah could hardly hear it, 'Michael's very down, Hannah. Rob says he's never seen such a case of Black Dog.'

'Does he.' Hannah deliberately missed off the question mark.

'Every time I've been round there he's been watching rugby or some sort of sci-fi rubbish on TV. I even caught him eating one of those disgusting supermarket pies.'

'Oh. What, like a pork pie?' That was what the Claridges tea needed, Hannah decided, something substantial that you could sink your teeth into, not these itsy-bitsy confections.

'No, more like a steak pasty type thing. It smelled revolting.' Lottie looked impatient at the digression and gave another, less obvious, look over her shoulder. 'He's so sorry, you know. He realises he's been the world's worst idiot.'

'That's one way of putting it,' Hannah said.

196

'So, how long do you think you'll be staying with whatsher-name?'

'Siobhan.'

'She's the one we met in the café that day, isn't she?'

'Yes, the one with the unglamorous hair.'

Lottie shrugged prettily. 'How did you get to know her?'

'We bumped into each other at the doctor's. She's great, really helping me out. And the baby is lovely. We should all get together,' Hannah added, eagerly. 'Nora and Ophelia are so close in age. What about a visit to Father Christmas?'

'They're too young, sweetie. We took Ophelia to Harrods and the guy just looked like Mike Yarwood. It was all horribly disturbing. Luckily Ophelia slept through the whole thing. So do you think you'll be there much longer? You know you're more than welcome to stay with us?'

'Thank you,' Hannah said, meaning it. 'But that wouldn't be fair on you. I'm fine where I am.'

'Have you started your NCT classes yet?' Lottie asked.

'No, not till February.'

'You'll meet nice people there.' The implication that Siobhan was not so nice resonated. Clearly, behind the scenes, she was being held at least partly responsible for the delay in Hannah's return to her rightful place by Michael's side.

'It's such a relief to meet similar couples in the same boat,' Lottie continued, topping up their tea. 'And in the same street as well. That's how we know John and Ali. We'd both lived on Bolingbroke for two years and only met at our NCT class. Amazing!'

Marianne returned. 'You will think about coming over at Christmas, or later, won't you? The pool is finished and the water's heated, of course. It's so relaxing.'

'I'll phone,' Hannah promised, smiling from one to the other. Lottie's saltiness and Marianne's sweetness were as well-balanced as the meal itself, yet they both wanted exactly the same thing:

the restoration of the status quo. And if, as she suspected, either had been commissioned personally by Michael to call this meeting, they'd be returning to him empty-handed. Her first peace offering, should she choose to offer anything at all, would be madc directly.

'Why don't I come and see you next week at your new place?' Lottie suggested. 'I want to drop off your Christmas present.'

'I'm not sure when Siobhan will be around.' *Or Larry*. 'Can I call you?'

'Well you will come to our drinks party on the twenty-ninth, won't you?'

'I'll phone,' Hannah said again. And they both seemed satisfied with that.

Chapter 17

Juliet waited for Hannah's car to pull up in front of the house. Sasha was working until Christmas Eve and the flat was empty: no bickering, no canoodling, no bathroom bottlenecks. As she did the last of the washing up, she half-hoped Hannah would be late, even though it meant they'd hit the evening traffic. The silence was a welcome tranquilliser; tidying up a bit made her mind feel more orderly, too, more in control of the situation.

When they'd spoken earlier in the week to make arrangements for the holiday neither she nor Hannah had made any reference to how sad or happy or surprised or unsurprised they were to find themselves, at their age, going to spend Christmas with their parents. They were both alone, both partnerless, and both pregnant, though only one foetus was the apple of its grandparents' eye this festive season, Juliet thought, and that was the way it would stay.

There was no mistake. She'd bought a twin pack of pregnancy tests and they were both positive (great psychological marketing, Larry had pointed out, that preying on the last vestiges of female hope; what percentage of women simply didn't believe their eyes the first time?). What's more, the medical websites she'd looked at explained that it was quite common to have a light period in the first months of pregnancy.

She wondered if it really were possible for her to get through this family Christmas without cracking. Hannah would be all ripe and glowing as she clucked over the inevitable early baby buys their mother would produce within seconds of them getting home. 'Home': Hannah still called it that, even though the cottage in Norfolk wasn't where they'd actually grown up and she was now well into her thirties and married. Or separated. It wasn't for long, though, Juliet was sure. She *knew* Hannah would be back with Michael, all forgiven and forgotten, before the baby was born. Then next Christmas Hannah would call her own house 'home', that pile in Battersea that Michael had just shelled out a fortune for. The arrival of children was the key; they legitimised a house, they made it a home.

For her part, she wasn't sure anywhere constituted home these days. Certainly the spare room at Sasha's felt the least like it in a long time; it was almost an anti-home, a jail made all the more miserable because her incarceration was voluntary. For years she'd lived with Luke in a succession of rented flats, sometimes a studio somewhere central, sometimes a bigger place further out, with the luxury of a roof terrace or communal garden. Then there'd been Hannah's place in Tufnell Park. Hers was the little room at the back of the flat with the wooden Venetian blind that always stuck on one side and shaded the room in a distracting diagonal – yes, that was probably the last time she'd been able to walk up her own street and not feel her heart sink if she saw that the lights were already on.

She dialled Hannah's mobile and for once her sister answered.

'Hi, how are you?'

'Fine. I rang you at work yesterday,' Hannah said, 'but they said you were off sick. What's up?'

'Just a bit partied out,' Juliet said. 'I'm OK.'

'Oh, good, I was worried.'

'Still up for later? I can drive if you're feeling too big?'

'No, it's fine,' Hannah said cheerily. 'I'm used to doing everything while getting booted in the bladder.'

There was a woman's laugh in the background, the 'amazing' Siobhan, presumably.

'Actually, it was a bit weird driving this morning,' Hannah said. 'It's been so long! Maybe because I've changed shape, I felt like I'd just passed my test.'

'How did you manage to get your car back without seeing Michael?'

'I asked him to leave the keys with the cleaner.'

'How's the new house looking?' Juliet asked.

'I didn't go in,' Hannah said. 'I don't think of it as mine.'

Juliet was impressed by this. Perhaps she'd underestimated her sister's stomach for independence after all. 'Larry said he's seen you a couple of times,' she said. This was a concession, not that Hannah would necessarily see it as such, but Juliet had not been overjoyed to hear that her best friend seemed constantly to be running into her sister and having spur-of-the-moment coffees all over the place.

'Yes, now he's defecting south,' Hannah laughed. 'He's a great guy, you're lucky to have such a good friend. Fab news that his flat's gone through, isn't it?'

'Is it?' Juliet felt her tone go stony. Hearing Hannah's news from Larry was one thing, but hearing Larry's from Hannah was quite another.

'On the flat in Sisters Avenue? My old road.'

'Oh, really?'

'It's quite a bargain, I think. Needs new floors and a kitchen, though. I'm sure he'll tell you the news himself . . .' She trailed off and a pause grew between them. Juliet felt very tired; all that cleaning must have been more strenuous than she'd thought. She sat down, wanting to hang up, but Hannah hadn't finished. 'You know, Larry really reminds me of . . . no, it doesn't matter.'

'Who?'

'No one.'

'Were you going to say Luke?' Juliet asked, her voice almost a whisper.

'Yes, sorry. It's just in a way, you know. Oh, it's not important.'

'What makes you think that?' Juliet persisted.

'Nothing, really,' Hannah said.

'I suppose they are sort of similar.' Juliet made a huge effort to sound normal as she tried to field the little hits of pain, like pebbles lobbed at her belly. She couldn't discuss him like this, in passing, as though he'd been consigned to a casual cross-reference. But Hannah was right: Larry and Luke *were* alike. Perhaps that was what had attracted her to Larry in the first place. She remembered being led around the pit by Michelle for team introductions and seeing him stretched back in his chair, one foot up on the edge of the desk. He was watching her, intrigued. OK, so Larry was lazy where Luke had been ambitious, but both had that manner of seeming so cynical while in truth caring properly about things. Then again, she thought, Luke hadn't cared properly in the end, not about her, anyway, not as properly as she'd believed.

'Did they ever meet?' Hannah sounded slightly breathless now and Juliet could hear Siobhan's voice in the background again. 'Coming!' Hannah shouted. 'Sorry, Juliet, lunch is ready. God, I'm hungry!'

'No, they didn't meet. I started at Imagineer afterwards, remember? Look, I've got to go as well. Shall I still see you here at four thirty?'

'Around then,' Hannah agreed. 'Maybe earlier if the traffic's not too bad.'

'OK, bye.'

Putting the phone down, Juliet found that her heart was pulsing so violently it was actually hurting her. Now she didn't enjoy the solitude at all, but envied Hannah her cosy little mothers'

202

club where lunch sat waiting on the table. Husband or no husband, Hannah always landed on her feet. *Where did it all go wrong for you, Juliet?* That was what Dominic had asked her. Her stomach groaned. She was hungry, too, but didn't bother looking in her own fridge; she knew there was nothing in it.

Chapter 18

The background sounds should have been comforting: Juliet and Laura giggling over an old set of Connect 4 that kept releasing all the counters at the wrong moment; their father lobbying for a partner to do the end-of-year quiz in the paper; their mother unloading the dishwasher in the kitchen over the murmur of a Christmas play on Radio 4. It was a lovely, familiar choreography of Boxing Day stereotypes. But Hannah, on the sofa in front of the TV, was distressed. Moments ago all had been well: the leopard minding the cub crèche was having a fine time watching the little ones roll around and bat their paws at one another. But now it seemed the second mother was lost and couldn't find her way back to the crèche. She paced on anxiously through the long grass but was heading in the wrong direction altogether. There were seven cubs in the single mother's charge but she had just four teats. Seven into four didn't go, whichever way you looked at it. For Hannah, that meant looking away: she couldn't bear it.

Her eye settled on Juliet and Laura, laughing together under the window like infants waiting for Santa's sleigh to come into view. She'd never noticed it before but at twenty Laura was shaping up into a rather beautiful adult, with a good dash of Juliet's leanness and natural grace. The two even shared a personal style, both dishevelled-looking dark-blondes with a fashion sense that was sort of sexy and distracted. Yes, that was exactly it, they looked as though they'd been distracted by sex from the business of getting dressed.

'Laura, don't scoff all the chocs,' Juliet shouted out. 'They were *my* pressie!'

'Sorry. I need to store energy for the Arctic trip.'

'You've had six in two minutes! Where're you storing them, in your cheeks?'

'You've had just as many, you fat pig! They're horrible anyway, they taste like Plasticine.'

'Child!'

'Old biddy! You're almost thirty!'

More giggles. It seemed to Hannah that a shift had taken place during this visit. For the first time she could remember Juliet had allied herself more closely with Laura, whose student preoccupations apparently presented no impediment to sororial bonding. Although Hannah and Juliet had driven up together in reasonable accord, the mysterious new fault-line had reappeared almost as soon as they'd arrived. Hannah supposed that it was this that had caused the other two plates to rub so closely together.

Over the past few days she had tried hard to join in her sisters' discussions about music, rent, debts, drinking, smoking and – more covertly – drugs, but time and again she felt separated from them. Her growing pregnancy and new marital status, on hold though it was and a subject conspicuously untouched by all so far, were twin wedges between them: the other two simply had no experiences in common with her.

'Are you all right, darling?' her mother asked, bringing mugs of tea, unbidden.

Hannah looked up at the older set of her own features, where common sense had come to outlaw fierce emotion. Juliet wasn't the only member of the family she'd neglected recently, but the difference was her mother didn't resent it. 'Yes,' she said, 'this programme is so unbelievably sad. Must be the hormones.'

'Do you want some shortbread? I've got that nice all-butter kind in the tin.'

'Oh, yes please.'

Gayle came back with a plateful and settled down next to her eldest daughter, who now sat up, right foot tucked under her left thigh in the position she'd discovered to be the most comfortable that week. She nibbled her shortbread, buttery and sweet as promised. The Chat had to happen sooner or later; she supposed it was only right that it should be just as she was actually contemplating her aloneness.

'It's a weird time, isn't it, being pregnant?' Gayle began.

'Everything seems so much more intense,' Hannah agreed. 'It's not paranoia, I don't think, though it feels like it sometimes. I just feel all *sentimental* about everything.'

'I know. It's right to feel like that. You must be thinking about the new house, as well.'

Yes, this was definitely it.

'It's lovely to be here, of course, Mum, but it was supposed to be our first Christmas as a married couple . . .' She didn't tell her mother that her fantasies of the first Fawcett Christmas were so torturously vivid they would probably, in time, be filed away as having been real. A garland for the front door with red roses and berries; poinsettias in heavy stone pots; tea lights in silver holders on every surface; presents wrapped in ivy-green paper with glossy scarlet ribbon; mulled wine permanently a-simmer for visiting friends and neighbours . . .

Her mother struck softly but swiftly: 'Are you really sure you want to end your marriage over this?'

'What, over this humiliating infidelity? As good a reason as any, I suppose.' Hannah began on a second piece of shortbread.

'God knows what Michael did was wrong, but I'm sure he deeply regrets it. You know what it's like at these work things, when there's a lot of drinking . . .'

'Mum, *I was there*. He hadn't been drinking. It wasn't like he

206

was on a work trip and I was ten thousand miles away out of sight and out of mind. He thought I was touring historic houses down the road!' She could feel her blood pressure escalate. 'I can't believe you're taking his side!'

'I'm not.'

'Well, you're certainly giving a good impression of it.'

Gayle looked at her mildly. 'All I'm saying is that what seems so unforgivable now may seem less so with time. Perhaps you're focusing too much on the drama of the circumstances?'

'But the circumstances are important, Mum,' Hannah argued. 'Being tempted is one thing, but calculated deception is another. Am I the only one who seems to see that?' She'd raised her voice and saw Juliet and Laura glance over then back at each other, widening their eyes at exactly the same instant, as if to agree, 'Let's keep well out of this one.' She breathed deeply. 'You know, this whole thing is *his* moral dilemma, not mine, don't you think?'

'Of course it is. You know I'm with you one hundred per cent, darling, but is there any harm in him driving up for the party on Monday? Or a bit earlier so you can have a proper talk? Lunchtime, say? It must be over a month since you've seen him.'

'You've already asked him, haven't you?' Hannah sighed. Now the leopard cubs were under attack from a male lion. Could the situation get any worse?

'Not exactly,' Gayle said, 'but I did say I'd ask you to call. He's absolutely distraught, you know.'

'So I hear.'

'Sitting in that big house on his own.'

Hannah looked up sharply. 'Yes, how tedious that he was expected to keep his wedding vows for longer than five months and is now forced to live in luxury accommodation all on his lonesome. My heart bleeds.'

'Oh, Hannah, think of the baby!'

This time only Juliet looked up. She stared at the sofa cushion between Hannah and their mother, then back to her game again.

'Come on,' Hannah protested. 'Two happy parents apart are better than two unhappy ones together.'

'What about two unhappy ones apart?' Gayle asked delicately.

The lion wasn't hungry enough to bother with the chase and he soon loped off. The cubs jumped up at their mother in relief. Hannah hit the 'Off' button on the remote control. 'Oh, OK, I'll phone him.'

'Thank you,' Gayle said.

When she and Michael spoke, an hour later, she could feel her natural affection for him rising and had to work hard at keeping her tone impersonal. She tried to model her voice on that of a waitron explaining how the fish of the day had been cooked. Anyone listening in would have been astonished to learn it was her husband she was talking to, her husband of just six months. But it was the fact that the phone call was taking place at all that was the message, and they all knew it.

Laura's new boyfriend Jay arrived that evening. To Hannah he looked about twelve, as though he'd just that week started shaving and still wore shirts ironed by his mother. She tried to calculate if *she* was old enough to be his mother. Only if she'd had him at thirteen or fourteen, but it was feasible enough. She felt a hundred years old.

After a while she saw that he had a quality about him that was very engaging. He was intense without being unsettling, polite without being sycophantic. He was also very good-looking, his dark hair trendily cropped, body long and lean, the usual choice of the Goodwin girl. Yes, she could see the attraction, and attracted Laura undoubtedly was for there was no escaping the steady crossfire of smouldering glances and sidelong smirks. Oh, for such uncomplicated relations between the sexes!

Drinks were circulated and guzzled at the speed of light and, after a couple of family-only days indoors, the atmosphere was noticeably improved with the buzz of new blood.

'Are you going on this Arctic expedition, Jay?' Juliet asked him.

'No, you must be joking, I couldn't hack that long in the cold. But it's great Laura's so into it.'

'It's a fantastic opportunity,' Laura said. 'I mean, my gap year was a laugh, but when will I ever do something as mad as this again?'

'You're just like Juliet,' their father, Christopher, said. 'A born traveller.'

Not like me, Hannah thought, the cautious one.

'Whereas Hannah has always liked her creature comforts,' Gayle said, bang on cue. 'I remember when we took you to Crete and you were so disappointed the hotel didn't have towelling robes, wasn't she, Chris? To think of that at the age of seven!'

'I wasn't that young,' Hannah protested. 'And it was cold.'

'We *all* like luxury hotels,' Juliet said, sounding friendly enough, but Hannah's guard went up at once. 'It's just that not all of us have the cash to afford them. Maybe Laura and I are *forced* to be adventurers.'

'Please don't mention the word cash when there's a student in the room,' their father said. 'It always leads to some sort of begging, borrowing or stealing.'

'I'm not that bad!' Laura giggled. 'But you won't believe how expensive rent is in York. Isn't it, Jay? You'd expect it to be so cheap up there, but we might as well be in London.'

'Don't exaggerate,' Christopher said. 'Top-up, anyone?'

'Well, don't talk to me about rent,' Juliet said. 'I'll take the handout, Dad, if there's one going?'

'What on earth do you do with all your money?' Gayle asked Juliet. Hannah listened, interested. She thought it very inappropriate of her sisters to angle for money when they knew their parents had spent much of the year struggling. But before Juliet could answer, Hannah was distracted by Jay asking when the baby was due.

'End of March,' she said. It still seemed a decade away.

'Have you been buying all the gear?'

'He's only interested in breast pumps, really,' Laura teased. 'This is his way of getting around to the subject.'

'Not true,' Jay said, obviously struggling to keep a straight face. 'I actually think they're a bit grotesque, if you must know.'

'So have you got a breast pump?' Laura asked Hannah. 'Have you practised yet?'

'Laura!' Gayle warned. 'Leave Hannah alone.'

'But it's so animal, so cowlike.'

'Bovine is the word,' Christopher corrected. 'Now make yourself useful, Laura, and pass these snacks around. What are they, by the way, cheese straws?'

Gayle confirmed this to be so and Laura made a big show of standing in front of each person in turn with the plate, refusing to budge until they took at least one and finally stuffing the remaining handful into her own mouth. 'There!'

Hannah, who was starting to feel like a freak show, tried to make herself heard over the titters. 'I haven't bought any equipment yet for anything,' she told Jay. 'Things are a bit uncertain. I'm not even sure where I'll be living.'

'Oh, you'll be OK,' broke in Juliet. It was definitely back again, that offhand attitude towards her she'd noticed that night at Sisters Avenue. It wasn't quite contempt, more mild sufferance, so mild she was probably the only one who sensed it.

'Really?' Hannah said, injured but trying not to show it. 'What d'you mean, Juliet?'

'Just that I'd say your life is pretty set,' Juliet said pleasantly.

'Yeah, me too,' Laura grumbled, rather less pleasantly and still with chewed-up cheese straws in her mouth.

'Oh you would, would you?' Hannah looked from one to the other. *Set*? What a joke. Had they forgotten she was camped out in the living room of someone she'd met in a café? That she hadn't received any post since the middle of November, was technically of no fixed abode? How was that 'set', exactly?

'Girls!' Gayle cried. 'What on earth's wrong with you? Don't upset Hannah, Juliet!'

So their mother had noticed, after all. This was like being nine years old again, only this time Juliet's crime wasn't a puerile pinch of the leg or a careless dog-earing of Hannah's favourite book. And this time Juliet didn't say sorry.

'Anyway, I'm not sure it's ever possible to say things are set,' Gayle said, with the all-encompassing smile of the experienced mediator. 'Not any more. We've certainly found that out this last year.'

Jay nodded. 'Our generation doesn't expect *anything* to be set,' he said. 'It's the one thing we don't expect.'

'We'll probably never have a job longer than a three-month contract,' Laura added. 'We'll have to do whatever's offered, work far from home, anything!'

'How tragic! We'll think of you when you're out on the rigs,' Christopher chuckled.

Hannah looked gratefully at her father. His brand of amused exasperation had never been more welcome as far as she was concerned. Now she came to think of it, he hardly ever spoke in these group situations in any other tone. She couldn't be sure if he was genuinely entertained or had simply realised that this was the only way to deal with more than one Goodwin female at once. Perhaps he'd learned something from the endless cycles of *Pride* and *Prejudice* the girls insisted on watching a few years ago when they were last at home together.

Goodwill duly restored, Jay turned back to Hannah. 'What do you do? Do you work? When does your maternity leave start?' He had the instinct of a puppy, singling out the person with the least energy to play. Or perhaps it was simpler than that, perhaps she just looked as in need of rescuing as she felt.

She made an effort to smile. 'I used to do conference organising, then I worked in an art school, but it closed down at the end of term. The owner was quite a well-known painter. So I suppose, yes, I'm on maternity leave now.'

'Hannah doesn't have to work,' Laura told Jay. 'Her husband's totally cashed up.'

'Cash again,' Christopher said, and Hannah watched him exchange looks with Gayle before shooting Laura a warning frown. She felt miserable. There was no satisfaction in having stirred her parents' instincts to protect her against her younger sisters.

'Oh, you're the one who got married last summer,' Jay said, ploughing gamely on. 'I remember Laura talking about it.'

'Jay and I were friends before we got together,' Laura explained. 'Well, we knew the same people, anyway. I thought he was one of those sad musos who couldn't actually play an instrument.'

'I thought she was straight out of the pony club,' Jay returned.

'I've never been on a horse in my life!' Laura protested.

Raising an eyebrow at her, Jay looked as though he was about to respond to this in less than innocent terms, but obviously thought better of it and kept his mouth shut. But the mood had lightened again. Hannah looked at the two students with envy. She wondered if they expected to be together forever, as she had when with her college boyfriend Matt. He was a psychology undergraduate with dreams of relocating to Japan to hang out with an island tribe of drummers or some such nonsense. He was constantly ringing the Japanese Embassy for advice, eventually using a false name so they wouldn't blacklist him as some kind of fanatic. She'd admired his passion.

As her father refilled their glasses she noticed Juliet watching Laura and Jay too, and there was no resentment in her face now, just pure pain. She chastised herself for forgetting Juliet's situation. Her sister was still, essentially, the grieving widow, and situations like family Christmases must surely be the worst to deal with. Two years ago it had been Luke who sat in Jay's armchair, the Goodwin girls' guest of honour, enjoying the steady stream of drinks and homemade snacks. Juliet had met him at college, too, she must have been close to Laura's age. They'd been together – how long? – seven years, it would have been almost nine by now. If he hadn't died, they'd probably be married, might have been expecting their first baby, too, just as the sisters had dreamed of when they were little girls following their mother around with their dolls in toy prams. Hannah's favourite doll, dressed in pale yellow, had been called Gayle. Juliet's, dressed in pink, had been called Hannah.

'Have you thought of any names yet?' Jay asked her. 'I like Quentin for a boy.'

'Quentin?'

'You know, after Tarantino?'

'Quentin's a rubbish name,' Laura sniggered. 'You wouldn't go for that, would you, Han?'

Hannah didn't have the heart to tell them that she hadn't even decided on the baby's surname yet.

Chapter 19

By the next morning, the neighbours' dog, a suspicious and highly strung Border collie, had been taken in by the Goodwins for a week while its owners went skiing. Gayle wasted no time in recruiting Hannah and Juliet for dog-walking duty on the grounds that Laura and Jay, being students, couldn't realistically be expected to present themselves during daylight hours. Every so often yelps of Laura's laughter escaped from her bedroom, tickling every corner of the house and accentuating the wordless chill that had settled between Hannah and Juliet as they drank coffee in front of the television.

'Come on, girls. You both need some air. You don't have to take him far, just around the green a few times . . .'

Hannah assented with her usual respect for her mother's nose for family politics. They both needed to *clear* the air, that's what she really meant. If she didn't know better she'd think Gayle had borrowed the dog specifically to engineer this sororial outing.

For the first time in almost three weeks it was a stunning winter's day. The duck-egg-blue sky was an immense screen lit up above the low, thin band of the horizon. Passers-by appeared to Hannah like actors on a sound stage, while Juliet, in her striped woollen hat and blood-red lipstick, was undoubtedly the headlining star. She found herself sneaking glimpses at her sister as she might a celebrity she'd spotted at the next table in a restaurant. But it soon emerged that this was to be a silent movie. Stalking up their lane with a sullen set about her mouth, Juliet looked as though she was prepared to endure the whole walk without speaking.

No sooner had they crossed the village green than the dog decided to dash off along its own route. Hannah eventually discovered it crouching by a little girl on her scooter like some sort of starving prairie dog and not a spoiled pet who'd been left fillet steak by its owners. It might even have been funny if the child hadn't started sobbing with real fear. It took several minutes to comfort her, locate the parent, and wrestle the dog back on to the lead, and then another couple to track down Juliet. She was sitting on the steps of the village pub, smoking and squinting into space.

'All sorted,' Hannah said. 'Ready?'

Juliet just blew out smoke and got to her feet in reluctant slow-motion. Hannah could bear it no longer. 'Why aren't you speaking?' she cried.

'I've got nothing to say,' Juliet replied. 'I'm tired, all right?' She walked off.

Hannah dragged the dog after her. 'I'm tired, as well, but I'm still able to make an attempt at conversation!'

Juliet said nothing.

'And what was all that about last night?'

'What?'

'You know, in front of Jay. All those snide remarks about my life being set and all that. Surely you can't believe all that? You know what's been going on with Michael. I could be bringing up a child on my own in a few months' time!'

'You'll hardly be struggling for the rent, though, will you?'

Hannah had had enough of apologising for her husband's wealth. God knew it was nothing special, not in Nappy Valley. 'No,' she said, 'but nor is it my fault if you *are* at the moment.

You've made your own financial decisions, Juliet, they're nothing to do with me.' Juliet stopped short and Hannah caught her breath. She'd hurled the grenade now, it was madness not to turn and run. She let the dog off the lead again as if to give one of them a shot at escape.

'I don't give a shit about money,' Juliet said, eyes burning.

'Good, because it's really not the only factor, never is.'

'Easy for you to say . . .' This was almost lost to the wind as Juliet suddenly started moving again, picking up the pace almost to a dash.

'Juliet,' Hannah called after her. 'Hold on! You know I can't walk that quickly! Tell me what's wrong.'

'Oh, just forget it,' Juliet sneered. 'You obviously have no idea what's going on in my life . . .'

'Then tell me!' Hannah cried, breathless and distressed now. 'Why are you being so horrible? What's changed? You were fine on the drive up . . .'

'I've never been *fine*,' Juliet said coldly. 'Oh, don't cry, for God's sake . . .'

'I can't help it,' Hannah sniffed, fighting hard to stem the flow. 'It happens when you're pregnant.'

'Of course, *I* wouldn't understand, then,' Juliet said. Again, she strode off.

Hannah got caught up in the dog's lead she'd been trailing and almost stumbled. 'Is this still about the flat?' she called, catching up. 'You *know* I had to sell it. I *had* to contribute to the wedding. Mum and Dad couldn't, not with their own problems and Laura being at college.'

'Oh, don't blame them,' Juliet said, flaring. 'You hardly needed a dowry! This is the twenty-first century! Michael could have paid for the wedding, you told me he wanted to. You could have kept the flat, I could have covered the mortgage and then you could have sold it later. Or I could have bought you out.'

Hannah was amazed by this outburst. 'But the only reason

216

you were living with me in the first place was to save money for the South America trip, and then when Luke died it made sense for you to come back.' At this, Juliet looked more thunderous than ever, so she hurried on: 'I wanted you to, of course, you know that. But I had no idea you saw it as anything long term. I mean, once you got into the swing of work you were going out so much more . . .'

Juliet glared at her. 'That didn't mean I didn't need you!'

Hannah didn't know what to say. She stood, waiting.

'God, I don't know why I was even surprised when you sold the flat from under me. You couldn't wait to move in with Michael and get away from me.'

It was the shrillness in her tone as much as the desperate eyes that told Hannah her sister had finally spat it out. 'It wasn't a case of choosing Michael over you,' she said gently. 'He was my fiancé and you are my sister. There was room for both. I just thought that as you seemed to be getting happier it was time for me to get on with my life as well. We hadn't even set a date for . . .'

Juliet interrupted: 'How could I *possibly* have been happier? God, you have *no* idea what that kind of unhappiness feels like.'

Hannah said nothing. In a competition of victimhood Juliet was always going to win hands down. 'Can I help you now?' she asked simply. 'What can I do? Do you need some money?'

'I don't want your charity,' Juliet said. 'Or anyone else's. I know it's up to me to sort my own stuff out. I'll get my own place in the New Year.'

'Maybe you and Guy could get somewhere together?'

Juliet turned. 'What *are* you on about? For starters we've split up, if you can remember anything that happens outside your own precious little world.' She was practically snarling again. 'And even if we were still together I wouldn't want to live with him. I don't want to live with *any* boyfriend.'

'Why not? Because of Luke?'

'No,' Juliet said, closing her eyes for a long second. It was a relief for Hannah to escape their glare. Juliet was breathing hard, obviously trying to calm herself down.

'Talk to me,' Hannah pleaded, stepping towards her.

Juliet looked up. 'I just know something will go wrong again, so it's better if I'm on my own, keep things uncomplicated.' This last comment reminded Hannah of Siobhan. But Siobhan was among the most contented people she'd met in her life, whereas anguish radiated from every pore of Juliet's body.

'What happened to Luke was an accident, Juliet. Those sorts of tragedies don't happen twice.'

'No, next time would be another kind. And it's not only him dying, anyway, you know that. It's . . . oh, everything!'

Her anger was completely gone now and between the cosy wrapping of hat and scarf her face was denuded, exposed. The skin was more lined than Hannah had noticed before; Juliet had aged noticeably in the last eighteen months.

She waited, watching.

'I know you think I'm mad,' Juliet went on, 'but I just don't trust, y'know, *life*.'

'Oh, Juliet!' Hannah moved towards her and hugged her tightly. At first, Juliet's body offered neither response nor resistance, then, slowly, it relaxed against hers. 'Nor do I trust it particularly,' Hannah laughed grimly. 'But I've still got to live it and so do you.'

They broke apart, lapsed into silence again, and Hannah busied herself fussing over the dog, who'd reappeared with a piece of old bark, pestering her to take it, then growling as she tried. I can't win, she thought, I can't win with any of these creatures. They want to fight me because I'm the easiest to beat.

'I know you're not happy at Sasha's,' she said, trying again. 'I wish you could come and stay with me. But obviously I'm at Siobhan's at the moment, I'm on the sofa as it is. But it won't be forever.'

218

'You're going back to Michael, aren't you?' Juliet said.

'I don't know.'

'Have you forgiven him?'

'I'd *like* to forgive him – and God knows everyone seems to think I should.'

'I don't,' Juliet said, voice flat. 'But maybe I take a bit of a hard line on such things.'

They looked at each other. 'I have to admit it would be a lot more convenient if I *could* forgive him,' Hannah said. All my plans are, *were*, with him: the baby, the house, even New Year.'

'New Year?'

'Yes, we were supposed to be going with Rob and Lottie to their place near Edinburgh. Michael still is, I expect.'

'I'm going to a party with Larry and Fulton,' Juliet said. 'You could come with us?'

'Maybe,' Hannah said, looking away.

'What's going on with you and Larry anyway?' Juliet asked. 'He's being very secretive about it. Are you two sleeping together?'

'Juliet!' Hannah was shocked, ridiculously so, and felt her heart batter at her ribcage. 'No!'

Juliet stared. 'He likes you, you know. I can tell.'

'I like him,' Hannah said. She prayed Juliet wouldn't press this. She felt utterly shattered. 'So tell me about this party, then?'

'It's at this artist's place, Joby. Larry knows him from college, he's really nice. It won't be too crazy or loud or anything. Anyway, it's not like you're an invalid, is it?'

'No.'

'Go on, it'll be like old times . . .'

This was the strongest appeal Juliet had made in such a long time that Hannah felt herself capitulating, and with real delight. How wonderful if they could recover their closeness; she'd be so much stronger about dealing with Michael, could help get Juliet back on track as well. 'OK, that would be great.'

219

'Let's head back,' Juliet said, looking across the fields to scan the distance they'd walked from the village. 'You must be tired.'

'What about the mad hound?' The dog was nowhere to be seen again.

'Oh, he'll find us eventually.'

On the way back they walked a little more closely together.

Chapter 20

The first hour of Michael's visit was taken up with a discussion, apparently turn-by-turn, of the route he'd taken from Battersea to the Norfolk coast. Juliet watched half-disgusted, half-admiring, as her parents behaved as though this were a perfectly routine Sunday lunch with their son-in-law.

'And how is the house, Michael? All the paperwork out of the way?'

'Oh yes,' said Michael, clearly relieved by the easy ride. 'It's great. I still miss the loft, though. I'd been there a few years. But this is more of a family home.'

'Nappy Valley, they call it, don't they?' Christopher asked, to sniggers from Laura and Jay.

'How funny,' Jay said. 'Where they make milk not wine.'

'I told you he was obsessed with breast-feeding!' Laura exclaimed.

'We went there for lunch in the summer, do you remember, Christopher?' Michael said. 'That restaurant on Northcote Road with the disappointing merlot?' Not like the gorgeous velvety Barolo he'd bought for them to have with lunch; even Juliet could tell it was exceptional and she still followed the strict £5-and-under rule instituted by Luke years ago – unless Imagineer was paying, of course. Yes, the wine was just one part of a shameless charm offensive that she suspected Michael normally reserved for clients and prospective bedmates. He was concentrating heavily on Christopher; presumably he thought Gayle was already in the bag since she was the one who'd engineered this cosy little lunch in the first place.

'I remember a noisy little Spanish place. Napa Valley it wasn't,' Christopher agreed.

'Nappy Valley doesn't sound much fun to me,' Laura said. 'Does *everyone* who lives there have kids?'

Michael turned to crinkle his eyes at her. 'Pretty much. It happens to the best of us, eventually. But the schools and nurseries are excellent in that area. Plus you have the two commons, of course. Fantastic for young children.'

Lay it on thick, why don't you, Juliet thought. He was behaving as though he were pitching for Hannah's hand all over again. How could her sister ever have fallen for this silver-tongued charmer? He was a classic Bachelor Skirt-chaser turned Serial Philanderer; you only had to look at him flashing that matinee-idol smirk all over the place to see he wasn't going to be faithful to anyone for more than five minutes.

For Juliet this whole occasion had an air of theatricality about it that she didn't think she could stand for long. After the confrontations of yesterday she'd been looking forward to spending some time with Hannah on their own, only to find Michael was already on the road with hopes of the same. Hannah had spent most of the morning in the bath and the rest on the sofa, so withdrawn she seemed almost to be meditating. Gayle had then recruited Juliet to help with cooking lunch, which meant the double dissatisfaction of knowing she was being deliberately distracted from bothering her sister and the ache in her arms from all that peeling and whisking was for the benefit of *Michael*'s stomach.

Hannah was still looking as glazed as the baked ham sitting in the middle of the table. 'She's absolutely exhausted,' Juliet had heard her mother say to Michael earlier. 'She needs a holiday.' She needs a husband who doesn't sleep with his twenty-four-year-old colleagues, Juliet had wanted to say. She looked around the table. It felt as though they had all gathered at Hannah's expensive nursing home and were going through the motions of a regular holiday meal with their recently lobotomised golden girl. No sooner had the thought occurred than she felt a rush of remorse. Perhaps Michael wasn't the only one to have had something to do with Hannah's subdued showing today. That row yesterday – she'd made her cry! Hannah, who was six months pregnant and whose only crime was to have thought it might be nice to live with the man she was about to marry. How could she have held a grudge over something so rightful, so perfectly *in order*? How had she allowed herself to become so unthinking?

'I have to say, I don't think *we'll* move house again,' Gayle was saying to Michael as she spooned the last of the dauphinoise potatoes onto his plate. 'Honestly, all that bidding and pulling out and gazumping and gazundering, or whatever they call it now. You just sit around for months waiting for chains to work, then they always unravel around your ears. No, we're here for the duration, aren't we, Chris?'

'Oh, yes, the duration, I should think.'

'Mum!' Laura cried. 'Don't say things like that!'

'I thought "duration" was quite a nice little euphemism.'

'Anyway, don't you get all sentimental, Laura,' their father said, raising an eyebrow. 'If any of us has their "duration" numbered, it's you, what with all your Arctic shenanigans. *We* could outlive *you*, you know. Or do you still suppose it will be like one of your ski-resort ice bars?'

'I heard about your trip,' Michael said to Laura. 'I'm impressed. Are you still looking for sponsors? When are you off?'

Buying them off one by one, Juliet thought. There was no

mention of the knicker rationing now. She'd never seen him so, so *straight*. She watched Laura extract his details, all smiles at this unexpected – and presumably substantial – donation and tried to catch her younger sister's eye. Did none of these people remember what Michael had done to Hannah in Cape Town?

'That's very generous of you, Michael,' Gayle purred. 'You know, people have been incredibly tight-fisted about this trip, even though it's entirely educational. It's because it's Christmas, I suppose.'

'Yes,' Christopher said. 'The season of overspending on things you don't want or need and cutting down on genuine charity.'

'I gave a cigarette to a homeless person the other day,' Juliet said, grinning at her father. 'And a lighter.'

'Marvellous, my dear. I'll look out for you on the New Year's Honours list.'

'Dad! It's all relative.'

Gayle sighed. 'Christmas does cost a fortune these days. You wouldn't believe what my shopping bill was for this party tonight, and it's just a few nuts and things.'

'That's no way to speak of your guests,' Michael chuckled. Even Juliet giggled at this. 'So how many people are coming this evening?' he asked, encouraged.

'Not too many,' Gayle said. 'Twenty or thirty.'

'Is your friend coming?' Laura asked Hannah. 'The one you're staying with.'

At this, the first suggestion of a reference to the situation they were all so politely overlooking, Hannah looked up and answered, without the slightest awkwardness: 'Siobhan? No, she was going to, but in the end she decided not to come because she's got a cold. It wasn't too bad, but now Nora's caught it.'

'They pick up so many bugs at that age,' Gayle said. 'She's lovely, Nora, isn't she? Hannah's shown us some pictures. Wonderful dark eyelashes. She's going to be a beauty.'

'She looks just like Siobhan,' Hannah said.

'I offered to give her a lift,' Michael put in. 'Haven't met her yet, actually.'

God, thought Juliet, souring again. He was so nauseatingly eager to demonstrate his helpfulness. And he was even talking as though it were a mere quirk of circumstance that he hadn't met Hannah's new friend. Didn't he feel any shame at all for not having been allowed anywhere near his wife for six weeks because of his own outrageous betrayal? How men deluded themselves. They just sat there rewriting history in their heads. Did they ever commit any confession of their transgressions to paper? No, they preferred the story of their lives to survive as an oral tradition, all the easier to gloss over the bits they preferred to forget. When Luke died, there was not a single scrap of physical evidence – bar an illegible postcard here and there – that told of his state of mind in those last few months; nothing that even hinted at the existence of another girl.

'Is Granny coming to the party, Mum?' Laura asked.

'Yes, but be warned, her malapropisms are getting worse by the day. When I was there last week I heard her tell her neighbour's son her star sign was labia. The poor boy was mortified.'

Juliet noticed Jay blush faintly at this. He was sweet. She was glad Laura was allowing herself to be attracted to nice guys. Perhaps Jay would turn out to be her Luke?

Michael laughed. 'Every family has their Mrs Malaprop, doesn't it? My Aunt Iris just told us over Christmas lunch that her man of the year was Charles Branson.'

'Did she mean Richard Branson or Charles Manson?' Christopher asked, tickled.

'I'm afraid that wasn't clarified.'

'How wonderful,' Gayle said. 'That'll be us in a few years' time.'

'Already is,' Laura muttered to Jay, ducking the napkin her mother flapped in her direction.

'She might have meant Charles Bronson?' Hannah said, suddenly interested. 'He died recently. Or she might have meant her man of the year 1965? She was probably confused. How is poor old Iris?'

'Fine,' Michael said. 'She asked after you.' Juliet watched as they met each other's eyes for a long moment. Michael looked as though he'd be willing to drop to the floor and pant at Hannah's feet if so directed. Hannah just smiled in distant amusement, as though remembering a joke from a decade ago.

'Who's Charles Bronson anyway?' Laura asked.

As the others laughed at her having never heard of Charleses Bronson *or* Manson, Juliet remembered the aunt Michael was talking about from the wedding, another one of the tall, superior women from his mother's side. They'd looked with horror at the succession of Goodwins, some of whom weren't wearing hats. How kind Hannah was, she probably really did think the old bat was just a bit befuddled.

'Who else is coming?' she asked her mother. Maybe this party was going to be fun after all.

'A few of the neighbours. Martin and Peggy, Auntie Maureen. Oh, and the Newells said they might come for a quick drink.'

'The Newells?' Michael asked politely.

It took a second or two for the penny to drop.

'Do you mean Jan and Tony?' Juliet asked aghast. '*Luke*'s parents?'

There was an uneasy silence during which no one met anyone else's eye; even Jay looked awkward, Juliet saw, he had obviously been briefed by Laura. She tried to catch her younger sister's eye – horrible little traitor. Only Michael was guiltless, working his eyes around the table from one person to the next with that same comfortable smile on his lips. 'What?' he said, finally sensing that something was awry. No doubt he feared he was the culprit.

'Tell me you're joking?' Juliet said to her mother when it

226

became clear no one else was going to explain. She couldn't believe this painful, hunted sound was her own voice.

'Well, I don't see what harm it can do?' Gayle said. 'They'd love to see you and they're just over the border, it takes no time at all to get here. We've seen them for lunch a couple of times since we moved here, you know . . .'

'*You* can see them all you want,' Juliet said. 'But I have no intention of going anywhere near them. I'm supposed to be forgetting!'

'There's a lot of good to remember as well,' Gayle said quietly. 'You were very close to them once, don't forget that.'

'How can I when you do this sort of thing? I'm amazed you even told me in advance, didn't have them jump out of a cake this evening to surprise me.'

'Darling, why shouldn't they come? Don't be so unreasonable. It's not always about you, you know.'

'Clearly,' Juliet glowered. Now she had the tension she'd been expecting and was distressed to be the one to have caused it. She wanted to sob until there were no more tears. Unreasonable! Not always about her! Hadn't she just come to that very conclusion herself? It was hard enough to admit you'd been a selfish cow without hearing your own mother say it in front of the rest of the family, not to mention Michael and Jay. She looked over at Hannah for help. It was impossible to tell whether she had been in on this, as well. Her instinct told her not. Hannah was unfashionably honest; had she known, she would have said something when they were out on their walk.

'It might not be that bad,' Hannah said, finally finishing chewing long after the others had put down their knives and forks. 'Anyway, with so many people coming you can easily avoid them.'

'Hmm.'

After lunch, Juliet grabbed Hannah and pulled her into their father's study. 'Can you take me to the station?'

227

'What?'

'You know there's no chance of a cab around here. Go on, it'll take you ten minutes.'

'When?' Hannah asked, confused. 'I thought we were going back together on Saturday?'

'I've got to go now. I *can't* see Jan and Tony.'

'But why not? I don't understand.'

'Hannah!' Juliet exploded. 'Stop acting like Mogadon woman! Please just help me get out of here. I'll run up and get my stuff and we'll just sneak off.'

'But my car's boxed in by Dad's, we'd have to get him to move his.'

'Fuck!'

They looked at each other. They could hear Michael helping Gayle clear the table, offering help with a cupboard door that had jammed.

'Use Michael's,' Juliet said. 'His must be parked out in the street.'

'Oh Juliet, it's a bit unfair to Mum, she'll be upset.'

'I don't care. She's got no right to put me through this and act like it's such great fun. She's always doing it. What about Michael coming today? I bet that was her idea, not yours.'

That seemed to swing it. 'OK,' Hannah said. 'Go and get your bag, I'll get the keys from Michael.'

They drove in silence, Juliet stony and shocked, forcing out of her mind the image of her father's puzzled face in the driveway. But she *had* to go. She remembered her near cardiac arrest when she'd seen Jan at Guy's bar. It was too soon. It might always be too soon.

'Is it still too awful to see them?' Hannah said, pulling up. 'They didn't do anything wrong, you know.'

'They let *her* come to the service. It was supposed to be just family and close friends. I won't ever forgive them.'

'We've talked about this, though, haven't we? They probably felt they had no choice. It's not that easy to ban people from a funeral. And imagine their own grief. Luke was their only son.'

This annoyed Juliet. Surely Hannah wasn't already pulling that 'only a mother understands' routine. Not unlike yesterday's 'only a pregnant woman cries' rubbish. At this rate there'd be no misery left for the rest of the population. For the first time she came close to confessing her own pregnancy, if only to find out if her feelings might be valued more highly if presented alongside evidence of fertility. She turned to open the door. She didn't want to feel bitter any more.

'I'll phone you tomorrow,' Hannah said. 'Try and forget all about this. Mum and Dad will be fine. I'll talk to them.'

'Thank you. And thanks for the lift,' Juliet said. 'I do appreciate it. Good luck with, well, everything.'

'OK,' Hannah said. 'Wait, the station looks closed!'

'No, the waiting room's open, look.'

'OK, but I'll wait till a train comes, just in case. It's creepy when it's deserted like this and it'll be dark soon.'

'No, you get back,' Juliet insisted. 'You'll need to help Mum with this evening. There'll be mulled wine to make and nuts to segregate and God knows what else.'

They managed to smile at one another, then Juliet clicked the door shut between them. 'See you next week,' she called, waving. 'New Year's Eve, don't forget!'

The journey was a disaster. Hannah had been right, there were no trains to London, though a shuttle to the coach station had been laid on, where a service was scheduled to make the journey to Victoria in three times the time it would have taken the train. The coach was late, the station bay freezing. On board, Juliet huddled against the window, trying to ignore the other passengers – losers and bruisers, Larry called people like this, people who didn't fit into society's idea of a traditional Christmas: in other words, people who neither owned a car nor had the social skills to stick out a family holiday beyond the day after Boxing Day. People like her . . .

229

As she finally walked down Murray Street and crossed Camden Square, she allowed herself to consider the evening ahead. If she could just avoid tormenting herself over the scene she'd left behind she could have a lovely, relaxing evening alone. She couldn't remember the last time she'd had the place to herself for a whole evening. Then she saw the light on at the living-room window and at once her heart was in her boots. Either the lights had been left blazing for three days or Sasha was also back early from her parents.

She let herself in and was at once assaulted by the smell of spirits. Sasha was lying under a throw on the floor of the living room the coffee table stacked with tissues, newspapers and the dregs of a bottle of Calvados. There'd been no Calvados in the flat before Christmas – like all committed drinkers Juliet kept a mental note of liquor stocks at all times, so Sasha had obviously brought in and consumed a new bottle.

'Sasha, are you ill?'

Her flatmate barely stirred. 'You had your mobile turned off.'

'Yeah, Guy's been calling, I couldn't handle a conversation with him over Christmas.'

'I needed you.' Sasha spoke in a pathetic childlike croak.

'What's wrong, tell me?' Juliet kneeled by the sofa and took in the puffy eyelids and dried saliva at the corners of Sasha's mouth. She looked in the thrall of some kind of unsupervised methadone-withdrawal programme. 'Why are you back from Winchester so early?'

'Couldn't stand it, I drove back yesterday, just wanted to be on my own.'

I know the feeling, Juliet thought. 'Has something happened with Callum?'

Sasha heaved herself into a sitting position and glared at her. 'Well, if you'd been on your mobile you'd know we split up on Christmas Eve.'

'No! You poor thing, what happened?'

Sasha clutched her hand as the unspectacular story spilled out: they'd rowed over Christmas arrangements, then, unable to agree, Callum had accused her of being self-absorbed and inflexible.

'He said we should quit while we're behind – how patronising is that? Do *you* think I'm self-absorbed?' Sasha asked.

Juliet paused, sensing that the severity of demands on her own energies that evening would hinge on this verdict. She needed to nip this in the bud while she could. 'I think we're all self-absorbed,' she said evenly. 'But it's better than being walked all over, isn't it? If he only wants to consider his own needs, then you're well out of it, if you ask me.'

It worked like a charm. 'Yes! Exactly!' Sasha was reinvigorated enough to pull her hand away and get up. 'Thank you, Juliet, thank you for stating the obvious! I'm going to make some tea.'

But thirty seconds later she was back, simmering afresh as she held out a handful of rubbish. 'And look what I found posted through the door when I got back!'

'What is it?'

'Look!'

Juliet peered into her hands at a shredded tangle of silver and orange.

'Satsuma skins,' Sasha announced with a whinny of indignation. 'Wrapped up like a proper pressie, with a gift tag and everything. We'd been laughing about getting them as stocking fillers when we were little. I thought it was a peace offering. But not even an *actual satsuma*, just the peel!'

'It could be worse,' said Juliet uncertainly. 'It could be, like, I don't know, a poo or something?'

Sasha looked crossly at her. 'Why would he post me a *poo*?'

'Well, why would he post you satsuma peel? He's obviously deranged!'

'You're right. I don't need this shit.'

231

'Good for you!'

Caliban had served six months with Queen Sasha, but it took Her Majesty less than six minutes to gather up the detritus of her mourning, open the windows to let in the quiet, icy North London air, and toast the end of an era with a mug of black tea. 'There's no milk,' she said, voice still defiant. Juliet saw that she was very drunk.

She huddled under the throw for warmth. 'Haven't had the greatest time myself,' she said. 'It turned out my mum had invited Luke's parents over, to sort of surprise me, can you believe it?'

'With ease,' Sasha said. 'Parents haven't got a clue. I couldn't believe the rubbish mine came out with about Callum. As though I was about fourteen. So much for unconditional support. They were almost *amused* by what he'd said to me.'

'I just had to get out of there,' Juliet said. 'I haven't spoken to them since before the funeral. They've sent me letters as well – I don't even open them.'

'So I got up early and just left them a note,' Sasha said. 'I know they're sorry 'cos they've rung loads of times, but I haven't picked up.'

'Right.' It seemed incredible to Juliet now that she'd ever confided in Sasha the circumstances of Luke's death. It must have been during those first forty-eight hours when they were still getting on. She shivered. It was very cold with the windows open. She would go and submerge herself in a hot bubble bath and spend a few private moments with her weirdly swelling stomach and breasts. The agony of suppressing all thoughts of her condition these last days had been almost physical – it felt as though she'd been knotted into the stiffest of corsets and denied all means of liberation. She was ready to cave in. Thank God Sasha was about as self-absorbed as it got (well spotted, Callum!) – just the merest hook of sympathy on her part and Juliet might have blurted out the whole thing. She willed herself to hang on. Just two more weeks and her body would be hers again.

'What am I going to do for New Year now?' Sasha cried, with fresh emergency. 'Oh, Juliet, can I come with you to Larry's thing?'

'Sure, if you want to.' That was all she needed, single girls together once more, but at least she could reliably expect Sasha to remove her companionship again as soon as Callum's replacement had been identified. 'I'm going to call it a night. Have a bath.'

'There's no water, something's wrong with the boiler,' Sasha said. 'The guy's coming tomorrow, charging me a fucking fortune, the bastard, it's not even a bank holiday!'

'Oh, OK. Well, let's catch up properly in the morning,' Juliet said. 'And you can tell me the whole Callum saga.'

'Nothing else to say,' Sasha said, picking up the TV remote control and releasing a whoosh of festive hysteria into the cold room. 'He can go and choke on a Brazil nut for all I care.'

Overwhelmed, Juliet withdrew.

Chapter 21

Hannah could see no way out of the MacFarlanes' drinks party on the twenty-ninth. Lottie, an enthusiastic believer in persistence paying, had called several times to campaign for her attendance. 'Come for a quick drink at least. The girls would love to see you – Anya and Fiona were asking after you only last night, they're worried they haven't heard from you. And Michael won't be there.'

'Are you sure?' Hannah asked.

'Yes, but you've seen him again, anyway, haven't you? In Norfolk? How did that go?'

So news was circulating with the momentum of a war effort, Hannah thought, every advance and retreat duly reported. Next they'd be running up dresses for her out of old curtains. But they cared, all right, the women in the group. She didn't need to clink glasses with them to know that it was each one's unspoken fear that what had happened to Hannah might happen to her. Except perhaps Lottie. As far as she could tell, Lottie had no fear. 'Fine,' she said. 'He came to my parents' place for a party.'

'And?' Lottie stretched the word to three syllables.

'And nothing,' said Hannah firmly. 'He drove home the same night.' She found it much easier to stand up to Lottie when she was sitting down with the phone in her hand.

'Well, he's still at Marianne's in Cheltenham for now,' Lottie said. 'He probably won't come to Edinburgh for New Year, either.'

'Why not?'

'He has to work on the second. Maybe he's not in the mood for a celebration, either . . .'

'I know the feeling,' Hannah said, determined not to get drawn in. 'Can I bring Siobhan to the party then?'

There was a pause. 'Of course, the more the merrier.'

'OK, I'd love to come.' Actually, she couldn't think of much she would have loved less – submitting herself to a full gynaecological examination on the bandstand in Clapham Common, perhaps – and was genuinely terrified of facing Michael's posse alone. She had never operated among them as a single entity, always appearing, if not on Michael's arm, safely under Lottie's wing. At least Siobhan would be there. It would be fun to mix Siobhan with the group. She had a natural directness that seemed to highlight other people's insincerities and Hannah was looking forward to getting her opinions on everyone.

However, on the morning of the party, Nora's cough was so much worse the doctor said she might even have bronchitis, so Siobhan decided she'd better cancel the babysitter and stay at home after all. Hannah considered asking Juliet to come with her instead, even left a message for her to call. But where Siobhan was candid, her sister could be openly scornful, and worse. Hannah had seen the way she'd looked at Michael during that lunch at home, as though she'd be satisfied with nothing less than death by guillotine – with a blunt blade. No, despite their recent rapprochement Juliet was still far too much of a loose cannon, so by the time she'd rung back, Hannah had changed her mind and instead invited her to the first antenatal classes.

'Hannah, come in! You look very festive!' Rob was at the door. She hadn't seen him for months, but, unlike her, he hadn't changed a jot. Even his cropped hair was maintained to within a millimetre of its standard length. He was neither short nor tall, the sort of height that worked well with Lottie whether she was in heels or not. Leering height was what it was, Hannah thought, as she smiled into his eyes, black, unreadable. He had a strong nose and jaw of the sort that looked better on an older face, when thrusting features helped make up for the receding authority of old age. But on a man a few years short of forty, his face was aggressive, intimidating.

Lottie appeared at his side. 'Hannah! Just look at that bump! It's really grown over Christmas, is it really only six months? Oh, no chum?' she asked before pushing shut the door.

'Nora's not well again,' Hannah said. 'So Siobhan had to stay with her.' She couldn't remember Lottie ever uttering Siobhan's actual name, was going to remark on this but found herself too distracted by Lottie's appearance. She looked absolutely lustrous, skin moist and facial-fresh, thick sable-blonde hair pinned up like Grace Kelly, long silver shirt over flared white trousers. And at her ears were the sparkliest diamonds Hannah had ever seen. She was like a winter bride. 'You look wonderful, Lottie!'

'Thank you, sweetie. The rocks were a Christmas pressie from Rob. Oh, and the shirt. Wrong size, of course, I had to change it, but at least he guessed too small, which is flattering in its own way.'

Rob grinned at this. 'Could have gone either way, though. If I bought a bra that was too small she'd have had my balls all right!' He handed Hannah's coat to a waiting serf and closed her fingers with his around a glass of champagne. 'You can have a couple, can't you? Those NHS guidelines are way too cautious if you ask me. Come on in, you probably know everyone, but just shout if you don't.'

She saw immediately that this wasn't going to be as horrendous as she'd feared. There were more than enough outsiders to dilute the inner circle – relatives, neighbours, even a few children, cheeks already flushed from stolen wine. She'd dreaded people's curiosity, but now realised that she could probably count on the majority to behave as though this particular marital blunder had totally passed them by. People had their own concerns, like hoovering up as much of the champagne as they could get their mitts on before their other halves noticed and narrowed a warning eye. Lottie had caterers in, of course; she always delegated Christmas. She'd told Hannah that last year, when Hannah had got herself into a flap about a drinks party for Michael's colleagues.

Sneaking a look at herself in one of the Venetian mirrors that lined the sitting room, Hannah wondered if her choice of dress – red velvet – had been a mistake. Her curves looked overripe, and there seemed something sinful about her, something *fallen*. She tried to picture the same image with Michael standing in the background, a tender hand on her stomach or hip: then she wouldn't be fallen, she'd be blooming, outshining every woman in the room, if only because – Lottie excepted – the rest all wore black. She stood, riveted, watching all the smiling faces in the mirror and feeling like a child peering through the banisters at an adult party, until a voice called out: 'Hannah, come and join us!'

She wasn't sure exactly who had spoken but obediently succumbed to kisses all round and planted herself at the edge of a group circling Marcus Blake's girlfriend Anya. Nearby, the other halves had created a loose scrum around Rob. It was like an arrangement from generations ago, all that were missing were the needlepoint and port.

'So I thought, fuck it,' a plump woman with her lower leg in a cast was saying to Anya. 'I'll just cancel the Harbour Club subscription, haven't been for three months anyway. Now I'm using the money for physio and massages.'

'Where did it happen?'

'Meribel.'

'We were there last year. My sister-in-law sprained *her* knee, actually. Getting out the car!'

'Shouldn't laugh! But it's such a pain when it happens early in the week, nothing to do but sit around eating all the cakes and waiting for everyone to come back. And Richard wasn't at all sympathetic.'

'Different story if it had been the other way around. God, men are about as useful as an ashtray on a motorbike, aren't they?'

'No skiing for you this season, eh?' Anya winked at Hannah. She meant the baby, Hannah reassured herself, not the fact that Michael was the skier and she the one who booked restaurant tables and waited for the others on freezing bar terraces. They'd been skiing twice together, but it had never quite lived up to her hopes of James Bonds zipping about on snowmobiles while the women watched from under big fur hats. Thank God Michael wasn't clinically obsessed, not like Rob and Marcus, who made three or more trips a season.

'How did your house move go?' It was Fiona Cummings, Adam's wife, short, squeaky-voiced, with watery eyes that always left her eye make-up smudged at the outer corners. Hannah had last seen her at dinner at the Cummingses just before the Cape Town trip. It occurred to her she hadn't ever called to thank Fiona. 'Are you all settled yet?'

'Great,' Hannah said. Fiona had to be bluffing; she must know Michael had moved into Salcott Road on his own. 'It's a beautiful house, Lottie found it for us.'

'She told us. There aren't very many with the basement floor Between the Commons, are there? We were thinking about digging ours out, but we've decided to extend upwards instead. I don't suppose you know any good builders?'

'No,' Hannah said. 'Sorry.'

'I'll put you in touch with someone,' Lottie said to Fiona, swooping in with a bottle of champagne in each hand. 'I know some guys who speak English and charge decent rates, and believe me that's not easy to find!'

'Thank you, Lottie! Adam said you'd be the one to ask.'

Hannah looked at Lottie with admiration. That's what she would do in the New Year, she decided, with a sudden flare of inspiration. She would reinvent herself as a Lottie-style dervish, start delegating anything she didn't fancy doing herself and make lists of key contacts. Before long, she'd be The One to Ask, too.

'Result, mate, it just shows it pays to be direct!' Rob had raised his voice and Hannah couldn't help tuning out of the women's conversation to listen to the men's. 'Let's put it this way, this bloke I know . . .' – he lowered his voice and raised his eyebrows, the classic precursor to some unsavoury revelation – '. . . chatted up this girl, fucking *stunning*, had her in the sack within an hour . . .'

A pulling tale. How tedious. Hannah turned back to the women.

'I mean, the guy who did the bathroom was *sooo* cheeky. I asked him if he wanted anything, you know, meaning a cup of tea or coffee, and he reeled off this sandwich order, chicken, tomato and lots of black pepper, like I was running a café or something.'

'Mine asked for sparkling mineral water!'

'Girls! You mustn't give them an *inch*,' Lottie advised. 'These are traditional men with traditional expectations. They'll have you wiping their arses if they can get away with it. Always remember you are paying for a service, not providing one.'

Hannah joined the nods of agreement.

'It worked like a charm,' Rob growled. 'Suggested they pretend to be film stars, not even tell each other their real names. Didn't use a condom, fucking maniac.'

The others laughed at this and Hannah thought she heard a mutter of 'Lucky bastard' amid the merriment. She puffed in irritation at their teenage grins, and it must have been louder than intended for Rob looked around at once, momentarily unnerved to spot her standing there, obviously listening.

239

'Oops, sorry, Hannah,' he said, with a sidelong glance at Marcus – and was that a hint of a wink, too? Now they were all looking at her and she had no idea what to do next. She had a fair idea of what they expected her to do, though, which was to skip back into the female fold like a good girl and let them get on with the rest of the story. What would Juliet do? she wondered; her sister spent virtually every night drinking with the boys. 'Don't worry, Rob,' she heard herself drawl. 'I've got nothing against a tale of romantic adventuring. Do go on . . .'

They snorted and shuffled at this, before turning inward again.

'Hannah, have you heard Fiona's news?' Anya exclaimed. Lottie had moved away, the home-improvements master class dismissed for now. 'She's been made client services director!'

'Sounds like a madam in a brothel, if you ask me,' Fiona said modestly.

'Congratulations, that's wonderful,' Hannah smiled mechanically. But she didn't care about Fiona's promotion; she felt as though the Oxford Street Christmas lights had been turned on in her head. My God! That story of Rob's was the same one Siobhan had told her about the man who'd got her pregnant. It was much too similar to be a coincidence. *Rob must know Nora's father*. She edged away from Fiona for a better view of her host. Satisfaction cloaked those jutting features as he tossed another detail into the scrum and lapped up the more envious sniggers. Her brain pogoed once more: *'This bloke I know . . .'*, wasn't that just a variation on *'I've got this mate, right . . .'*? What if Rob didn't just *know* Nora's father, what if Rob *was* Nora's father?

Out of nowhere, Juliet's words came out of her mouth again. 'Which bloke was that, Rob? He sounds like quite a character . . .' For an instant, Rob looked straight at her, truly aghast, but managed to recover by the time the other faces had swivelled back from Hannah's to his. 'Oh, no one I actually know, Han, just a mate of a mate. You know, it's probably just one of those urban myths.'

'See the rugby?' Marcus asked him. 'Absolute scandal, that disallowed try.'

Sport, the classic male salvage tactic, Hannah thought, but duly withdrew. She turned to a new face in the women's cluster and, impatient of preamble, asked: 'Does Rob still work at Proctor Mitchum, do you know?'

'Yes, unless you've heard something I haven't,' the woman said. Hannah now recognised the sultry, mannered drone of Victoria, the wife of a colleague of Rob's.

'I *knew* it!' Hannah burst out, exhilarated. 'I wonder if he might know my friend Siobhan. She used to temp there.'

'Oh, right.' Victoria was looking at her strangely. 'I have no idea, Hannah, sorry. Neil's at CSFB now.'

'How's he getting on?' Hannah switched back on to autopilot. She knew Victoria knew she'd forgotten who she and Neil were but she didn't care. It *had* to be Rob. Same company, same chat-up line, same dark eyes ... No wonder Lottie was getting diamonds for Christmas. She felt like dropping to the floor and crawling right into that tight little male knot to confront the bastard there and then. But hang on ... if Rob and Siobhan worked together then they could hardly have been strangers play-acting in a bar, could they? They'd know each other's names, at the very least.

Her whole body slumped an inch at the wholescale evacuation of adrenalin. She considered a second glass of champagne but there were no trays anywhere near her. Then she saw Rob glance in her direction, lift his chin a little in acknowledgment. He looked guilty. The adrenalin started trickling back. Did he suspect she was on his case? He probably viewed her as one of Lottie's spies, in which case why on earth talk so openly about his conquests? Arrogance, that was why, she thought, watching him grab Adam and administer some sort of neck lock – they were still going on about the rugby. Good. She would make sense of this, somehow. Banks were huge, she'd seen the Proctor Mitchum building near Liverpool Street and you could play tennis in the lobby. Thousands worked there and most of them were men who looked exactly the same. Siobhan must have worked in a different department from Rob, she'd probably never laid eyes on him before that night. Perhaps he'd eyed her up in the lift once or twice, nothing more. Then they'd both turned up to the same birthday drinks and watched the sparks fly like November the fifth.

No, that sounded like a bad romantic novel. She needed to do a lot more delving before she thought about confronting anybody. What was it Siobhan had said, *He'd probably laugh in my face, deny the whole thing*. She was probably right. Rob was a professional, lies and denials were the air he breathed, were the air all these men breathed. Unless they were caught *in flagrante*, like Michael, in which case they had to fall back on the good old-fashioned biding of time.

Lottie shimmered into view again, nodding across at Rob like a satisfied general as she delivered to Hannah her sister Emily, a younger, drabber version of herself and someone Hannah had liked from the very first.

'Hannah! You look so well!' Emily cried, kissing her cheeks. 'So tell me everything, when do two become three?'

Chapter 22

Hannah wore the same red dress to the party Juliet and Larry took her to on New Year's Eve, though there she felt less the fallen woman than Little Red Riding Hood in a forest full of wolves. The host, who she didn't lay eyes on until a good hour after arrival, even had a set of teeth that could, without too much exaggeration, be described as fanged. The party was far from being the intimate gathering trailered by Juliet, but a huge event with at least a hundred and fifty people crammed into the Hackney Wick live/work space of Joby and his girlfriend – what was her name again, something that rhymed with his? Jodie, possibly. Everyone was smoking and the music, less thumping than stamping, seemed to enter Hannah's body through her whole skin, even through her *hair*. She held her bag over her belly, not allowing herself to think about what all of this might be doing to those softly sprouting eardrums tucked away inside.

There was no escaping Joby's art. Positioned on a series of dais, like podium dancers in a club, were life-size inflatables: a woman, back contorted to bring her head between her legs, tongue outstretched towards her own crotch; twin babies lying under a mobile with huge shiny-gummed grins, the toys that dangled above them human organs. She came to a halt next to a figure in a wheelchair, cigarette glued between his lips, ashtray

243

built into the arm of the chair. She had a feeling she'd seen this sort of thing before.

'Hilarious, aren't they?' Larry said, sneaking his hand into hers behind their backs. That felt lovely, natural, all the protection she needed from the assaults of the night. It was odd that she still felt as close to him as before, even though she'd seen Michael again and survived her first re-entry into his orbit. What was happening with Larry, it seemed, was happening to a parallel Hannah, some kind of detached, anonymous Hannah who was permitted by the prototype to operate quite autonomously.

'I'm not sure "hilarious" is the word I'd choose,' she said, smiling at him, and he moved his face a bit closer to hers. She loved his smell, had broken its blend down to smoke and sweat and mint and lemon.

'OK, then, waste of space, but still hilarious. Tell you what, by the end of the night I bet you won't be able to tell the sculptures from the guests.'

'That's what worries me,' Hannah giggled.

'Ah, here's Joby, finally!' Larry said, as a man in his early thirties approached, a cocktail glass in each hand. Though his clothes – jeans of some expensively mutated denim and a pink vintage shirt – told of self-conscious styling, his eyes blazed with childlike eagerness. Was he even *panting*, Hannah thought, blinking. Then she spotted the fangs and took a small step back.

Larry introduced them. 'What do you think of my work?' he asked her at once. She was disappointed that the voice matched the clothes and not the eyes.

'Well, I guess they're shocking,' she said politely. 'I assume that's what you intended.'

'Quite the opposite,' Joby said. 'They're actually just a joke. A big fat send-up. That's what we'll call the show, maybe. I wanted to test how baseless our shock is. I mean, it may *seem* outrageous to see a baby playing with a penis-shaped toy, but why? The child has no idea what the toy represents; we're just foisting our own sense of sin on its innocence. I mean, we all suck our mother's tits and have no memory of it.'

'Thank the Lord for that,' Larry said, taking an enormous gulp of vodka.

'But breastfeeding is totally natural,' Hannah protested.

'Why should art be natural?'

'Shut up, you phoney bastard,' Larry said, laughing. 'You've got to stop spouting this rubbish, mate. But I like the guy in the wheelchair, I have to say. It *does* look shocking to see someone in a wheelchair smoking, but if you think about it he's already fucked, so he might as well have a fag.'

'Exactly,' Joby said. 'I knew you'd get it, Laurence.'

'Where d'you find the wheelchair?'

'Got a mate to nick it from St Barts.'

'That's awful,' Hannah said, frowning. 'You must return it, afterwards.'

'After what?' Joby asked. 'These pieces might still be standing in a hundred years.'

'I'd just get them through the night first, if I were you,' said Larry, grinning. He was fidgeting again; she could see he wanted a cigarette.

'And how's the corrupt and greedy world of advertising?' Joby asked. 'Sorry, brand consultancy. Was that Juliet you came in with?'

Hannah hadn't seen Juliet since the unexpected arrival of Guy twenty minutes ago. And she was only too aware of how Juliet felt about unexpected arrivals, having been grilled earlier in the evening on the Jan and Tony situation. (Had Hannah spoken to them at their parents' party? Did they mention her? Did they talk about Luke? Did they ask about the letters?) Funny how she drew strength from what she thought of as her sister's greater confidence, yet Juliet was no more capable of a real confrontation than she was. She wondered where the two of them had got this defeatist gene from? Perhaps it had skipped a generation, been passed down from their great uncle, who'd been a deserter during the war.

'I think you might've scared her off by inviting an ex of hers,' Larry was saying to Joby. 'You know what women are like if they don't get full guest-list approval.'

'They're fanatical, aren't they?' Joby agreed. 'Makes you wonder why more doormen aren't women.'

'Or why more doormen aren't doorwomen,' Larry laughed. 'Any sign of Fergus yet? Can you believe he's working in a *call centre*?'

As the two men caught up on old college friends, Hannah spotted Guy making his way through the crowd towards them, apparently heading for the front door. There was no sign of Juliet so Hannah decided to intercept him. 'Guy, how are you? How are things at the bar?'

He looked surprised to see her. 'OK,' he said. 'I'm just going back there now.'

'You're working tonight?'

'It's a private party,' he shrugged. 'Joint New Year's with someone's thirtieth birthday, a regular.'

'You look tired,' Hannah said. It was true. Although from a distance he'd looked as glamorous as ever, close up the whites of his eyes were grey.

'Yeah, I'm burnt out, you know. Benjy just resigned. I've got to find a new chef.'

'Sounds like you need a break.'

'I'm spending all of February in France,' Guy said. 'There's already fantastic snow, I hear.' Another ski nut. They were everywhere.

She smiled. 'Did you know Juliet's here? We came together.'

'Did you?' He sounded amazed. 'You two getting on again, then?'

'Yes.' It struck Hannah that she had thought so little until recently of the slide in her friendship with her sister that she

246

hadn't once discussed it with Michael. Guy, on the other hand, had obviously been briefed on an official estrangement several months ago.

'And you two?' she asked.

'I've just seen her,' Guy said. 'No change there.' She saw that he knew she'd guessed he was there expressly to see Juliet. She wanted to take him aside and explain Juliet's insecurities, tell him to keep trying; but having seen Juliet's fury at their mother over that business with Luke's parents, she decided it best not to interfere.

'You must be getting excited about the baby?' he said, clearly looking to change the subject.

'Yes, I am. But it still seems so far away.'

'How many weeks?'

As she explained she wondered if Guy would question the fact that she and Larry were standing hand in hand, to all intents and purposes a couple, just seven months after her wedding to Michael. She had no idea whether to expect a reaction from him. It struck her that she didn't know Guy at all, this man who'd been seated with her closest sister at the top table at her wedding. There she was criticising Juliet for being too quick to judge Michael, but she hadn't even made the time to form an opinion of Guy – and now it was too late to make any difference.

'How d'you know Joby?' she asked.

'I don't really. I know Josie; she's from Wellington as well. This art is complete bollocks, though, that's for sure. Look, Hannah, I've really got to go, good to see you all . . .'

Joby drifted on, too, and she was on her own with Larry. He smiled down at her and pressed the top of her head into his neck. She marvelled at the ability he had to create a sense of aloneness together, even though they were standing in the middle of a mob, like he'd cuddled her to him under a big, cosy coat. With Larry there was no looking over her shoulder for someone more interesting, no uninvited pawing, none of that proprietorial handling she was used to with . . . with other men.

'So,' Larry said, speaking right in her ear. 'If you were a deluded modern artist, who would you be?'

She smiled. 'Juliet used to get me to do this all the time when we lived together. What do you two call it again?'

'The Kipling game.'

'That's it! The "If" game. It got ridiculous. Like, "If you were a breakfast cereal, which would you be?"'

'Kellogg's Frosties, definitely,' said Larry seriously. 'I have an affinity with Tony the Tiger.'

'And the artist?'

'Well, I wouldn't be Joby, that much I know,' Larry said.

'Oh, he's all right,' Hannah said. 'At least he's passionate about something.'

'People say that all the time,' Larry replied. 'But why's it so good to be passionate if the passion is totally misguided? If it's going nowhere?'

She knew he wasn't talking about Joby now, and felt too weary to follow where he was going. Why now, when she'd been loving just being with him? 'You know, I tried that "If" game with Michael once,' she said, not sure why she was so keen to mention the name she knew Larry so disliked hearing. 'He just didn't get it. He wanted someone else to say what sort of animal he would be or what sort of car. He found that much more interesting.'

'The sign of a true egomaniac,' Larry said. 'No self-knowledge.'

'Hard to argue with that,' Hannah said.

Just then a girl in a belted pea-green coat shimmied through the crowd to reach them. Hannah was reminded of the Owl and the Pussycat. 'Larry, there you are! Can I borrow you? Apparently, you're the only person in the room who knows how to mix a proper margarita . . .'

Looking at the monumental levels of consumption taking place all around her, Hannah found that hard to believe, but Larry followed the pea-green woman anyway, leaving her where she'd feared she'd end up this evening: on her own. Or not quite, as she'd edged perilously close to the nearest set of figures: two elderly creatures with puckered plastic skin, locked together on a swing hanging from the joist fifteen feet above. The old woman was straddling the man, his tweedy trousers pulled down over his hips. As another guest walked by he pushed at the swing so it rocked back and forth and Hannah had to move out of the way to avoid being kicked. She gazed out the window for a while at the view: glaring streetlights, cheap cars, sad little supermarts, and one solitary tree, its branches like animal bones held up in sacrifice. Rescue me, she whispered to herself, turning back.

It was at this point that the music was turned up so high it seemed to slam off the walls, and Juliet reappeared with her American friend, the smooth-skinned handsome one who always managed to work it into the conversation that he'd been to Brown University, like the average Brit had ever heard of the place. They were with a dazzlingly pretty blonde girl who had commandeered a tray of canapés and kept trying to feed them to the other two. All three of them looked completely out of it.

'You know Fulton and Rachel,' Juliet said to Hannah.

They all said hi. 'Bunch of freakin' stoners here,' Fulton offered by way of conversation. He was sucking at a yellow drink through a curly straw.

Juliet frowned at Hannah. 'Can you *believe* Guy was here? The way he just *popped up* in the kitchen like that . . .'

The music was louder than ever and Hannah tried to man-oeuvre Juliet closer to her, away from the other two who had now begun kissing. Juliet continued to engage her sister with fierce eyes. 'I would *never* have come if I'd known.'

'But you didn't break up badly, did you?' Hannah realised she didn't actually know why it was that things had fallen apart between Juliet and Guy in the first place. 'Maybe it wouldn't hurt to talk things through again?'

'I couldn't hear what he was saying,' Juliet said. 'There were blenders going crazy all over the place. Joby's on some kind of cocktail frenzy. How does Guy even know Joby, anyway?'

'He knows the girlfriend . . .' Hannah could no longer hear her own voice through the din.

Juliet looked distressed. 'What? A new girlfriend? Was she here? Did you see her?'

'No, he *knows* . . .'

'Everyone!' The music was suddenly killed and a voice boomed from a skylight above their heads. 'Come on up to the roof! It's time for Joby's Act of Illusion!'

Doubtless balancing on his head in some ironic statement of anti-balance, Hannah thought, or dangling by a nose hair above the traffic while someone tickled him with a sex toy. A ladder had been lowered into the room and guests started scuffling towards it. She looked around for Larry. Where was he? He'd been ages.

'What, Joby's naked on the *roof*? What a laugh, hold my bag, Han, will you,' Juliet squealed.

'We're coming, too,' Rachel said, passing Hannah her drink.

She was suddenly a human cloakroom, with bags, jackets, even a hat, piled around her as people abandoned their possessions to climb up onto the roof. I'm like one of Joby's installations, she thought, giggling to herself. If I stand here long enough, someone might put a little red sticker on my nose and make arrangements to ship me off to a private collection somewhere. All at once, in the deadened, emptying room, she was delighted by the prospect of her own future. If it meant family life of any description then it had to be better than what was on display here. How could she have ever felt alone when a life was taking shape inside her? She looked at her watch, reminded herself to call Siobhan at midnight. She felt happy.

It was then that the police arrived and she was shipped off all right, to Hackney Wick police station. In all, they found eight wraps of cocaine on her, admittedly in different pockets and wallets, and God knew how many pills – there were quite a few in one big bagful. They were uninterested in her argument that she'd been a hatstand. It did sound implausible in the cold light of the interview room, but it was the very implausibility of the situation that made her feel so protected. In many ways the station was preferable to the party, though she didn't like using the loo.

She heard the roars and whistles at midnight from her holding cell – how male crowds always sounded – and wondered how long it would take Michael to get to London. She hadn't needed to think twice about calling him first, he would know exactly what to do, she'd just hoped he hadn't gone to Edinburgh after all. When he picked up and confirmed himself to be at his parents' house in Cheltenham it seemed to her incredibly significant that he was willing to drive up to rescue her. She prayed he wouldn't be pulled over for drink driving; it wouldn't do for them both to be arrested. And then he was there, buttoned into a long, dark blue coat, a vision of well-heeled familiarity in this scuffed and alien place. His voice was still tight with anger when she was handed over to him, but his fingers were gentle on her elbow as he led her to the car.

'Fucking outrageous, keeping a pregnant woman down there. Have they got nothing better to do on New Year's Eve? Isn't this when all the losers jump off Hungerford Bridge?'

'Not their patch,' said Hannah, enjoying the softness of the upholstered headrest on her skull. She'd missed being a passenger in Michael's car, that feeling of being armoured by luxury against the outside world.

'Gun crime, then? They've got maniacs walking the streets with Kalashnikovs and they're worried about a woman holding someone else's handbag! It's like fucking *Monty Python*!'

'They thought I was some kind of crack whore,' Hannah said. 'The weird thing is, I feel like I *have* taken something, I feel so wide awake.'

Michael looked at her anxiously. 'Did anyone give you anything? At that party? Maybe we should go to the hospital just in case?'

'No, I didn't even have a drink, just mineral water. It must be adrenaline.'

'If you're sure. Bloody Juliet. It was her coke, I suppose?'

'I think it must have been *everyone*'s. Did you manage to speak to her?'

'Yes,' said Michael grimly. 'She had no idea you'd been arrested. Dozy tart.'

'She was on the roof,' Hannah remembered. 'Joby was doing an Act of Illusion.'

Michael just snorted, but he wasn't angry with her, she could tell.

After that they travelled in easy silence. The journey through the City and the West End took just minutes on the emptying predawn roads and soon they were was turning onto Chelsea Bridge, past the park and the new glass apartment buildings, accelerating into the curve of Queenstown Road. They passed the furniture shop where she'd ordered a cot and linen chest for the baby's room: she wondered if they'd arrived yet, couldn't remember them being mentioned in Michael's phone-message updates. She was still thinking about nursery furniture when they took a right between the twin mansion blocks on Clapham Common Northside: they were heading towards Battersea Rise, towards home, Salcott Road home, his home.

'Would you take me to Siobhan's please,' she said quietly.

He stopped at the next lights and gave her a long look. His eyes were so filled with pleading that she turned away, unable to bear their pull. Instead she flipped down the mirror to look at herself. That was scarcely more bearable. Her skin was pale, as

252

though her features had been carved out of soap, her eyes volcanic dark: she looked half-savage. Yes, hers was a glamour that required regular retouching, not police surveillance. 'God, I look a right state.'

'You look fine. You've had a scare,' Michael said. He was driving faster, cutting through the dark core of the common. 'Siobhan's place, OK. Which way once I get to Brixton Hill?'

She directed him to the flat, thought about inviting him in for a coffee, but it was quiet, Siobhan and Nora still asleep, so she kept him in the hallway.

'What does O.R.A. stand for?' Michael asked, peering down the narrow passageway. 'Is that some kind of Brixton black-power thing?'

Hannah looked. 'Don't be ridiculous. It's N.O.R.A. *Nora*. The "N" must have fallen off. That's her bedroom.'

'I thought her name was Siobhan?'

'Nora's her baby. I *told* you.' She was finally exhausted, looked at the clock in the tiny hallway: five thirty. 'Thank you,' she said to Michael. 'You saved my life tonight.'

'Not quite,' Michael said. They stood looking at each other for a minute.

'Why didn't you go to Scotland?' she asked, finally.

He just shrugged. 'Didn't fancy it, all that Hogmanay hysteria. Maccas wasn't bothered either way.'

Her mobile was ringing and she clicked it straight on to voicemail, though not before recognising Larry's number.

'Will you call me?' Michael said.

'Yes, I will.' She closed the door, heard him wait a beat or two on the other side before he went up the steps.

'Michael was *here*? In this flat?' Siobhan asked a few hours later. 'I wish you'd woken me up, I'm dying to see what he's like.'

'Not worth waking a baby for,' Hannah said with a smile.

'But how great of him to rescue you! I can't believe they

thought you were involved! They need to spend a bit of time down in Brixton if they can't recognise a dealer when they see one.'

'I know. It didn't seem real.'

'I mean, you're so obviously *pregnant*!'

'Maybe they thought the bump was my stash,' Hannah said.

'Maybe when they heard you use words like "stash" they knew you weren't their man after all.'

They both giggled.

'Where was Larry when all of this was going on?' Siobhan asked.

'He'd gone to buy cigarettes, he said. I got a text saying he'd come to the station but they wouldn't let him see me.'

'All these white knights,' Siobhan sighed. 'I wouldn't mind one myself.'

'Really?' Hannah asked eagerly. She'd had a lot of time to think on that grubby little mattress at the police station, time to think about Siobhan and Nora and Rob. What had Michael said? *Maccas wasn't bothered either way*. Well, she'd see about that. 'Do you think you need rescuing, then?' she asked.

Siobhan looked taken aback for a second. 'Only from the drudgery of nappies and Infant Nurofen. You'd never guess she'd been screaming until three in the morning, would you? Mind you, the fireworks didn't help. But the cough's much better, thank God. Isn't it, sweetheart?'

Nora was on her tummy on the striped rug at their feet, rearing up now and then to flash a three-toothed smile or contribute a roar of delight, a miniature heckler to Hannah's tale. Hannah tickled her, then stroked a bit of her own baby, an elbow or knee, maybe, it was hard to tell.

'How about you? Are you feeling any better?' she asked Siobhan.

'Much better. I think we're both on the mend.'

'Good. I think this is going to be a great year for you.'

254

'It'd be hard to beat the last one,' said Siobhan with a huge grin. 'So tell me, is Michael back in favour?'

Hannah looked down. 'Maybe.'

'I suppose you ought to decide, one way or the other.'

'I know. I will. There's just some stuff I need to sort out first.' She had to be sure Siobhan and Nora would be cared for when she left. She could see that Siobhan meant it when she said she was happy, but surely she'd be even happier with a decent contribution from Rob and all that improved finances bought: a holiday in the sun, clothes for Nora from cute little boutiques and not supermarkets, the opportunity to delay her return to work . . .

'What kind of stuff?' Siobhan asked. 'Can I help?'

Hannah thought quickly. 'Oh, like all the antenatal classes. I've got my first hospital session next week. I've decided to do those as well as the NCT ones next month. You can't be too prepared.'

'I'll come with you if you like,' Siobhan offered.

'Thank you,' Hannah said, 'but I've already asked Juliet. That reminds me, I must call her. I think Michael must have shouted at her, he blames her for last night.'

'Do you?' Siobhan asked.

'No.' Now she came to think of it, she never blamed Juliet.

Chapter 23

'So how've you found being pregnant?' the man with the 'Jonath' sticker on his jumper asked Juliet. 'You're not showing much yet, are you?'

'Oh, I'm not having a baby,' Juliet said. 'I'm just here with my sister. How about you and . . . ?' She nodded towards the smiley, dark-haired space-hopper now chatting to Hannah.

He turned, too, revealing a stark, square profile that looked as if it had been dashed off by a cartoonist. 'We're *very* excited,' he told her, though totally deadpan. 'We've had a really easy pregnancy, actually, no sickness or anything.'

'So, all set then.' Juliet feared she was already running out of conversation and the group activity had only just begun. 'Is your name really "Jonath"? Is that a variation on Jonah?'

'It's Jonathan,' he said, surprised. 'Oh, I see, you know how you run out of space on the labels? Anyway, I keep having these anxiety dreams about finding a parking space on the night. I mean, what if there's a queue? It took me twenty-five minutes to park today. That's why we were late.'

'You could get a cab instead,' Juliet suggested.

'That's a point. Will cabs take women in labour?'

'I don't see why not, if they'll take vomiting and fornicating women every night of the week.'

'Oh!' Jonathan looked as though he wasn't sure whether to let himself laugh.

Juliet got up. 'Want some tea?'

'No thanks, we've both gone decaf since we found out we were pregnant.'

You're not the one who's pregnant, you great blockhead, she wanted to say to him. Why did they all speak in those ghastly coupley plurals? It was driving her nuts already. That and the constant stroking of bumps and napes and lobes and just about anything else within fingering distance. There were about eight couples in all, most unable to stop twiddling with one another even though the object of the exercise was to separate and exchange notes with their counterparts in a neighbouring duo.

She poured herself a coffee and flipped 50p into the pot. The contributions would go towards the unit's new birthing pool, said the handwritten notice. Juliet pulled a face: the exchange of one vessel of murky warm liquid for another, that made sense. The coffee was too hot to drink straight away so she filled a plastic beaker with water and gulped that down. It was hideously sweaty in the hospital antenatal unit; she should never have worn a cashmere polo neck (a sweetly generous Christmas present from Kate), however good it looked. Then she looked at the minuscule nappies pinned to the board behind her and at the pictures on the wall. They were cross-section illustrations of a pregnant woman, month by month, the growing baby gradually colonising her entire body, squishing the intestines and bladder and God knows what else into flat hinterlands. It took some effort not to pause at the third month.

She'd known this was going to be difficult from the moment Hannah had asked her to come. She'd instinctively wanted to decline, but it had been just days since their dog-walking run-in, not to mention that mad dash departure when she'd virtually forced Hannah into Michael's car to drive her to the station.

Then, after the débâcle of New Year's Eve, she'd needed to make amends, *wanted* to make amends.

'Ready, Juliet?' The instructor was a squat athletic woman called Celia who looked as though she knew exactly how to handle one of those scary suction thingamies displayed on a table in the corner. She was handing out cards and telling everyone to put them in order of importance, from 'Sit back and wait' to 'Call 999 at once'. Hannah distributed the cards among their group, eyes sparkling, smiling at everyone. How must she really feel, thought Juliet, the only woman in the group to bring a sister and not a father-to-be? Actually, there was one other woman on her own, a beetle-eyed character whose every comment and question began, 'Mike and I heard that . . .' and ended, 'I must tell Mike we were right about that.' Unfortunate that her partner had the same name as Hannah's. Hannah hadn't mentioned her Michael once so far, nor did she respond in plurals when asked a question. Perhaps she really was going to go through all this on her own. Juliet linked her wrist through her sister's arm and saw the look of pleased surprise before she smiled back.

'"*Contractions every ten minutes lasting thirty seconds*",' Jonathan read aloud. 'What do we think? Sit back and wait?'

'Yes. "*Painless and irregular Braxton Hicks contractions*"?'

'Same.'

'"*The urge to scrub kitchen floor and make a large casserole*"?'

'Same.'

'Your turn, Juliet.'

'Er, "*Diarrhoea*",' she read. 'Call 999 at once?'

It was getting even steamier. Perhaps they'd turned up the heating a notch in preparation for the *pièce de résistance* of the session: the bathing of a newborn from the postnatal ward. Quite a treat for all these cooing rookies. Juliet wriggled in her seat at the sensation of a sweaty film settling between clothing and skin, even in her cleavage. Juliet and cleavage! They were not two words normally used in the same sentence. Shouldn't get too attached to the idea, she thought to herself, taking another big swallow of coffee and trying to pull herself together. The next time she walked through the doors at Imagineer she'd be herself again.

The first few days of work this year hadn't been so bad, partly because Dominic was still away snowboarding. An account director from another team was standing in for Michelle, so Juliet and Phil were bonding over their mutual failure to secure the promotion. She'd been amazed by the relief she'd felt at this; that morning, she'd even filled him in on last night's EastEnders without the slightest temptation to make something up. So Imagineer hadn't worked out; she could cope with that. At least it would pay the rent – and Sasha was on about putting that up by £150 a month from February – until she found something else. She had the *Guardian* in her bag, was going to start applying for new jobs next week.

'OK, everyone ready?' Celia asked. It took a while for the Weebles to get up from the floor, where they'd been spreading out the cards. Jonathan made a big show of helping Hannah up, once Debs was safely seated, before settling himself between the two women like a fertility god. Juliet half-expected him to assume patting and stroking rights for Hannah forthwith. What on earth would Michael say? But she had a funny feeling that had the Fawcett marriage made it to this juncture even without such catastrophic thickening and thinning, Michael still probably wouldn't have come to the class. He was too busy, his work too important. This stuff was for women and Jonathans.

Her thoughts were interrupted by Celia, hovering inches from her face and telling them: 'Diarrhoea is a classic sign of pre-labour. No need to call 999 or even get excited, it's just a very good sign that you're on your way.' At this, Debs pulled a packet of biscuits from her bag and inserted two thick chocolate discs into her mouth at once. Then she offered one to Hannah, but not to Jonathan or Juliet.

'Charming,' Jonathan smirked. 'We obviously don't count!' He looped a stray strand of his wife's hair behind her ear as if to give the next biscuit a cleaner trajectory.

'Now, have a look at these leaflets on perineal massage while I go and get the baby,' Celia said. 'Just take one per couple, please.'

That shut Jonathan up. He looked genuinely appalled.

'Are you going to do this?' Juliet asked Hannah, showing her the diagrams. 'It looks a bit obscene!'

'I don't intend to have an audience,' Hannah laughed. 'Are you OK? Your face is very red?'

'It's so hot in here. Sorry, I'm not being very helpful, am I? I had no idea about the diarrhoea.'

'You've been great,' Hannah said. 'I really didn't want to come on my own. But don't worry, I won't ask you to be the birth assistant. Mum will do it if, well, you know . . . This is actually quite fun, though, isn't it?'

'Yeah,' said Juliet, lowering her voice. 'But I can't stand the KIA, can you?'

'KIA?'

'The Know It All, that woman over there. Wife of the missing Mike. No wonder he's done a runner.'

Hannah followed her nod to watch the woman pull a bottle of oil out of her bag and show the group around her. '*Never* use mineral oil,' she was saying to them. 'Only grape seed or sweet almond.' For a horrible moment Juliet feared she was going to slip her knickers off and demonstrate the massage there and then.

'Oh, one of those,' Hannah laughed. 'Probably a defence mechanism because she's so scared about the birth, don't you think? I tell you, Juliet, it's the weirdest thing, knowing that it's ahead of you, and so *unstoppable*.'

'I can imagine.' Except she wasn't allowing herself to imagine, was she? She'd made her decision; there could be no change of heart.

Hannah seemed to sense her discomfort and changed the subject. 'How are things with Sasha?'

Juliet rolled her eyes. 'Same as ever, getting more strained by the day. Callum's back, of course. The break-up lasted precisely one week. They got back together on New Year's Eve.'

'Oh. An eventful night all round, then.'

'Hmm.' Now Juliet felt nervous that Hannah was going to reopen the case of her disappearing act on New Year's Eve. She was not proud of the fact that she, Fulton and Rachel had climbed across to a neighbouring roof garden and hidden, giggling, while everyone else was summoned inside. She remembered hearing Joby's protests; he'd whined like a five-year-old who'd had a game of Pass the Parcel called off just as he'd reached the innermost layer. Having assumed Hannah and Larry would just head off home, she'd been horrified to discover Hannah had been bundled off in a police car along with several other guests, more horrified still to register her own relief that it had been Hannah instead of her.

Luckily the lights now dimmed and Celia called out, 'Here we are! Everyone come and meet little Daniel!' She had returned with what looked like a marmoset restrained in a blanket full of holes. It was letting out a steady pulse of very feeble squeaks. 'He's exactly one day old and still getting used to the world!'

'Ahhh!' Everyone crowded around as Daniel was unwrapped. His legs began instantly to shudder as though they'd been plunged into icy water and the squeaks intensified. Juliet noticed a woman in pyjamas come into the room walking like a penguin and start taking photos. This was getting surreal.

'That must be the mum,' Hannah said, nudging her. 'Isn't the baby adorable? She must be *so* happy.' Juliet saw that her sister's eyes were shiny with tears and, looking around, that everyone else's were, too. Couples were nuzzling up against one another, exchanging looks as if to say, *That'll be us in a few weeks' time*.

She felt a gush of sheer desperate envy, then, as Daniel was

261

dipped into the baby bath, was seized by a compulsion to snatch up the helpless thing. And what? Run? She imagined the scene. Even if she managed to keep a hold of the slippery creature, she wouldn't get very far, particularly as you needed to know the security combination to get in and out of the unit. Celia would bring her to the ground with a deft swipe of the forceps, the penguin woman would be hysterical. She'd be arrested, of course, or maybe they'd call upstairs for a psych consult like on ER, when Doctor Carter had run out of better ideas. Hannah would never forgive her, would probably have to transfer to another hospital to avoid the humiliation.

Not to run, then, but just to cuddle it, get a little taste of what these women were so ravenous for. She thought again of Luke; he'd been broody in his mid-twenties, often used to ask her what she thought their child might look like, whether it would have her long, slender toes or his chunkier ones. For a while after his death, her worst nightmare had been that the Spanish girl would come forward and announce she was pregnant with his child, that she alone took a real, juicy, living piece of him into the future. As Luke's girlfriend of seven years, and the only serious relationship of his adult life, Juliet would have been forced to withdraw and watch her own stake disintegrate. But the girl hadn't been pregnant, of course, and, a year and a half on, Juliet's stake felt worthless anyway.

'Always keep baby's head and neck supported with one hand,' Celia commanded, 'and keep talking softly, reassuring him everything's OK . . .'

She wondered what would happen if she raised her hand and announced the truth to this group: that she was having an abortion at eight thirty the following morning; that she *did* have an opinion, as it happened, about how it felt to be pregnant; that for today at least she *was* entitled to the chocolate biscuit.

'Will it pee in the water?' Debs asked Celia, notebook and pen in hand.

'You'll be unlikely to notice,' said Celia briskly.

'What happens if it does a *number two*?' one of the husbands asked amid delighted chuckles.

'Then I'm guessing bath time is probably over,' Celia replied, now patting Daniel's scalp dry with a hand towel.

Juliet whispered to Hannah, 'Just going to the loo, I'll be back in a sec.'

'OK.' Her sister's eyes didn't move from the baby in the bath, now kicking quite contentedly and gazing, unblinking, at its mother.

When she came back, ten minutes later, Daniel was gone and a new activity had begun: they were passing around albums of pictures labelled '*Photo diary: Maddy's first twenty-four hours!*'

'Look, Julie, isn't it incredible how she's copying her father by sticking out her tongue?' Jonathan said to her in proud wonder. He held up a picture of a man with a double chin leaning over a shrivelled baby, both with pink tongues poking out.

'Sweet,' Juliet said, passing the picture on. The way she saw it, it was the father who was copying the baby, not the other way round. But when she heard the next group exclaiming exactly the same as Jonathan, she realised she was the only one who saw it differently, the only one who saw any of this differently.

Chapter 24

Bed four was exactly the same as all the other beds: soft narrow mattress, single pillow pressed flat by a thousand heads, bedside table, stiff, waterproof curtain.

'Would you like tea and toast afterwards?' the nurse asked Juliet. She couldn't have been older than nineteen or twenty but already had the bright, disengaged manner of a veteran.

'Yes, no, I mean yes, please.'

'Marmalade?'

'Yes, thank you.'

The nurse wrote this down and moved on. Juliet waited. She almost expected her name to be called over a Tannoy system like in an airport lounge. Would she need to present a boarding pass before they took her into surgery? After all, booking the abortion had been disconcertingly similar to booking a flight.

'I can do a ten a.m. at the Royal Free on January the eighth,' the voice had said. It was some sort of central helpline, impossible to tell where the voice was based: Bristol, maybe, or Bombay.

'January the eighth, but that's weeks away!'

'It's because of the Christmas break,' the voice said. 'Everyone's away. There's nothing available until at least the New Year.'

'What if I go private?' Juliet asked, burgeoning overdraft

forgotten, along with the fact that she still owed Sasha for the last phone and gas bills and hadn't bought her family's Christmas presents yet. 'I really want to get this sorted as soon as possible, preferably before Christmas.'

'That's not going to be possible. You can go to a Marie Stopes clinic out in the East End on January the sixth, but it'll cost you £420. Oh, look, here's an NHS slot in Central London on the fifth, that will be free . . .'

Her mind struggled to follow. 'OK, great, I'll go for that.' *Great*? Not the right word, but the voice didn't care. 'Where is the hospital?'

'Euston. Here's the address . . .' The voice rattled it off, then added, 'Remember that's just for your initial consultation, not for the actual procedure.'

'Well, when will that be? It won't be much longer after, will it?' She was starting to unravel.

'It shouldn't be more than a week later, the doctor will give you a date for the procedure when you go in.'

The 'procedure', that was how they'd referred to it all along. At the consultation, when she'd been examined inside and out and told, 'Yes, you're about ten or eleven weeks,' she had wanted to joke, 'Plus the extra week spent reading magazines in the waiting room.' A further hour was spent in a corridor, next to a girl reading *Gawain and the Green Knight*, a student probably. Juliet thought of Laura. She and the clean-cut Jay wouldn't be so stupid as to find themselves in this corridor, at least she hoped not.

Finally, she was called in to see the counsellor, another proponent of the even, non-judgemental delivery, though this time the face was more watchful.

'It's not the right time for me to have a baby,' she said to the woman, surprised by her own sudden meekness. 'I know I'm nearly thirty, but I'm not in a relationship at the moment.'

'Ever been pregnant before?'

'No.'

'No previous termination?'

'No.'

'Miscarriage?'

'Not if I've never been pregnant before!' Juliet burst out. This was unendurable. She looked around, noticed for the first time that there were no windows. Could there be any place more dismal?

'Now, any questions for me?' The woman didn't even look up from her notes.

Juliet paused. 'No. I mean, yes, if I, y'know, go through with this, will it affect future pregnancies, or whether or not I can get pregnant again?'

'No, shouldn't do, though obviously there is a small risk with every procedure and we can't say for certain. Each woman's body is different.'

Now each woman's body was remarkably similar, Juliet thought, as she caught glimpses of the other girls in their pink gowns, knees bare and vulnerable. The nurse was going around with pessaries, coaching each patient about its insertion, explaining that it would help soften the cervix. Juliet knew the instructions by heart by the time it was her turn.

Occasionally, a low, suppressed murmur could be heard on the ward, spine-stiffening, almost alien – the voice of the male. Boyfriends, not husbands, she guessed. Supportive boyfriends, but unfit fathers. Poor bastards.

She lay back, the pessary doing its unfelt work, and thought of Guy. She had no idea how he would respond if he knew what she was doing at that moment. No doubt he pictured her at her desk, joking on the phone, ping-ponging emails back and forth with Larry about Friday drinks. That was if he still pictured her at all. She wished she'd talked to him on New Year's Eve, even if what Hannah had said was true and he did have a new girlfriend now. But she didn't handle surprise appearances well, never had.

'Bed one.'

'Bed two.'

'Bed three.'

'Three left half an hour ago,' the nurse's voice sang out, making no attempt at confidentiality. 'Slovakian girl. Changed her mind.'

Juliet wondered what percentage of smiley, pink-cheeked babies had once been near-terminations. Her own appointment today had been brought forward by a week thanks to another cancellation. If he knew, the father of her child, would he race over in a taxi and talk her out of it? Would he help her back into her knickers, take her straight home and start planning their future together as a family?

Then it came: 'Bed four.'

Juliet had considered asking Hannah to come and collect her from the clinic, but rejected the idea for the same reason she hadn't told her she was pregnant in the first place: how could you tell someone about to give birth to a baby that you preferred to erase yours?

Instead the job fell to Kate, who arrived too late to witness Juliet's first attempt at standing up, which involved the sloshing of what seemed like a pint of blood down her legs and onto the floor tiles.

'Nothing to worry about,' the nineteen-year-old said. 'You've just filled up a bit, like a cup. Go and pee and you'll flush it all out.'

She burst into tears at the sight of her friend armed with the sort of fruit basket your mother would give you for harvest festival day at school.

'Is it the grapes?' Kate asked anxiously. 'I thought they might be a bit too retro. I've never visited anyone in hospital before!'

'No, they're lovely, thank you for coming. Look at your tan!' Kate had just come back from skiing with her family. Juliet had missed her; there was no one she would rather have with her in this situation.

'Stops at the neck,' Kate said. 'So, did it go all right?'

'I think so, come on, let's get out of here.' She couldn't believe it was finally over. The damp grey walk through Camden and King's Cross that morning now seemed like something from *last* January.

Kate had borrowed her mum's car, which made the whole thing seem all the more teenage. They ate blackcurrant and liquorice sweets from the glove compartment.

'How was your first day back at work? Any news?' Juliet asked.

Kate pulled a face. 'Dominic's back. We think he might be wearing tinted contact lenses, though I suppose it could just be the tan making his eyes look brighter. Larry's still all vague and dreamy. It must be love, and it must be your sister – I saw his tube ticket from Brixton this morning. But he won't tell me anything.'

'He *is* seeing Hannah,' Juliet said. 'It was obvious on New Year's Eve that they were together.'

Kate turned, eyes wide. 'Did you actually *see* them snog?'

'No, but they were holding hands. It was weird, as if Larry was the father of her child.'

'What does Hannah say about it?'

'I asked her at Christmas, but she was very cagey.'

'D'you think they're, you know . . . ?'

'Having sex?' Juliet shrugged. 'She says not. God, this is weird, I can still feel blood seeping out of me . . .'

'Did you get to look at the baby?' Kate asked.

'Of course not. They don't want people freaking out on them, do they? They don't call it the baby anyway.'

'What, foetus? Or, what's it called, embryo?'

'No, not even that.'

'What then?'

Juliet breathed. 'The product.'

'*Product*? Really? That's so cold.'

'Well, it's not exactly a warm and cuddly thing to do, is it? So I guess I'm now back to my old unproductive self.' Juliet adjusted the seat and sank back into a mood of freedom, *renewal* almost, that was completely unexpected. She could see Kate shooting puzzled sidelong looks at her. 'Don't worry, I have taken this very seriously and I don't intend doing it ever again. But I don't want to mope about it. All of this craziness is over. As far as I'm concerned, my New Year starts tomorrow.'

'That's the way to look at it,' Kate agreed. 'Are you going to say anything to Guy?'

'Guy? No, I don't think so.'

'Larry said he was at that party on New Year's Eve as well?'

Juliet turned to look out the window. 'Yes, we said hello. I was a bit out of it, actually, you know when you're on a mission to obliterate everything?'

'You've had a lot to obliterate,' Kate said.

They drove in silence for a while. 'Will Sasha be in?' asked Kate.

'No. Hopefully they'll be out tonight as well. Even she and Caliban go for drinks on a Friday occasionally.'

'She doesn't know about today?'

'No. The only abortion she cares about is the one she's going out with.'

'I can't believe you said that!' Kate giggled.

'Only to you,' Juliet said.

They were approaching Sainsbury's on Camden Road and Kate switched to the inside lane. 'Shall we pick up some chocolates and a DVD? And magazines, we need magazines. I love the January issues.'

'Yeah, New Year, New You,' said Juliet. 'Perfect.'

The next morning, having slept for almost twelve hours, Juliet felt as though she'd undergone deep sleep therapy in a Swiss spa. There was still an ache in her abdomen and some bleeding, so she showered and went back to bed with a glass of water and the last of the paracetamol. It was eight a.m. She couldn't remember the last time she'd been awake at this time on a Saturday.

The whole weekend would be devoted to recovery: she'd have lots of baths, drink and eat nice things from Marks and Spencer (bought with a Christmas voucher to avoid further damage to the overdraft), listen to music with optimistic lyrics, and then start again on Monday where she'd left off. She wasn't exactly sure what she meant by 'left off', only that it had taken place long before yesterday, months ago, maybe years. You've had a lot to obliterate, Kate had said, but she was never going to be able to delete the last eighteen months of her life, however efficiently she pickled her brain. In any case, there had been gains, too: her friendships with Larry and Kate, for instance, and the experience, however chequered, of being independent. Yes, it was time to stop blaming other people.

There was a thump on her bedroom door. She had a funny feeling her new outlook wasn't going to extend to Sasha. Bloody woman. Why didn't she ever go on holiday? Or a weekend away? What did she do with all that salary and rent and the parental handouts Juliet knew she still received? Stasha, Larry called her after she'd joined them for drinks one night and not bought a round in three hours.

Before Juliet could decide whether to admit to wakefulness or not, Sasha marched into the room. She'd obviously forgotten quite how small the room was and came to a slightly unbalanced halt at the foot of Juliet's bed, face set in an unfriendly glower. Juliet could sense Caliban hovering in the hallway.

'Juliet! There's *another* glass broken!'

'What?'

'Yes, this time one of my new wine glasses.'

Oops, Kate must have cracked it when she was washing up

yesterday. They hadn't even used any glasses themselves, prefer-ring dozens of mugs of tea and, finally, a giant hot chocolate with fake cream from one of those spray-gun things. But Kate had been unstoppably helpful, had insisted on washing up a week's worth of dishes and spring-cleaning the whole kitchen while Juliet watched back-to-back old *Dawson's Creek*.

'Wine glasses?' She tried to concentrate on looking serious, but it was difficult lying in bed; she wanted to laugh.

'That's *three* you've broken now!' Sasha's voice was fast rising to a shriek.

Juliet couldn't be bothered to wait for her to get to the point. Why did she always get her knickers in a twist about such insignificant things? 'What do you want, exactly? I'll buy you some new glasses on Monday, plus a couple of extras to make up for it.'

'No, I want them replaced today.'

'Sasha, it's eight in the morning and I've got no plans to go out today anyway. I'm not feeling well, to be honest, and I need to get some more sleep. Shall we talk about this later?'

'No, I want you to *get* up and *go* and get glasses. I'm sick of you disrespecting my things.

'That's it,' Juliet said, pulling the covers off reaching for her dressing gown. 'You know what, Sasha? You can fuck right off.'

Sasha looked at her, astonished. 'What?'

'You heard. You can fuck off, you pikey cow. Is this really all you've got to worry about in the world? I wouldn't give a damn if you broke one of my glasses. Feel free to go and smash what-ever you like! These things happen. Now, please get out of my room.'

'No,' Sasha shot back. '*You* get out of *my* flat!'

'With pleasure.'

'Good!' Sasha stood for a moment as though not quite believ-ing what had taken place, then withdrew at a trot. There were sounds of a scuffle, so she must have backed straight into Caliban. She was like a pony refusing a jump, thought Juliet. She'd be back.

Shaken, she pulled on jeans and a jumper and hunted through her pockets for her mobile phone. 'Hey, Larry. I'm so glad you're up.'

'Juliet? Is everything OK?' After Sasha's histrionics, Larry sounded reassuringly sane. 'Sorry I didn't call last night, I thought you might just want to be on your own with Kate. Did it go all right?'

'Yes, fine, thanks. I'm really glad it's all over. Look, sorry to call so early, I just wondered if I can stay with you for a bit?'

Larry didn't hesitate. 'Sure, it's a bit of a mess, though, I'm not doing very well with the packing.'

'I could help you? Can I come over straight away?'

'Er, I'm not at home at the moment.'

'Oh yeah?'

'I'm at Hannah's.'

'Oh, OK.' Two nights in a row. This was getting worrying. Larry didn't fall very often but, according to Kate, when he did it was more splatter than sprain. There was an awkward pause and Juliet worried she might have spoken her thoughts aloud. 'It's just I've had a row with Sasha,' she said quickly, 'and I'm moving out today. I could try Kate, but she's at her mum and dad's and they're just back from holiday . . .'

'I'll come back now,' Larry said. 'I'll pick you up on the way. Are you OK to get your stuff together on your own?'

'Oh yes, I haven't got much. Thank you.' The benefits of living light. She had no more than a wardrobe of clothes and shoes and a shelf of books, plus an ashtray or two and a few files from the office. The rest of her stuff was at her parents' place in the spare room. She decided to tell them to give anything decent to charity and take the rest to the tip.

'Oh, Larry?'

'Yeah?'

'You haven't said anything to Hannah, have you? About yesterday.'

'No, not a word.'

'Thank you, I don't want to upset her. See you in a bit.'

Listening to her flatmate stomping around the living room and kitchen she couldn't help feeling smug. She wondered how long it would take for Sasha to remember that Juliet had moved in on May the eleventh last year and always paid Sasha her rent on that date, rather than at the beginning of the month. (Amazingly, Sasha hadn't thought to extract a deposit from her.) Today was January the tenth.

'Er, Juliet?'

'Yes?' She smiled sweetly at Sasha's flustered face.

'I've decided you can stay another month if you need to. You probably don't have anywhere to go.'

'Oh, I do, but thanks for the offer. I'll be out of here this morning and the rest of your glass collection will be quite safe.' Would Sasha actually spell it out, she wondered.

'But your rent is due tomorrow . . .' Sasha fidgeted with her ponytail, plainly flummoxed by her own uncharacteristic error.

'I know,' Juliet said, 'it's all worked out very neatly. I'm sure you'll find someone else soon, you're such a lovely laid-back flatmate. Totally un-self-absorbed.'

'You fucking cow!' Sasha pounded back down the hallway and Juliet heard her banging about in her wardrobe and yelling something at Callum. Calmly, Juliet continued folding her clothes into a holdall. Could she dare to hope she'd never have to see either of them again? She was optimistic: the friend Sasha had originally had in common with Hannah had not been mentioned by either of them for months.

She looked out of the window at the garden, owned by the couple in the basement flat who both worked away a lot. It was small for the size of the house and entirely paved over.

They'd had a potted tree in the summer, an olive or orange tree or something totally unsuitable for the climate, but it had soon died. Juliet pulled down the blind. She'd never liked the view.

Chapter 25

Tipped into the corner of a leather sofa, oversized hot chocolate on the table in front of her, Hannah wondered if this investigative jaunt might not have been a mistake after all. She hated being in the City, felt like Nelly the Elephant plonked down on a savannah full of gazelles. Gazelles who all wore slate-coloured Gucci and had New Year skiing tans. Had she ever been one of these animals herself; had she ever been so urgent, so *forbidding*? She supposed the answer must be no, otherwise she'd still be among them now, rushing – well, lumbering – to meetings until the day before her delivery date.

She checked her watch again: one o'clock, forty minutes since Larry had set off in pursuit of Rob. She'd expected him to be back by now. Operation Skirtchaser, he called it. Saving Siobhan, she called it. Saving her from doing anything silly, like letting Rob off the hook and refusing his money.

She'd chosen her moment carefully (Nora in bed, second glass of wine half-finished) and asked Siobhan outright if she'd met Rob MacFarlane during her time at Proctor Mitchum. 'He's tall-ish, dark hair, quite-good looking in a sharp sort of way.'

'You've mentioned him before,' Siobhan said. 'I don't think we did ever meet, but don't worry, I can just imagine the sort of man Lottie is with.' She added that she'd moved from desk to desk at the bank and hadn't had a regular team position, so it was possible that she *had* met him but just couldn't remember how or when. Hannah, who was in no doubt that her sixth sense was spot on about all of this, was undeterred. Of course Siobhan wouldn't know she'd met Rob because she'd never found out her seducer's name. One thing didn't make sense, however. Once she had realised she was pregnant, wouldn't it have been human nature to find out the man's name, even if she didn't intend acting on it immediately? OK, so the company occupied several floors of a huge building, each probably chocker with tallish, quite good-looking types, but it still wouldn't have taken that long to identify Daddy-to-be. Wasn't Siobhan being a bit casual about all of this, too casual to be true, in fact?

So when, later that evening, Hannah came back from her bath to find her friend sneaking her diary into the bottom of a desk drawer, it was only natural that a new suspicion should strike: Siobhan knew exactly who Rob was, was in touch with him already and was feigning ignorance with Hannah because she didn't want her to say anything to Lottie! The next morning she waited for Siobhan to leave with Nora for a check-up at the clinic before going straight to the drawer. She almost cried out in triumph, for there it was, the very next day, January the 15th, in Siobhan's spiky black hand: '*12.30ish – lunch R, Café Septima*'. This was followed by a phone number, which Hannah deliberated over for all of ten seconds before tapping into her mobile. When the voice at the other end announced, 'Proctor Mitchum, can I help you?' she almost gasped from the blood rush. She knew just what she had to do.

'Right. So, I'll be waiting in the coffee place across the road from his office,' she told Larry on the phone after outlining her plan. 'If I'm not there for whatever reason, call me on my mobile.'

'Why not just follow *her*?' Larry asked. 'Why follow Rob? She might not even be meeting him.'

'Of course she is, why else would she be hiding the diary? She must have been rattled by my questioning.'

'Are you sure she was hiding it and not just putting it back where it belongs?' Larry asked.

'Well, who else would "R" be, then?' Hannah countered.

'Er, Rosie, Rebecca, Ralph, Richard, Raquel . . .'

'No one actually knows anyone called Raquel,' she interrupted impatiently. 'Anyway, you can't follow her because she'll recognise you straight away. Just follow Rob to the café and glance in as you walk past to confirm that it's her he's meeting. She'll be concentrating on greeting him so she won't notice you. Then we'll know for sure.'

'That's what I like, strong documentary evidence,' Larry snickered.

'Larry! This is for Siobhan's future. Why should he be allowed to get away with it?'

'Well, if he's meeting her he's hardly getting away with it, is he? And if she's doing exactly what you wanted, then why are you getting involved at all?'

'I just want to check!' She was barely aware of how frantic she sounded. 'That way I can broach the subject with her again this evening. I want to make sure she hasn't let him talk her out of the whole thing.'

'OK, OK, God, remind me never to father a child of any friend of yours! You should work for the CSA.'

Hannah sighed. 'Are you going to help me or not?'

'Yes, of course,' said Larry. 'But what if I bump into her in the street as I'm following him? She might be coming from the same direction?'

'Then just say you're going to a meeting for Imagineer and move quickly on. Better carry a portfolio or something.'

'Yes, sergeant major.'

It all made rather less sense now, of course. As soon as she'd seen Larry stride into view and linger with a couple of smokers to the side of the Proctor Mitchum main entrance, she'd begun worrying. The problem was he was just so conspicuous here among the granite-jawed City boys with their closely cropped haircuts and flashy watches. What had he been thinking of, wearing a battered leather jacket and jeans that obviously hadn't seen the inside of a washing machine this millennium? He looked like a roadie. She watched as he kicked his cigarette end into the road and pulled out his mobile. Her own phone vibrated in her pocket.

'Larry? I can see you. I'm in position across the road.'

'Cool. Listen, I just had a thought, where does *Michael* work? Isn't he somewhere around here? He'll definitely recognise me.'

Hannah had thought about this. 'Not a problem. His firm has just moved to Canary Wharf. Anyway, I think he's in Brussels this week.' She didn't say how she knew this and Larry didn't ask.

'OK, whoops, here he comes, that's Rob, isn't it? The one with the big nose?'

'Yes, get going!'

Rob was on his own and bang on time, twelve twenty. Larry had done a reccy and it was exactly ten minutes from Proctor Mitchum to Café Septima, an old-style Italian place in a side street so small they'd almost missed it on the *A to Z*. Hannah frowned as Rob crossed onto Liverpool Street and headed off in the wrong direction entirely. Covering his tracks, no doubt, just in case anyone saw him with Siobhan and Nora and put two and two together. What were these men like? They made her sick.

She waited till she could no longer see either of them before turning back to her birth plan. It was weird reading notes she'd made back in the autumn. '*I would like my husband to be present in the event of an emergency Caesarean*.' She popped the lid off her pen and wrote '*mother*' over the top of '*husband*'. Then she changed it to '*birth assistant*', but decided to cross that out as well. She *had* to make a decision about whether or not it was going to be Michael. She tried to picture him by her side in the delivery room, but all she could see was that image of him and Nicola together. They were like snakes coiling around one another so you couldn't tell their skins apart, Nicola gripping her thighs at Michael's hips and leaning forward to savage his lips with her own, her long hair splayed over both their torsos, his horrible paws at her breasts . . .

The laughable thing was she hadn't actually seen them having sex, only heard them. She wondered if Michael remembered the exact physical choreography that had blown his marriage apart, or if he'd already blocked it from memory with a firewall of guilt and remorse? If only she had a sense, an instinct, however fleeting, that everything was going to be all right, then she could begin to build a wall of her own. She closed her eyes. Visualisation, that was the key according to a magazine article she'd read about betrayal. She needed to start visualising Nicola from a distance, in faded black and white, as a cartoon character with a silly voice – all techniques that were supposed to help you move away from memories that tortured you.

When she opened her eyes again Larry was there and it was a second before she remembered where she was. She made room for him on the sofa. 'Any luck?'

'I fear you're going to be disappointed,' he said, not sounding at all afraid. 'He didn't go to Café Septima for lunch. He went to some place near the ice rink. Had a drink in the bar first, I think a vodka and tonic. I had a look at the menu – fucking expensive, but then he'll soon find out that fucking can be very expensive, won't he?'

'Ha ha,' Hannah said. 'So you mean he didn't meet Siobhan, then?'

'No. He did meet a woman, though.'

'What did she look like?'

'Blonde, thin, pretty. Dark grey suit.'

That could be anyone. Hell, that could be Lottie. 'Bugger. Anything else?'

'Nope, don't think so. What did you have in mind?' Larry asked.

Hannah bristled with impatience. 'I don't know, some sort of suspicious behaviour.'

'What, like another stab at the marital act in a public place? A half-sister for Nora so she won't be a lonely only?'

'Don't laugh! I know you think I'm nuts!' She felt beyond disappointed by this report, it was more a feeling of being *dismantled*. How could Rob not be the one meeting Siobhan? It was illogical. She couldn't begin to imagine how real detectives lived with the agony of these red herrings and false trails.

'Sorry,' Larry said, taking her hand.

She glared back at him. 'So did you go via Café Septima on the way back and see who Siobhan *was* meeting?'

'No, it was in the other direction. I could go now? But my humble guess is she's meeting an old colleague whose name begins with "R". Rosie, Raquel . . .'

Hannah sighed and Larry began massaging the palm of her hand, squeezing the skin between thumb and index finger until it ached. 'Did you actually ask her what she was doing today?' he asked finally.

'Yes, she just said she was meeting a friend. But I don't understand why she didn't ask me to babysit? Why take Nora with her?'

'Why not? It's the Square Mile not Hamelin.'

'Hamelin?'

'You know, Pied Piper, child snatching and all that?'

'I never said Rob was going to snatch Nora! Oh, don't you see, he could be on his way to Café Septima now!' She was getting hysterical, losing track of her arguments.

'I don't think so. Look, let me just get a coffee,' Larry said. Hannah blinked away tears as she stirred the thickening remains of her hot chocolate. She had no idea why this had become such an obsession, why she was so determined to suspend the rest of life's business until she'd resolved it. She certainly didn't agree with Larry's theory that she was punishing Michael by punishing Rob. 'Classic displacement,' he'd said. 'Either that or you're just off your head of course.' And who could blame him for leaning towards the latter? Following Rob from his office to the lunch restaurant of his choice didn't prove anything except he was a man in possession of a normal appetite and an expense account.

'I thought you might like this marshmallow biscuit,' Larry said when he came back. He'd picked up a *Standard* at the counter and started flapping through it. God, I remind him of marshmallows, Hannah thought glumly.

'I've had a thought,' he said, looking up.

'What?'

'Why don't you have a look at Nora's birth certificate? That will say who the father is, won't it? It must be hanging around the flat somewhere.'

'Oh, Hannah said. 'That's a good idea.'

He put the paper down again. 'If you don't mind me saying, I don't think you're cut out for this sleuthing game. I mean, have you even thought what you're going to do if you're right, if it is Rob? What can you do that Siobhan can't?'

Hannah frowned. 'I can do what she *won't*! Confront him, get him to start paying her regular money. And if she really doesn't want to know, then he could at least start a bank account for Nora or something. Siobhan doesn't realise how expensive Nora is going to be – university is going to cost an arm and a leg in eighteen years' time!'

'What about his wife? I know she's supposed to be a bossy old trout, but aren't you two mates?'

'You can take it from me that it's better to know these things,' Hannah said, cheeks flaming. He'd hit on a point that she'd been deliberately avoiding tackling. If she was right about Rob – and no instinct this powerful could be wrong – did she really have the right to publicly expose his infidelity, his second family? It was obvious that Larry thought not, that she should just let sleeping dogs lie. She repeated the words to herself: *sleeping dogs*. That was exactly what they were, the Robs and Michaels of this world.

'What do *you* think we should do, Larry?'

He tore open a sugar and stirred it into his drink with a plastic stick. 'Shouldn't we just respect Siobhan's privacy? Whether it's Rob's baby or not? She's always very respectful of yours, of *ours*.' Larry had become quite a fan of Siobhan's in the last month or so. 'She's incredible,' he'd said a couple of times. 'She does all this on her own and never complains. My sister never stopped moaning when she had her first child. Anyone would have thought she'd had quadruplets the way she went on about the workload.'

'Yes, maybe you're right,' Hannah said dejectedly.

'Promise me you won't do anything based on a hunch?' he said, graver than she'd ever seen him.

'OK.'

'Being a father is a big deal, you can't just go around accusing anybody . . .'

'I know, I know.' She unwrapped the marshmallow. 'Thanks for helping me today. Are you sure it was all right for you to take the afternoon off again?'

'Don't see why not, everyone's entitled to a sickie now and then. Not much going on with the Smithfield's account anyway. Dominic's been in meetings with them all week. We reckon they might be talking to another agency.'

'Really? That's terrible? Will you still have your jobs?'

Larry pulled a face. 'Couldn't give a monkey's. What's that you've got? Not your private detective's log?'

'It's my birth plan,' Hannah said, showing him.

His eyes scanned the page. '"*I would like to be present in the event of an emergency Caesarean*"? I'm no medical expert,

Hannah, but isn't a Caesarean going to be pretty hard without you?'

Hannah giggled. Larry could always make her laugh. She was glad that nothing physical had happened between them since that first grapple on the sofa, nothing except a little friendly hand-holding and some nice hugs. Yes, she was lucky to have Larry as her friend.

Chapter 26

On the last Saturday in January Hannah woke up late after a particularly uncomfortable night. She immediately knew that something had taken place in her head; her brain felt rinsed out. Finally, she could see her position as it really was: she was almost thirty-four, married, pregnant and sleeping on a sofa. She'd begun the year in a prison cell. How on earth would it end if she didn't take control now? In seven weeks' time she'd be giving birth! OK, so the nocturnal brain irrigation hadn't quite removed the thought of Nicola, but she'd at least become a still rather than a moving image. The visualisation exercises would take care of the rest.

Yes, it was time. She picked up the phone and dialled Michael's mobile. 'It's me, Hannah. Can we meet for lunch?'

'Er, yes, sure.'

'You're not busy?'

'No, I was just going to watch the rugby with the boys.'

'Nothing special then,' Hannah said dismissively.

He didn't come back with some quip about the Five Nations being more important than a moon landing as he would certainly have done a year ago. His breathing sounded careful; she could tell he was standing very still. She had his full attention.

'Can you come to Brixton?'

'Yeah, of course. Shall I meet you at Siobhan's place?'

'No,' Hannah said. 'Let's meet in a restaurant. Nothing too smart, I'm bringing someone.'

'I don't know Brixton at all,' Michael said doubtfully.

'There's a little pizza place on Atlantic Road. Opposite the noodle bar. Can you make one thirty?'

'Atlantic Road . . . OK. Great.'

'Are you sure about this?' Siobhan asked when Hannah rang off.

'I think so.'

'I can cancel work if Nora's a problem.'

'Oh no, not at all,' Hannah said. 'I'll just take her with me. They like babies in there, don't they? And don't worry, there won't be any shouting.'

'Lucky for him,' Siobhan said. 'But don't let him get off too lightly.'

'What makes you think he's getting off?'

Siobhan just gave her a look.

'Some people just do, don't they?' was all Hannah could think to say.

'I'm heading off,' Siobhan said, kissing Nora on the nose. 'There's a jar and some rice cakes in her bag if you need them. Good luck with Michael. Come into the shop later and tell me what happened.'

'Yes, don't worry. It'll be fine.'

Hannah loved being out with Nora on her own, looked forward to the afternoons Siobhan worked at the deli near the station, helping out for cash three times a week. Of course, with her dark hair and darker eyes everyone thought Nora was hers and she'd come to enjoy the sororial frankness open to her as a local mother. Once, queuing up for a coffee in the café in the park, a woman had nodded at Hannah's bump and said, 'That's right, get them out of the way all at once. I had my two sixteen months apart.' She smiled back, liking the idea of Nora being a big sister to her own little man.

Today, she nodded as usual as the other parents at the swings peered at the long-lashed little girl wrapped up in her fairy princess fleece and matching hat, both Christmas presents from Hannah. Then she decided to walk to the restaurant the long way round, past the cinema and through the market. She knew it wasn't just because she was running early that she'd chosen this route: it was a sort of farewell tour. She wanted to remember how she'd felt the first time she'd been shopping on a Saturday morning in Brixton market. She'd been jostled all over the place, shouted at to get on with it, heckled repeatedly for clogging the walkways with Nora's pushchair. In the end, she'd given up and returned to the flat with a single mango. Siobhan had laughed, 'Just ask them where you're supposed to put the bloody buggy? On your head? You need to give as good as you get down here!' Now, as she weaved between shopping bags and shins with expert care, she thought to herself, I must come back here for fruit and veg some time, I'll never find avocados this cheap in Northcote Road.

In the restaurant, Michael was already seated. He wore that rapidly spruced-up look she recognised from hungover work mornings when he was running late to meet a client, still brushing his teeth when Charlotte called to chivvy him along. She felt a surprising gleam of attraction towards him as he sprang up to greet her, kissing her on the corner of her mouth. He smelled of lavender. 'Who's this?'

'Nora, Siobhan's baby. Isn't she a sweetie?' Hannah screwed Nora's portable seat to the table end, settled her in it and gave her a spoon to play with.

'I didn't realise she's had you on babysitting detail all this time,' Michael said, wincing at the sharp crack of Nora's spoon.

'It's the least I can do. And I love it, it's great practice.'

They both looked down at her stomach, bulging through her

beige cashmere V-neck. She'd made no special effort to look desirable but somehow every inch of her skin looked smooth and glossy, even her fingernails looked as though they'd been dipped in baby oil.

'So how's the bump doing?' Michael asked.

'Fine.'

'It's bigger.'

'That's the idea, I believe.'

The waitress approached. 'Our special today is calzone with caramelised shallots, goat's cheese, sliced potato and thyme.'

'I'll have that,' Hannah said. 'And an apple juice and mineral water – sparkling, please.'

'Piccante for me,' Michael said. 'And another beer.'

The waitress left and there was a pause. 'This is all a bit more sophisticated than I expected,' he said. 'Maybe Brixton has changed after all.'

'What were you expecting, fried chicken and corn bread?' Hannah laughed. 'There is life outside SW11, you know. And it's really not that bad down here, actually.'

'Of course. It's very . . . *vibrant*.' He was obviously determined to be agreeable no matter what. 'Are you allowed goat's cheese?' he asked dutifully.

'It's one of those things that I have no idea if it's pasteurised or not,' she said. 'If I want it, it must be good for me.' She was pleased with the attitude she'd pulled off so far, not as ball-breaking as Siobhan would have preferred, but pretty assertive considering the circumstances of their last meeting. He nodded, more humbly than she'd seen before, and clearly puzzled. She couldn't blame him. He'd probably assumed his rescue mission on New Year's Eve had sealed the reconciliation deal, only to be foiled by the single phone call she'd made to him since then, when she'd told him that she was still unsure about things and would be in touch again when she was ready.

'Is he kicking much?' Michael asked, eyes back to her stomach.

'Non-stop, every day. Listen, Michael, the reason I wanted to meet is that I thought I'd come back, move into the new house. That's if it's still what you want, too?'

'Of course it is.' Now his face expressed pleased disbelief.

'And if you genuinely believe you can behave like a normal husband and father.'

'Of course,' he said again. 'This is fantastic.'

'And I don't want to talk about what happened,' Hannah said, eyes narrowing. 'I want to look forward, not back. This is going to be such a special year.'

'I know.'

Nora squealed and held out a napkin to Michael.

'Is that your white flag she's got?' he joked.

'Don't ignore her, Michael, it's a game. She wants to play tug-of-war.'

He gave the napkin a gentle pull and turned back to Hannah. 'I could bring you back today?'

'No, I need to sort things out with Siobhan first, make sure I'm not leaving her in the lurch.'

He nodded, eyes eager. 'We could hire someone to mind Dora if you're committed to any more days?'

Hannah tutted in exasperation. 'It's Nora, not Dora! I hope you won't be so bad at remembering your own child's name!'

'Sorry, Nora. Anyway, Lottie says she knows a good nanny agency.'

He and Lottie must have talked about how he would manage with his visits if he and Hannah divorced; or perhaps they'd even cooked up a plan to go for sole custody. The New Year's incident wouldn't have helped Hannah's cause, she was only too aware of that. 'No, I can still help Siobhan out myself, while I've got the energy at least; it's just a few minutes from us by car.'

'Hmm.'

Hannah cast another unimpressed glance at him. 'That's another thing. You and Lottie seem determined to see Siobhan as a bad influence when you don't even know her,' she said. 'Well, I'm sorry, Michael, but that's just not acceptable. Believe me, your unborn son owes a lot to her kindness.'

'Oh, come on,' Michael said, smiling. 'You were never on the street.'

'How would you know?' Hannah said. 'I could have been sleeping in Brockwell Park for all you know.'

'Where?'

'Anyway, I'm not interested in arguing with you. You'll just have to accept the fact that Siobhan is now a good friend and I hope our son and Nora will be close, too.'

'OK, but I'm not sure Junior will be into older women, not at first, anyway.'

Hannah had to smile. 'Give them a chance.'

They were both watching Nora now. Napkin dropped, her attention was divided between their faces and the bowl of oil and vinegar in the middle of the table. Was it Hannah's imagination or was that splash of Rob stronger than ever in the curve of the child's chin? Her nose was small, but they sprouted later, didn't they? She thought about what had happened with the birth certificate. She'd been prepared to snoop but hadn't had to; Siobhan had been doing some decluttering and had had a pile of Nora's papers out on the kitchen table. Hannah had been so certain of what she would find she'd been dialling Larry's number in her mind before she'd even scanned down to the section headed 'Father'. But all there was was a black dash. Father's details not recorded. That was that then, Larry had said, but Hannah saw it differently. OK, so Siobhan might not be in touch with Rob after all, or even know his name, but that didn't mean he wasn't the father. After all, the child was practically a deadringer.

'Michael, do you think Rob is faithful to Lottie?'

'What?' Michael was visibly rocked by this and even flushed slightly. 'I imagine so.'

'I mean, it's obviously easy to sleep around in that environment – sexual morals aren't too high on the list in the City, are they?'

'Maccas is more interested in money than sex,' Michael said, squinting at her over the top of his glass. 'And so would you be if you saw the bonus he trousered last year.'

'But say he was,' Hannah persisted, 'in those situations, you know, one-night stands, would condoms be used?'

'I thought you didn't want to talk about this?' Michael said, shifting in his seat.

'I'm not talking about *you*. I can only hope you were careful and your office lover isn't pregnant with your child?'

'She's not in my office any more,' Michael said.

'I also assume she's not your lover any more?'

'Of course not.'

Hannah chuckled to herself and Nora joined in, doing her funny snorting face. Michael looked back and forth between the two of them with something close to fear. 'What do you mean about Rob? Are you saying you think he's been playing away? That he's got someone *pregnant*?'

His eye had settled on Nora and Hannah saw she'd gone too far. 'Of course not,' she said quickly. 'I just see him and Lottie as being very compatible, more than we are, for instance, and I just wondered if there were any cracks, you know, underneath that perfect public face.'

'I'd hardly call their public face perfect,' Michael said. 'They're always bickering. Anyway, there are cracks in all relationships, aren't there?'

'Are there?' He gave the impression that this was brand-new conversational territory for him. Was it possible that he hadn't properly discussed his own predicament with a soul? Lottie would have bullied a few details out of him, she was sure, during those sessions when she'd found him eating innutritious snack foods in front of the TV, but she could imagine Rob and the boys carrying on as though nothing had happened, just as they had with her at the MacFarlanes's party.

'I think everyone expects that, don't they?' Michael said. 'We all go through thick and thin, don't we?' This was a common Fawcett strategy, the invocation of some invisible army of the likeminded. 'Everyone' had marital difficulties, therefore by definition it couldn't be anything special, could it?

'I'm not sure,' Hannah said. 'It seems to me that "nobody's perfect" is a very convenient argument for those who obviously aren't.'

She could tell he was itching to use some blinding bit of rhetoric to shoot her down, but instead he said, 'Oh, look, here's our food.'

'Fab, I'm absolutely *starving*.' She cut a huge piece and began chewing.

'I'm so pleased you're coming back,' Michael said, spotting his opportunity to get the conversation back on track. 'I'm not sure I've made Salcott Road very homely on my own.'

'There's lots of stuff we need to buy,' Hannah said. 'Are there even any curtains up?'

'Helena left the blinds,' said Michael. 'And Lottie says there's a sale on at the Designers Guild.'

'Right.'

'I've bought some baby clothes,' he added. 'And my mother dropped off a load of old stuff. But I can't see you wanting Junior in purple crocheted trousers and matching waistcoat.'

Finally, Hannah allowed herself a giggle 'What a shame her Chanel rule doesn't extend to babies! Maybe you should come to the NCT antenatal classes,' she added. 'Juliet's been with me to the hospital ones, but I'm not sure it's really her thing.'

'Just let me know the dates and I'll get Charlotte to block out my diary.'

To Michael's plain relief the conversation continued in this way as they ate their pizzas. She wondered if he would want to have sex with her as soon as she returned, or whether they would wait until after the baby. Deep inside her body, through the layers of food and drink and baby and fluid, she thought she felt something that might be lust. But then she identified it as a little lunge of regret for Larry.

Chapter 27

Lottie was on the phone ten times a day the week before the baby shower. Her vast extended kitchen with its polished marble floor and walnut table for twelve was the natural operations HQ and Hannah had got into the habit of popping in first thing in the morning for an update and a decaf cappuccino. She was busier now than ever before, shopping for things for the house, reconfiguring Michael's attempts at layout and decoration, finally getting around to choosing wedding photos for framing and arranging the rest in albums. There was something about this last task that helped make her feel the marriage was real again. OK, so things with Michael weren't quite as they'd been before, but it was good enough. He was even coming home at a civilised hour each day, making a point of noticing everything she'd done with the house, praising her fabric and colour choices and not once questioning the cost. Finally, they were living somewhere with her stamp on it.

'For once there's something in this American schmaltz,' Lottie said, looking up from her gift registration file and remembering to wink at the Virginian nanny. 'No offence, Hilary, you're practically a Brit yourself these days. But I mean gifts, Hannah, you'll get truckloads of good stuff. There'll be the usual Tiffany trinkets, of course, but you might just get a

293

nappy bin or something useful as well. Maybe one of those nappy-wipe warmers.'

'They're good,' Hilary agreed. 'Ophelia hates cold wipes on her bottom.'

'But they made her giggle when it was really hot, do you remember?'

Every so often Lottie would say something that made Hannah see that she was a more hands-on mother than everyone gave her credit for. Those months with Siobhan had taught her that motherhood was not just a double but a triple shift, with all weekend and holiday entitlement suspended till further notice. So even with nanny, au pair, cleaner, gardener and whoever else Lottie conducted with such virtuoso ease during the day, in the dead of night it was she who was on duty.

'We'll need to set up a play area for the kids in the sitting room. The playroom is just too far away. Hil won't mind supervising.'

'Sure,' Hilary said. 'They'll have fun. Maybe I'll sort out all Ophelia's drums and xylophones and stuff.'

'That's the music taken care of, then,' Lottie laughed.

Hilary got to her feet. 'I'm upstairs if you need me. I'm just gonna check on her.'

'I'd like her to nap for longer if possible,' Lottie told her. 'She had a very early start today.'

'Will there be children at the shower, then?' Hannah asked when Hilary had gone.

'Well, Ophelia, of course. She's looking forward to showing off her new cruising skills. Emily will be bringing Stanley and Rosie and I assume whatshername will also bring, oh, whatshername?'

'Lottie! You know their names: Siobhan and Nora.'

'Of course, sorry, Siobhan and Nora,' Lottie repeated with an indulgent smile. 'Now, food. We need minimum stain snacks if we're going to be in the sitting room. Are there any vegetarians coming? Let's have another look at the confirmed guest list.'

Hannah didn't like to admit that she'd be hard pushed to pick out a vampire from this list, let alone a vegetarian, as half those coming were Lottie's friends. It had been a bit embarrassing to discover she'd now given up on almost every pre-wedding friendship she had cared about. Or was it merely that she'd finally let go of the pre-Michael friendships that had managed to survive as long as the wedding? Either way, she was too ashamed to renew contact with people with the express purpose of inviting them to another event that occasioned an expensive gift. To make matters worse, Marianne and Gayle would both be away for their annual winter sun rations, having strategically scheduled breaks to allow a generous countdown to the big day. Laura, of course, was pleading poverty over the train fare. She tried to concentrate on Lottie's list. 'Vegetarians, no, I don't think so. But I suppose everyone will be on a diet, except me of course.'

In the end she'd included Rani – who she knew would be amazed at the invitation – and a handful of brand-new acquaintances from her antenatal course. With Juliet, Juliet's friend Kate, Anya, Fiona, and Lottie's sister Emily, in town that weekend for a Sunday wedding, the numbers were respectable enough. And Siobhan, of course. The two of them hadn't been able to meet up nearly as much as Hannah would have liked since she'd moved out, for it seemed impossible to find a time when she wasn't shackled to the house for deliveries or for supervising the new bathroom and decorating works. The one time Siobhan had visited her at Salcott Road she'd had to abandon her for an hour while she refereed an argument between the decorator and the delivery guys trying to squeeze a new fridge through the newly painted basement door.

If that wasn't bad enough, she'd then forgotten a longstanding babysitting arrangement because Michael wanted her to go with him to dinner with Simon and Alice – the last time she'd seen them was at the hotel in Stellenbosch – and she'd got into such a frenzy about it Siobhan and Nora had totally slipped her mind. Siobhan had been fine about it, of course, said she'd been able to get her new childminder at the last minute, but Hannah still felt awful. She didn't want what had happened with Juliet to happen with Siobhan; she wouldn't allow their friendship to slip.

'I'll get Kasia to do something for the kids' tea,' Lottie was saying, scribbling a memo as she spoke. 'Maybe sausage and mash, that's easy for all ages. Will that be OK for Nora? Is she a good eater like Ophelia?'

'I'm sure she'll be fine with that.' For the first time Hannah considered the fact that Ophelia and Nora were going to be together in the same room, in the same infant orchestra! Would anyone notice a likeness? Probably not, as Ophelia was pale and dainty like Lottie, whereas Nora was dark-haired and robust like Siobhan, like Rob . . .

Lottie's mobile rang. 'I'd better take this,' she said.

'I'll just go for a pee,' Hannah told her, pulling herself up.

Time spent visiting the loo was almost starting to exceed that spent on all other activities put together, but she enjoyed using the Floris goodies in Lottie's cloakroom (her guest brand only – upstairs, in the master en suite, were products Hannah knew for a fact were wait-listed at Selfridges). When she came back, Lottie was still talking, so she looked in the fridge for something sweet, settling in the end for a fromage frais and a banana.

'I'm sorry, but that's not acceptable,' Lottie said into the phone, as fiercely as Hannah had ever seen her. 'Please interrupt his meeting. I'll hold.' She put her hand over the receiver and hissed to Hannah, 'I've got ten grand commission sitting in this idiot's client account. That's made with formula milk, you know, Han, are you sure you want it? Hello? Yes, still here. OK, bear with me, I just need to get that document from another room.'

As she swished off down the hall, Hannah thought about Siobhan behind the counter at the deli. Ten grand! *Her* earnings must barely cover what she paid the childminder, and the extra babysitting session must have been a blow. And yet it could all be solved with a simple paternity suit! There she was, vowing not to let things slip with Siobhan and yet she'd done nothing to help with the paternity case since finding the birth certificate. She blamed Larry for the temporary lapse in investigations; they'd even had a row about it the last time they'd met. 'Just give it up,' he'd pleaded, more impatient than she'd seen him before. 'Let Siobhan decide for herself.' They hadn't even hugged when they'd parted, and when she'd later phoned to say she was moving back in with Michael he'd been distinctly chilly, even though it could hardly have come as a surprise. Well, Larry might have lost faith in her mission, but she hadn't. Lottie would be fine whatever happened, anyone could see that, but nothing could change the fact that Rob had responsibilities. All Hannah needed was something to get her back on track, a new clue, a sign.

And then she saw them. Sitting on the lower shelf of the side table by the sofa, two DVD box sets still in their shrink wrap. The first one was *Big Screen Legends: Cary Grant*. She had to squint a little to see the second but her brain had already anticipated the words: *Big Screen Legends: David Niven*. This was a sign all right, a great big glittering, neon-lit sign. Before she could stop herself she had picked up the nearest phone and was ringing the number she'd committed to memory since first seeing it in Siobhan's diary. Silently, she began rehearsing Siobhan's accent, a sort of even, neutralised Northern. *Hello, is this Rob MacFarlane? My name is Siobhan Barnes . . .*

'Proctor Mitchum, can I help you?'

'Rob MacFarlane, please.'

'One moment.'

'Yep? This is Rob. Hang on.'

She waited for him to come back on the line, thrilled with herself for not succumbing to cowardice and hanging up. 'Is this

Rob MacFarlane?' Not a bad impersonation at all, just needed a little extra dash of no-nonsense.

'Yep, speaking.'

'Rob, it's Siobhan.' Too much no-nonsense now, she felt like a headmistress.

'Who?'

'Actually, you won't know my name.' Yes! Perfect Siobhan: even, direct, pleasant.

'You what?'

'I used to work for Proctor Mitchum.'

'Oh, right. What's up?'

She took a deep breath. 'We had sex, Rob. In a bar near work, about eighteen months ago.' The voice was getting nervous now, turning Welsh. Hannah sensed this was going wrong.

Rob spoke: 'Are you having a laugh? What did you say your name was?'

'It doesn't matter,' Hannah said, timid now.

'Well, I can assure you we have not had sex, whoever the fuck you are!' He was brusque, impatient, and totally one-hundred-per-cent genuine: he had no idea who she was. Bugger. *Bugger.* Then, unexpectedly, he hooted with laughter. 'Hang on a second, who put you up to this? Was it Scummings? That dirty bastard . . .'

Hannah hung up, shaking badly, but the landline rang straight away. Without thinking, she picked up. 'Hello, MacFarlane residence.'

'This is Rob. Who's that?'

'It's Hannah. Hi, Rob, how are you?'

'Oh, hi there, Hannah. Did someone just call me?' Disaster! He must have caller ID, what had she been thinking of taking such a risk? She imagined him scouring the ranks of Lottie's helpers in his mind, trying to put a face to Adam Cummings's accomplice. Hearing Lottie's footsteps in the hallway she toyed with the idea of faking a waters-breaking moment and getting off the hook that way. Or just bundling the phone into the nearest cupboard and dashing home. Then she remembered the handset in the cloakroom. Rob had landlines in every room in the house, he even made phone calls when he was shaving, Lottie said. He'd obviously been juggling calls just now, so maybe he'd assume he'd made a mistake and forget all about this. Calmness descended.

'Hannah? You still there?'

'Yes, sorry. No, I don't think Lottie called you, she's taking a business call on her mobile right now. And Hilary's upstairs with Ophelia. And I think Kasia's at Sainsbury's.' *Too much information, stop now.* 'And I was just in the loo.' *Shut up.*

'All right,' said Rob. 'The system must be playing up again. Everything OK with you?'

'Yes, fine thanks.'

'You and Tappy still coming for dinner on Saturday?'

'Yes, looking forward to it.'

'Not long to go before D-day, eh? Look, I've got to go, cheers, bye.'

'Bloody conveyancers,' Lottie said, returning to the kitchen a minute later. 'No sense of urgency whatsoever. This was supposed to have completed before Christmas.'

Breathing quickly as she struggled to separate disappointment from relief, Hannah thought it best not to mention Rob's call.

Chapter 28

Juliet was late again. At least it wasn't her own fault this time, she wasn't even hungover, but the Northern Line had signal problems and they'd been stuck in a tunnel outside Kennington for twenty-five minutes. Correction: thirty minutes. Clearly the tube was no better south of the river than north. What was more, Larry found it amusing to pass the time recalling his top ten most claustrophobic tube experiences. She tried to listen but kept getting distracted by the flaps of extra heat from either side of her as people wrenched off first scarves and coats, then jackets and ties. One man in particular worried her: he looked like he was seconds from freaking out – maybe Larry was pushing him over the edge as well. She could count the individual droplets of sweat that had gathered at his hairline.

'It was like that scene in *The Great Escape*,' Larry said. 'You know, when Donald Pleasance goes ape . . .'

'I know the bit,' Juliet frowned. 'Shh!'

'I'm just saying it's unnatural, being all the way down here . . .'

The man was searching the rows for reassurance, but no one wanted to catch the eye of the One Most Likely to Be a Crazed Killer. Juliet stopped counting the sweat drops, didn't want to be his first victim when the lights failed . . . Then the train jolted forward and everyone got back to their newspapers, not incinerated, not murdered, just late.

At her desk, the Post-its were everywhere, and an email waited that had been sent an hour ago. It was flagged urgent. Dominic wanted to see her. Michelle's stand-in Sylvie was giving her the evil eye, she could feel the death rays cauterising the side of her neck, and she was certain other people were staring, too. If only Larry or Kate sat up here and not in the pit, they'd give it to her straight. *Yep, sorry Juliet, but you're a goner.*

She took the plunge and met Phil's eye. 'You'd better go straight up,' he said quietly. There was no mistaking it, she was experiencing *pity* from Phil Swain. In a way it was decent of him, for he must have guessed it was between the two of them. Dominic had fired two account executives the week before – didn't call it 'firing' of course, it was voluntary redundancy and seemed to be picking one off from each team. He was swift, systematic, probably saw himself as a World War Two sniper. *Nothing personal, Juliet.*

She'd checked her contract as soon as the redundancies started and found that were it to happen to her she'd be entitled to just two weeks' pay. She did the mental calculations as she checked the rest of her emails (lunch with Mark K? Not if her company credit card was toast). Two weeks' money would pay off her overdraft, but then what? She hadn't had a single response from the seven jobs she'd applied for and the two headhunters she was using were behaving as though theirs were the only heads worth hunting. Well, at least rent wasn't a problem. She was staying at Larry's new place in Sisters Avenue for the time being, paying him in alcohol; there was a pub on Lavender Hill he'd grown attached to. He wouldn't take money, especially as she was sleeping on an airbed until the sofa arrived.

'Good luck,' Phil said as she stood up. She prayed she wouldn't cry.

As she walked through the office she felt that everyone knew she was on her way out. She cursed herself for not taking her bag; now she'd have to go back and get it rather than slipping straight into the lift from the third floor and leaving Imagineer for good. What was weird was that she loved the company at that moment. Loved it in spite of the politics and the gadget porn and the ridiculous paper-free procedures instituted after Dominic's visit to an agency in San Francisco (following a campaign led by Larry, Post-its had been declared exempt); in spite of the tube horror stories and competitive hangovers and £3 takeaway coffees drunk out of that little slot thing in the lid – why did no one ever take the lid off? She loved it in spite of the *spite*. She *liked* the spite.

Dominic was sitting at his corner desk on the fourth floor. The combination of the sharpest shave and costliest suit she'd ever seen was intimidating. He had a cardboard cut-out of Top Cat silhouetted against the window. A Christmas present, perhaps, or a bit of ironic self-gifting to celebrate his second successive appearance in a national newspaper's annual rich list the previous weekend.

'Got a new imaginary friend?' she asked him. My God, she even loved Dominic this morning. Where the hell was this sentimental strain coming from? It was disarming, just when she needed to feel fully armed.

Dominic looked up. 'Not imaginary, Juliet, just two-dimensional, therefore closer to the human model than you might think.' What did *that* mean? Was she being fired for being too thin? 'Come on,' he said, standing. 'Let's go down to the boardroom. This is confidential.'

'I'm sorry I've been late a few times recently,' she said, scurrying to catch up with him, 'I'm getting used to a new commute.' She couldn't believe she was scurrying; scurrying was not cool, especially when combined with pre-emptive apologies. Never apologise, never explain: Larry was constantly trying to drum it into her and Kate, said it was the difference between men and women. Juliet just thought it was the difference between people who dealt directly with the client and those who whiled away their time reading the paper and playing the Kipling game. *If you were about to be sacked and had one chance to save your skin . . .*

'Where've you moved to?' Dominic asked.

'Sisters Avenue, near Nappy Valley.'

'Where the fuck is that?'

'Battersea, or Clapham – to be honest I can't work out which.'

'I thought you said you'd never live south of the river?'

'It's just temporary.' Like everything else lately, everything since Luke. And now, just as she was craving permanence again, she was about to get the boot.

He slid the boardroom door closed behind them and closed the blinds. *In case I cry*, she thought. 'Right, I've got some news. Shall we sit down?'

'Of course.'

Dominic paused. She knew he was enjoying her fear. 'You may know from Sylvie I've been meeting with Smithfield's all week about renewing contracts.'

'Yes.'

'I had lunch with Polly and Sir Alfie a couple of days ago.'

'Oh?' She strained to think of something to say to this. 'Are they still shagging?'

'What?' Dominic looked appalled.

'Sorry, that's not relevant.' She was nervous, nerves always made her blurt.

'Not *relevant*? It's beyond the scope of human comprehension! Glad I didn't know that the other day, it would have put me right off my beef Wellington.' He grinned and she relaxed. 'Anyway, they've just signed with us for another year.'

'Congratulations.' Maybe she'd get more than two weeks after all, for old times' sake.

'Your name came up,' Dominic said. The expression on his face was strangely benevolent.

'Oh?' She squirmed, then sat on her hands.

'Apparently the job swap wasn't quite the waste of time we all thought.'

'I never said it was a waste of time,' she protested.

'I didn't mean you. To cut to the chase, your idea is going into the tunnel as of next week.' The *tunnel*. Another thing she wouldn't miss, the jargon. Hang on, *her* idea?

'What idea?'

'Cuff him! Classic Juliet – their first new range in two years and you don't even remember! The unhealthy treats for carb-craving pissheads, that's what. Your Morning After range.'

Juliet looked at him agape. 'Oh, I'd forgotten about that. I didn't think Polly particularly liked it.'

'Well, Sir Alfie particularly did. They hope to launch in less than eighteen months if we can get the marketing right. Part of their ongoing strategy, as you may know, is to target students and first-jobbers. They're finally being perceived as cheaper than Tesco and Safeway.'

'Great.'

'By the time we've finished, Smithfield's will *own* hangovers. As far as I'm concerned, if you're not dependent on alcohol already then you'll want to be when you see this brand. Hey, that's an angle, Jules! Cool guy *fakes* hangover just so he can eat The Morning After bagel!'

'That's fun,' Juliet said. This was surreal.

'I'd like you to start thinking about celebrity endorsements straight away. Someone famously clean-living would be good. Obviously that cuts out your immediate circle.'

'Ha ha.'

He leaned forward, elbows on the table. 'And the other thing is they've suggested that you take over as account director. Branding the new range will be a big part of what we do for them this year and it's obviously your baby. Of course, it's my call.'

This was beyond surreal, this was fairy godmother territory. 'What about Michelle?' she asked.

'Oh, she probably won't come back. If she does, we'll find something for her.' He's dismissed her completely, Juliet thought, she no longer exists. Remind me never to have a baby while I'm working here. She felt herself grimace and tried to turn it into a smile.

'What's up?' Dominic asked. 'Not Sir Alfie and Polly again?'

'No, nothing.'

'So, account director? You up for it?'

'Of course.'

'Cool. And they wanted me to let you know that because you were working at Smithfield's at the time you submitted the idea, you're eligible for their in-house staff reward scheme. Not a lot, just a couple of grand I think. I'll find out and pay it through your salary.'

'Right.' She couldn't decide whether she was going to punch the air or fall down faint.

'I'll also be adding an Imagineer bonus to your salary this month. I sometimes do this when an account director helps bring in new business. Goes without saying that it's at my discretion and totally confidential.'

Juliet had a sudden, faint memory of the Negotiation Strategy for Nice Girls. 'How much?'

'I thought two months' salary would be about right.'

Wow. She didn't know what to say, but one look at the inflated satisfaction on his face made her shelve any immediate plans for a show of gratitude. She forced her grinning lips into a pout. 'I'm not sure, Dominic. I mean, I didn't get a Christmas bonus, or the quarterly bonus in October.'

'Didn't you? Well, let me look into that and rectify the over-sight,' Dominic said hastily. 'And of course the new business bonus will be two months of your *new* salary.'

'New salary?'

'Yes. I need to talk to finance about figures, but I imagine we can do something in the region of a twenty-five per cent increase. And I'll get Emma to talk to you another time about the share options for the senior team.'

He grinned at her and at last she grinned back. 'Do I need to know a secret handshake as well?'

'Only Top Cat knows that.'

'That's fair.'

'So, tell me, how did you come up with the idea?' Dominic asked.

She thought. She remembered the meeting now. She'd been out with Fulton the night before, had meant to say something to him about that weekend with Rachel, but in the end they'd just downed martinis and danced around the subject until Rachel herself had pitched up, even drunker than they were and with clear ambitions for round two. And wasn't that also the day she'd finished with Guy? Had so much time passed already?

She saw that Dominic was waiting for her answer. 'Er, I don't know, to be honest. I just imagined what I fancied eating at that moment.'

'Well, for once I have to approve of my staff getting wankered every night. I'll ask Emma to announce this company-wide, of course, but let's get the team together now and tell them the news. Sylvie'll round them up . . .' He was thumbing through the numbers on his mobile – this was Dominic all over, he never used landlines – when she heard herself speak up suddenly: 'Dominic, before we tell the others, I wanted to ask you . . .'

'Yes?' The phone still hovered at his ear.

'What was it that happened at the Grosvenor that night, y'know, back in November?'

He snapped the phone shut. 'How d'you mean?'

'It's just that you said no hard feelings, that time I fainted, something like that.'

'Remind me which night?'

'It was the *Media Today* awards do at the Grosvenor, we went with Phil Swain and the three Marks. Polly was on holiday, so we gave the spare tickets to some of the creatives.'

'Oh, yeah, I remember. You did rush off a bit abruptly, maybe it was that.'

'Rush off? I just sort of need to know, did we . . . ?' This was excruciating. From tomorrow every word she uttered to Dominic would be purely professional, no syllable would ever again betray the fact that she'd once touched his penis. From tomorrow, as far as she was concerned, he didn't even have one.

'Did we what?' he asked, starting to grin. 'Are you *blushing*, Juliet?'

She was. 'Well, did we sleep together that night? In the cloakroom maybe?'

Dominic let out a shout of laughter.

'Tell me!' she pleaded. 'I drank so much, I just can't remember anything from about nine o'clock onwards!'

He walked around the table, pulled the back of her chair out, as though helping an infant down from the adults' dining table. 'Fuck the hangover range, Juliet, you could do with eating a bit more the night before! How often do you black out like this?'

'Only that night,' she muttered, humiliated. She was glad he was still hovering somewhere behind her and she didn't have to see his face.

'And do you really go around having sex in cloakrooms? Get a room, for God's sake, you were in a hotel after all!'

'Please,' Juliet said, eyes closed.

Dominic sat down beside her, so close she could see the shine on his lips where he must have licked them. 'Well, no, we did not have sex. But I do seem to remember a conversation about the times we did. Not all of your remarks were the most flattering I've received, I have to say, and I was less than delighted to have them aired in front of the Smithfield's marketing team.'

'Oh.' So not Dominic, then, and not that night.

'But I suggest we forget all of that now,' he said, 'and start afresh.'

'Yes, afresh.' She liked that.

'Exactly. A clean slate.'

'A new leaf,' she added.

'Now, is this a Radio Four nerdy-wordy quiz or shall I call the team in and make this announcement?'

'Yes, please.'

He turned back to his phone. 'Polly and Sir Alfie, eh? The horny old goat.'

Juliet had no idea which of them he was talking about.

Chapter 29

Ringing Lottie's doorbell with Kate by her side, one clutching silver-wrapped packages and the other a bunch of gerberas, Juliet found that she was really rather excited about the baby shower. She hadn't thought about it properly before, but this was going to be her first nephew, her parents' first grandchild. He would outlive them all – now that was a pretty permanent fixture in the temporary shack that was her life.

'This place is *huge*,' Kate whispered. 'What's Lottie like?'

'She's OK,' Juliet said. 'She was very bossy when she was helping Hannah organise the wedding. Kept tasking me with all the things they obviously didn't want to do themselves. Her husband's been shagging around as well, according to Larry.'

'Oh, is he the one who . . . ?'

'Shh! Someone's coming.'

The door swung back and Lottie beamed down at them, casually perfect in dark blue flares and a zipup top. 'Hello, girls, come on in.'

Juliet had never seen anyone as charged, as *in charge*, as Lottie. She could run for prime minister. So what if her husband was playing away, she looked like she'd have him successfully rehabilitated before breakfast if she ever got around to giving two hoots. Her manner was a perfect balance of regal and chummy, as she spoke first to a waitress patrolling the room with canapés and then to a pink-cheeked minion guarding a cage full of babies. She shepherded Juliet and Kate towards Hannah, who was sitting in the middle of a huge room in what looked like a bath chair. Had she lost the use of her legs? She looked as though she'd need to be airlifted to the maternity unit any minute now.

'Gifts go on the table, please,' Lottie told them. 'Hannah will be with you in a jiffy. Oh, and congratulations on your promotion, Juliet, she's so proud of you.'

Yes, she could learn a lot from this woman, and God knew she needed a few new tricks to keep her team under control. It hadn't been easy making the transition from notorious boozer who couldn't keep track of her sexual shenanigans to respected account director and shareholder. She'd even cut out midweek drinking to keep a clear head for the morning catch-ups she'd instituted for the first few weeks. *That* hadn't been popular with the gang. And behind her though Dominic was (literally behind her, as it turned out, forever pressing the trades at her, bringing clients to meet her, even delivering Starbucks), he was still Dominic, a royal pain in the proverbial.

'Juliet! And Kate! Thank you so much for coming!'

'You look like you're almost there,' Juliet said, kissing her sister.

'I look like a bus,' Hannah replied. 'A big, fat, *parked* bus. Thanks for the pressies, I hope you didn't feel pressured into buying anything too expensive?'

'We got the list,' Juliet said. 'But we didn't think we could carry a maternity rocking chair with foot stool on the tube.'

Hannah laughed. 'It's great you're here. Laura claimed she couldn't raise the train fare, of course, and Mum's still in Portugal.'

'Well, I'm just up the road now,' Juliet said. 'It's all very convenient.'

'Oh yes. Funny, I never think of Sisters Avenue these days. Except to think that you're there, of course.'

And Larry, Juliet thought to herself.

'Everyone's here now, Hannah,' Lottie said, before clearing her throat and calling out, 'Have we all got bubbles? Here's a glass, Juliet. All teenies in a safe place? Good. Then let's open the presents!'

As the booty piled up at Hannah's feet – cashmere blankets, sheepskin hat and mittens, embroidered laundry bags, appliquéd sailing-boat bed linen – Juliet found herself staring at a woman on the other side of the room who had a very beautiful round face and dark hair unravelling from pigtails. There was something about her, something serene, almost moral, that set her apart from the rest of this sharp-eyed, designer-shrink-wrapped bunch. She tried to catch her eye, but gave up when an Asian woman in vertical stripes squeezed onto the sofa next to her and began talking with great determination.

'Wow! What a gorgeous cosytoe,' Hannah was exclaiming. 'Thank you so much, Fiona!'

A short-legged woman with panda eye-make-up beamed and said, 'I couldn't resist going for the fur-lined suede.'

Juliet, who had no idea what a cosytoe was, was starting to fret that her own gift, a teddy holding a keyboard that played lullabies, might seem a bit pedestrian compared to this mass of luxury fabrics. This whole thing was way over the top – someone was now wheeling up a chest of drawers!

'Has your sister found a nursery yet?' asked the woman sitting on the other side of Kate.

'Oh, I don't know,' Juliet said politely. 'Sorry.'

'Surely it's too early for that?' Kate said. 'The baby's not even born yet.'

The woman looked at Kate as though she was the most tragic case of special needs she'd encountered in a long time. 'But she'll need to get her name down straight away. It's probably too late already for anywhere decent.'

'Oh, rubbish,' said Lottie from a couple of seats away.

'Hannah hasn't even decided on her childcare yet. She's talking about doing it all herself.'

Juliet watched as Lottie and the woman exchanged 'She'll learn' looks.

'Anyway, people really do need to stop following the crowd,' Lottie continued. 'I heard about one place where the nursery assistant told one of the kids she'd seen a mouse, and before Old MacDonald could say "squeak squeak" every single mother had pulled her child out. I mean, *come on*. At any given moment there are rats running around a foot away from us . . .'

'And that's just the husbands,' Juliet joked. Kate giggled.

'Now, now,' Lottie said. 'You'll find when *you* start having babies that men can have their uses after all.'

'Lottie,' a voice called out from the baby-cage zone. 'Where shall I change Stanley's nappy?'

Lottie sprang up. 'Come with me, Em, there's a changing mat set up in the downstairs cloakroom. I think Hilary's in there at the moment with Donald . . .'

'Why do the kids all have old people's names?' Kate asked Juliet in an undertone.

'Maybe so their names will suit them when they *are* old. As opposed to the ridiculousness of being called Boo or Kitten when you're eighty-five. What are you called, sweetie?' A small child had approached Juliet, was looking at her with a solemnity that was almost mesmerising.

'Wosie. Would you like my 'nana?' She offered Juliet an unpeeled banana and then closed her tiny teeth around the stalk.

'Oh, no thank you, Rosie, I've got some smoked salmon. Shall I peel that for you?'

'I do it. You not like 'nana?'

'Actually, no, not today.'

'Why?'

Juliet smirked at Kate. 'Because it's Satan's stools.' Kate spluttered into her champagne. That's what Larry called bananas. He'd

312

once submitted some copy about organic fruit and veg with all references to bananas replaced by the phrase. It was the one thing he wouldn't eat. There would be no banana sandwiches in the Morning After range.

'What's Satan?' Rosie asked, squashing the banana into her pinafore pocket.

'Don't do that,' Juliet said, looking around for a likely mother.

'What's Satan?'

'Satan is the devil.'

'What's stools?'

'It's another word for poop.' Juliet gave her a big smile and turned back to the unwrapping frenzy. She could barely see Hannah behind a pair of pyjamas that would fit Hattie Jacques.

'It takes a while to shift those pregnancy pounds,' explained the size eight mini-girl who'd given them. Smug old trollop, Juliet thought. These characters were truly dreadful.

'Why his poo white?' Rosie was asking.

'Because he eats innocent children. Like the giant at the top of the beanstalk.'

Rosie's lip wobbled and Juliet saw she'd made a mistake. 'I mean, because he eats lots of yummy vanilla ice-cream.'

'Wosie wants ice-cream.'

Finally, the mother of Stanley came to claim Rosie, saying, 'Don't bother the nice ladies, Rosie,' in the sort of voice that Juliet knew really meant, 'Don't go near the barren freaks.'

'Do you get the feeling we don't fit in?' she asked Kate, giggling.

'Just a bit! God, you must find this all very weird, Juliet? After, you know . . .'

Juliet looked down. 'No, not really, I suppose it's just confirmed that I'm not ready for this yet.'

'I know. Me neither.' They both sat watching the small children for a moment. 'I'd like the house, though,' Kate sighed.

'Yeah,' Juliet said. 'But to get a house like this you need a husband like Rob or Michael. A Serial Philanderer.'

'Poor Larry,' Kate said, leaning back and looking up at the high ceilings as though they were the sky itself. 'He can't compete with this, can he?'

'No. I'd say Hannah's back in this world for good now,' Juliet said.

'Do you think she ever liked him in that way? It's so difficult to tell from what he says.'

'I think she probably thought she did but in the end he just helped her realise Michael was for her.'

'Poor Larry,' Kate said again. 'I'll go and get us another drink. I think we're the only ones who've had more than one.'

'I heard what you said to that child,' said a voice to Juliet's right. It was the Asian woman.

'Oh, hello.'

'There's a lot of chi in a stool, you know.'

'Is there?' Juliet said. 'I'm Juliet, by the way. Are you a friend of Hannah's?'

'I'm Rani. Hannah and I worked together at Grace's.'

'Grace's?'

'The art school. I'm working at the Northcote Yoga Sanctuary now. So you're Hannah's sister. You have a very different spirit. Are you older or younger?'

'Younger, four and a half years younger. I'm obviously in need of a bit of chi myself if you can't tell that,' Juliet giggled.

Rani just said, 'No, you seem much older. More burdened, less centred.'

'Right!' Who was this character, some sort of rent-a-guru? She was a relief from the mothers, but, on balance, Juliet thought she preferred the toddler with the banana. From across the room, the serene woman with pigtails nodded at her with an expression of part mischief, part sympathy. Juliet made a 'Rescue me' face.

'Have you ever been to Santorini?' Rani now asked her.

'Yes, no, I can't remember. Oh, is that the one with all the gay clubs?'

314

'Rani! Hannah's opening your gift now!' Lottie interrupted. 'It's the last one, and then I think we all deserve another drink. Oh, I see Kate's already found them. Well done!'

'How lovely,' Hannah said. 'A mother-and-baby yoga mat. Thank you, Rani. I'll need something to help me get back in shape.' She put the mat on top of the outsize pyjamas and used her hands to ease her body forward in the bath chair. 'Right, it's time I got off my bum . . .'

Juliet and the serene woman both stepped forward to help her. 'Juliet, have you met Siobhan yet?' Hannah asked, breathing heavily through her open mouth.

So that's who she was. The single-minded single mother. The feisty one who'd, by everyone's reckoning but Hannah's own, put Hannah up to the rather lengthier estrangement from Michael than had been expected. The 'amazing' one.

'Back in a minute,' Hannah said, 'I need the loo *again*.'

'That Rani's a strange one, isn't she?' Siobhan said to Juliet. 'She told me I had an infant's spirit.'

'You were lucky,' Juliet said. 'I have less chi than the contents of a toilet bowl. Also, I'm a geriatric trapped in the body of a twenty-nine-year-old.'

'Same age as me,' Siobhan exclaimed. They smiled at each other. 'Hannah's told me a lot about you,' she added. 'She really admires you.'

'Can't imagine why,' Juliet said honestly. After a pause, she added, 'Thank you so much for taking her in last year. You were much more like a sister than I was.'

'I'd do the same for any friend,' Siobhan said. 'No one should be alone when they're pregnant. Though, actually, as soon as you're pregnant you never really feel alone again. Sorry, that's the sort of remark people without children find extremely annoying! I know I used to.'

Juliet thought she knew exactly what Siobhan had meant, but didn't say so. 'Are you working again now?'

'I'm doing some shop work locally, just part-time. But I'm running out of money, so I suppose I'll have to get something better paid. I always said I'd take a full year with Nora, and I should be able to hold out till then.'

'What do you want to do?'

'Project management of some sort. But not in the financial sector, where I used to work. I want something a bit less *male*, if you know what I mean.'

'Oh yes,' Juliet said, 'only too well. I'll tell you what, I should be looking for a new account exec in the spring, just a junior position. I work for a brand consultancy.'

'I remember Hannah saying.'

'It's really interesting work. You should think about coming in for an interview.'

'You don't have to do that,' Siobhan said. 'I don't know anything about advertising or brands.'

'Well, do you know what an emotional bucket is?'

'Haven't got a clue.'

'Good, then that's all I care about! It's only an interview, anyway. We'll have the usual five thousand applicants as well, of course.'

'Of course,' Siobhan said. 'Sorry, but I'd better go and rescue Nora. I can hear her yelling for me.'

'Oh, is she in the baby cage?'

'I believe mothers prefer to call them "dens"!'

'Oops, I'll try and remember that.'

'Juliet,' Kate hissed. 'That Rani's made me sign up for a course at her yoga centre. She says I have a natural yogic artlessness! How can I get out of it, it's miles from home? Will you go instead?'

In the end it was all so much briefer than the social events Juliet was used to. By five thirty the last of the mothers were wrestling children into snowsuits and shipping them off for baths and bedtime. Lottie loomed and Juliet recognised her delegation face from the previous summer. 'Juliet, would you mind helping Siobhan carry the smaller gifts round to Hannah's place? I'd come myself but I've got calls to return and we're about to do Ophelia's bath.'

'Of course. Kate will help us as well, won't you, Kate?'

'Sure,' Kate agreed. 'But then I have to shoot off home. It's my dad's birthday. I still live with my parents,' she added to Siobhan and pulled a face. 'Up in Palmer's Green.'

'You're so lucky to have them in town,' Siobhan told her. 'I envy you.'

Hannah was back and wrapped an arm around Siobhan's waist. How close they were, Juliet thought with a pang. 'Siobhan hasn't seen the house now it's finished,' Hannah said to her sister. 'I can't wait to show her. Now, what shall I carry?'

At Hannah's, Juliet saw Kate off and went to join the tour, which had begun at the top of the house, where builders were putting finishing touches to the new guest en suite.

'We're paying the plumbers a cash bonus if they finish by Tuesday,' Hannah puffed as she reached Juliet on the first-floor landing. 'Lottie says it's the only way. I absolutely cannot have them under my feet when the contractions start.'

'I don't know, some of their equipment could come in handy,' Juliet joked.

Siobhan giggled. 'There are similarities, I have to say.'

'Where next?' Juliet asked. 'The nursery? Where are you going to put that chest of drawers, Han?'

It took ages to get through the five bedrooms and assorted bathrooms, the hidden storage solutions and quirky period nooks and crannies, all of which Hannah explained with great passion, but eventually they reached the sitting room.

'Hannah! How many wedding photos have you had framed?' cried Juliet. 'It's like a gallery in here! I thought you'd become a frustrated estate agent but now I see you're still a frustrated curator!'

'There's only six,' Hannah laughed. 'I just really liked the sepia ones. They make the whole thing seem so *traditional*, like stills from an old movie. This one's my favourite. Michael looks gorgeous, doesn't he?'

'And also taller,' Juliet agreed. 'He's *got* to be standing on the step behind you.'

'Juliet!'

Siobhan chuckled and leaned in for a closer look.

'That's definitely the best shot of you two,' Juliet said. 'But I look *awful*, like a right hippie. And so miserable.'

'No you don't, you silly moo. Everyone looks perfect.' Hannah rubbed at a tiny smear on the glass.

'Imagine what it's going to be like when there are baby pictures in here, as well!' said Juliet. 'You'll have to get a catalogue printed up.'

'Look, that's me with Dad at the church,' Hannah told Siobhan. 'Just before we went in. I remember *exactly* how I felt. I had absolutely no nerves, it was extraordinary.'

'You look lovely,' Siobhan said. Both Juliet and Hannah looked at her in surprise: she sounded as though she were choking. 'You know, I'd better get going, Nora needs to go to bed soon . . .'

'She's still sleeping in her pushchair,' Juliet said, poking her head round the door to check. She wondered if Hannah had noticed that Siobhan hadn't even got to the picture outside the church.

'Are you all right?' Hannah asked as Siobhan stepped away in obvious agitation, eyelids blinking madly as though she'd lost a contact lens. For a second it looked as if she might even projectile vomit all over Hannah's extremely expensive-looking woven rug, but luckily she pressed her hand over her mouth and scuttled to the nearest door.

Hannah followed. 'That one's nailed shut, Shiv, we don't use it. Go this way . . .'

'Sorry. I must just go to the loo . . .'

318

'I'll go after her in a minute,' Hannah whispered to Juliet. 'She's fallen out with her parents over Nora. I think the picture of me with Dad must have upset her. You heard what she said to Kate. It's so sad, isn't it?'

'I'll be downstairs,' Juliet said. 'I'll put the kettle on and we'll start sorting out the presents.'

From the kitchen, she could hear Siobhan fobbing off Hannah, amiably enough, of course, before, with a swift three-point turn of the buggy, closing the front door behind her.

Hannah came down, looking well and truly shattered. 'I would say it's been a long day, but actually it's been a short one. I was in bed till ten this morning.'

'Come and sit down,' Juliet said. 'Here's your tea. Just look at all this stuff! Do babies *really* need a man-size Piglet? Even in Nappy Valley?'

'That was sweet of Emily,' Hannah said. 'Lottie's sister. It's such a shame she doesn't live in the area any more. And I do like Kate, it was nice of her to come.'

'She's lovely,' Juliet agreed. 'A really good friend.'

'Siobhan left in a hurry, didn't she?' Hannah said. 'I hope she was OK.'

Juliet shrugged. 'She was probably just tired. Don't worry about it.'

'But I feel guilty,' Hannah said. 'I barely had a chance to talk to her today. Maybe I shouldn't have shown her the house and the wedding pictures. It probably looked like I was showing off.'

Juliet pulled a face. '*Everyone* likes to see other people's houses. There'd be no cable TV otherwise.'

But Hannah still looked anxious. 'It's just that she was the only one, well, *one* of the only ones, who was there when I needed a friend.' Kind of her to correct herself for my benefit, Juliet thought. 'I feel like I've betrayed her somehow. I really want to help. I mean, I've tried . . .' She broke off to drink from the glass of water Juliet passed her.

She must mean that stalking nonsense with Lottie's husband, Juliet thought, drinking her tea. Larry had told her about their trip to the City, where he and Hannah had pursued the poor man like something out of *The Secret Seven*. 'What do you mean, you feel like you've betrayed her?'

'Oh, nothing,' Hannah said. 'Just by getting back with Michael, I suppose. In a way, she and I coupled up, you know, looked after Nora together.'

'It can't have been that much of a surprise that you got back with your own husband,' Juliet said, watching. 'What does she think of Michael anyway?'

'They haven't met yet,' Hannah said. 'God knows what she'll think when they do. It's so difficult, isn't it, when you hear all the bad stuff first and then have to just get on with them and pretend you don't know any of it?'

'Oh, people understand. I mean, no one expects perfection, do they?'

Hannah nodded. 'Exactly. One thing I've learned is that if you expect perfect behaviour you'll wait your whole life for it. Not because people don't know how to behave *decently*, but because no one else can ever interpret what *you* mean by perfect. Especially when you're changing your own definition every day. And even if you do find yourself attracted to someone who's willing to be controlled, then that's not a partner anyway, that's a slave.'

'Like Sasha and Caliban!' Juliet thought about what Hannah had said. 'Yes, that's true, I think you're totally right.'

Hannah looked so startled by her agreement that Juliet wanted to weep with remorse. How many times must she have scorned her sister's advice to earn a reaction like that?

Hannah went on: 'Anyway, unless you're with someone all day every day, you can never know what they're doing. And even if you were together all the time, you don't know what they're *thinking*.'

'Yes,' Juliet said again. She paused. 'So do you think it's all right to not feel totally certain about someone, you know, all the time?'

'Definitely,' Hannah said, looking at her. 'Do you mean Guy?'

'Maybe. But he's got a new girlfriend now anyway, hasn't he?'

'Has he? I'm sorry, I didn't know.'

Juliet stared. 'I thought it was you who told me?'

'When?'

'At Joby's party? I'm sure it was you, you know, before everything happened.'

Hannah looked puzzled. 'Do you mean when I said he was there because he knew *Joby's* girlfriend?'

'Oh! I just assumed . . .' Juliet's eyes widened. She'd already decided what to do about Guy before today, but this made it better, this meant she'd be stepping on no other toes to get to him. It was strange to feel her spirits skip and jump again. She could hardly wait. But first she needed to take care of this other business. 'Shall I help you do your thank you letters, Han? Where's your address book?'

'Oh, would you? Lottie did a spreadsheet with all the guests' home addresses. It's in my bag upstairs.'

Wonderful 't'-crossing, 'i'-dotting Lottie, Juliet thought. She'd be needing that list.

'Right, let's put this stuff away first. What shall I do with this breadmaker?'

'It's not a breadmaker, you idiot, it's a nappy bin!'

'No way,' Juliet said. 'That's gross.'

Chapter 30

She didn't ask Larry which bus went to Brixton, just did the quiet thing and consulted the map at the bus stop at the end of the road. The thirty-seven was the one. It was Sunday and she expected to have to wait for an age, but one came bundling along straight away. At every stop she watched the people get on and off and wondered if anyone else travelled with dread in their stomach. She was grateful when someone was particularly slow or when, as it did twice, a row broke out between driver and passenger to cause an additional delay. She considered going all the way to Peckham, where the service terminated, and then staying aboard for the trip home. She even prayed for a breakdown. But the bus rattled out a reasonable progress and soon she saw the sign for Brockwell Park lido and knew she was there.

She'd been prepared to wait on the doorstep if necessary, but Siobhan answered the door at once. 'Juliet. Come in.'

She knows I know, Juliet thought. Might as well get straight to the point. But it was hard. Siobhan was still the luminous, unpretentious breath of fresh air she'd liked instantly yesterday in that room full of Nappy Valley's finest. She needed to confront her quickly, before she changed her mind. Following her into the living room, she said to the back of her head, 'Michael is Nora's father, isn't he?'

Siobhan turned and speared Juliet with the sort of look that made her body brace itself instinctively for an attack. But when Siobhan answered at last, her voice was yielding, resigned. 'Yes, he is. Do you want to grab a seat and I'll make some tea.'

'OK.' Juliet looked around the room. The flat was shabby, really down-at-heel compared with the finery of Lottie's and Hannah's houses. Even Larry's place was whitewash fresh, with newly waxed floorboards and smartly painted woodwork. The carpet here looked about a hundred years old and the faded floral curtains were a funny three-quarter-length, like cut-off trousers. So this was the difference between marrying Michael and just fucking him. It was a big difference. And where were Siobhan's things, anyway? There was not a single square foot that hadn't been claimed by the child: chairs, mobiles, boxes, bibs, beakers, caterpillars, ponies . . . Even Juliet had more possessions in evidence in Larry's living room than this mother did here.

Siobhan came back and set down two mugs on the coffee table. 'Sorry about the mess. I manage to keep mine and Nora's rooms tidy but the living room is so much more difficult to contain.' So she did have her sanctuary tucked away somewhere back there. Juliet was glad.

'Where's Nora today?' she asked.

'She's out with my mum at the swings.'

'I thought you weren't in touch with your parents?'

Siobhan raised an eyebrow. 'I suppose Hannah told you they didn't like me having a baby on my own. They're very old-fashioned. But I think Christmas made them rethink a bit, especially when they found out one of my aunties has been diagnosed with breast cancer. So my mum came down for the day. I'm really glad Nora's met her.'

'Sorry,' Juliet said. 'I mean, that's great. But why didn't you say anything to Hannah about it yesterday? She's worried about you being on your own with no one to help.'

'It wasn't my day,' Siobhan replied.

Juliet paused. They looked at each other.

'I swear to you I had no idea who he was until I saw that photo,' Siobhan said. 'That was the first time I've seen Hannah's husband.'

'The first time since you slept with him, you mean?' Juliet knew she sounded hostile, couldn't help herself.

'Yes.'

'So it was just a coincidence that you became friends with the wife of the father of your child?'

'Of course it was!' Siobhan was frowning so hard her eyebrows almost touched in the middle. 'I met Hannah in a café. I remember it quite well. Nora was tiny then, she'd been crying all morning and I took her out in the sling. I used to walk around for hours in those days to get her to go to sleep. We stopped for a coffee and Lottie began talking to me. Otherwise I don't suppose I would even have noticed them.'

'And how did you meet Michael?'

'Through some bloke at work, an old boss of a friend of mine. It was someone's birthday in Front Office and Sal and I tagged along for drinks.'

'I suppose you mean Rob, Lottie's husband, also in the wedding photo – Michael's best man?'

'I didn't notice anyone else in the photo,' Siobhan said simply. 'Hannah's mentioned Rob a few times, though. To be honest, I wasn't sure who she meant. Now I see the connection, of course. I suppose it must have been Rob who invited Michael along that night. I'm sure Sal used to call him Mac or something.'

'Hmm.'

'You know, Michael wasn't married then,' Siobhan added. 'I did ask.'

'He was engaged,' Juliet said. 'They were engaged for almost a year before they got married.' She'd done the maths. Nora must have been conceived in August or September of the year before last, just after Luke had died. That was when Hannah had

324

taken Juliet back into her flat and looked after her. She'd taken time off work so Juliet wouldn't have to be alone, and she'd told Michael she wasn't going to be staying over at his for a while.

'I didn't know,' said Siobhan. 'Obviously.'

'*Obviously*,' Juliet repeated. She was alarmed by the aggression rearing in her ribcage; her blood was hot and her skin was burning up. *She* had helped cause all of this! If she hadn't monopolised Hannah, Michael would never have been out on the pull with Rob. 'So how many times did you and Michael see each other, then?'

'Just that once, at the bar near work.'

'You mean you shagged in the bar?'

'In the cloakroom, yes.'

'How seamy.' She'd convinced herself she must have had sex with Dominic again that night at the awards dinner when she'd woken up under the coats and found she'd lost at least an hour. Kate had dismissed the idea but couldn't account for Dominic's movements either, so the next morning Juliet had got up early to beat Sasha and Callum to the shower and try to wash him off her. As it turned out, she'd just been sleeping. As it turned out, she'd already been made pregnant by then.

'And you didn't have sex with anyone else around that time?'

'No!' Siobhan frowned bitterly. 'With all due respect, this isn't really your business, Juliet.'

'Yes it is,' Juliet burst out, shocked to feel the snarl on her lips. 'Hannah's my sister, she's about to give birth and now you drop this bombshell!'

'I'm not dropping any bombshell. And nor should you. No one else knows.'

'For how long? I don't see how you can continue to be friends with her and keep this secret. You can't avoid meeting Michael forever. It's amazing it's gone on this long, they've been back together for weeks now. God, weren't you even invited to my parents' place at Christmas when he was there?'

'What do you think I spent all of last night thinking about?' For the first time there was a frantic inflection in Siobhan's steady voice. 'This is a nightmare. Thank God it was a photo and not him in the flesh!'

Juliet nodded.

'Anyway, I've already decided I'm going to drop out of the scene,' Siobhan said, sounding controlled again.

'But you live down the road. Hannah won't *let* you drop out. She adores you. She won't understand.'

'I'll say I'm moving back up north to be with my family. She'll forget. People do.'

Juliet thought about the baby shower; there'd been so many faces she'd expected to see who weren't there, including Hannah's circle from her last full-time job, all of whom had been at the wedding. Yesterday they'd gone completely unmentioned. And what about Larry? Hannah hadn't even asked after him when they'd been talking about Sisters Avenue and not so long ago the two of them had been inseparable. 'So you haven't ever contacted Michael?' she asked Siobhan. 'In all this time?'

'I swear to you I didn't even know his name.'

Juliet knew about the random charmer trotting out some guff about being David Niven. Larry had told her and Kate all about it and they'd laughed at the erotic extension of their If game. But Michael as *David Niven*? Someone must have suggested that to him – the man was into sci-fi, for God's sake. 'You *never* heard his name? Not even afterwards?'

'I did hear the others call him by some stupid nickname, Taphead or something like that.'

Juliet gaped. Thank God Siobhan had never thought to mention this to Hannah.

Siobhan went on: 'Anyway, as I keep trying to tell people, I have no desire to contact the father, whatever his name. Why is that so hard to get your head around?'

'You know Hannah thought *Rob* was Nora's father?' Juliet said.

'What? That's just crazy.'

'No more crazy than this!'

Siobhan stood up and drew the curtains. Juliet could see her hands were shaking. 'It's getting dark. My mum will be back with Nora soon.'

'Why did you do it?' Juliet asked. 'Y'know, go ahead with the baby? In those circumstances? I mean, we've all been there, one-night stands, whatever . . .'

Siobhan regarded her with dignity. 'There are many reasons why people go ahead with unplanned pregnancies,' she said, 'and many reasons why they don't. I don't think I need to explain mine to you or anyone else.'

'That's kind of the point, though, isn't it? Hasn't it occurred to you that there might be people who need explanations down the line? Nora, for instance.'

'Yes, it's occurred to me. But when you're making a decision as important as that, well, that kind of thing isn't as big as giving life. *Nothing* is.'

Juliet swallowed some of the cooled drink, not registering whether it was tea or coffee. 'Look, I just want you to guarantee you won't contact Hannah again, *ever*, that you'll keep out of her life? Will you?'

Siobhan didn't bother answering and Juliet couldn't blame her. She set down her mug and Siobhan said, 'I think it's time for you to go.'

Juliet followed her back down the hallway to the front door.

'I'll keep away,' Siobhan said. 'But don't judge me when you don't even know me.' She shut the door.

As Juliet sidestepped the potted plants she saw Siobhan inside the front window, face in hands, obviously sobbing. She wanted to fall against the window and join in.

Chapter 31

'Gatwick, please,' Juliet said to the minicab driver.

'No bags, mate?'

'No, just this.' 'Mate' again. She wondered if cabbies called Hannah 'mate'. It seemed unlikely, what with her impeccable make-up and Nicole Farhi coat. Anyway, pregnant women were 'darlin' by rights, weren't they? But 'mate' was OK; she could get used to 'mate'.

Tucking her overnight bag beside her, she took a quick back-long glance through the early morning at Larry's flat window – it was still so dark it was like squinting through bonfire smoke. Larry wouldn't be up for hours; even though there were no blinds or curtains the winter light was so dingy he could sleep until noon at weekends.

She hadn't told him where she was going, but had left a note for him saying she'd be away for the rest of the weekend, a spur-of-the-moment thing. He'd probably think that meant she was doing something with Hannah. All roads seemed to lead to Hannah at the moment. How cruel it was that Larry had ended up living so close by; if he didn't run into her in person, he'd be hard pushed not to pass her old building at least once a day.

She and Larry had been out drinking last night, to Guy's bar, now being run with acceptable familiarity by a relief manager. It had been just the two of them for the first part of the evening, Kate having broken ranks to go to a dinner party with Phil. 'Just so long as you're not *throwing* the dinner party with Phil,' Larry had said to her. 'That would be too much too soon.'

'Nothing's the same any more,' he complained later. And he was right, it wasn't like the old days when they'd overpowered the other drinkers with their loud laughter, pooled coins for the cigarette machine, plotted grisly ends for Dominic and Phil, played endless rounds of the Kipling game. That all seemed a bit hollow now, or, worse, *irrelevant*.

'I'm glad it's not the same,' Juliet said. She watched Ewan, the new manager, uncork a bottle of house white and ask one of the girls to get more ice. He was even staying in Guy's flat upstairs for the month. Who was Ewan's girl, she wondered, the one he had a drink with after locking up? Martine would be her guess; she'd grown her hair and was wearing darker lipstick.

She tried to think of ways to cheer up Larry, who was still down about Hannah. She felt awful for him, was sorely tempted to tell him about the baby shower and her dealings with Siobhan, to tell him that he wasn't the only one to check the screen for Hannah's name every time his mobile rang. She'd been expecting the call ever since she'd walked away from Siobhan's door and flagged down the bus back to Battersea, certain that a tearful Hannah would soon be in touch with the news that it was all over, *really* all over this time. But the only call from her sister had been routine: she'd wanted Kate's email address to add her to the list of people Michael was going to contact when the baby came, before the announcement cards did the job more formally. No, thought Juliet, Siobhan had obviously kept her mouth shut and it was vital she did the same. Larry would only want to use the news as a way to get Hannah back from Michael, and Juliet wasn't going to be the one to put her sister through all that again. Her baby was due in three weeks.

'I just wish women would make up their minds,' Larry said,

screwing up an empty cigarette pack and flicking it across the table. 'At least Kate likes the Swine, whatever anyone else says about him.'

'You know we're not supposed to call him that any more,' Juliet said and grinned. Larry didn't. Everyone was a swine today as far as he was concerned. 'What I mean is, she's not using him to make a point to someone else,' he said.

'I don't think Hannah was using you, if that's what you mean,' said Juliet, carefully. 'Obviously I don't know the details, but she just doesn't think . . .'

'No, you don't know the details,' Larry said simply. 'But fuck it, let's drop it. Where's Fulton tonight?'

'I don't know.'

'You two fallen out?'

'No, I just feel like calming down for a while and he's not the greatest influence in the world.'

'Whatever you say, Shirley Temple.' Now Larry was grinning. 'So no more three-way action, then?'

'No more three-way action,' she repeated. She hoped he hadn't told her sister about all that. All those Fridays he spent with Hannah before Christmas, not to mention the skived after-noons and cosy evenings, they must have talked about something. She couldn't expect him to withhold all the juicy details of her life, and God knew there'd been a whole orange grove of them recently.

She was relieved when Joby joined them and started grum-bling about the departure of Josie, who, it turned out, had called their relationship off soon after the New Year's raid. It seemed appropriate to leave the two of them together – she didn't fancy having to defend the whole of the female population for the rest of the night. Besides, she had her own private life to rescue. Back at Larry's she didn't even take her coat off before turning on the PC. She tried a few travel sites and fairly quickly found a flight to Geneva for the following morning. It was Saturday tomorrow and the last-minute seats were scandalously overpriced, but she hit 'Buy Now' anyway, thanking God and Dominic for the bonuses sitting in her account. But she knew she would have done the same if work had gone the other way and she was out of a job.

She liked the taxi-run to the airport on early empty roads, when London looked at its most friendless, and this morning was no exception. And when the suburbs gave way to airport country she liked wondering who lived in those houses right near the runways – as if the screaming planes weren't enough, the roads out front were choked with airport traffic, too. Luke once said that people who ended up having to live next to airports were exactly the people who couldn't afford to travel very often and therefore take advantage of the one benefit their location afforded. It was one of those classic city ironies. Juliet said that if she lived so close by she'd like to go to Departures occasionally and fantasise about walking up to a sales desk and asking for a ticket for the next flight out of there, regardless of where it was headed. If possible, she'd want to avoid knowing the destination until she was actually on the plane.

Luke had laughed at that. 'What a cliché! What if the next flight was to Karachi, you'd soon want your money back. And what about visas?'

'Where's your sense of romance?' she'd asked him. 'That trip could be a life-changing experience.'

Luck was on her side this time: the cabbie was playing half-decent music and not singing or whistling or treating her to a run-down of the anti-social scheduling of his day and the havoc that played with family life. She gave him a generous tip, checked in ahead of the crowds and went straight through to the departure gate, where she sat for some time looking through the glass at the white and orange plane and at the reflections of the other travellers. Everyone was trailing scarves and moving slightly blurrily in fat jackets and sturdy boots. She'd almost forgotten she was going to the mountains, had just thought of it as going to Guy. She realised she was going to need to buy some gloves and a hat as soon as she reached Geneva.

There weren't enough seats at the gate for passengers and people started sitting on the floor. Some of them weren't very pleased about not getting a seat, they didn't like feeling like surplus. That made her think about Siobhan and Larry. Somehow those two were losers in recent events, while Hannah and Michael stood rejoined and elevated, like the figures on the top of the wedding cake. She was sorry for Larry, but she couldn't blame Hannah. All Hannah had done was to opt out of losing. Now she wanted to do the same, if it wasn't too late.

'Excuse me, madam, are you joining us for the flight to Geneva?'

'Yes, sorry.' She jumped up; the gate had emptied and she was the last to board. It was a while since she'd been on a plane, she'd forgotten the pure, irresistible buzz of air travel, however local the destination, however simple the service – no-frills they called it. Luke had written about this airline for a travel magazine soon before they'd left for Mexico. He'd thought he had a better chance of placing proper travel pieces later if he accepted commissions for the dull stuff now. He had always been curious about people on aeroplanes, never took it for granted that everyone was either off on holiday or returning from one. 'Could be pleasure or pain,' he said once. 'Could be going to a wedding. Could be bringing a body home.' She felt her heart catch. Did she only imagine he'd said that last bit? It seemed incredible that she would only now remember it.

'Seatbelt, please.' Mechanically she slotted the buckle together, barely looking up. Would it ever be possible to travel anywhere again without thinking of Luke? Juliet the traveller, that's how her parents referred to her, even now, said she had 'the bug'. But he had been the traveller of their partnership, and it had been more drug than bug. At college he'd belonged to that coterie of gap-year undergraduates who'd varied the standard Eurorail or Thailand–Australia route prescribed by the travel agents and done something different. He'd been to China and Vietnam, had had a story published in *Time Out* – the usual stuff about having to eat his own chopsticks when he'd run out of money but amusingly told. They'd got together just before the first summer vacation, which he'd spent in Canada, she waitressing in a café on Tottenham Court Road. The tips had been insulting. The following summer, she'd gone with him. She would have gone if it had been Karachi.

But Luke hadn't always been the leader. There'd been the time she'd badgered him into a package holiday. They were a year into working life and, shattered by the transition from university, she'd decided she was damned if she was going to spend her one precious break sitting with the ants on some sticky station steps, running through the *Lonely Planet* listings for the cheapest hotels with indoor plumbing. Ditto the two-hour discussions over which was the most vital to their survival, the ceiling fan or the mosquito net, because they couldn't use both at once. No, she wanted air con, a minibar, and a steps-from-the-beach hotel.

Finally he'd agreed. They'd gone to Corsica. Transferring from the airport on a coach with people their parents' age, they listened to the patter of the tour rep ('The road to the resort is old and twisted – and so is our driver.') without daring to look at one another. Their beachside 'cottage' was a soulless unit with 'Romania' stamped on the back of the plates and mugs. At the welcome meeting another rep shared a season's accumulated wisdom ('In Corsica, you can use any bin you like') and distributed English beer.

'See, this is grim as fuck,' Luke whispered, giving her that faux long-suffering grin she found so sexy.

'I think it's funny,' she said. She hated admitting she was wrong.

And, in the end, she *had* rather enjoyed it; drinking rosé in the bar, watching the oldsters write their postcards with the gravity of a captain at his last log. She vowed to read her own parents' cards more closely in future if this was the level of concentration devoted to them. As for Luke, by day three he was hanging out with the watersports guys, who would see off the braver of the grey-haired couples in their canoes before lying on beached Hobie Cats smoking. It was only a matter of time before he'd got them invited to the staff quarters for drinks and signed up for some off-the-beaten-track mountain trek on the staff day off.

But with Luke, one place always led to another, and by the time they were boarding their charter back to London a scheme was afoot to save for a trip to Latin America. By the time they'd landed, the Inca Trail had been added, along with the Colca Canyon, Lake Titicaca and God knew where else. 'All these old folks are cramming it all in now, worried they'll die before they see it all. Let's do our mid-life crisis trip while we've still got the energy.' Of course she'd agreed, she didn't want a whole year in London without him. She would do the Mexico leg, come home to earn some cash while he travelled to Guatemala and Ecuador, then fly back out to rejoin him for Peru.

'Would you like something to drink?'

She looked up. 'Oh, yes please, a coffee.'

'One pound seventy-five.'

Soon she wished she hadn't bothered, had forgotten you paid for drinks on these low-cost flights, scuffled for some coins in her bags.

'Sorry, we don't take anything smaller than a one-pound coin.'

'But the drink is one seventy-five?'

'You could pay in euros?'

She handed over a ten-euro note.

'Are you a bit nervous? We're through the worst of it now. And it's been much smoother than the inbound flight.' It turned out her cheeks were wet, the attendant thought she was frightened by the turbulence.

'Just weeping at your prices,' she joked. The attendant gazed back, uncomprehending, and she looked to her right for support, but her neighbour had his nose in the in-flight guide.

'Thank you,' she said, taking her change and sipping. She couldn't taste anything so added a sachet of sugar. It was a short flight. They were already starting their descent.

It was so easy to find a taxi and the route to Morzine so direct that she was there before she felt mentally ready, standing on the iced kerb as the driver pulled away with a brief mutter of 'Merci, Madame' (since when had she become 'Madame' rather than 'Mademoiselle'? Presumably around the time she became 'mate'). She didn't know where Guy was staying and, having pictured some sort of cobbled ski village with a couple of bars next door to each other, now saw that she might never find out. This place was a real town, a town at the peak of the season, with an ice rink, Olympic swimming pool, good shopping, and streets and streets of hotels, bars and restaurants. The resort slogan was everywhere: '*Le plaisir ça s'apprend*!' She wondered what it meant.

She sat in a bar overlooking a car park and drank vin chaud while studying maps of the town and the Portes du Soleil ski area. She had only one clue to Guy's whereabouts: his brother was married to a ski instructor, who presumably worked for the Ecole du Ski Français. It was just after lunch and people were gathering in groups to take the télécabine up the mountain. The instructors were easy to spot with their red ski gear and chestnut faces. She found the enquiries desk. It had just reopened after lunch and there was already a queue.

'*Excusez-moi, je cherche Madame Morrison.*'

Blank look.

'*Elle est un instructeur pour l'école de ski.*'

Shrug. Was *instructeur* even a word? She tried to take her brain back to the classroom.

'*Elle travaille ici. La professeur ...?*' Very poor. No wonder Hannah had taken to booking herself on intensive language courses before every holiday – Michael could speak several languages and she hated to look like the uneducated Brit. Maybe Guy's sister-in-law used her maiden name; but she had no idea what that was and couldn't remember her Christian name, though she knew Guy had mentioned it several times. The brother's name she was sure she knew, something Scottish-sounding. What was it again? Robert or Finn. She turned back to the man. '*La femme qui je cherche, elle est mari a un homme qui apelle Finn?*'

This gained her a half-shrug and a look over her shoulder to the next in line. It was hopeless. She was getting nowhere and the couple behind her were very anxious about a lost lift pass. She went to sit at a terrace table of the nearest bar and ordered another vin chaud, this one nicer, less sweet. All she could do was watch the faces as they came and went. Then, as the sun dipped, she retreated inside and sat by the window, still watching.

She switched bars twice. Three more vins chaud. Skiers started to return from the slopes, crashing through the door in those stupid astronaut boots, shouting in hectic voices. She turned hopefully every time she heard an Australian or Kiwi accent, but it seemed mainly to be Brits, so many of them she feared she might run into someone she knew. Everywhere she turned, big, flushed faces were yelling about the black run they'd just done, the total blowout they'd just survived, the nightmare queues for the drag lifts. What had Luke thought he was going to find in every last corner of the known world? Holidaymakers were exactly the same everywhere: they did their daylight activities and then they bored each other rigid with an evening debrief. The bar: that was where you really earned the stamps in your passport.

Just as she couldn't delay the hunt for a hotel any longer, she saw him. She didn't recognise him at first, for his head was shorn of its curls, his face deeply tanned; he no longer looked like someone who lived in London, but like someone who'd left and wasn't looking back. He was in a huge group, a mix of instructors and ordinary skiers. Everyone seemed to have at least three drinks – that ski thing where people had beers and brandies and coffees all at the same time.

The last time she'd felt as nervous as this was when she'd first got her new team together and given a presentation about her plans for the Smithfield's account – and that had been *seriously* run-away-and-cry scary. This was worse, though, because it meant so much more. Couldn't he just come over and order at the bar rather than using the waitress? Did she have to risk rejection in front of all these people? What had he said to her at that New Year's Eve party? What had she said to him?

'Guy.'

She was not prepared for the look on his face, which fell short of the shock-gives-way-to-delight she'd hoped for. It was more a lack of recognition followed by involuntary painful memory and, soon after, plain irritation. But at least the rest of the group carried on as before and didn't fall into an open-mouthed hush as she'd feared. If anything, it was hard to tell if Guy could even hear her as she stuttered out how lucky she thought she was to spot him in such a crowded place. Either way, he waited for her mouth to stop moving before putting down his beer and shouting, 'Juliet, why are you here? Are you skiing?'

Ah, she thought, he just thinks this is an unhappy coincidence. 'No! I came to find *you*!'

He frowned. She remembered to smile. 'Guy, I've got a lot to tell you. I mean, well, I've changed my mind.'

'Changed your mind about what?'

It hit her that quite a long time had passed since they'd been together, four months in fact. There was every chance she'd misjudged all of this and was about to discover she'd just been the same convenient fling to Guy that she'd thought he'd been to her.

She saw herself returning to London, perhaps not even telling anyone about this twenty-four-hour bout of insanity. Larry and Kate would understand if she didn't want to go back to Guy's bar once Guy was back in it; in fact, they'd expect it. That was if Guy ever returned and it wasn't about to be Ewan's Bar indefinitely. The thought made her feel desolate.

It took exactly two seconds to process all of this before she blurted out, 'I never changed my mind. God, I'm sorry I was such a freak, Guy.'

He actually took a step back. She felt very thin and unprotected in her London clothes, her London skin. He was narrowing his eyes now, intent, motionless, studying her. She told herself to stay positive: she'd been wrong about that meeting with Dominic and she might be wrong about this. But hadn't Dominic been the one to summon *her* . . . ?

'Will you at least give me half an hour,' she asked. 'Can we go somewhere quieter?'

'Never thought I'd hear Juliet Goodwin say that.'

No smile, but a crack, a tiny hairline crack, of humour. A good sign.

'OK,' Guy said. 'Half an hour.'

She told him everything, everything she thought helped account for the way she'd behaved towards him. About Luke, mainly. When she got to the bit about the stabbing she found it reasonably easy to get through, not like when she'd told Larry and had broken into those horrible cartoon sobs.

'He was intercepting a mugging? In Lima? The *idiot*.'

'I know, we weren't even on the street, we were in a taxi. We saw these guys, boys, practically, pushing the girl against the wall. The driver didn't want to pull over, but Luke made him; they were arguing, he was trying to open the door when the car was still moving.'

'How many attackers?'

'Two. I doubt they planned to actually use the knife, but the girl was refusing to give up her bag.'

'Then what?'

'It was all, God, exactly like they say, y'know, a dream sequence. It happened so quickly. I could hear shouts in Spanish, then Luke was on the ground, the girl was shrieking, she'd been cut as well, but only on her hands. At the time it was hard to tell how badly either of them had been hurt. The muggers just vanished. I swear I didn't even see them run off. There was blood everywhere. Luke didn't seem like he was dying, I mean his eyes were open, he was breathing, he was *alive*.'

'Did you get him to a hospital?'

'Eventually. I didn't know what to do, the girl was hysterical and even though she was Spanish herself and I couldn't speak a word of the language, she just couldn't calm down enough to help. I didn't know if there was even an ambulance service or where the hospital was. I'd just arrived, I barely had a clue where we were, just that we were somewhere downtown. I tried to stop taxis, cars, no one would come near us. He was dead by the time we got him to a doctor. He'd been stabbed in the chest. Right into the lungs.'

'It's hard enough to lose someone,' Guy said. 'But to witness a murder, jeez.'

'It was so terrible,' Juliet said. 'Having to phone his parents. And the girl, Cristina she was called, just didn't go away. It turned out she knew Luke. She said they were sleeping together. Thought they were some sort of an item. She obviously knew about me.'

'How do you know she was telling the truth?'

'Other travellers in the apartment where he'd been staying, they confirmed it, though I never found out how long it had been going on. Probably since he'd arrived in Peru two weeks earlier. Maybe even in Ecuador – a whole bunch of them had travelled down together on some dodgy bus. Luke had moved to a hotel the day before I arrived. Of course he must have known her and cared about her, why else would he have intervened? Everyone knows you stay away from that sort of situation.'

'Of course.' She'd run out of cigarettes and Guy lit her one from his pack of a French brand. It tasted like a hundred cigarettes condensed into one and she couldn't stop coughing. She'd thought about all of this endlessly, never really understood what was running through Luke's head that night. Would he have got involved if he hadn't recognised the girl being attacked? Even in London you wouldn't try to help, let alone South America. But Luke was a doer, he seemed to lack the gene that regulated fear and caution. They'd been drinking as well, big, touristy pisco sours, one after the other. She'd been tired, wanted to get back to the hotel to sleep, had rested her head against his shoulder. Perhaps if she'd been sitting up, keeping the conversation going, he wouldn't have been staring out the taxi window, wouldn't have seen the girl . . .

'We got the same plane back to London, Cristina and me.' Not sitting side by side, that would have been too sick, but separated by a few rows. 'I could hear her crying, it was horrible. The air hostesses kept going to see how she was. They gave her a sleeping pill, an extra blanket.'

Guy signalled to the waiter for more wine.

'I didn't even feel sorry for her. I felt she had caused his death and then stolen my grief as well.'

'Did she try to speak to you?'

'She didn't speak particularly good English. I wasn't very receptive anyway.'

'How did Luke get to know her then, if she didn't speak English?' Guy asked.

'The language of love?' Juliet laughed, a little bitterly. 'No, he spoke fluent Spanish. He'd done it at college. He always wanted to be a travel writer and he thought it would be useful.'

The wine came and she fished a new pack of cigarettes out of her duty-free carton. 'She was very young,' she said. 'It was probably her first time out of Europe. When I got off the plane in London I thought that would be the last I saw of her. But then she turned up at the service, had somehow got to know Jan and Tony – that's Luke's parents.'

'How did that go?'

'I don't know. I left as soon as I saw her. I couldn't bear it, I felt betrayed by them. Luke and I had been together for seven years, for fuck's sake. She was some student traveller he'd known for five minutes. Of course, now I know they were in the same hell as me, worse, probably.'

'You just walked out?'

'I was with Hannah, she came with me, we drove to her flat in London. But my parents stayed. I wish I'd stayed now.'

'Yes?'

'I know what you're going to say,' Juliet said. 'I didn't have closure. But I did. I went back to the grave every week for the next two months.'

'Have you seen this Cristina since?'

'No. I heard she stayed with Jan and Tony for a few days, then went back to Madrid.'

'I wonder if he was going to tell you about her,' Guy said.

Juliet pulled a face. 'What, like Michael was going to tell Hannah about Nicola? What do *you* think?'

Guy looked puzzled. Of course, the Nicola fiasco had happened after she and Guy had split; she had so much to update him on, if he wanted to hear any more, that was. 'They separated,' she explained. 'But now they're back together again.'

He nodded. 'I wondered what was going on when I saw her at that party with Larry.'

They finished their drinks. 'Where are you staying?' Guy asked.

'I haven't found a hotel yet,' Juliet said. 'I have to go back to London tomorrow.'

'You can stay with us. The apartment's in town.'

'Thank you.'

It was so cold outside it choked the back of her throat and made her blink. She pulled on the new hat – red and fluffy, with a dangly bit hanging down between her shoulder blades – and felt like Santa's elf. But it was several degrees below freezing. 'Can I be really cheeky and borrow a jumper as well?'

Guy led the way downhill; it was steep and icy and she had to concentrate in her leather-soled shoes. Big groups were gathering outside bars, most showered and shiny-nosed and ready for the evening and another round of war stories. Others were still in their ski clothes, passing the other way. There wasn't a single miserable face among them.

They stopped at a doorway on the main street and Guy let them upstairs and into a hallway, then a living room. It was cosy, with pictures on the wall and rugs on the floor, someone's home, not a ski apartment. 'This was Jeanne's place before she got married,' he said. 'They're moving in the spring. They're planning on trying for a kid.'

'*Jeanne*. I wish I'd remembered that earlier. And your brother's not called Finn, is he?'

'Craig.'

'That's right.' She couldn't think what else to say and sat on the sofa.

Guy poured them both a drink. 'Why tell me all this now and not before?'

Juliet looked at him. 'I couldn't talk about it. I was angry; angry with everyone.'

'Angry with me?'

'No, but angry with myself for letting it all get in the way.'

'Of us?'

'Yes.'

'So why come all the way here?' he asked quietly.

'I wanted to say sorry face to face, I was wrong to end things the way I did. I was behaving like a maniac. I didn't know how I felt.'

342

'Well, how do you feel?'

'I love you.' She felt herself blush, hoped he'd think it was her skin reacting to the indoor heating. She couldn't meet his eye but didn't want to look away either, so she stared at the three new freckles on his nose instead.

Guy picked up a grey sweater from the arm of the sofa and handed it to her. She pulled it over the top of her jacket. It smelled of Guy smells: cigarette smoke, coffee, something woody and dark.

'The others will be back soon. Do you want to go out for dinner?'

'Yes, I'd like to meet Craig.'

'I mean just us.'

'OK,' Juliet said. She fought hard not to agonise over what it meant that he hadn't said 'I love you' back. That would have been too easy, she supposed. The important thing was that he hadn't said she was too late because he was now married to Jeanne's sister/friend/pupil, and he also hadn't said 'Leave, you must be joking, go back home'. This was the moment in a movie where the music would let her know it was all going to be all right. But the only music she could hear was overexcited guitar rock belting out from the bar across the road. It was ancient Bon Jovi, 'You Give Love a Bad Name'.

She turned back to Guy. 'Believe it or not, I can actually pay for dinner as well. I have some money.'

He grinned. 'You do?'

'Pots of the stuff. Well, a lot for me anyway! Work seems to have turned around. But that's another story.' She thought about reaching for his hand but decided not to. She wished she'd taken off the elf hat.

'Right, well let's go.'

'Can we have fondue?' she asked. 'Or have you had it a thousand times already this trip?'

'One more won't kill me.'

As they walked, they passed a wall plastered with posters of

343

the resort ads she'd seen earlier. 'What does that mean?' she asked, pointing. '"*Le plaisir ça s'apprend!*"? I've seen it everywhere.'

Guy looked. 'It means, "Pleasure is something you learn".'

'Oh, I like that,' Juliet said.

Chapter 32

'Can you believe he's ours?' Hannah asked Michael. 'We *made* him.'

'Well, *you* made him really,' Michael said. 'I just got the creative process started.'

It was only when studying baby James that Hannah realised how similar she and Michael looked. It was impossible to tell who had given him those dark eyes, tar-black from day one, as both she and Michael had them too. 'I think the nose is mine,' she said, kissing it. 'It's got that funny little tilt at the end.'

'The nose is both of ours,' Michael said. 'Everything about him is both of ours, and always will be.' She squeezed his hand, moved by this rare show of sentimentality from her husband. 'Six days old. Can you imagine?'

The doorbell rang. She was still getting used to its merry, singsong notes, so different from the machine-gun rattle at the loft that made you want to dive for cover in case the windows blew in.

'OK,' Michael said, getting up from the kitchen table, James a soft creamy bundle on his shoulder. 'It's showtime! Come on, back into your basket, little man, so everyone can admire you properly.'

'You make him sound like a puppy,' Hannah giggled. 'Like we keep him in a kennel in the garden.'

'I think you'd be hard pushed to improve on his current accommodation,' Michael grinned. 'The amount of money you've spent on the nursery.'

'Oh, shut up and get the door,' Hannah smiled. She settled James and wondered where best to place his Moses basket. It was the first week of March, but a beautiful spring day, so they'd opened the conservatory doors on to the garden and put out the garden furniture from their old roof terrace. It wasn't quite the style she had in mind for a tranquil walled garden, but she'd get something new ordered in time for the summer. She placed the baby just inside in the shade near the doors. He was already sleeping, as he had done through most of his life so far.

'Hannah, you look wonderful. And here he is! Oh look, Arthur, what a precious little morsel!'

It was Michael's parents. Hannah hadn't seen Arthur since the wedding, but it was surprisingly easy to behave as if nothing of note had taken place between then and now. She'd been told that after the birth she'd feel different about all sorts of things and it was true. All her old social guilt and anxiety was empty nonsense compared to the job at hand.

'Hello, son,' Arthur said, embracing Michael in that firm, dry Fawcett way. Hannah wondered if any of Arthur would trickle through to James. She'd always found her father-in-law refreshing; he was single-minded, fair, untouched by family politics, and extremely successful in his property business, based mainly on the south coast. He and Marianne were the perfect demonstration of an old-fashioned marriage: he concentrated on making the money while she kept the world sweet. Hannah watched Michael compliment his mother on her jacket, adding a comment about her hair. So how did it work, exactly, when the husband made the money *and* dispensed the charm?

Arthur handed Michael an envelope. 'Just a little something towards James's school fees . . .'

'Thanks, Dad. We'll tot up the booty later,' Michael grinned. He'd already told Hannah he knew his parents were secretly scouting for a beach house to give them, somewhere for James to enjoy when London summers got too overwhelming. It was Marianne's personal project.

'And Hannah,' Marianne said. 'You look, what's the word? *Beatific.*'

'I'm not entirely sure what that means,' Arthur chuckled. 'But I'd take it as a compliment if I were you.'

'You *all* look well,' Marianne said. 'All *three* of you. I think this is the most special time in a couple's life. More so even than a honeymoon. Did you remember the camera, Arthur? Let's get some pictures before anyone else arrives. The three generations of Fawcett men. Oh, I do hope I live to meet a fourth!'

Juliet was ready and waiting when Kate arrived at Larry's place. 'You might as well move down here, too,' she told her. 'The number of times you've been here recently.'

'I know,' Kate said. 'I think I've been south of the river more times this year than the rest of my life put together. Still no furniture yet, then?' They looked at Juliet's quarters, a corner of the living room with airbed and clothes rail. 'I can't believe he still hasn't sorted out curtains? Doesn't it get cold? I might ask my mum to make him some for his birthday.'

'When's his birthday?' Juliet asked in mild panic. 'I haven't missed it, have I?'

'End of the month,' Kate said.

'Let's do something for him, a surprise dinner somewhere?'

'Definitely. Anything to cheer the grumpy sod up. You look great, by the way! What a fantastic suede skirt.'

'Thank you,' said Juliet. She had to admit she was pleased with herself today. Her skin looked healthy, a real peachy-pink *skin* colour, and the whites of her eyes were actually white, which made the green greener. It was incredible what halving your alcohol intake could do for your appearance. 'I went on a bit of a spree yesterday. There are some amazing clothes shops in Nappy Valley, believe it or not, catering for the yummy mummies, I suppose, and assorted transients like myself. Guy's coming back today, so I wanted to make a bit of an effort.'

'Is he going to be back in time for the party?' Kate asked.

'I hope so. His flight was delayed, but he's going to get a train to Clapham Junction with all his gear and come in a cab to Hannah's.'

'It's so fab how things have worked out,' Kate said, squeezing her hand. 'I'm still not sure what made you go out there?'

Juliet kept hold of her friend's hand. 'I didn't want to wait a second longer. I just thought that if I told him everything and he still liked me then I'd know it was the real thing. I hate secrets. They just grow bigger the longer you keep them and then eventually everything just spontaneously combusts.'

'I know what you mean. I hate keeping Phil and me a secret at work.'

'I think everyone knows about that, darling,' Juliet said. 'You can't meet in the shower room for a secret snog two minutes after the five-a-side team finish their practice and expect no one to come in!'

'That was a pain,' Kate agreed. 'We had to leave at the same time, either that or one of us would have had to have hidden and watched someone take a shower.'

'Urgh, don't. I think I'd rather watch you and Phil snog! Shall we go?'

'Yep.' Kate followed her out. 'Where is Larry today anyway?'

'He's at some Sunday lunch thing in Tooting with his old flatmate,' said Juliet, locking the door behind them. 'It was a bit awkward actually. I feel terrible about this whole Hannah thing. And they live so close as well.'

'Does he know what we're doing?'

'Yes, I told him Hannah was having people over to meet the baby. He just shrugged. He wouldn't expect to be invited.'

'Poor Larry.'

Yes, poor Larry. That was how they thought of him at the moment, *poor*. And so much for not keeping secrets; she might have cleared the decks with Guy but there suddenly seemed to be so many things she couldn't tell *Larry* at the moment. For starters there was the Siobhan and Michael situation, though 'situation' hardly did justice to this latest near-ruinous twist. Larry had asked her only yesterday whether Hannah still suspected Rob of crimes against the sisterhood and she'd just fobbed him off, said maybe, you know what she's like, hormones and all that.

And then there was the fact that Dominic wanted Larry out of Imagineer. 'I'm sick of that too-fucking-cool-for-school malarkey. Sylvie saw him in the City with his portfolio a while back and she didn't know anything about a client meeting. I bet he was going for an interview with Cherry Brand. Well, I hope he gets it.'

'No, he wasn't,' Juliet said. 'I know for a fact he wants to stay here. He's just got a new mortgage. Maybe Sylvie was the one going for the interview? She wasn't very pleased to be taken off Smithfield's so soon.' She'd argued hard for him to stay, and she'd won, but she hadn't told him, didn't want him to feel he owed her a favour.

She was walking so quickly Kate had to skip a couple of steps to keep up. 'D'you think they'll bump into each other a lot then, Larry and Hannah?'

'Maybe not. He's by Clapham Common and she's closer to Wandsworth. And they're both car people, I suppose. Hannah's just swapped hers for one of those SUV monsters so she'll probably never walk again. Can someone explain to me why having a seven-pound addition to the family means you need a car the size of a rhinoceros?'

Kate giggled. 'This'll be us one day.' She was so sure, Juliet thought, as they weaved through the crowds on Northcote Road, and it wasn't just youthful optimism, it was just Kate. She couldn't remember ever being so trusting of the future, even when Luke had been around to plan it all out for them.

'It's a bit hot for a jacket, isn't it?' Kate said. 'What a beautiful day for a "welcome to the world" party.'

'Here we are,' Juliet said, stopping to admire the rows of box hedges in their slim slate planters. 'God, it's like a garden centre out here. I'd be scared someone was going to nick expensive pots like these.'

'Hannah is so lucky,' Kate said, looking up at the gleaming windows and pristine brickwork. 'She's got *everything*. I can't wait to see the baby.'

'He is *gorgeous*. Already like a real person, even though he was a bit early. He kept sneezing when I saw him at the hospital, they had to take the flowers out of her room.'

Michael opened the door. 'Come on down. The conservatory seems to be where all the cooing and clucking activity is based.'

He looked more handsome than Juliet had ever seen him, and smelled expensive. She managed to kiss his cheek and introduce him to Kate without once meeting his eye.

'Champagne, girls?' he asked from the kitchen. 'Or I could do you a bellini? That's the ad bunny's favourite, isn't it?'

'Michael!' Hannah rolled her eyes. 'They're not playmates!'

'Champagne would be lovely.' Juliet watched Michael as he poured. He was visibly on a high. She wanted to punch him, but in a strange way she also felt sorry for him, indignant, even. What right did Siobhan have to carry and raise his child without his knowledge, let alone his blessing? She supposed it was the same right that she herself had exercised when she'd chosen to stop a man's child from existing at all. But who could possibly gain from knowing, after the fact, about an abortion? Yet every day Nora gained was a day Michael lost to

Siobhan. And every day lost to Michael was a day gained by Hannah.

It was making her head hurt. She *had to* forget all about that Nora business, and not just for today but for as long as Siobhan was willing to do the same. She turned to look at her nephew, who was sleeping. His eyelids were paper-sheer, perfect as butterfly wings. The last time she'd seen such a young baby was when her mother had brought Laura home from the hospital twenty years ago. She and Hannah had stood at the front door with their aunt, waiting to see the presents they'd been told their sister had bought for them. Juliet had thought it unfair that Laura already had pocket money.

'Oh, he is absolutely incredible,' Kate said reverently. 'So tiny, like a teddy-bear cub.'

'He was almost two weeks early,' Hannah said. 'He was six and a half pounds but they lose a few ounces in the first week.'

'He'll soon pork out, though,' Michael said. 'You can tell he's going to like his tucker. Look at the way his lips move in his sleep.'

'Thank you so much for inviting me,' Kate said to him. 'I know it's just family today, isn't it?'

'You're very welcome,' he smiled. 'If you're Juliet's date.'

'Actually,' Juliet said. 'Guy might be coming, too, if that's OK. He's just back from France.'

'Oh, Juliet, are you back together? That's wonderful!' Hannah looked as though a thousand happy endings had come true in one go.

'I know, it's great. But don't go asking him about marriage yet, I don't want to scare him off!' Juliet waited for Michael and Kate to drift out of earshot before asking, as casually as she could manage, 'Have you heard from Siobhan?'

'No.' Now Hannah's face fell. 'I don't know if she even knows about James yet. Michael got her answerphone when he rang with the news and then again when he rang to invite her to come today. I know she never checks those BT Answer things. The last time I spoke to her was, God, it must have been just after the baby shower and she was about to go and stay with her parents for a while. I suppose I should be pleased for her, and I am, of course, but she was such a big part of my pregnancy – I really wanted her to be one of the first to meet James.'

'Sometimes people just grow apart, don't they?' Juliet said delicately. 'Her role was to support you when you needed it and now you don't need it any more.'

'Yes, I do,' Hannah protested. 'Now more than ever! This is bloody terrifying you know, Juliet. And the fact that you love the helpless little thing so much makes it more so.'

Juliet took her arm. 'Well, I'll help you as much as I can. I'll come every night after work if you like. And you've got Michael and Mum and Michael's mother and Lottie . . .'

Hannah interrupted her, her mind clearly still on Siobhan. 'Besides, I want to support *her*, too. She's got far fewer people around her than I have.'

'OK,' Juliet said, alarmed by this intensity. She wished she hadn't introduced the subject.

'I've called so many times, I don't see what else I can do. I think I'll drive round there next week.'

'Oh, I'm sure she'll be back in touch soon,' Juliet lied. 'She's probably just giving you some space, knowing family will be descending. You should just concentrate on this little one.'

'I'm sure you're right,' Hannah said.

It was starting to feel a bit unreal, like a sequence from a dream, their guests no more than trompe l'oeil figures on the conservatory walls. She couldn't remember a single thing she'd said to anyone for the last twenty minutes. The combination of adrenaline, her first alcohol splurge in eight months, and having all her special people around her at once was making her dizzy. Luckily Michael was in fine fettle, keeping the champagne brimming, fielding the queries and tips with equal affability.

All the Goodwins were here now, along with Rob and Lottie, who were to be James's godparents. Hannah had agreed at once when Michael had suggested they be asked. She hoped that somehow it might make amends, in her own head at least, for all that business over Rob and Nora. Thank the Lord Lottie knew nothing about that; she'd been so lucky the phone call was never followed up. She didn't know what she'd been thinking. Nora's father was probably thousands of miles away by now.

It struck her that Lottie and Rob seemed very close today – they were even holding hands. How nice that this sort of celebration made people really appreciate what they had. She watched as Lottie settled into a chair in the garden and appeared actually to *relax*. She even allowed herself to be offered food and drink and didn't once attempt to restructure the organised chaos of Michael's kitchen HQ. Sweet that he'd insisted on organising all the refreshments himself so Hannah didn't have to worry.

'Is Jay not with you?' she asked Laura, suddenly thinking of him.

'We split up ages ago.' Laura's hair was shorter now, you could see her ears with their multiple piercings, and she was smoking more than Hannah remembered.

'Oh, why? Did your expedition give you a new perspective on things?'

'No,' Laura said. 'He just turned out to be a bit of a gimp.'

Kate giggled.

'Don't encourage her,' Christopher said. 'When perfectly pleasant young men are despatched for being "gimps", I lose faith in the future of human relationships. Personally, I don't see the institution of marriage lasting much beyond the next generation.'

'I didn't know you were a *Star Trek* fan,' Michael said at his shoulder with a freshly popped bottle of bubbly. 'Do you like *Deep Space Nine* as well?'

'What?'

'Geek,' Laura giggled, and Michael winked at her.

'You'll notice she confines her slurs to monosyllables beginning with "g",' Christopher said to him. 'She never wins Scrabble; that's usually Juliet. She has a much more extensive vocabulary of insults.'

'Where *is* Juliet?' Gayle asked.

'She's here somewhere,' Hannah said, squinting into the sunshine. 'She must have gone to the loo. Oh, there's the phone again, Michael.'

'I'll get it, excuse me . . .'

'I'll look after the champagne,' Kate offered, taking the bottle from him and beginning with a top-up of her own glass.

'She sounded much happier the last time I spoke to her,' Gayle said to Hannah. 'We were so worried at Christmas.'

'I know, but she's back with Guy now and everything seems to have settled down. And it's great having her so close by.'

'How strange that she's ended up on your old street,' Gayle said. 'Perhaps you'll move to Sisters Avenue one day, too, Laura?'

'I will *never* be able to afford this area,' said Laura. 'Unless I get a hundred-year mortgage or something. Oh, look, I think James is awake! Does that mean we can cuddle him now? Can I go first?'

'Have you put your cigarette out? Good, now remember to support his neck and head . . .' Gayle followed her youngest daughter into the conservatory and they came back with the baby, still swaddled in his blanket. Hannah had to make a big effort not to take him straight into her own arms. She kissed his ear.

'Did I tell you I'm going to save ten pounds a month for him?' Laura said to her. 'By the time he's a student that should be enough to fund drinks during Freshers' week. Juliet should do the same to cover his fags.'

'I'm sure Hannah and Michael will be thrilled with your thoughtfulness,' Christopher said, chuckling.

The doorbell rang. 'I'll get it,' Lottie said, springing up. 'You've got your hands full, Hannah.'

'Thank you.'

'Who else are you expecting?' Gayle asked her.

'It must be Guy,' Kate said. 'Juliet said he was on his way.'

'Oh, that's right.' Secretly, Hannah hoped it might be Siobhan, back from her reunion with her parents and delighted to discover the news of James's early arrival. That might have been her on the phone, telling them she was on her way. Only with Siobhan here would things really be as they ought to.

'I can't wait to see Guy again,' said Laura. 'He looked absolutely gorge at the wedding.'

'I wouldn't kick him out of bed,' Kate agreed. 'Oops, sorry, Mr Goodwin.'

'Don't mind me. I'm aware that men are now viewed as mere commodities.'

Hannah liked the tender look he shared with her mother.

'Not all of them,' she said. 'It is Guy, look! Guy! It's great to see you. And what a tan! You remember my mum and dad from the wedding, don't you?'

It was a few seconds before she registered that Lottie was signalling to her from inside the house, pulling her rarely seen 'We've got a loose cannon' face. And then Larry lurched into the garden.

Every time Juliet came to Hannah's new house there seemed to be a dozen new things, beautiful new things: chairs, pictures, rugs, throws, vases. Glass seemed to be her sister's latest passion, there were lots of green glass boxes about and a new mirrored console table on the landing. When they'd lived together it had been velvet, so much velvet the place had come to resemble a Versailles boudoir. She tried to imagine a flat belonging to her and Guy: it would be empty but for their clothes, a row of optics, maybe a rack or two of cheap red.

They'd build up gradually, though. By the time they were ninety they might have enough possessions to fill one of Hannah's smaller spare bedrooms.

She was in the guest bedroom at the top of the house, with its floor-to-ceiling window at the back. You can come and stay in this room for as long as you like, Hannah had said to her when she'd shown her the work in progress on the new en suite shower room. Even the tiny pink tiles seemed to have been chosen with her in mind, they looked like a wall of strawberry Starburst chews.

Funny how things had changed: these days she had accommodation options coming out of her ears. The tenant in the studio above Larry's flat was moving out next month and she had the landlady's number; she and Kate had been talking about getting a place together; and now Guy was back on the scene, to be reinstalled in the flat above the bar that very evening. She didn't think Kate would mind if new developments overrode their initial plans, especially as she spent several nights a week at Phil's place now. Besides, the situation with Sasha had made Juliet very wary of sharing – she had no intention of losing Kate as a friend.

She tried to resist the yearning to hear Guy's voice again, though they'd spoken only an hour and a half ago when he'd touched down at the airport. No harm in finding out how close he was, maybe he was in the taxi already. Her longing to be in his arms was almost dizzying. She picked up the phone on the bedside table.

'What was that?' said Michael's voice.

'Nothing, I think I just nudged the buttons,' said a woman's voice. 'So don't change the subject, how about later?'

'I told you, I'm going to have to lie low for another week or two.'

'Then lie low with me.'

'*Fleur!*'

356

'I'm feeling seriously horny. Shall I tell you what I want you to do to me?'

There was a pause. Sleazy bastard, Juliet thought. Sleazy, weak, arrogant, worthless bastard. You certainly will be lying low, sunshine, when I chuck a glass pot between your legs! She sat on the edge of the bed, free fingers playing with the tassels on an embroidered cushion, keeping her breath as silent as she could.

'God, I really want you to come over here now, this minute, and when I open the door not even speak to me, just put . . .'

'*Fleur*,' Michael said. 'Stop. I mean it. I have to go now.'

'When, then? Come on, just an hour, later.'

Say no, Juliet prayed, but she knew he wouldn't. She could almost hear him panting.

'Maybe later,' he growled, 'but only if I can get away.'

'Well, I'm about to go and meet the girls for a drink, so I'll call you when I get back in, see if the coast's clear.'

'No, *I'll* call you, when I'm leaving, *if* I'm leaving.'

'What shall I wear?'

Another pause, then, 'Wear my Christmas present.'

'I can see what sort of mood you're in.'

'Er, pot, kettle, missy . . .'

Juliet hung up. God, who was this sex-line floozy? Another one of Michael's 'colleagues', no doubt. She lay back on the bed, crushed flat with sadness for Hannah. Then she sat up again. She wasn't going to pretend not to know about this one as well: she would *have* to tell her sister. Not today, though, not in front of everyone. First she'd talk to Guy and get his advice.

She decided to stay upstairs until Michael was safely back in the garden – presumably even he wouldn't risk too long a conversation with his mistress while his wife breast-fed their newborn in front of both their families. Looking out of the window her heart soared as she spotted Guy. Despite the heat he was in the bobbly grey sweater he'd lent her that night in Morzine. He leaned in to kiss Hannah, who was holding James, shading his face from the sun with her hand. Thank God she'd chosen Guy and not a Serial Philanderer like Michael. Thank God Guy had agreed to be re-chosen.

She watched as Kate approached, glugging away at another full glass of champagne. How lovely she looked today; Juliet hoped she'd remembered to say that to her earlier. She'd lost weight, grown her hair past her shoulders and flicked it out at the ends. As she whispered into Guy's ear she looked so confident and poised, like a different person.

Then Guy's whole body went completely still and Juliet felt herself freeze, too. Kate was still touching his arm and chatting on, but he pulled abruptly away from her and headed out of frame towards the house. He must be looking for me, Juliet thought. Then she heard the front door open and close. What on earth . . . ?

As she rushed down she passed Michael on the landing. 'The house looks great, doesn't it?' he asked her, smile as wide as a game-show host's.

'Yes,' she said, flying by. 'Hannah's done you proud.'

Over Guy's shoulder, Hannah watched Lottie handle Larry, successfully coaxing him back into the conservatory and then beyond into the kitchen. Half of her was anxious to join them, the other half wished she could hide behind Guy for the rest of the afternoon.

'Is Larry all right?' Guy asked, looking. 'I picked him up in my cab down the road, he'd forgotten your address. He looks a bit out of it.'

'I'd better go and see. Can I leave you with Kate? Mum, can I give you James for a bit?'

'Of course, darling. Careful I don't take him home with me, mind!'

'Guy, it's so great you're back!' Kate cried, and Hannah breathed very deeply before leaving them.

358

In the kitchen Lottie looked relieved to see her. It was not a good sign if Lottie felt she couldn't deal with this on her own.

'Thanks for dropping in,' she said to Larry pleasantly. Meeting his eye wasn't as guilt-inducing as she'd expected, especially as he was having trouble focusing. 'Do you want to come and meet James?'

'I came to see Siobhan,' Larry said, sullen, childlike.

'I told you she's not here,' Lottie said. 'It's just family.'

'*You're* not family,' Larry said.

'Siobhan couldn't come,' Hannah said. 'I think she must still be visiting her parents in Manchester.'

'Bollocks,' Larry said. 'She wouldn't miss this.'

'I don't know then,' Hannah said. 'Michael couldn't get hold of her.'

'Bet he didn't even try,' Larry muttered.

'Larry!'

'It doesn't matter where she is,' Lottie said wearily. 'It's not as if she's a godparent or anything.'

'She should be,' Larry sneered. Then, ominously, he was grinning and nodding, looking at Lottie as though it was all starting to make sense to him. 'Oh my God! You know what I think?'

'Not really,' Lottie said.

'No, Larry,' Hannah added quickly. She didn't like this one bit.

'I think Siobhan hasn't come because she knew she'd run into Rob.'

'Rob?' Lottie asked. 'What's he got to do with it?'

'Siobhan doesn't know Rob,' Hannah said loudly. '*Really*, she doesn't.' She tried to give Larry a warning look but he might as well have had a pair of glass eyes for all the good it did.

'That's a laugh,' Larry said, and to prove his point began chortling to himself.

'What *is* your problem?' Lottie said.

Just then, Marianne appeared. 'Hannah, darling, we want a photo with all the mothers together.'

'I'm a bit busy. Could you give me a minute?'

'Just two seconds, everyone's in position and James is looking *so* alert. *Please.*'

'OK. Where's Michael?' Hannah asked in desperation.

'He's here somewhere, don't fret. Wasn't he on the phone? We're doing fathers next, though, so send him out, Lottie, if you see him.'

'Sure.'

'I'll be back,' Hannah said to Larry. 'Don't say *anything* else. Not a word.'

Larry just wrinkled his nose and sat down on the nearest chair.

'I'll get you some water,' Lottie sighed.

As she turned, Hannah collided with Kate, whose chest was flushed deep pink. 'Larry! I didn't know you were coming. Have you seen Juliet? I think I might have put my foot in it with Guy. I thought she said she'd told him *everything*?'

Chapter 33

Juliet raced the full length of Salcott Road to the corner of Northcote Road before she caught sight of Guy. He was moving in long, unstoppable strides, scattering dawdlers in his wake. 'Guy, wait! Guy, please! Kate told you about the abortion, didn't she?'

He stopped dead and turned, forcing two women to sidestep around him and lose their balance. They looked about to grumble until they saw the mutinous expression on his face. 'She didn't *tell* me,' he said. 'She just assumed I knew. So what was all that bullshit about telling me everything in France?'

'I did tell you everything, everything to do with us, everything that affects us.'

'And this doesn't? The fact that you aborted my child?'

'Guy, don't do this, everything was fine again between us.'

'Are you mad? This changes everything. *Everything*.' His body had gone still again, but his eyes were livid.

She threw up her hands. 'So I've had an abortion! So have half the women in London!'

He paused. 'That's their business. Half the women in London have not been pregnant with *my* child.'

People were gaping now, mothers and fathers and toddlers on shoulders, huddling together in their perfect family units and

361

gaping. Juliet ignored them and pulled Guy into the doorway of an estate agent's. It was no use, she was going to have to tell him. 'The baby wasn't yours, Guy. I slept with someone else after we split up.' Almost true, only the word 'after' was open to debate.

He snatched his arm away. 'I don't believe you.'

'It's true, I swear to you. I would have told you if it had been yours. I mean, beforehand, we would have made the decision together.' For a while back there she'd even hoped it was Guy's, hoped he might persuade her to keep it, that they would change their own two lives together for the sake of a third.

He continued to glare at her. 'Who then? Not that arsehole Dominic? I thought that was over long before us?'

'It was. No, not him. Of course not.'

'Who?' They waited for some house hunters to finish browsing.

'It's nice, but it's not actually Between the Commons,' the woman said to the man.

'No point seeing it then,' he agreed.

'If you don't tell me,' Guy said, 'I'm getting on that train and you'll never see me again.'

Juliet took a breath. 'Fulton.' It was Fulton's. By process of elimination the baby had to have been Fulton's. Things had been over with Guy too long ago, Dominic had denied any kind of reprise, but she'd seen a lot of Fulton around that time.

Guy snorted. '*Fulton?* Exactly when did you start sleeping with *him*?'

'It was a one-off.' A two-off, a few-off. 'Well, it happened a few times, but it was nothing serious.' Don't mention the Rachel factor, she told herself, that really would be too honest.

'Wasn't he with someone around then?' Guy asked, frowning.

'On and off,' Juliet said.

'I don't believe this. Why didn't you tell me this in France?'

'I didn't think it was relevant.'

'You have unprotected sex with that goose and it's not relevant!'

362

Juliet suppressed a snicker, she'd never heard Fulton called a goose before, but Guy's face was inches from hers and he'd seen her lips twitch. 'Jeez, you think this is *funny*?'

'No, no, of course not, I'm sorry. I didn't mention it because I was trying to forget the whole thing. It wasn't exactly a highlight of our time apart. Come on, Guy, I haven't asked you if you've been seeing anyone.'

'Well, I certainly haven't been going around creating new life.'

Why did people have to use such dramatic language about pregnancy and babies? What was it Siobhan had said? Nothing was as important as giving life.

'How can you be sure?' Juliet asked him quietly. 'The fallout tends to be left to the woman, doesn't it?'

Guy just looked at her now, really looked. He'd always done that, examined her face as though he'd never seen the seductive smile or sarcastic sneer or whatever happened to be the Juliet attitude *du jour*. He'd never been interested in what she was wearing on her body *or* her face. 'Does Fulton know?'

'No. And he doesn't need to.' Wouldn't want to, either, Juliet was sure about that at least.

'How do I know you're telling me the truth?'

'Because I am. Guy, you must believe me or there really is no point, is there?'

He stepped away and sat on a nearby wall, still staring at her. 'Is there anything else I need to know? Including anything you think I don't need to know?'

'I swear that's it. Please come back to the party.'

'I might come back in a bit. I need a second on my own.'

She turned. 'I have to go. I'm sorry. I told Hannah I'd be there all day and I haven't even spoken to my parents yet.'

'Who else there knows about this?' Guy asked. 'Kate, I suppose. What about Larry?'

'He knows, but you won't see him today.'

'I already have. We arrived together.'

'Oh,' said Juliet. 'That's not good.'

As she hurried back up Hannah's path she could see Larry in the sitting-room window. What was he doing here? Now all they needed was for Siobhan to turn up and the world's worst baby party was complete. If James could survive this, he could survive anything.

'Juliet!' Her mother answered the door. 'Where on earth have you been?'

'Oh, I just needed to talk to Guy on my own.' Why was it that mothers were the last people you wanted to explain things to when things got complicated, and yet probably your best bet for sorting things out?

'Well, I'm glad I've got you on *your* own,' said Gayle, 'especially as we haven't seen you since Christmas.'

'Can we talk about that in a little while?' Juliet asked, impatient to get into the sitting room and find out what the hell Larry was doing here. Her mother just nodded, resigned. 'Sorry, Mum, I'm not avoiding you. I promise I'll be down in two minutes. I've just got to see Larry.'

'Yes, I'm sure that's more important,' Gayle said. They were professionals, mothers, the slickest guilt-trippers in the business. 'I just need to make sure I give you this.'

'What is it?' But Juliet recognised the writing on the envelope. It was a letter from Jan and Tony. She hadn't had one for months, not since moving in with Sasha, at which point she'd begged her parents not to pass on the new address.

'I told Jan you hadn't opened the others. She asks that you please read this one,' Gayle said.

'Mum!'

'It's important to *her*, Juliet.'

Juliet sighed. 'OK, I will. Just let me talk to Larry and I'll come straight back down.'

'Fine, far be it from me to interfere.'

Juliet waited for her to disappear down the stairs before she tapped on the closed sitting-room door and went in. Larry was shuffling about at the window looking sulky, while Lottie hovered by the sofa, apparently guarding the exit. They both looked around.

'Juliet, I'm glad you're here,' Lottie said.

'What's up, Larry?' Juliet said, walking over to him. 'What are you doing here? God, you look hammered.'

He just laughed grimly. 'So that's why I haven't been offered a proper drink.'

'We've only just managed to get him out of the loo,' Lottie said. 'He was unable to operate a simple household bolt. Hannah's organising some very strong coffee and then he's leaving.'

Larry sent a poisonous look Lottie's way and let it smoulder. 'If anyone should leave it's your old man.'

'He keeps muttering on about Rob,' Lottie told Juliet. 'I don't think they even know each other, do they?'

'Larry, shut up,' Juliet said. 'You're completely wrong.'

'That's all the Goodwin girls say today. *Shut up*, Larry, *shut up*! Is the other sister here as well? Maybe she'd like to take a shot at me, too.'

'Why don't we go home? We can get some coffee there.' Juliet tried to take his hand but he pulled it away and rubbed his nose. Poor Larry, poor, *dangerous* Larry.

'Can I leave you to handle this now?' Lottie said, opening the door.

'Doesn't she know, then?' Larry said, not mumbling now.

Lottie spun back round. 'Know *what*? I'm getting bloody sick of this. Just spit it out, you moron!'

'With pleasure, m'lady, with pleasure.' Larry spoke with the slow, exaggerated enunciation of the drunk whose pride had been injured. 'Rob, your esteemed husband Rob, Mr Snotty Lottie, is the father of Siobhan's baby.'

'I hardly think so,' Lottie said witheringly. 'Are you mad?'

'Hannah told me. She's got proof.'

'He's making this up,' Juliet said to Lottie. 'Just ignore him. You go back down and I'll get him out of here.'

But Lottie looked shaken; she'd really lost her cool. She unhooked her hand from her waistband and touched her tummy. It reminded Juliet of the women at Hannah's antenatal class. 'I'm going to have a word with Hannah about this. What's she doing, spreading this sort of rubbish about Rob?'

'Rubbish about Rob,' Larry mimicked, like a pantomime dame. Juliet wanted to shut him in a cupboard and leave him there.

She was running out of ideas. 'Look, she hasn't been spreading rubbish, Lottie. Larry's got totally the wrong end of the stick. Rob isn't Nora's father.'

Larry lurched towards Lottie. God, was he going to push her? 'He is! He had sex with Siobhan when she was working for him. He said he was Errol Flynn.'

'David Niven,' Juliet couldn't help correcting him. She didn't dare look at Lottie. 'Look, that wasn't Rob, Larry, so just leave it.'

'Yes, it was,' Larry said.

'No, it wasn't.'

'What do you know anyway?' Larry said to Juliet. 'Just keep out of it.'

'I've had enough of this,' Lottie said. 'I could sue you for slander. I'm going to get Rob.'

Juliet closed her eyes. 'Lottie, listen, both of you . . . Rob is not Nora's father. *Michael* is.'

'*What?*' Lottie looked even more appalled. Even Larry looked shocked. Eyes fixed on Juliet, Lottie fumbled for the end of the sofa and sat back down. Finally, there was silence. Then came a voice from the doorway. 'Did you just say *Michael* is Nora's father?' It was Hannah. Juliet couldn't look.

Then came another voice from behind Hannah, this one loud

and uncontrolled. 'Juliet! *There* you are! I need to talk to you. I've really screwed up. I didn't realise Guy didn't know about the abortion!'

'Shh!' Larry said in a scandalised stage whisper. 'That's a secret, Kate.'

Hannah just managed to slosh down the mug of coffee she was carrying before slumping back against Kate, who reacted remarkably deftly considering the amount she'd drunk and was able to hold Hannah's weight until Juliet and Lottie could help.

The weird dreaminess of an hour ago had vanished and now Hannah was alert, combative, wired to survive. She turned to face Juliet. 'Are you absolutely sure about this? How can you possibly know?'

Juliet looked close to tears. 'I've spoken to Siobhan. She recognised Michael in the wedding photos when she was here. You saw how weird she was. I'm so sorry, Hannah.'

'That's why she didn't come,' Hannah whispered. James and Nora, brother and sister. Did they really think they were going to keep this from her?

'Oh Hannah, I'm sure this can't be true,' Lottie said, squeezing her arm. 'Don't worry about it.'

'It's definitely true,' Juliet said simply. 'I'm sorry.'

'Does Michael know?' Hannah asked her.

'No.'

'Well, we should tell him about these *suspicions* before someone else does.' Lottie rolled her eyes in Larry's direction. He was quiet now, had drifted off from the conversation as though its disastrous turn had had nothing to do with him.

Hannah jumped at the sound of footsteps in the hallway outside. Not Michael, please, not in front of everyone.

Rob stuck his nose round the door. 'Hannah, James has been sick all over Arthur's trousers. D'you want to come and . . .' He noticed Kate, Larry and Juliet and stopped. 'What's going on? There's more people up here than downstairs.'

'Nothing,' Lottie said. 'Go back down, darling.'

Hannah spoke. 'Just tell him, Lottie. I don't care.'

'Tell me what?'

No one said anything, so Hannah opened her mouth again, marvelling that words could travel smoothly through so dry a throat: 'It's Michael. It seems he's the father of another child.'

'What?' Rob said. 'Fleur's pregnant?' He saw his mistake instantly and bumped against the doorframe as he backed away.

Lottie gave a huge sigh. 'Go away, Rob, please.'

'Who *is* this Fleur?' Juliet asked. 'She was on the phone earlier . . .' She tailed off.

The more tightly Hannah's heart was squeezed, the clearer her voice rang out. 'The only Fleur I know is the girl who bought our flat.'

'Fleur?' Larry said politely, as though roused from his reverie by the introduction of a new guest. 'The giantess? Is she here?'

'Get him home,' Lottie commanded Juliet. 'And sober him up there.'

'I'll try.'

'No, I want Juliet to stay,' Hannah said.

'I'll take him,' Kate said. 'Come on, Larry, it's time to get going.'

'Don't treat me like a child,' Larry protested, but allowed her to steer him out of the room. There was an almighty crash and a yelp from Kate.

'What now?' Lottie asked.

'Guy's skis,' Juliet said. 'He left them behind.'

Hannah looked up. 'When did Guy go? He just got here.'

Juliet sighed. 'We had a slight disagreement.' The two sisters looked at each other.

'Juliet, how do you know all this stuff?' Hannah asked. 'About Siobhan, about Fleur?'

'I know because people aren't very good at keeping secrets. And now *you* know because I'm not very good at it either. Hannah, please forgive me.'

'You've done nothing wrong,' Hannah said. 'And I'm glad you're not good with secrets, I really am.' She stood up. 'Look, everyone, I need to find Michael.'

'Shouldn't we wind this party down first?' Lottie said gently. 'Then you can talk to him alone.'

'Oh God!' All the details of domestic arrangements, the dinners and beds and towels and breakfasts, mobbed her brain in an unmanageable jumble. What was she going to do? 'This is a nightmare. Mum and Dad and Laura are supposed to be staying here tonight and tomorrow!'

'They can stay at ours,' Lottie said. 'I'll go down and tell everyone there's been a catastrophic plumbing breakdown and we'll soon be knee-deep in sewage.'

'We already are, aren't we?' Juliet said. 'Why don't we get out of here, Han? Leave Michael to it. We could go to my place, or to Lottie's, anywhere?'

'No,' Hannah said. 'This time I'm not the one who's going.'

'Leave it with me,' Lottie said. 'I'll give them all a drink at ours and try to explain.' As she stood she looked thoroughly drained. Hannah had seen her like this just once before, when she'd first been pregnant with Ophelia.

'Thank you, Lottie, I really appreciate it. Juliet, when everyone's gone could you look after James while I talk to Michael upstairs?'

'Of course.'

'We can take James as well,' Lottie offered.

'No. He stays with me,' Hannah said. 'I'll be in our bedroom. Can someone send Michael up?'

Lottie brought James to Juliet. He was back in his Moses basket, tucked up and oblivious of his transfer from woman to woman.

'Did you have to get this started?' she asked Juliet, but not crossly.

'I'm sorry. But what Larry was saying to you, well . . . I've never seen him like that.'

'This is far, far worse than anything he could have said to me. Rob would have explained it wasn't true and that would have been the end of it.'

'Did you know about Fleur?' Juliet asked.

'No, I didn't actually. I told Rob that after that business in Cape Town I didn't want to hear about Michael and this sort of thing any more. Hannah is my friend.'

'But you suspected?'

Lottie shrugged. 'You know, there's always going to be someone, Juliet. With these men, there's always going to be someone.'

Juliet didn't dare ask if 'these men' were men in general or just men like Michael. She longed for Guy, wanted to weep for having blown it a second time.

'OK,' Lottie said, turning to go. 'Rob's bringing the troops up so keep this door closed or you'll get badgered with questions. Ask Hannah to call me later if she's up to it.'

'I will.' Juliet listened to them all trailing through the hallway, fussing and speculating. She heard her mother's voice above the others: 'Is this something to do with Juliet being a lesbian, Rob?'

Laura said: 'Mum, I told you, she's not gay!'

'But Kate said she was her date, you know, her *partner*.'

How many more cats had Kate set among the pigeons this afternoon, Juliet wondered. She prayed this new lesbian angle was the worst she'd have to contend with when she joined them later.

'Can't we say goodbye to little James?' That was Marianne, indignant, but, like the others, just a little too well-oiled with champagne and good food to make any trouble.

'I'm sure Hannah will bring him along in a while,' Lottie said. 'Just let me get you all home for a drink and I'll bring you up-to-speed. We're just around the corner, Chris and Gayle, overlooking the common. It's not far at all.'

'Oh, just look at that blossom! You'd never believe it was March!'

'It could be June!'

'Did you read in the paper about how the birds think it's summer already?'

And they were gone. The silence made Juliet's skin itch. Don't think about Guy, she repeated to herself, just stay calm and look after James. She peered into the basket, hoping Hannah wouldn't spend too long giving the Philanderer his marching orders. She had no idea how to change a nappy or soothe the hunger pangs of a breast-fed newborn.

After a while, James woke up and gave a little squeak. Her heart choked at the sight of his tiny innocent face. Then the eyelids wobbled and he was off again. She noticed Jan's letter, face down on the coffee table, and decided to obey her mother for once and read it. She was confused to find a card with a picture of a stork on it and a Coutts cheque for twenty thousand pounds. Then she saw it was addressed to James. 'Well, every cloud has a silver lining, mate,' she whispered to him, and leaned down to kiss his tiny fist.

Jan's letter was in her pocket and she tore it open before she could change her mind. It was no more or less comforting than she'd expected to read of the Newells' continuing grief and to learn of their lifelong commitment to Juliet as the most special person in their son's short life *above and beyond any other figure*. They added, '*We enclose a photo for you from your time together in Mexico. We think it will help you remember him at his happiest.*'

She looked at the photo. It had been taken in a bar near Tulum, just before she'd left for Cancun for her flight home. They'd stayed in the area for several weeks, sleeping in a beach hut with iguanas threading in and out of the gaps around the door. Luke had his arm around her as he laughed into the camera lens, and she was laughing at his laughter. She tried to remember some of the faces at the neighbouring tables – they'd got to know most of the long-term travellers there. The Scot with weedy little dreads and a crusty rash on his neck; his new best friend, an Aussie from a chicken farm in Queensland who was helping out behind the bar in return for free accommodation.

And then she saw her among the faces in the background. Most of her hair was obscured by a shoulder in the foreground, but you could clearly see the clean, sharp profile: it was Cristina all right. The Cristina who'd been a bit hazy about when she and Luke had actually met, though she thought it was around the time they'd both arrived in Lima. Juliet had suspected they might in fact have got together earlier, en route from Ecuador; she'd imagined them 'thrown together' in sub-standard travel conditions. But had Luke met Cristina before Juliet had even left Mexico? Had he already slept with her in another of those little huts on the ocean's edge? Juliet had lined up four months' work in London before she was due to rejoin him in Peru. Four months for the romance to wend its way south, last stop Lima.

There's always someone with these men, that's what Lottie had said. Juliet went to have a look at the picture of Hannah and Michael kissing on the church steps, the one Siobhan had seen. She considered putting it in the bin with her own photograph, but decided to leave that for Hannah to do.

Then she heard the trudge of footsteps and something heavy scraping against the wall. She peeked around the door. It was Michael, carrying an overnight bag. He looked pale and dazed, as though punched by a boxer who knew exactly how to strike without leaving a bruise. She watched him open the front door and then hesitate, turning his head to look back up the stairs. Then they both started at the sound of Guy's voice.

'Michael! I didn't see you earlier, mate. Congratulations! Hey, everything all right?'

'No,' Michael said, voice grim. 'All wrong, actually, all wrong.'

'What . . . ?' The door shut and Juliet went out into the hall and hugged Guy, didn't want to let go. 'What's going on?' he said, stroking her head. 'Michael looked like he was about to *cry*. Is something wrong with the baby?'

'Hannah's had some bad news,' she said. 'Come into the living room.'

Guy followed her in. James's eyes were open properly now, so she picked him up, slotting her flat hand beneath his back and neck as she'd seen Hannah do. He was very interested in a nearby potted lily.

Hannah came in. 'It's over,' she said. 'I can't believe it.' But she looked as if she could believe it, which Juliet thought was a good sign.

Guy put an arm around Juliet and held his other hand out to Hannah. 'Come on, we can sort all this out together.'

Juliet cuddled James against her and kissed the top of his little head. 'Thank you,' she said.